VICTORIA HOLT is at her spellbinding best in this new romantic adventure of intrigue and suspense.

Set against exotic backgrounds ranging from Victorian England to the mysterious islands of the South Seas, *THE SECRET WOMAN* unfolds the spine-tingling drama of a lonely woman's daring quest for love—and her discovery of a scandalous secret that threatens to destroy not only her dream but her life as well.

Fawcett Crest Books
by Victoria Holt:

THE
Secret Woman

by Victoria Holt

A FAWCETT CREST BOOK

Fawcett Books, Greenwich, Connecticut

THE SECRET WOMAN

THIS BOOK CONTAINS THE COMPLETE TEXT OF THE
ORIGINAL HARDCOVER EDITION.

Published by Fawcett Crest Books, CBS Publications,
CBS Consumer Publishing, a Division of CBS, Inc.,
by arrangement with Doubleday & Company, Inc.

Selection of the Reader's Digest
Condensed Book Club, July 1970
Selection of the Doubleday Book Club, December 1970

Printed in the United States of America

29 28 27 26 25 24 23 22 21 20

****

THE QUEEN'S HOUSE

1

When my Aunt Charlotte died suddenly many people believed that I had killed her and that if it had not been for Nurse Loman's evidence at the inquest, the verdict would have been one of murder by some person or persons unknown; there would have been a probing into the dark secrets of the Queen's House, and the truth would have come out.

"That niece of hers obviously had the motive," it was said.

The "motive" was Aunt Charlotte's possessions which on her death became mine. But how different everything was from what it appeared to be!

Chantel Loman, who had become my friend during the months she lived with us at the Queen's House, laughed at the gossips.

"People must have drama. If it isn't there they invent it. Sudden death is manna from Heaven. Of course they talk. Take no notice of them. I don't."

She did not have the same need to do so, I pointed out to her.

She laughed at me. "You're always so logical!" she said. "Why, Anna, I do believe that if those wicked old gossips had had their wish and you had stood in the dock you would have got the better of the judge as well as the jury and counsel for the prosecution. You can look after yourself."

If only it were true! But Chantel did not know of those sleepless nights when I lay in my bed making plans, trying to work out how I could dispose of everything and start a new life in a new place and so free myself from this haunting nightmare. But in the morning it would be different. Practical considerations forced themselves on me. I *could* not go away; it was not financially possible. Little did the gossips know the true state of affairs. Moreover I was not going to be a coward and run away. As long as one was innocent what did it matter what the world thought of one?

6

A foolish paradox, I told myself immediately, and an untrue one. The innocent frequently suffer when they are suspected of guilt, and it is necessary not only to *be* innocent but to prove that one is.

But I could not run away; so I put on what Chantel called my mask and turned a face of cold indifference to the world. No one was going to know how deeply I cared about the slander.

I tried to see everything objectively. In fact I could not have endured those months if I had not looked upon what happened as an unpleasant fantasy like a drama being played out on a stage, the chief characters being the victim and the suspect—Aunt Charlotte and myself—and in the minor roles, Nurse Chantel Loman, Dr. Elgin, Mrs. Morton the cook-housekeeper, Ellen the maid, and Mrs. Buckle who came in to dust the cluttered rooms. I was trying to convince myself that it had not really happened and one morning I should wake up to find it was nothing but a nightmare.

So I was not logical but foolish and even Chantel did not know how vulnerable. I dared not look back and I dared not look forward. Yet when I saw my reflection in the mirror I was aware of the changes in my face. I was twenty-seven and looked it; before, I had appeared young for my age. I imagined myself at thirty-seven ... forty-seven ... still living in the Queen's House, getting older and older, haunted by the ghost of Aunt Charlotte; and the gossip would go on, never to be entirely forgotten and those not yet born would one day say: "That's old Miss Brett. There was some scandal long ago. I never heard quite what. I believe she murdered someone."

It must not come to that. There were days when I promised myself I would escape, but the old stubbornness returned. I was a soldier's daughter. How many times had my father said to me: "Never turn your back on trouble. Always stand and face it."

That was what I was trying to do when once more Chantel came to my rescue.

But the story begins before that.

When I was born my father was a Captain in the Indian Army; he was Aunt Charlotte's brother; there was a great deal of the soldier in her. People are unpredictable. They appear to conform to patterns. Often you can say he or she is such and such a type, but people are rarely types, or not completely so. They conform up to a point and then they diverge wildly. So it was with both my father and Aunt Charlotte. Father was dedicated to his profession. The Army was more important than anything in the world; in fact little else existed for him. My mother often said that he would have run the household like a military camp if she had let him and treated us all as though we were his "men." He quoted Queen's Regulations at breakfast, she said mockingly; and he would grin sheepishly at her for *she* was his divergence. They had met when he was on his way home on leave from India. She told me about it in what I called her butterfly way. She never kept to the point and she would stray off so that one had to guide her back to the original theme if one were interested in it. Sometimes it was more intriguing to let her run on.

But I was interested to hear about my parents' meeting so I kept her to it.

"Moonlit nights on deck, darling. You've no idea how romantic ... Dark skies and the stars like jewels ... and the music and the dancing. The foreign ports and those fantastic bazaars. This heavenly bracelet ... Oh the day we bought that ..."

She would have to be led back. Yes, she had been dancing with the First Officer and she had noticed the tall soldier, so aloof, and she had made a bet that she would make him dance with her. Of course she had and they were married two months later in England.

"Your Aunt Charlotte was furious. Did she think the poor man was a eunuch?"

Her conversation was light and frothy—racy even. She fascinated me as she must have fascinated my father. I was far more like him, I feared, than like her.

In those early days I lived with them though I was more often in the company of my ayah than in theirs. There are vague memories of heat and brilliantly colored flowers, of dark-skinned people washing their clothes in the river. I remember riding in an open carriage with my ayah past the cemetery on the hill where I was told the bodies of the dead were left out in the open that they might become part of the earth and air again. I remember the wicked-looking vultures high up in the trees. They made me shiver.

There came the time when I must return to England and I traveled back with my parents, and myself experienced those tropical nights at sea when the stars seemed to have been placed like jewels on dark blue velvet as though to show off their brilliance. I heard the music and saw the dancing; and for me everything was dominated by my mother, the most beautiful being in the world, with her long draperies, her dark hair piled high on her head, and her incessant, inconsequential chatter.

"Darling, it will only be for a short time. You have to be educated, and we have to go back to India. But you'll stay with Auntie Charlotte." It was typical that she should call her Auntie. Aunt Charlotte was always Aunt to me. "She'll love you darling, because you're named after her—well, partly. They wanted Charlotte for you, but I wasn't going to have my darling daughter called that. It would remind me of *her* ..." She caught herself up sharply, remembering she was trying to put Aunt Charlotte in a good light. "People always like those who have their names. 'But not Charlotte,' I said, 'That's *too* severe ...' So you were Anna Charlotte to be known as Anna and so avoid having two Charlottes in the family. Oh, where was I? Your Auntie Charlotte ... Yes, darling, you have to go to school, my precious, but there are holidays. You can't come all the way out to India in the holidays can you? So Auntie Charlotte will have you at the Queen's House. Now doesn't that sound grand? Queen Elizabeth slept there, I believe. That's where it gets its name. And then ... in no time ... my goodness how time flies, you'll be finished with school and you'll come out to us. I can't wait, my darling, for the day. What fun I shall have launching my daughter." Again that attractive grimace which I believe is called a *moue*. "It will be my compensation for getting old."

She could make anything sound attractive by the way she spoke of it. She could dismiss years with a flick of the hand. She made me see not school and Aunt Charlotte but the days ahead when the ugly duckling I was would be transformed into the swan, looking exactly like my mother.

I was eight years old when I saw the Queen's House for

the first time. The cab which had brought us from the station took us through streets very different from those of Bombay. The people looked sedate, the houses imperious. Here and there was a touch of green in the gardens, such green as I had not seen in India, deep and cool; there was a light drizzle in the air. We caught a glimpse of the river for the town of Langmouth was situated on the estuary of the River Lang and it was for this reason that it had become the busy port it was. Scraps of my mother's chatter lived on in my mind. "What a big ship! Look darling. I suppose that belongs to those people ... what's their name, darling? —those rich and powerful people who own half Langmouth and half of England for that matter?" And my father's voice: "You mean the Creditons, my dear. They do in fact own a very prosperous shipping line but you exaggerate when you say they own half Langmouth, although it is true that Langmouth owes a certain part of its growing prosperity to them."

The Creditons! The name stayed with me.

"They would have a name like that," said my mother. "The creditable Creditons."

My father's lips twitched as they did for my mother; it meant he wanted to laugh but felt it was undignified for a Major to do so. He had gained his majority since my birth and extra dignity with it. He was unapproachable, stern, honorable; and I was as proud of him as I was of my mother.

And so we came to the Queen's House. The carriage drew up before a high red brick wall in which was a wrought-iron gate. It was an exciting moment because standing there looking up at that ancient wall one had no idea what one would find on the other side. And when the gate was opened and we went through it and it shut behind us, the feeling came to me that I had stepped into another age. I had shut out Victorian Langmouth, made prosperous by the industrious Creditons, and had stepped back three hundred years in time.

The garden ran down to the river. It was well kept, though not elaborate and not large either—I should say perhaps three quarters of an acre at most. There were two lawns divided by a path of crazy paving, and on the lawns were shrubs which would doubtless flower in spring or summer; at that time of year they were draped with spiders' webs on which globules of moisture glistened. There was a mass of Michaelmas daisies—like lovely mauve stars, I thought them—and reddish and gold-colored chrysanthemums. The fresh smell of damp earth, grass and green foliage and the faint scent of the flowers was so different from the heavy frangipani perfume of the blooms which grew in such profusion in the hot steamy Indian air.

A path led to the house, which was of three stories—wider than it was tall; it was of the same red brick as the wall. There was an iron-studded door and beside it a heavy iron bell. The windows were latticed, and I believed that I was aware of a certain air of menace, but that may have been because I knew that I was to be left here in the charge of Aunt Charlotte while my parents went away to their gay and colorful life. That was the truth. There was no warning. I did not believe in such things.

Even my mother though was a little subdued on that occasion; but Aunt Charlotte had the power to subdue anyone.

My father—who was not nearly such a martinet as he liked to pretend—may have been aware of my fear; it may have occurred to him that I was very young to be left to the mercy of school, Aunt Charlotte and the Queen's House. But it was no unusual fate. It was happening to young people all the time. It was, as he told me before he left me, a worthwhile experience because it taught one to be self-reliant, to face up to life, to stand on one's own feet; he had a stock of clichés to meet occasions like this.

He tried to warn me. "This is reckoned to be a very interesting house," he told me. "You'll find your Aunt Charlotte an interesting woman. She runs this business ... she's clever at it. She buys and sells valuable old furniture. She'll tell you all about it. That's why she's got this interesting old house. She keeps the furniture she buys here and people come here to see it. She couldn't keep it all in her shop. And of course this sort of business is not ordinary business, so it is quite proper for Aunt Charlotte to do this. It is not as though she were selling butter or sugar over a counter."

I was puzzled by these social differences but too

overawed by my new experiences to bother with such trifles.

He pulled the rope, the old bell clanged and after a wait of some minutes the door was opened by Ellen who dropped a flustered curtsy and bade us come in.

We stepped into a dark hall; odd shapes loomed up all about us and I saw that it was not so much furnished as full of furniture. There were several grandfather clocks and some elaborate ones in ormolu; their ticking was very audible in the silence. The ticking of clocks was something I would always associate with the Queen's House. I noticed two Chinese cabinets, some chairs and several small tables, a bookcase and desk. They were simply put there, not arranged.

Ellen had run off and a woman was coming toward us. I thought at first she was Aunt Charlotte. I should have known that her neat white cap and black bombazine dress indicated the housekeeper.

"Ah, Mrs. Morton," said my father who knew her well. "Here we are with my daughter."

"Madam is in her sitting room," said Mrs. Morton. "I will inform her that you have arrived."

"Pray do," said my father.

My mother looked at me. "Isn't it fascinating?" she whispered, half fearfully, which told me she didn't think so but wanted me to. "All these priceless, precious things! Just look at that escritoire! I'll bet it belonged to the King of the Barbarines."

"Beth," murmured my father in indulgent reproof.

"And look at the claws on the arms of that chair. I'm sure it means *something*. Just think, darling, you may discover. I'd love to know all about these lovely things."

Mrs. Morton had returned, hands neatly folded over bombazine stomach.

"Madam wishes you to come at once to her sitting room."

We ascended a staircase lined with tapestries and a few oil paintings which led us straight into a room which seemed to be filled with more furniture; another room led from this and from that another and this third was Aunt Charlotte's sitting room.

And there she was—tall, gaunt, looking I thought like my father dressed up as a woman; her mid-brown hair with streaks of gray in it was pulled straight back from her big strong face and made into a knot at the back of her head. She wore a tweed skirt and jacket and a severe olive green blouse, the same color as her eyes. I knew afterward that they took their color from her clothes; and as she usually wore grays and that dark shade of green they seemed that tinge too. She was an unusual woman; she might have lived on her small income in some quiet country town, genteelly calling on her friends, leaving cards, perhaps having her own carriage, helping to organize church bazaars, doing charity work, and entertaining in a modest way. But no. Her love of beautiful furniture and porcelain was an obsession. Just as my father had stepped out of line to marry my mother, so had she with her antiques. She had become a businesswoman—a strange phenomenon in this Victorian age: a woman who actually bought and sold and who knew so much about her chosen subject that she could compete with men. Later I was to see her hard face light up at the sight of some rare piece and I have heard her talk with passion about the finials on a Sheraton cabinet.

But everything was so bewildering to me on that day. The cluttered house was not like a house at all: I could not imagine it as a home. "Of course," said my mother, "your true home is with us. This is just where you will stay during holidays. And in a few years time ..."

But I could not think of the passing of the years as lightly as she could.

We did not stay overnight on that occasion, but went straight down to my school in Sherborne, where my parents put up at a hotel nearby and they stayed there until they returned to India. I was touched by this because I knew that in London my mother would have led the kind of life that she loved. "We wanted you to know we weren't far off if school became a little trying just at first," she told me. I liked to think that her divergence was her love for my father and myself, for one would not have expected a butterfly to be capable of so much love and understanding.

I think I began to hate Aunt Charlotte when she criticized my mother.

"Feather-brained," she said. "I could never understand your father."

"I could understand him," I retorted firmly. "I could understand anyone. She is different from other people." And I hoped my withering look conveyed that "other people" meant Aunt Charlotte.

The first year at school was the hardest to endure, but the holidays were more so. I even made plans to stow away on a ship that was going to India. I made Ellen, who accompanied me on my walks, take me down to the docks where I would gaze longingly at the ships and wonder where they were going.

"That's a ship of the Lady Line," Ellen would tell me proudly. "She belongs to the Creditons." And I would gaze at her while Ellen pointed out her beauties to me. "That's a clipper," she would say. "One of the fastest ships that ever sailed. It goes out and brings back wool from Australia and tea from China. Oh, look at *her*. Did you ever see such a beautiful barque!"

Ellen prided herself on her knowledge. She was a Langmouth girl and I remembered that Langmouth owed its prosperity to the Creditons; moreover she had an added distinction: her sister Edith was a housemaid up at Castle Crediton. And she would take me to see that—but only from the outside of course—before I was many days older.

Because I dreamed of running away to India I was fascinated by the ships. It seemed romantic that they should roam round the world loading and unloading their cargoes—bananas and tea, oranges and woodpulp for making paper in the big factory which the Creditons had founded and which, Ellen told me, provided work for many people of Langmouth. There was the grand new dock which had been recently opened by Lady Crediton herself. There was a "one," said Ellen. She had been beside Sir Edward in everything he had done and you would hardly have expected that from a lady, would you?

I replied that I would expect anything from the Creditons.

Ellen nodded approval. I was beginning to know something of the place in which I lived. Oh, it was a sight she told me to see a ship come into harbor or sail away—to see the white canvas billowing in the wind and the gulls screaming and whirling around. I began to agree with her. There were Ladies—she told me—Mermaids and

Amazons in the Lady Line. It was Sir Edward's tribute to Lady Crediton, who had stood with him all the time and had a business head which was remarkable for a woman.

"It's really very romantic," said Ellen.

Of course it was. The Creditons were romantic. They were clever, rich, and in fact superhuman, I pointed out.

"And don't you be saucy," said Ellen to that.

She showed me Castle Crediton. It was built high on the cliff facing out to the sea. An enormous gray stone fortress, with its battlemented towers and a keep, it was just like a castle. Wasn't this a little ostentatious, I asked, because people did not build castles now, so this was not a real castle. It had only stood there for fifty years. It was a little deceitful, wasn't it, to make it look as though the Normans had built it?

Ellen looked about her furtively as though she expected me to be struck dumb for uttering such blasphemy. It was clear that I was a newcomer to Langmouth and had not yet discovered the power of the Creditons.

But Ellen it was who interested me in Langmouth and to be interested in Langmouth meant to be interested in the Creditons. Ellen had heard tales from her parents. Once ... not very long ago, Langmouth had not been the grand town it was today. There was no Theatre Royal; there were no elegant houses built on the cliffs overlooking the bridge. Many of the streets were narrow and cobbled and it wasn't safe to wander out to the docks. Of course the fine Edward Dock had not been built then. But in the old days the ships used to sail out to Africa to capture slaves. Ellen's father could remember their being auctioned in the sheds on the docks. Gentlemen came all the way from the West Indies to bargain for them and take them off to work on their sugar plantations. That was all over. It was very different now. Sir Edward Crediton had come along: he had modernized the place: he had started the Lady Line; and although Langmouth's very situation and its excellent harbor had given it some significance, it could never have been the town it was today but for the magnificent Creditons.

It was Ellen who made life bearable for me during that first year. I never could be fond of Mrs. Morton: she was too much like Aunt Charlotte. Her face seemed like a door that was kept tightly shut; her eyes were windows—

too small to show what was behind them and they were obscurely curtained—inscrutable; she did not want me in the house. I quickly learned that. She complained of me to Aunt Charlotte. I had brought in mud from the garden on my boots, I had left the soap in the water so that half the tablet was wasted (Aunt Charlotte was very parsimonious and hated spending money except to buy antiques), I had broken the china teacup which was a part of the set. Mrs. Morton never complained to me; she was icily polite. Had she raged at me or accused me to my face I could have liked her better. Then there was plump Mrs. Buckle who mixed the beeswax and turpentine, polished the precious pieces and kept a watch for that ever threatening enemy: woodworm. She was talkative and I found her company as stimulating as that of Ellen.

I began to have odd fancies about the Queen's House. I pictured how it must have looked years ago when it had been treated as a house. In the hall there would have been an oak chest, a refectory table and a suit of armor at the foot of the beautiful staircase. The walls would have been decorated with the family portraits, not the occasional picture, and those enormous tapestries which were hung irrespective of color—sometimes one over another. I used to fancy that the house resented what had been done to it. All those chairs and tables, cabinets, bureaus, and clocks ticking away sometimes fussily as though exasperated with their surroundings, sometimes angrily so that they sounded ominous.

I told Ellen that they said "Hurry up! Hurry up!" sometimes to remind us that the time was passing and we were growing older every day.

"As if we need reminding of that!" cried Mrs. Buckle, three chins shaking with laughter.

Ellen jerked a finger at me. "Missing her Ma and Pa, that's what. Waiting for the time when they come and get her."

I agreed. "But when I haven't done my holiday task they remind me of that. Time can remind you of quickness and slowness but it always seems to *warn*."

"The things she says!" commented Ellen.

And Mrs. Buckle's plump form shivered like a jelly with secret mirth.

But I was fascinated by the Queen's House and by Aunt

Charlotte. She was no ordinary woman any more than the Queen's House was an ordinary house. At first I was obsessed by the idea that the house was a living personality—and that it hated us all because we were in the conspiracy to make it merely a store for goods—precious as they were.

"The ghosts of people who lived here are angry because Aunt Charlotte has made their home unrecognizable," I told Ellen and Mrs. Buckle.

"Lord a' mercy!" cried Mrs. Buckle.

Ellen said it wasn't right to talk of such things.

But I insisted on talking. "One day," I said, "the ghosts of the house will rise up and something fearful will happen."

That was in the first months. Later my feelings toward Aunt Charlotte changed and although I could never love her, I respected her.

Practical in the extreme, down to earth, unromantic, she did not see the Queen's House as I saw it. To her it was rooms within walls—ancient it was true and the sole virtue in this was that it made an appropriate setting for her pieces. There was only one room in the house which she allowed to keep its character and she had even come to this decision for business reasons. This was the room in which Queen Elizabeth was reputed to have slept. There was even the Elizabethan bed, reputed to be the bed itself; and as a concession to this legend—if legend it was—everything in the room was Tudor. It was for business, she said hurriedly. Many people came to see this room; it put them in the right "mood"; they were fascinated and because of this prepared to pay the price she asked.

I often went to that room and found some comfort there. I used to say to myself: "The past is on my side . . . against Aunt Charlotte. The ghosts feel my sympathy." That was my fanciful notion. And during those months I needed sympathy.

I used to stand in that room and touch the bedposts and think of the famous Tilbury speech which my father had often quoted to me. "I know I have the body of a weak, feeble woman; but I have the heart and stomach of a king—and of a king of England too . . ." And then I was as certain that I would come through this unhappy period as she had been of victory over the Spaniards.

So it was understandable that the house offered me compensation and I began to feel that it was alive. I became familiar with its night noises—the sudden inexplicable creak of a floorboard, the rattle of a window, and how when the wind moaned through the branches of the chestnut tree it sounded like whispering voices.

There were days when Aunt Charlotte went away to buy. She would visit sales at old houses sometimes quite far away and after she returned we would be more cluttered than ever. Aunt Charlotte had a shop in the center of the town and there she displayed certain pieces but most of the goods were in the house and strangers were constantly visiting us.

Miss Beringer spent all her time at the shop to allow Aunt Charlotte to absent herself, but Aunt Charlotte said the woman was a fool and had little appreciation of values. That was not true; it merely meant that Miss Beringer lacked Aunt Charlotte's knowledge. But Aunt Charlotte was so efficient herself that she thought most people fools.

For at least a year I was what Aunt Charlotte would call "a cross," in other words a burden; but that changed suddenly. It was a table which caught my attention. I was suddenly excited merely to look at it and I was crouching on the floor examining the carvings on the legs when Aunt Charlotte discovered me. She squatted on the floor beside me.

"Rather a fine example," she said gruffly.

"It's French, isn't it?" I asked.

Her lips turned up at the corners which was as near to a smile as she could get.

She nodded. "It's unsigned but I believe it's the work of René Dubois. I thought at first his father Jacques was responsible for it, but I fancy it's a year or two later. That green and gold lacquer on the oak carcase, you see! And look at those bronze mounts."

I looked and found myself touching it reverently.

"It would be the end of the eighteenth century," I hazarded.

"No, no." She shook her head impatiently. "Fifty years early. Mid-eighteenth century."

After that our relationship changed. She would sometimes call me and say: "Here! What do you think of this?

What do you notice about it?" At first I felt a certain desire to score over her, to show her that I knew something about her precious goods; but later it became a great interest to me and I began to understand the difference between the furniture of various countries and to recognize period by certain features.

One day Aunt Charlotte went so far as to admit: "You know as much as that fool Beringer." But that was when she was particularly incensed by that long suffering lady.

But as far as I was concerned the Queen's House took on a new fascination. I began to know certain pieces, to regard them as old friends. Mrs. Buckle dusting with deft but careful hands said: "Here, are you going to be another Miss Charlotte Brett, Miss Anna?"

That startled me; I felt then as though I wanted to run away.

It was one morning in the middle of the summer holidays, about four years after my parents had brought me to England, when Ellen came to my room and told me that Aunt Charlotte wished to see me at once. Ellen looked scared and I asked if anything was wrong.

"I've not been told, miss," said Ellen, but I was aware that she knew something.

I made my way—one made one's way in the Queen's House—to Aunt Charlotte's sitting room.

There she was, seated with papers before her, for she used the place as her office. Her desk on that day was a sturdy refectory table—sixteenth-century English, of a type that owed its charm to its age rather than its beauty. She sat very upright on a rather heavy chair of the Yorkshire-Derbyshire type of carved and turned oak, of much later period than the table, but as strong and sturdy. She chose these strong pieces for use while they were in the house. The rest of the office did not match the table and chair. An exquisite piece of tapestry hung on the wall. I knew it to be of the Flemish school, and guessed it would not be there for long; and crowded together were heavy oak pieces from Germany side by side with a delicate French eighteenth-century commode and two pieces in the Boulle tradition. I noticed the change in myself. I could sum up the contents of a room, date them and note their qualities even while I was eager to know what this summons meant.

"Sit down," said Aunt Charlotte, and her expression was more grim than usual.

I sat and she went on in her brusque way. "Your mother is dead. It was cholera."

How like her to shatter my future with two brief sentences. The thought of reunion had been like a lifebelt, which had prevented my being submerged in the misery of my loneliness. And she said it calmly like that. Dead . . . of cholera.

She looked at me fearfully; she hated any display of emotion.

"Go to your room. I'll send Ellen up with some hot milk."

Hot milk! Did she think that could console me?

"I've no doubt," she said, "your father will be writing to you. He will have made arrangements."

I hated her then, which was wrong for she was breaking the news in the only way she considered possible. She was offering me hot milk and my father's arrangements to console me for the loss of my beloved mother.

2

My father did write to me. We shared our grief, he said; he would not dwell on that. The death of his beloved wife and my dear mother had meant his making great changes. He was thankful that I was in the hands of his dear sister, my Aunt Charlotte, on whose good sense and great virtue he relied. It was a great comfort to him to know that I was in such hands. He trusted I was suitably grateful. He thought he would be leaving India shortly. He had asked to be transferred and he had good friends at the War Office. He had received the utmost sympathy and as there was trouble brewing in other parts of the world, he believed that very soon he would be doing his duty in another field.

I felt as though I were caught in a web, as though the house was laughing at me. "You belong to us now!" it seemed to say. "Don't imagine because your Aunt Charlotte has filled the house with these alien ghosts you have ousted us." What foolish thoughts. It was fortunate that I kept them to myself. Only Ellen and Mrs. Buckle thought me an odd child, but even Mrs. Morton had some sympathy for me. I heard her say to Miss Beringer that people shouldn't have children unless they could look after them. It wasn't natural for fathers and mothers to be on one side of the world and their children on another in the hands of those who knew nothing of them and paid more attention to a piece of wood—and often riddled with the worm at that! As for me I had to face the fact that I should never see my mother again. I kept remembering scraps of her conversation; I idealized her beauty. I saw her in the figures on a Grecian vase, in the carving of a tallboy, in the gilded beauty supporting a seventeenth-century mirror. I would never forget her; the hope of that wonderful life she had promised me had gone and I was certain now that the ugly duckling would never turn into a swan. Sometimes when I had looked into old mirrors—some of metal, others of mottled glass—I had seen her face, not my own rather sallow one with the heavy dark hair which was the same color as hers. My deep-set dark eyes were like hers too; but the resemblance ended there for my face was too thin, my nose a little too sharp. How was it that two people who were fundamentally alike could look so different? I lacked her sparkle, her gaiety, but when she was alive I could imagine myself growing like her. After she was dead I could not.

"It's a long time since you've seen her," soothed Ellen, seeking to offer comfort with the hot milk.

"Children forget, quick as lightning," I heard her say to Mrs. Buckle.

And I thought: Never. Never. I shall always remember.

Everyone tried to be kind—even Aunt Charlotte. She offered me the greatest consolation she could think of.

"I have to go along to see a piece. I'll take you with me. It's at Castle Crediton."

"Are they selling something?" I stammered.

"Why else should we go there?" demanded Aunt Charlotte.

For the first time since my mother's death I forgot her. I was sorry afterward and apologized to my reflection in the mirror where instead of my own face I made myself see hers, but I could not help the excitement which came to me at the prospect of visiting Castle Crediton. I remembered vividly the first time I had seen it and my mother's comments and I wanted to know more about that important family.

It was fortunate that I had learned to hide my emotions and that Aunt Charlotte had no notion of how I was feeling as we drove under the stone gatehouse and looked up at the conical turrets.

"Fake!" snapped Aunt Charlotte. It was the biggest insult she could offer.

I wanted to laugh when I entered that house. The inside of Castle Crediton should have been the inside of the Queen's House. The Creditons had made a great effort to produce a Tudor interior and had succeeded. There was the big hall with long refectory table on which stood a large pewter bowl. There were firearms on the walls and the inevitable suit of armor at the foot of the staircase. Aunt Charlotte saw only the furniture.

"I supplied the table," she said. "It came from a castle in Kent."

"It looks very well here," I commented.

Aunt Charlotte did not answer. The manservant returned to say that Lady Crediton would receive Miss Brett. He looked at me questioningly and Aunt Charlotte said quickly: "You may wait here for a while!" in such a manner as to defy the servant to object.

So I waited in the hall and I looked at the thick stone walls partially covered with tapestries—lovely French Gobelin type in beautiful blues and stone color. I went up and examined one. It depicted the labors of Hercules. I was studying it intently when a voice behind me said: "Like it?"

I turned and saw that a man was standing close to me. I was startled. He looked so tall and I wasn't quite sure what he was thinking of me. The color heightened in my cheeks but I said coolly, "It's beautiful. Is it really Gobelin?"

He lifted his shoulders and I noticed the interesting way his eyes seemed to turn up at the corners when his lips did. He was scarcely handsome but with the blond hair bleached by sun at the temples and blue eyes that were rather small and crinkled as though he had lived in brilliant sunlight, his was the sort of face which I felt I would not easily forget.

"I might ask," he said, "what you are doing here. But I won't . . . unless you want to tell me."

"I'm waiting for my aunt, Miss Brett. She has come to see some furniture. We're from the Queen's House," I said.

"Oh, that place!"

I fancied there was a hint of mockery in his voice and was warm in its defense. "It's a fascinating house. Queen Elizabeth once slept there."

"Such a habit that lady had for sleeping in other people's houses!"

"Well, she slept in ours, which is more . . ."

"Than you can say for this one. No, we're imitation Norman, I admit. But we're firm and solid and this is the house that will withstand the winds of time. We're built on a rock."

"Ours has proved it could do that. But I find it very interesting here."

"I'm delighted to hear it."

"Do you live here?"

"When I'm ashore. Mostly I'm not."

"Oh . . . you're a sailor."

"How discerning you are."

"I'm not really about people. Though I am learning about some things."

"Tapestries?"

"And old furniture."

"Going to follow in Auntie's footsteps?"

"No. No!" I spoke with great vehemence.

"I expect you will. Most of us go where we're led. And think what you already know about Gobelin tapestry."

"Did you . . . go where you were led?"

He raised his eyes to the ceiling in a manner which, for no reason I could think of, I found very attractive. "I suppose you could say that I did."

I was filled with a desire to know more about him. He was just the sort of person I should have expected to meet in Castle Crediton and he excited me as though he were an unusual piece of furniture.

"What should I call you?" I asked.

"Should you call me?"

"I mean . . . I should like to know your name."

"It's Redvers Stretton—usually known as Red."

"Oh!" I was disappointed and showed it.

"You don't like it?"

"Well, Red is not very dignified."

"Don't forget it is really Redvers which you must admit is more so."

"I've never heard that name before."

"I must say in its defense that it's a good old West Country name."

"Is it? And I thought it should go with Crediton."

That amused him secretly. "I couldn't agree more," he said.

I had a notion that he was laughing at me and that I was being very naïve.

He said: "I must ask yours, mustn't I, otherwise you may think me impolite."

"I shouldn't but if you really want to know . . ."

"Oh, I do."

"It's Anna Brett."

"Anna Brett!" He repeated it as though memorizing it. "How old are you, Miss Anna Brett?"

"I'm twelve."

"So young . . . and so knowledgeable."

"It's living in the Queen's House."

"It must be like living in a museum."

"It is in a way."

"It makes you old before your time. You make me feel young and frivolous."

"I'm sorry."

"Please don't be. I like it. I'm seven years older than you."

"So much?"

He nodded and his eyes seemed to disappear when he laughed.

The manservant had come back into the hall.

"Her ladyship is requesting the young lady's presence," he said. "Will you follow me, miss?"

As I turned away Redvers Stretton said: "We'll meet again . . . less briefly, I hope."

"I shall hope so too," I replied sedately and sincerely.

The manservant gave no indication that he considered Redvers Stretton's behavior in the least strange and I followed him past the suit of armor up the wide staircase. I was almost certain that the vase at the turn of the staircase was of the Ming reign because of the rich violet color of the porcelain. I could not prevent myself gazing at it, then I turned and saw Redvers Stretton standing looking up at me, legs slightly apart, hands in pockets. He bowed his head in acknowledgment of the compliment I had paid him by turning round and I wished I hadn't because I felt it showed a rather childish curiosity. I turned away and hurried after the servant. We came to a gallery hung with oil paintings, and I felt a little impatient with myself because I could not assess their value. The largest of the pictures in the center of the gallery was of a man and I was able to guess that it had been painted some fifty years before. I was certain it was Sir Edward Crediton, the founder of the shipping line, the dead husband of the woman I was shortly to see. How I wished I might have paused longer to study it; as it was I caught a fleeting glimpse of that rugged face—powerful, ruthless, perhaps yes, and with a slight tiptilt of the eyes which was so pronounced in the man I had met a few minutes ago. But he was not a Crediton. He must be a nephew or some such relation. It was the only answer.

The servant had paused and tapped on a door. He threw it open and announced: "The young lady, my lady."

I entered the room. Aunt Charlotte was seated on a chair, very straight-backed, expression grim, in her best bargaining mood. I had seen her like this often.

Seated on a large ornamental chair—Restoration period with the finely scrolled arms and the crown emblems—sat a woman, also large but scarcely ornamental. She was very dark, her skin sallow and her eyes looked as black as currants and as alert as a monkey's. They were young eyes and defied her wrinkles—young and shrewd. Her lips were thin and tight; they reminded me of a steel trap. Her large hands, quite smooth and white were adorned by several rings—diamonds and rubies. They lay on her voluminous lap and from the folds of her skirt jet-beaded satin slippers were visible.

I was immediately overawed and my respect for Aunt Charlotte rose because she could sit there looking so unperturbed in the presence of this formidable woman.

"My niece, Lady Crediton."

I curtsied and Lady Crediton gave me the full attention of her marmoset eyes for a few seconds.

"She is learning to know antiques," went on Aunt Charlotte, "and will be accompanying me now and then."

Was I? I thought. It was the first time it had been stated, although I realized that for some time it had been implied. It was enough explanation of me. They both turned their attention to the escritoire which they had evidently been discussing when I entered. I listened intently.

"I must call your attention, Lady Crediton," Aunt Charlotte was saying almost maliciously I thought, "to the fact that it is only accredited to Boulle. It has the richly scrolled corner pieces, true. But I am of the opinion that it is of a slightly later period."

It was a beautiful piece, I could recognize that, but Aunt Charlotte would not have it so. "It is definitely marked," she said. Lady Crediton had no idea how difficult it was to dispose of furniture that was not in first class condition.

Lady Crediton was sure that any defects could be put right by any man who knew his business.

Aunt Charlotte gave a hoarse cackle.

The man who knew that business had been dead more than a hundred years—that is if André-Charles Boulle was really responsible, which Aunt Charlotte gravely doubted.

And so they went on—Lady Crediton pointing out its virtues, Aunt Charlotte its defects.

"I don't think there is another piece like it in England," declared Lady Crediton.

"Would you give me a commission to find you one?" demanded Aunt Charlotte triumphantly.

"Miss Brett, I am disposing of this one because I have no use for it."

"I doubt whether I could find an easy buyer."

"Perhaps another dealer might not agree with you."

I listened and all the time I was thinking of the man downstairs and wondering about the relationship between him and this woman and the man in the portrait in the gallery.

Finally they came to an agreement. Aunt Charlotte had

offered a price which she admitted was folly on her part and Lady Crediton could not understand why she should make such a sacrifice.

I thought: They are two of a kind. Hard both of them. But the matter was completed and the escritoire would arrive at the Queen's House in the next few days.

"My patience me!" said Aunt Charlotte as we drove away. "She makes a hard bargain."

"You paid too much for it, Aunt?"

Aunt Charlotte smiled grimly. "I expect to make a fair profit when the right buyer comes along."

She was smiling and I knew she was thinking that she had got the better of Lady Crediton; and I wished that I could have crept back to Castle Crediton and heard Lady Crediton's comments.

The man I had met in the hall of the Castle would not be dismissed from my mind so I judiciously set about discovering if Ellen knew anything about him.

When we went for our walk I led the way up to the cliff top facing the Castle and we sat on one of the seats which had been put there by something called the Crediton Town Trust, the object of which was to add amenities to the town.

The seat was one of my favorites because I could sit on it and gaze across the river at the Castle.

"I went there with Aunt Charlotte," I told Ellen. "We bought a Boulle escritoire."

Ellen sniffed at what she called my "showing off" so I came quickly to the point which was not on this occasion to show my superior knowledge.

"I saw Lady Crediton and . . . a man."

Ellen was interested.

"What sort of man? Young?"

"Quite old," I replied. "Seven years older than I am."

"Call that old!" laughed Ellen. "Besides, how did you know?"

"He told me."

She looked at me suspiciously so I decided to come straight to the point before she accused me of doing what she called "playing the light fantastic." She used to say:

"The trouble with you, miss, is I never know whether you've dreamed half you tell me."

"This man was in the hall and saw me looking at the tapestry. He told me his name was Redvers Stretton."

"Oh him," said Ellen.

"Why do you say it like that?"

"How?"

"Scornfully. I thought everyone in that place was a sort of god to you. Who is Redvers Stretton and what's he doing there?"

Ellen looked at me obliquely. "I don't think I ought to tell you," she said.

"Whyever not?"

"I'm sure it's something Miss Brett wouldn't want you to know."

"I'm fully aware it's not connected with Boulle cabinets and Louis Quinze commodes—and that's the only thing Aunt Charlotte thinks I should concern myself with. What is it about that man that mustn't be talked of?"

Ellen looked over her shoulder in that now familiar fearful way, as though she believed the heavens would open and dead Creditons would appear to wreak vengeance on us for having committed the sin of lese majesty— or whatever one would call showing lack of respect to the Creditons.

"Oh come on, Ellen," I cried. "Don't be silly. Tell."

Ellen pressed her lips tightly together. I knew this mood and had never so far failed to wheedle from her what I wanted to know. I cajoled and threatened. I would betray her interest in the man who came with the firm of furniture movers and who often conveyed pieces to and from the Queen's House; I would tell her sister that she had betrayed certain Crediton secrets to me already.

But she was firm. With the expression of a martyr about to be burned at the stake for her faith she refused to talk of Redvers Stretton.

If she had it would have been easier perhaps to forget him. But I had to have something to stop my brooding on my mother's death. Redvers Stretton supplied that need; and the fact that his presence at Castle Crediton was a mystery helped in those weeks to lighten the melancholy caused by my mother's death.

The escritoire was put in the large room at the top of the house which was even more overflowing than the rest. This room had always fascinated me because the staircase leading to it was one of those which opened into the middle of it; the roof sloped at each end so that the ceiling was only a few inches from the floor. I thought it was the most interesting room in the house and tried to imagine what it had looked like before Aunt Charlotte had turned it into a store room. Mrs. Buckle always complained about it. How she was expected to keep that lot free from dust, she did not know. When I had come home from school last holidays Aunt Charlotte told me that I should have to sleep in the room which led off this top room because she had bought a new tallboy and two very special armchairs which had to be kept in my old room, so that I would not very easily be able to reach my bed. At first I had felt it rather eerie up there, but later I had begun to like it.

The escritoire was put between a cabinet full of Wedgwood china and a grandfather clock. When a piece came it was always thoroughly cleaned and I asked Aunt Charlotte if I could do this. She gruffly said I might and although it was against her principles to show pleasure she could not hide that this was how she felt about my interest. Mrs. Buckle showed me how to mix the beeswax and turpentine which we always used and I set to work. I polished that wood with extra loving care and I was thinking about Castle Crediton and chiefly Redvers Stretton and telling myself that I *must* find out from Ellen who he was when I was suddenly aware that there was something unusual about one of the drawers in the escritoire. It was smaller than the others and I could not understand why.

Excitedly I ran down to Aunt Charlotte's sitting room where she was busy with her accounts. I said I thought there was something rather strange about the escritoire, and that brought her up to the top of the house at great speed.

She tapped on the drawer and smiled. "Oh yes. An old trick. There's a secret drawer here."

A secret drawer!

She gave me the benefit of her grim mirthless laugh. "Nothing extraordinary. They had them made to conceal their jewelry from casual burglars or to put in papers or secret documents."

I was so excited that I could not restrain my feelings and Aunt Charlotte was not displeased.

"Look here, I'll show you. Nothing very special about this. You'll often come across them. There's a spring. It's usually about here. Ah, there it is." The back of the drawer opened like a door and displayed a cavity behind it.

"Aunt, there's something there."

She put in her hand and took it out. It was a figure, about six inches long. "It's a woman," I said. "Oh ... it's beautiful."

"Plaster," she said. "Worthless."

She was scowling at it. Clearly it had no value. But to me it was intensely exciting, partly because it had been found in a secret drawer but chiefly because it had come from Castle Crediton.

She was turning it over in her hand. "It's been broken off from something."

"But why should it have been in the secret drawer?"

She shrugged her shoulders. "It's not worth much," she repeated.

"Aunt, may I have it in my room?"

She handed it over to me. "I'm surprised you are interested in a thing like that. It's of no value."

I slipped the figure into my apron pocket and picked up my duster. Aunt Charlotte returned to her accounts. As soon as she had gone I examined the figure. The hair was wild, the hands were outstretched, and long draperies were molded to look as though they were blowing in a strong wind. I wondered who had put it there in the secret drawer and why, if it were of no value. I also wondered whether we ought to take it back to Lady Crediton, but when I suggested this to Aunt Charlotte she pooh-poohed the idea. "They'd think you crazy. It's worthless. Besides I overpaid her anyway. If it had been worth five pounds it would have been mine ... for the price I gave her. But it's not. It's not worth five shillings."

So the figure stood up on my dressing table and comforted me as I had not been comforted since my mother's death. I very quickly noticed the half obliterated writing on the skirts and with the aid of a microscope I made out the inscription: *The Secret Woman.*

My father came home that year. He was changed, more remote than ever without my mother's softening influence. I realized that the future I had looked forward to could never be. I had always known it could not be ideal without her but I had had dreams of joining my father, becoming his companion as she had been; I saw now how impossible that was.

He had become very silent and he had always been undemonstrative, and I had not the power to fascinate him that my mother had had.

He was leaving India, he told me, and was going to Africa. I read the papers and would know that there was trouble out there. We had a large Empire to protect and that meant that there would always be trouble in some remote spot on the globe. He had no desire now for anything but to serve the Queen and the Empire; and he was grateful—as I must always be—to Aunt Charlotte, for making it possible for him to feel at ease as to my welfare. In a year or so I should go to Switzerland to finish my education. It was what my mother had wished. A year there, say, and then we would see.

He went off to join his regiment and take part in the Zulu War.

Six months later we heard that he had been killed.

"He died as he would have wished to die," said Aunt Charlotte.

I did not mourn as I did for my mother. By this time he had become a stranger to me.

I was seventeen. Aunt Charlotte was now my only relative, as she was fond of telling me, and I relied on her. I was beginning to think that to some extent she relied on me; but this was never mentioned.

The household seemed to have changed little in the ten years since I had first walked through that gate in the red wall, but life had changed drastically for me, though not for the inhabitants of the Queen's House. They were nearly all ten years older, it was true. Ellen was now twenty-five; Mrs. Buckle had had her first grandchildren; Mrs. Morton looked almost exactly the same; Miss Beringer was now thirty-nine. Aunt Charlotte seemed to have changed less than any of us, but then I had always seen her as the grim old woman she appeared to be at that time. There is something timeless about the Aunt Charlottes of the world; they are born old and shrewd and stay so until the end.

I had discovered the reason why Redvers Stretton was at Castle Crediton. Ellen had told me on my sixteenth birthday because I was, as she said, no longer a child and it was time I started learning something about life which I couldn't from a lot of worm-eaten old furniture. This was because I was increasing my knowledge considerably and even Aunt Charlotte was beginning to have a mild respect for my opinions.

"He's got a sort of right to be up at the Castle," Ellen told me one day when we were sitting on the seat looking across the river to that pile of gray stone, "but it's what you might call a left-handed right."

"What on earth is that, Ellen?"

"Ah, Miss Clever, you'd like to know, wouldn't you?"

I said humbly that I would. And I heard the story. You had to learn about men, Ellen informed me. They were different from women; they could do certain things which while deplorable and not exactly right were to be forgiven if performed by men, whereas if a woman had done the same thing she would have been cut off from society. The fact was that Sir Edward was a very *manly* man.

"He was very fond of the ladies."

"The ships you mean?"

"No, I don't. I mean flesh and blood ladies. He'd been married to Lady Crediton for ten years and there was no child. It was a blow. Well, to cut a long story short. He took a fancy to his wife's lady's maid. They say he wanted to know whose fault it was, his or his wife's that there weren't any children, because what he wanted most of all was a son. It was a bit comic in a way ... if you can think of anything so sinful as being comic. Lady Crediton found that at long last she was going to have a child. So was the lady's maid."

"And what did Lady Crediton say to that?" I pictured her seated in her chair, hands folded on her lap. Of course she would have looked different then. A young woman. Or comparatively young.

"They always said she was a clever woman. She wanted a son the same as he did, for the business, you see. And she was nearly forty. It was the very first and that is not the best time for having children, not first ones at least."

"And the lady's maid?"

"She was twenty-one. Sir Edward was cautious. Besides he wanted a son. Suppose Lady Crediton was to have a girl and the lady's maid a son. You see, he was greedy. He wanted them both. And Lady Crediton, well, she's a strange woman and it seems they came to terms. The two babies were to be born at about the same time and they were both going to be born in the Castle."

"How very strange."

"Well, there's nothing ordinary about the Creditons," said Ellen proudly.

"So the babies were born?"

"Yes, two boys. I reckon if he'd have known Lady Crediton was to have a boy he wouldn't have had all the scandal. But how was he to know?"

Even Sir Edward didn't know everything, I pointed out ironically, but Ellen was too carried away by the story to complain of my disrespect this time.

"So the two boys were to be brought up in the Castle and Sir Edward claimed them both. There was Rex."

"He was to be the King."

"Lady Crediton's son," said Ellen, "and Valerie Stretton's was the other."

So *he* is the other.

"Redvers. Valerie Stretton had the finest red hair you've ever seen. His turned out fair but he's more like Sir Edward than like his mother. He was brought up with Master Rex; the same tutors, same school, and both brought up for the business. Young Red, he wanted to go to sea; perhaps Mr. Rex wanted it too, but he had to learn how to juggle with the money. So now you know."

Ellen then went on to talk of something of greater interest—to her—than the Creditons' "goings-on": her own relationship with the fascinating Mr. Orfey, the furniture remover who would one day marry her, when he could offer her the home he considered worthy of her. Ellen sincerely hoped he would not wait too long for she was no longer so young and she would be content with one room and as she put it "Mr. Orfey's love." But Mr. Orfey was not like that. He wanted to be sure of what he called a settled future; he wanted to put the money down for a horse and cart of his own from which he would expand.

It was Ellen's dream that one day a miracle would happen and the money would come from somewhere. Where did she think? I asked her. You never knew, she replied. Aunt Charlotte had once told her that if she was still in her employ at the time of her death there might be a little something for her. That was when Ellen had hinted that she might find more congenial employment elsewhere.

"You never know," said Ellen. "But I'm not one to like waiting for dead men's shoes."

I listened half-heartedly to an account of the virtues of Mr. Orfey, and all the time I was thinking of the man I had met—long ago now, the son of Sir Edward and the lady's maid. I could not understand why I continued to think of him.

I was now eighteen.

"Finishing schools," snapped Aunt Charlotte. "That was your mother's nonsense. And where do you think the money would come from for finishing schools? Your father's pay stopped with him and he saved nothing. Your mother saw to that. When he died I believe he was still paying off the debts she incurred. As for your future—it's clear that you have a flair for this profession. Mind you, you have a lot to learn ... and one is always learning, but I think you might be fairly promising. So you'll leave school after next term and begin."

That was what I did and when a year later Miss Beringer decided to get married, the arrangement from Aunt Charlotte's point of view was ideal. "Old fool," said Aunt Charlotte. "At her time of life. You'd think she'd know better." Miss Beringer might have been an old fool but her husband wasn't and, as Aunt Charlotte told me, Miss Beringer had put a little money into the business— that was the only reason why Aunt Charlotte had taken her in—and now that man was making difficulties. There were visits from lawyers which Aunt Charlotte did not like at all, and I supposed that they came to some arrangement.

It was true that I had a flair. I could go to a sale and my eyes would alight as if by magic on the most interesting pieces. Aunt Charlotte was pleased, though she rarely showed it; she stressed my errors of judgment which were becoming rarer and lightly passed over my successes which were growing more and more frequent.

In the town we became known as Old and Young Miss Brett and I knew that it was said that it was somehow not *nice* for a young girl to be involved in business; it was unfeminine and I should never find a husband. I should be another Miss Charlotte Brett in a few years time.

And it was borne home to me that that was exactly what Aunt Charlotte wanted.

3

The years were passing. I was twenty-one. Aunt Charlotte had developed an unpleasant complaint which she called "rheumatics"; her limbs were becoming more and more stiff and painful, and to her fury her movements were considerably restricted.

She was the last woman to accept illness; she rebelled against it, was impatient with my suggestion that she should see a doctor and did everything she could to continue with her active life.

Her attitude was slowly changing toward me as she relied on me more. She was constantly hinting at my duty, reminding me how she had taken me in, wondering what would have become of me if when I was orphaned she had not been at hand. I became friendly with John Carmel, an antique dealer who lived in the town of Marden some ten miles inland. We had met at a sale at a manor house and become friendly. After that he was constantly calling at the Queen's House and inviting me to accompany him to sales.

We had not progressed beyond an interested friendship

when his visits ceased abruptly. I was hurt and wondered why until I overheard Ellen say to Mrs. Morton, "*She gave him the order of the boot. Oh yes, she did. I heard it all. I think it a shame. After all Miss has her life to lead. There's no reason why she should be an old maid like her.*"

An old maid like her! In my cluttered room, the grandfather clock in the corner ticked maliciously. Old maid! Old maid! it jeered.

I was a prisoner in the Queen's House. One day it might all be mine. Aunt Charlotte had hinted as much. "If you're with me," she had said significantly.

"You'll be here! You'll be here!" Why did I imagine the clock said these things to me? The date on the old grandfather was 1702, so he was old already. It was unfair, I thought, that an inanimate piece of furniture made by a man lived on and we had to die. My mother had lived for thirty years only, yet this clock had been on earth for more than a hundred and eighty years.

One should make the most of one's time. Tick, tock! Tick, tock! All over the house. Time was flying past.

I did not believe I should ever have wanted to marry John Carmel, but Aunt Charlotte was not going to give me the chance to find out. Strangely enough when I thought of romance a vision of a laughing face with tiptilted eyes came to my mind. I was obsessed by the Creditons.

If the time came, I promised myself, that I wanted to marry, nothing and nobody should stop me.

Tick, tock! mocked the grandfather clock, but I was sure of this. I might be like Aunt Charlotte but she was a strong woman.

I was in the shop and on the point of fixing the notice on the door "If closed call at the Queen's House" when the bell over the door tinkled and Redvers Stretton came in. He stood smiling at me. "We've met before," he said, "if I'm not mistaken."

I was embarrassed to find myself coloring. "It was years ago," I mumbled.

"You've grown up in the meantime. You were twelve at the time."

I was ridiculously delighted that he remembered. "Then it must be nine years ago."

"You were informative then," he said, and briefly he looked round the shop at the circular table inlaid with ivory, and the dainty set of Sheraton chairs and the tall slender Hepplewhite bookcase in a corner. "And you still are," he added looking back at me.

I had recovered my calm. "I'm surprised that you remember. Our meeting was so brief."

"But you are not easily forgotten, Miss ... Miss ... Miss Anna. Am I right?"

"You are. Did you come in to see something?"

"Yes."

"Then perhaps I can show you."

"I'm looking at it now, although it's extremely uncivil of me to use that word when describing a young lady."

"You cannot mean that you came to see *me*."

"Why not?"

"It seems such an extraordinary thing to do."

"It seems to me perfectly reasonable."

"But suddenly ... after all these years."

"I am a sailor. I have been very little in Langmouth since our last meeting or I should have called before."

"Well, now you are here ..."

"Should I state my business and depart? Business? Of course you are a businesswoman. I must not forget that." He wrinkled his eyes so that they were almost closed and gazed at the Hepplewhite bookcase. "You are very direct. So I must be. I'll confess that I did not come in to buy those chairs ... or that bookcase. It was merely that as I was driving past that long red wall of yours I saw the inscription on the gate, *The Queen's House* and I remembered our meeting. Queen Elizabeth once slept over there, I said to myself, but what is far more interesting is that Miss Anna Brett sleeps there now."

I laughed. It was a high-pitched laugh—the laughter of happiness. I had sometimes imagined I should see him again and that it would be something like this. I was becoming speedily fascinated by him. He did not seem quite real; he was like the hero of some romantic tale. He might have stepped out of one of the tapestries. He was, I was sure, a bold adventurer who roamed the seas; he was elusive for he disappeared for long periods. He might walk out of the shop and I might not see him for years and years ... not until I had become Old Miss Brett. He had that quality which Ellen would describe as "larger than life."

I said: "For how long will you be in Langmouth?"

"I sail next week."

"For what part of the world?"

"To Australia and the Pacific ports."

"It sounds ... wonderful."

"Do I detect signs of the wanderlust in you, Miss Anna Brett?"

"I should love to see the world. I was born in India. I thought I should go out again but my parents died and that changed everything. I came to live here, and it looks as though this is where I shall stay."

I was surprised at myself offering so much information for which he had not asked.

He took my hand suddenly and pretended to read my palm. "You'll travel," he said, "far and wide." But he wasn't looking at my hand; he was looking at me.

I was aware of a woman standing at the window. She was a Mrs. Jennings who often came to the Queen's House and bought very little. She was an inveterate looker-round and an infrequent buyer. I suspected it was curiosity to get her nose into other people's houses rather than an interest in antiques which made her visit us. Now she would have seen Redvers Stretton in the shop. Had she seen him holding my hand?

The bell tinkled and she came in.

"Oh, Miss Brett, I see you have someone here. I'll wait."

Such alert eyes behind her pince-nez! She would be asking whether that Miss Brett had an admirer because Redvers Stretton was in that shop with her and did not appear to be buying.

Redvers looked momentarily dismayed, then with a faint lift of the shoulders said, "Madam, *I* was on the point of departure."

He bowed to me and to her, and left. I was infuriated with the woman, for all she wanted was to ask the price of the bookcase. She stroked it and commented on it and hunted for signs of woodworm merely to chatter as she did so. So Redvers Stretton from the Castle was interested in an antique. He was only home for a short time she believed. There was a wild one, very different from Mr. Rex who must be a great comfort to his mother. Redvers was another kettle of fish.

"Anyone less like a kettle of fish I never saw," I said with asperity.

"My dear Miss Brett, a figure of speech, but that young man is by all accounts *wild*."

She was warning me. But I was in no mood to be warned. I was late back at the Queen's House and Mrs. Morton told me that Aunt Charlotte was waiting to see me. I found her peevish. She was lying on her bed; she had had a sip of laudanum to bring her relief. I was late, she reminded me, and I told her that Mrs. Jennings had been to inquire about the Hepplewhite and had kept me.

"That old busybody. She'll never buy it."

But she seemed satisfied, which was more than I was.

I was becoming obsessed by that man.

Two days later Aunt Charlotte announced her intention of going off to a sale. It was too good to be missed and although she was scarcely fit for it she decided to dose herself liberally and set out. She would take Mrs. Morton with her for she would need someone in attendance as she was to be away for two nights; travel for one afflicted with her infirmity in addition to the discomfort of hotel bedrooms was well nigh intolerable. It would have been far more satisfactory if I could have accompanied her, but obviously we could not both be away . . . for business reasons. If that absurd Beringer had not made such a fool of herself by getting married I could have gone and Beringer have been left in charge. Aunt Charlotte disliked Miss Beringer more since her marriage even than before.

She left in due course and I continued to hope that Redvers would call in again at the shop. I wondered why he did not because he had come in for the purpose of seeing me and had seemed to take the excuse of leaving with alacrity. Why, since he had come in in the first place.

Perhaps he had already sailed.

It was the evening of that day after Aunt Charlotte had

left. I had shut up the shop, come back to the Queen's House and I was in my room when Ellen came running up to say that a gentleman had called and was asking to see me.

"What does he want?"

"To see you, miss," Ellen smirked. "It's Captain Stretton from the Castle."

"Captain Stretton from the Castle!" I repeated her foolishly. I looked at my reflection in the glass. I was wearing my gray marino which was not very becoming, and my hair was untidy.

"I could tell him you'll be with him in ten minutes, miss," suggested Ellen conspiratorially. "After all you wouldn't want him to think you were rushing."

I said rather tremulously, "Perhaps he has come to see some piece of furniture."

Ellen said: "Yes, miss. I'll tell him."

She was gone; and I rushed to the wardrobe I was using and took out the light navy silk which my father had brought me from Hong Kong. It had been made up by the local dressmaker and was certainly not in the latest style— for I had had it some time—but the material was lovely; it had a ruching of velvet at the neck which I had always thought becoming.

So I hastily changed, straightened my hair and ran downstairs.

He took my hands in his free and easy way which might have been unconventional but which I found charming.

"Forgive my calling," he said, "but I had to come to say goodbye."

"Oh . . . you are going?"

"Tomorrow."

"I can only wish you bon voyage."

"Thank you. I hope you will think of me while I'm away and perhaps pray for those in peril on the sea."

"I hope you won't need my prayers."

"When you know me better you'll realize that I need them more than most."

When you know me better! I should have guessed at the state of my feelings when a simple phrase like that and its implication could delight me. He was going away, but when I knew him better . . .

"You strike me as being very self-sufficient."

"Do you think any of us really are that?"

"I think some of us may be."

"You?" he asked.

"I have not yet had the time to discover."

"You have always been cosseted?"

"Hardly that. But you have just made me realize that I have never exactly been on my own. But what a profound conversation! Won't you sit down?"

He looked round him and I laughed. "That's how I felt when I first came here. I used to sit on a chair and say to myself, Perhaps Madame de Pompadour once sat here, or Richelieu or Talleyrand."

"Being less erudite such a thought would not occur to me."

"Let us go into my aunt's sitting room, that is more . . . habitable. That is if you have time to stay for . . . a little while."

"I'm sailing at seven in the morning." He gave me that quizzical look. "I should leave before that."

I laughed as I led the way up the stairs and through our cluttered rooms. He was interested in some of the Chinese pieces which Aunt Charlotte had recently bought. I had forgotten how she had to make room for them in her sitting room.

"Aunt Charlotte bought rather lavishly on this occasion," I said. "They belonged to a man who had lived in China. He was a collector." I felt I had to go on talking because I was so excited that he had come to see me. "Do you like this cabinet? We call it a chest-on-chest. The lacquer is rather fine. See how it is set with ivory and mother-of-pearl. Heaven knows what she paid for it. And I wonder when she will find a buyer."

"How knowledgeable you are."

"Nothing compared with my aunt. But I'm learning. It takes a lifetime though."

"And," he said gravely studying me, "there are so many other things in life to learn."

"You must be an expert on . . . the sea and ships."

"I shall never be an expert on anything."

"Who is? But where will you sit? This is perhaps more comfortable. It's a good sturdy Spanish chair."

He was smiling. "What happened to the desk you had from the Castle?"

"My aunt sold it. I don't know who was the buyer."

"I did not come to talk about furniture," he said.

"No?"

"But to talk to you."

"I don't think you'd find me very interesting ... apart from all this."

He looked round the room. "It's almost as though they're trying to make a period piece of you."

There was a moment's silence and I was suddenly aware of all the ticking clocks.

I heard myself say almost involuntarily: "Yes, I think that is what I fear. I see myself living here, growing old, learning more and more until I know as much as Aunt Charlotte. As you say, a period piece."

"That mustn't happen," he said. "The present should be lived in."

I said: "It was good of you to call, on your last evening."

"I should have called before, but ..."

I waited for him to go on but he had decided not to.

"I heard about you," he said.

"You heard about me?"

"Miss Brett the Elder is well-known in Langmouth. I heard that she drives a hard bargain."

"Lady Crediton told you that."

"She was under the impression that she drove a harder one. That was the occasion when we first met." And then: "What do you know about me?"

I was afraid to repeat Ellen's story in case it was wrong.

"I had heard that you live at the Castle, that you are not Lady Crediton's son."

"Then you will understand that I was in a somewhat invidious position from the beginning." He began to laugh. "I can talk to you of this somewhat indelicate matter. That is why I find your company stimulating. You are not the sort of woman to refuse to discuss a subject simply because it is ... unconventional."

"It is true?"

"Ah, so you have heard. Yes, it's true. Sir Edward was

my father; I was brought up as a son of the house, and yet not with the same status as my half brother. All very reasonable, don't you think? It's had its effect on my character, though. I was always trying to outdo Rex in everything, as much as to say, 'See I'm as good as you are.' Do you think that excuses a boy for being shall we say arrogant, eager to attract attention, always wanting to win? Rex is the most patient of fellows. Far more worthy than I but then I always say he didn't have to prove he was as good. He was accepted as being better."

"You aren't one of those tiresome people with a chip on your shoulder, I hope?"

He laughed. "No, I'm not. In fact trying so hard for so long to convince people that I was as good as Rex meant that I succeeded in convincing myself."

"That's all to the good. I could never bear people who are sorry for themselves, perhaps because there was a time when I started to feel life had treated me rather harshly. That was when my mother died."

I told him about my mother, how beautiful she was, how enchanting, her plans for my future, how my father and I had doted on her; and then I went on to speak of his death and how I was left, an orphan, at the mercy of Aunt Charlotte.

I was unusually animated. He had that effect on me. I felt I was being amusing, interesting, attractive and I was happier than I had been since my mother died. No, I was happier than I had ever been in my life. I wanted this evening never to stop.

There was a gentle tap on the door and Ellen came in, bright-eyed and conspiratorial.

"I was going to say, miss, that there's supper nearly ready and if Captain Stretton would be joining you for it, I could serve in fifteen minutes or so."

He declared his delight in the suggestion. His eyes rested on Ellen and I noticed that the color deepened in her cheeks. Could it be that he had the same effect on her as he had on me?

"Thank you, Ellen," I said, and I was ashamed that I had felt a little jealous. No, it was not really that, but the thought occurred to me that his charm was not for me alone; he possessed it in such abundance that he could

afford to squander it so that even a maid announcing a
meal was aware of it. Was I attaching too much importance to his interest?

Ellen had set a meal in the dining room and had, greatly
daring, put two lighted candles in the lovely carved gilded
seventeenth-century candlesticks and had set them at either
end of the Regency table; she had placed two Sheraton
dining-room chairs opposite each other and the table
looked delightful.

About us loomed the bookcases and chairs and two
cabinets filled with porcelain and Wedgwood pottery, but
the candles lighting the table shut off the rest of the room
and the effect was charming.

It was like a dream. Aunt Charlotte never entertained. I
wondered fleetingly what she would think if she could see
us now, and I thought too how different life here would be
without Aunt Charlotte. But why think of her on such an
evening?

Ellen was in high spirits. I imagined her giving an
account of it all to Mr. Orfey the next day. I knew she
believed—for she had told me often—that it was time I
had "a bit of life." This would be in her opinion a very
delectable slice of life, not just a bit.

She brought in the soup in a tureen with deep blue
flower decorations and the plates matched. I caught my
breath with horror that we should be using such precious
plates. There was cold chicken to follow and I was thankful that Aunt Charlotte was to be away another day which
would enable us to replenish the larder. Aunt Charlotte
ate little herself and kept a very meager table. But Ellen
had worked wonders with what she had; she had turned
cold potatoes into delicious sauté and had cooked a
cauliflower which she served with a cheese and chive
sauce. Ellen seemed to be in possession of new powers on
that night. Or perhaps I imagined that everything tasted
different from what it had before.

We talked and every now and then Ellen would come in
to serve, looking very pretty and excited; I was sure there
had never been a happier scene in the Queen's House,
even when Queen Elizabeth was entertained here. I was
full of fancies. It was as though the house approved and

the alien pieces retreated as I sat in the dining room at the Regency table entertaining my guest.

There was no wine—Aunt Charlotte was a teetotaler—but that was of no importance.

He talked about the sea and foreign places and he made me believe I was there, and when he spoke of his ship and his crew I could guess what it meant to him. He was taking out a cargo of cloth and manufactured goods to Sydney and when he was there he would do a certain amount of trading with the Pacific ports before bringing wool back to England. The ship was not big; she was under a thousand tons but he would like me to see how she could cut through the water. She was in the clipper class, and you couldn't find anything speedier than that. But he was talking too much about himself.

I protested. No. I wanted to hear it. I was fascinated. I had often been down to the docks and seen the ships there and wondered where they were going. Were they entirely cargo ships, I wanted to know.

"We take some passengers, though cargo's the main business. As a matter of fact I have a very important gentleman sailing with me tomorrow. He's primarily a diamond merchant and going out to look at Australian opals. He has quite a conceit of himself. There are one or two other passengers too. Passengers can present problems on ships like ours."

And so we talked and the clocks ticked on furiously and maliciously fast.

And as we talked I said: "You haven't told me the name of your ship."

"Haven't I? It's *The Secret Woman*."

"*The Secret Woman*. Why . . . that's what it said on the figure which was in the desk we bought from Castle Crediton. It's in my room. I'll go and get it."

I picked up the candlestick from the table. It was heavy and he took it from me. "I'll carry it," he said.

"Be careful with it. It's precious."

"Like everything in the house."

"Well, not everything."

And I turned and side by side we went up the stairs.

"Be careful," I said, "as you see we're very cluttered."

"I understand it's the shop window," he replied.

"Yes," I chattered. "I found this figure in the desk. I suppose we should have returned it to you but Aunt Charlotte said it was worthless."

"I'm sure Aunt Charlotte, as usual, was right."

I laughed. "She almost always is, I have to admit." And thinking of Aunt Charlotte I marveled afresh that I could have dared to invite him to supper as I had—although Ellen had made that inevitable. But I was very willing, so it was no use blaming her. I refused to think of Aunt Charlotte at such a time; she was safely out of the way in some dingy hotel bedroom—she would never stay at the best hotels and poor Mrs. Morton was no doubt having a very trying time.

We stepped up into the room above. I always thought the house was eerie in candlelight because the furniture took on odd shapes—some grotesque, some almost human, and as they changed constantly they rarely became familiar.

"What an odd old house!" he said.

"Genuinely old," I told him. And I laughed aloud to think of Aunt Charlotte's verdict on Castle Crediton: Fake! He wanted to know why I laughed and I told him.

"She has the utmost contempt for fakes."

"And you?"

I hesitated. "It would depend on the fake. Some are very clever."

"I suppose one would have to be clever to be a successful faker."

"I suppose so. Oh mind this, please. See how that edge of that table juts out. I didn't see it in the shadow. It's rather dangerous there, so near the stair."

We had reached my bedroom.

"Miss Anna Brett slept here," he said with mock reverence.

I was very lighthearted. "Do you think we should fix a plaque on the wall? 'Queen Elizabeth and Anna Brett . . .' Perhaps they ought to call it Anna Brett House instead of the Queen's House."

"It's an excellent idea."

"But I must show you the figure." I took it from the drawer in which I kept it. He put down the candlestick on the dressing table and took it from me. He laughed. "It's the figurehead of *The Secret Woman*," he said.

"A figurehead."

"Yes, no doubt there was a model of the ship and this was broken off."

"It's of no value?"

"None whatever. Except of course that it represents the figurehead of *my* ship, which might give it a little value in your eyes."

"Yes," I said. "It does."

He handed it back to me and I must have held it somewhat reverently, for he laughed.

"You can take it up now and then, look at it and think of me on the bridge as it plows through the waves."

"*The Secret Woman*," I said. "It's a strange name for a ship. Secret, and Woman. I thought all the Crediton ships were ladies."

At that moment I heard the sound of a door being shut; I heard voices below and felt the goose pimples rise on my flesh.

"What's wrong?" he asked and he took me by the arms and held me close to him.

I said weakly: "My aunt has come home." My heart was beating so wildly that I could scarcely think. Why had she come home so soon? But why not? The sale had not been so interesting as she had hoped; she hated hotel bedrooms; she would not stay in one longer than she could help. It didn't matter for what reason she had come. The point was that she was here. Perhaps at this moment she was looking at the remains of our feast ... the lighted candle—only one because we had the other here—the precious china. Poor Ellen, I thought. I looked wildly about the room—at my bed, the here-today-and-gone-tomorrow pieces of furniture, and the candlelight throwing elongated shadows on the wall, the tallboy and . . . ourselves.

Redvers Stretton was actually alone with me in my bedroom and Aunt Charlotte was in the house! I must at least go downstairs as quickly as possible.

He understood and picked up the candle which he had put on the dressing table. But we could not hurry of course; we must pick our way carefully. As we came to the turn of the staircase and looked down at the hall, Aunt Charlotte saw us. Mrs. Morton was standing beside her; Ellen was there too, white-faced and tense.

"Anna!" said Aunt Charlotte in a voice which reverberated like thunder. "What do you think you are doing?"

The Queen's House could never have known a more dramatic moment: Redvers towering above me—he was very tall and he was standing one stair up; the candlelight flickering; our shadows on the wall; and Aunt Charlotte standing there in her traveling cloak and bonnet, her face white with the strain of fatigue and pain, looking more than ever like a man dressed up as a woman, powerful and malevolent.

I walked down the stairs and he kept close to me.

"Captain Stretton called," I said trying to speak naturally.

He took the matter out of my hands. "Perhaps I should explain, Miss Brett. I had heard so much of your wonderful treasure store that I could not resist coming to see it for myself. I was not expecting such hospitality."

She was a little taken aback. Was she, too, susceptible to that charm?

She grunted and said: "You can scarcely judge antiques by candlelight."

"Yet it must often have been by candlelight that those wonderfully wrought pieces were shown in the past, Miss Brett. I wanted to get the effect by candlelight. And Miss Brett kindly allowed me to do this."

She was assessing his possibilities as a buyer. "What are you particularly interested in, Captain Stretton?"

I said quickly, "Captain Stretton was greatly impressed by the Levasseur cabinet."

Aunt Charlotte grunted. "It's a fine piece," she said. "You'd never regret having it. It would be very easy to place if ever you wanted to pass it on."

"I am sure of it," he said earnestly.

"Have you seen it in daylight?" Her voice was ironical. She didn't believe for one moment in this act. To her it was an absurd charade.

"No. That's a pleasure in store for me."

Aunt Charlotte was staring at the candlestick in his hand.

"Aunt Charlotte," I said, "you must be very tired after your journey."

"Then I should take my leave," said Redvers. "And thank you for your kind hospitality."

"And the Levasseur?"

"In daylight," he said. "As you tell me I should."

"Come tomorrow," she said, "I'll show it to you myself." He bowed.

"Ellen will show you out."

But I was not having that. I said firmly: "I will."

And I went with him to the door. I stood in the garden with him. I was talking wildly about the cabinet. "That marquetry of brass on the tortoiseshell background is really very beautiful. There is no doubt that it is genuine Levasseur . . ."

"Oh, no doubt at all," he said.

It was autumn and I could smell the peculiar odor of chrysanthemums and the dampness of the ground and the mist on the river. Whenever I smell those smells I remember that night. My enchanted evening was over; and he was going away. I was shut in my prison; he would leave me for his life of adventure and I would go back to my infuriated jailer.

"I think she is a little put out," he said. "I'm sorry."

"I thought she would be away another night."

"I meant I'm sorry I'm going away. I'm leaving you to face that . . ."

"I could face it if . . ."

He knew what I meant. If he were there to face it with me, if I could see him now and then, even if they were stolen meetings, I would not care. I was twenty-one years of age. I did not have to be Aunt Charlotte's slave forever.

"I wish it had been different," he said, and I wondered what he meant by that. I waited for him to go on, and I knew I could not stay long. Inside the Queen's House Aunt Charlotte was waiting.

"Different?" I insisted. "You mean you wish you hadn't come?"

"I couldn't wish that," he said. "It was a wonderful evening until the ogress returned. She didn't believe me, you know, about that . . . thing."

"No," I said, "she didn't."

"I hope it is not going to be ... disagreeable."

"But the evening before she came was so very agreeable."

"You found it so?"

I could not hide my feelings. "The most agreeable evening I have ..." No I must not be so naïve. I finished, "That I have spent for a long time."

"I shall be back," he said.

"When?"

"Perhaps sooner than you think."

He took my face in his hands and looked at me; I thought he was going to kiss me, but he seemed to change his mind and suddenly, he was gone and I was alone in the autumn-scented garden.

I went back into the house. Aunt Charlotte was not there. Ellen was clearing the table.

"Your aunt's gone to bed," she said. "Mrs. Morton's helping her. She's worn out. She says she'll see you, and me, in the morning. Oh miss—we're in for it, we really are."

I went back to my room. Such a short time ago he had been there with me. He had brought a magical touch to my life and now he was gone. I had been foolish to imagine ... What had I imagined? What did a young woman who was not outstandingly attractive have to interest a man who must surely be the most charming in the world?

And yet ... there was something in the manner in which he had looked at me. Had I shown too clearly my feelings?

I took out the figurehead and set it on the dressing table. Then I undressed and when I got into bed I took the figurehead with me—a foolish childish gesture, but I found it comforting.

It was a long time before I could sleep but at last I dozed. I awoke with a start. It was the creak of a floorboard—the sound of a footstep on the stair which had disturbed me. Someone was coming up to the top of the house . . . footsteps and the tap-tap of Aunt Charlotte's stick.

I sat up in bed; I stared at the door which slowly opened and she stood there.

She looked grotesque in her camel's-hair dressing gown with the military buttons, her long gray hair in a coarse thick plait, and in her hand the ebony-topped stick which she used since her arthritis made it difficult for her to walk about. She carried a candle—in a plain wooden stick, not one of our valuable ones.

She glared at me. "You may well look ashamed of yourself," she said. Her laughter was horrible, sneering and in a way coarse. "I couldn't sleep for thinking of what happened tonight."

"I have done nothing of which to be ashamed."

"That's what you tell me. So you waited until I was out of the way before you brought him in. How often has he been here? You're not telling me this was the first time."

"It was the first time."

She laughed again. She was angry and frightened. I didn't know it then but she needed me far more than I needed her. She was a lonely old woman who had to rely on people like Mrs. Morton; but I was to be her salvation. I was going to look after her and the business; she had trained me for just that. And what she feared was that I would marry and leave her—as Emily Beringer had.

She looked round the room. "You're feeling lonely now he's gone, I daresay. Don't tell me he wasn't up here. I saw the light from the garden. You ought to have thought to draw the curtains. But then you weren't expecting to be seen, were you? You thought you had the place all to yourself and that Ellen, she was in it, too. A nice example to her, I must say."

"Ellen was not to blame."

"She served your supper on the Delft, didn't she?"

"That was foolish but . . ."

"But not so foolish as bringing him up here to your bedroom."

"Aunt Charlotte!"

"Don't play the innocent with me. I know you were up here. I saw the light. Look. There's candle grease on the dressing table. Didn't I see you come down together? Oh,

I wonder you can lie there, so brazen. You're another
such as your mother, you are. I said at the time it was a
pity your father ever took up with her."

I said: "Be silent, you wicked old woman."

"That sort of talk will get you nowhere."

"I won't stay here," I said.

It was the worst thing I could have said.

She turned her rage on me. "You ungrateful girl! I did
everything for you. What would have happened to you if I
hadn't taken you in, eh? It would have been an orphan-
age, I can tell you. There was nothing, nothing left for
you. I kept you. I've tried to make you useful. I've taught
you all you know ... to give you a chance of paying me
back and this is what you do. Bring strange men into the
house as soon as my back's turned. Your mother all over
again ... I shouldn't wonder."

"How dare you say such things. My mother was good,
better than you could ever be. And I ..."

"And you are good, too? Oh, very good. Very good to
young men who visit you when my back's turned."

"Stop it! Stop it!"

"You dare to order me in my house."

"I'll go if you like."

"Where to?"

"I'll find some post. I know something about antiques."

"Which I have taught you."

"I could be a governess or a companion."

She laughed. "Oh yes, you're very clever. I know. Has it
occurred to you that you might owe me something? You
might think about that. A fine fool you are. Making
yourself cheap to the first man who comes along. And
from that place too. I should have thought you would
have known better where someone of *that* reputation is
concerned."

"What reputation?"

She chuckled. "You ought to select with more care. I
can tell you that Captain Redvers Stretton has not a very
good name in this town. He's the sort who's going to take
his fun where he finds it. And I'll daresay that he's ready
to try all sorts."

I could only cry: "Go away. I don't want to hear what

you have to say. I'll leave here. If you want to get rid of me, if I'm such a burden . . ."

"You're a rash and foolish girl," she said. "You need me to look after you. Your father was my brother and I've got my duty. I'll have a good talk to you in the morning. I'm worn out . . . and my pain is terrible. I couldn't sleep for thinking about you. I thought I'd speak to you tonight. But tomorrow perhaps you'll be in a more contrite mood."

She turned and went out. I stared at the door. I was hurt and angry; the evening had changed. She had smirched it with her evil thoughts and her talk of his reputation. What did she mean by that? What did she know?

And then suddenly there was a piercing scream and the heavy thud of something falling. I got out of bed and ran to the stairs.

Aunt Charlotte was lying at the foot of that flight, groaning.

I ran down. "Aunt Charlotte," I said. "Are you hurt?"

She did not answer; she was breathing heavily.

I called Mrs. Morton and Ellen. Foolishly I tried to lift my aunt; I couldn't, so I found a cushion and put it under her head.

Mrs. Morton came hurrying. With her fine hair in curlers under a net she looked different, grim, excited.

"My aunt must have slipped coming down the stairs," I said, I remembered warning Redvers.

"At this time of night," said Mrs. Morton. She picked up the candle which Aunt Charlotte had dropped. There was the faintest moonlight shining through the window. Aunt Charlotte began to groan again.

I said: "Put on your cloak, Ellen, and go and ask Dr. Elgin to come."

Ellen ran off and Mrs. Morton and I stayed with Aunt Charlotte.

"How did it happen?" asked Mrs. Morton. She looked rather pleased, I thought, and I imagined what it had been like traveling with Aunt Charlotte.

"She came to my room to talk to me and fell on the way back to her own."

"She was in a rage, I daresay," said Mrs. Morton.

She looked at me obliquely; I realized that I had never understood Mrs. Morton at all. She seemed to be shut in with some secret life of her own. I wondered why she endured Aunt Charlotte's tantrums. Surely she could have found more congenial employment elsewhere? I could think of no reason for her staying but that of Ellen: that she would be remembered in my aunt's will if she were still in her employ.

It seemed a long time before Ellen returned. Dr. Elgin would be with us shortly, she said.

When he came he said we should get Aunt Charlotte to bed at once. I was to make hot sweet tea for her because she was suffering from shock. He thought she had been lucky for no bones were broken.

As I made the tea Ellen said: "What a night this has been! Do you know, I reckon this could knock years off her life. A fall like that, at her age . . ."

And I know that she was thinking of taking her legacy to Mr. Orfey.

Life changed after that. It was the beginning of the disastrous period. Aunt Charlotte had injured her spine in the fall and this had aggravated her arthritis. There were days when she could not walk except to potter about the house and sometimes she could not even do that. She could not always go to sales; I had to go. I became a well known figure at them. At first I was treated with mild contempt; but this so angered me that I determined not to miss anything and I became more and more knowledgeable, so that they had to respect me. "She's her aunt all over again," it was said. And I was rather pleased because the only way in which I could bear to resemble Aunt Charlotte was in her knowledge.

More than anything Aunt Charlotte had changed. I made excuses for her in the beginning. A woman with her energetic mind must find it tragic to be physically incapacitated. It was small wonder that she was irritable and bad tempered; she had never been convivial but now she seemed to hate us all. Continually she reminded me that I was responsible for her condition. It was her concern for me that had made her come to my bedroom; it was because she was so upset by my conduct that she had carelessly walked into the edge of that table and tripped. I had cost her her health and vigor; I owed it to her to repay her in any way I could.

The household had never been gay; it now became grim and melancholy. She would sit propped up in her chair in her sitting room on her good days and go through the accounts. She never allowed me to see them; she herself did most of the buying. She would allow me no authority although my knowledge was growing and was not far behind her own.

I began to experience once more that feeling that the Queen's House was a prison; and just as in the old days I had dreamed of reunion with my mother as my means of escape, now I thought of that evening with Redvers and I told myself: He will come home from his voyage and when he does he will come to see me.

The months passed and I heard nothing of him. The autumn was with us—the smell of dahlias and chrysanthemums in the garden; the damp mist was rising from the river and it was the anniversary of that evening and still I heard no news of him.

Aunt Charlotte was getting more crippled, more irritable. Scarcely a day passed during which she did not remind me where my duty lay.

I went on waiting and hoping that one day Redvers would seek me out, but he never did.

It was Ellen who brought news to me. Her sister still worked for the Creditons. She had married the butler and had come up in the world. Lady Crediton was pleased with her and although she was not exactly a housekeeper, she was in charge of the maids which, being the butler's wife, was very convenient.

Ellen said to me one day when she was helping me to take some Ferrybridge pottery from one of the cabinets and pack it for a customer: "Miss Anna, I've been wondering whether to speak to you since yesterday morning."

I looked at her in some alarm; she was clearly distressed and I wondered whether Mr. Orfey had grown tired of waiting for her legacy and turned to someone else.

"I went up to the Castle, yesterday to see our Edith."

I avoided looking at her; I must handle the pottery very carefully. "Yes," I said.

"There's news of the Captain."

"The Captain," I repeated foolishly.

"Captain Stretton. Something awful's happened."

"Not ... dead?"

"Oh no, no ... but some awful disgrace or something. He lost his ship."

"You mean it was ... sunk."

"Something like that. They're all talking about it up at the Castle. It's something dreadful. And he's miles away. And it's some disgrace, but there's something else, Miss Anna."

"What, Ellen?"

"He's married. He's been married some time. He's got a wife in foreign parts. He must have been married when he came here that night. Who'd have thought it!"

I didn't believe it. He would have said so. But why should he discuss his private affairs? I must have misunderstood bitterly. I had thought ... What had I thought? I was a simpleton. I was all Aunt Charlotte said I was. That evening had meant nothing to him. Two people could see the same event entirely differently. He had called on me because he had nothing else to do before he sailed. Perhaps he knew how I felt about him and was amused. Perhaps he had told his wife about that last evening. The meal by candlelight, the arrival of Aunt Charlotte. I suppose it could be seen as comic.

"How interesting," I said.

"I had no idea, had you, miss?"

"Of what?"

"That he was married of course. He kept it dark. There's trouble about that, too. Whoops! You nearly dropped that. There would have been trouble if that had been broken."

Broken, I thought dramatically, like my dreams, like my hopes. Because I had been hoping. I had really believed that one day he would come back to me and then I would begin to be happy.

Captain Redvers Stretton was married. I heard it from several sources. He had married somewhere abroad, married a foreigner, so they said. He had been married for some time.

When Aunt Charlotte heard, which she did inevitably, she laughed as I had rarely seen her laugh before. And from that day she taunted me. She never lost an opportunity of bringing his name into the conversation. "*Your* Captain Stretton. Your evening visitor. So he had a wife all the time? Did he tell you that?"

"Why should he?" I asked. "People who come to look at the furniture don't feel it necessary to acquaint one with their family history, do they?"

"Perhaps people who come to look at Levasseurs might." She laughed. She was better tempered than she had been for a long time, but spiteful and malicious.

He came home I believe but I didn't see him. I heard from Ellen that he was there. And the time passed—one day very like another, spring, summer, autumn, winter; and nothing to make one week different from another except perhaps that we sold one of the Chinese pieces which nobody seemed to want, for what Aunt Charlotte called an excellent price but which I believed was what she had paid for it. She was relieved to see it go. "You wouldn't find another like that," she said. "Carved red lacquer. Fifteenth century of the Hsüan Te period."

"And you wouldn't find another buyer either," I retaliated.

We were like that together, constantly bickering; I was getting old and sour and so was everyone in that house. Ellen had lost some of her exuberance. Mr. Orfey was still waiting. Poor Ellen, he wanted the legacy she would get more than he wanted her. Mrs. Morton was more withdrawn than ever; she went off on her free days once a fortnight and we never knew where she went. She was mysterious and secretive in her ways. I was twenty-five—no longer young. Sometimes I thought: It is four years since that night. And it meant nothing to him because all the time he was married and he didn't tell me. He implied ... But had he implied or had I imagined it? Aunt Charlotte never forgot. She was constantly reminding me that I had behaved like a fool. I had been an innocent and he had known it. It seemed amusing to her; she would titter in an infuriating way when she spoke of it. It was the only subject she ever found amusing.

Oh, the dreariness of the Queen's House with four women growing old and sad, all waiting for something to change their drab and dreary lives. I knew what it was: Aunt Charlotte to die. Ellen could marry Mr. Orfey. Mrs. Morton was no doubt waiting for what she would get. And I . . . At least I thought I should be free. Why didn't I go away? Could I have found a post? Perhaps somewhere in England there must be an antique dealer who could make use of my services; and yet much as I hated her—for hate her I did at times—I felt a responsibility toward Aunt Charlotte. If I went she would be bereft. I was doing more and more of the essential work. I could run the business alone—except of course that I was never allowed to see the accounts. But in my heart I believed that I had a duty to her. She was my father's sister. She had taken me in when my parents left me in England; she had looked after me when I became an orphan.

The clocks ticked on. There was a very special significance in their ticking now.

Aunt Charlotte had grown worse; she could not move from her bed. The injury to her spine aggravated her complaint, said Dr. Elgin. Her bedroom had become an office. She still kept a tight hold on the books and I was never allowed to see them; but I was taking over all the selling and a great deal of the buying, though everything had to be submitted to her first and accounts passed through her hands. I was very busy. I devoted myself passionately to my work and if ever Ellen or Mrs. Buckle started to talk about what was happening up at Castle Crediton I implied that I was not interested.

One day Dr. Elgin asked to see me; he had just come down from Aunt Charlotte's room.

He said: "She's getting worse. You can't manage her without help. There'll come a time very soon when she'll be completely bedridden. I suggest you have a nurse."

I could see the point of this but it was, I said, a matter I should have to discuss with my aunt.

"Do so," said the doctor. "And impress on her that you can't do all that you do and be an attendant in the sick room. She needs a trained nurse."

Aunt Charlotte was against the idea at first but eventually gave in. And then everything changed because Chantel Loman had arrived.

4

How can I describe Chantel? She was dainty and reminded me of a Dresden china figure. She had that lovely shade of hair made famous by Titian, with rather heavy brows and dark lashes; her eyes were a decided shade of green and I thought her coloring the most arresting I had ever seen. She had a straight little nose and a delicately colored complexion which, with her slender figure, gave her the Dresden look. If she had a fault it was the smallness of her mouth but I thought—and this had occurred to me with some of the finest works of art I handled—that it was the slight imperfection which added something to beauty. Perfect beauty in art and nature could become monotonous; that little difference made it exciting. And that was how Chantel seemed to me.

When she first came into the Queen's House and sat on the carved Restoration chair which happened to be in the hall at that time, I thought: "She'll never stay here. She'll not come in the first place."

But I was wrong. She said afterward that the place fascinated her, as I did. I looked so . . . forbidding. A regular old maid in my tweed skirt and jacket and my very severe blouse and my really lovely hair pulled back and screwed up in a way which destroyed its beauty and was *criminal*.

Chantel talked like that—underlining certain words and she had a way of laughing at the end of a sentence as though she were laughing at herself. Anyone less like a nurse I could not imagine.

I took her up to Aunt Charlotte and oddly enough—or

though perhaps I should say naturally enough—Aunt Charlotte took a fancy to her on the spot. Chantel charmed naturally and easily, I told Ellen.

"She's a real beauty," said Ellen. "Things will be different now she's come."

And they were. She was bright and efficient. Even Aunt Charlotte grumbled less. Chantel was interested in the house and explored it. She told me later that she thought it was the most interesting house she had ever been in.

When Aunt Charlotte had been made comfortable for the night Chantel would come and sit in my room and talk. I think she was glad to have someone more or less her own age in the house. I was twenty-six and she was twenty-two; but she had lived a more interesting life, had traveled with her last patient a little and seemed to me a woman of the world.

I felt happier than I had for a long time and so was the entire household. Ellen was interested in her and I believe confided in her about Mr. Orfey. Even Mrs. Morton was more communicative with her than she had ever been with me, for it was Chantel who told me that Mrs. Morton had a daughter who was a cripple and lived with Mrs. Morton's unmarried sister five miles from Langmouth. That was where she went on her days off; and she had come to the Queen's House and endured the whims of Aunt Charlotte and the lack of comforts because it enabled her to be near her daughter. She was waiting for the day she would retire and they would live together.

"Fancy her telling you all that," I cried. "How did you manage to get her to talk?"

"People do talk to me," said Chantel.

She would stand at my window looking out on the garden and the river and say that it was all *fascinating*. She was vitally interested in everything and everybody. She even learned something about antiques. "The *money* they must represent," she said.

"But they have to be bought first," I explained to her. "And some of them have not been paid for. Aunt Charlotte merely houses them and gets a commission if she makes a sale."

"What a clever creature you are!" she said admiringly.

"You have your profession which is no doubt more useful."

She grimaced. At times she reminded me of my mother; but she was efficient as my mother would never have been.

"Preserving lovely old tables and chairs might be more useful than preserving some fractious invalids. I've had some horrors I can tell you."

Her conversation was amusing. She told me she had been brought up in a vicarage. "I know now why people say poor as church mice. That's how poor we were. All that economy. It was soul-destroying, Anna." We had quickly come to Christian names, and hers was so pretty I said it was a shame not to use it. "There was Papa saving the souls of his parishioners while his poor children had to live on bread and dripping. Ugh! Our mother was dead—died with the birth of the youngest, myself. There were five of us."

"How wonderful to have so many brothers and sisters."

"Not so wonderful when you're poor. We all decided to have professions and I chose nursing because, as I said to Selina, my eldest sister, that will take me into the houses of the rich and at least I can catch the crumbs that fall from the rich man's table."

"And you came here!"

"I like it here," she said. "The place excites me."

"At least we shan't give you bread and dripping."

"I shouldn't mind if you did. It would be worth it to be here. It's a wonderful house, full of strange things, and you are by no means ordinary, nor is Miss Brett. That is what is good about this profession of mine. You never know where it will lead you."

Her sparkling green eyes reminded me of emeralds.

I said: "I should have thought anyone as beautiful as you would be married."

She smiled obliquely. "I have had offers."

"But you've never been in love," I said.

"No. Have you?"

That brought the color flooding my cheeks; and before I could prevent myself I was telling her about Redvers Stretton.

"A roving Casanova," she said. "I wish I'd been here then. I would have warned you."

"How would you have known that he had a wife abroad?"

"I would have found out, never fear. My poor dear Anna, you have to see it as a lucky escape." Her eyes shone excitedly. "Think of what might have happened."

"What?" I demanded.

"He might have offered marriage and seduced you."

"What nonsense! It was all my fault really. He never gave the slightest indication that he was ... interested in me. It was my foolish imagination."

She did not answer but from that moment she became very interested in Castle Crediton. I used to hear her talking about it and the Creditons with Ellen.

My relationship with Ellen had changed; Ellen was far more interested in Chantel than in me. I could understand it. She was wonderful. By a deft touch of flattery she could put even Aunt Charlotte in a good mood. Her charm lay in her interest in people; she was avidly curious. After Ellen's day off she would go to the kitchen to prepare a tray for Aunt Charlotte and I would hear them laughing together.

Mrs. Buckle said: "That Nurse Loman's a real bit of sunshine in the house."

I thought how right she was.

It was Chantel who had the idea about our journals. Life, she said, was full of interest.

"Some people's," I said.

"All people's," she corrected me.

"Nothing happens here," I told her. "I lose count of the days."

"That shows you should keep a journal and write everything down. I have an idea. We both will and we'll read each other's. It'll be such fun, because, you see, living as close as we do we shall be recording the same events. We'll see them through each other's eyes."

"A journal," I said. "I'd never have time."

"Oh yes, you would. An absolutely truthful journal. I insist. You'll be surprised what it will do for you."

And that was how we began to keep our journals.

She was right, as she always seemed to be. Life did take

on a new aspect. Events seemed less trivial; and it was interesting to see how differently we recorded them. She colored everything with her own personality and my account seemed drab in comparison. She saw people differently, made them more interesting; even Aunt Charlotte emerged as quite likable in her hands.

We had a great deal of pleasure out of our journals. The important thing was to put down *exactly* what one felt, said Chantel. "I mean, Anna, if you feel you hate me over something, you shouldn't mince your words. What's the good of a journal that's not truthful?"

So I used to write as though I were talking to myself and every week we would exchange our journals and see exactly how the other had felt.

I often wondered how I had got through the days before Chantel came. She was as much a nurse to me in a way as she was to Aunt Charlotte only I didn't need the physical attention.

It was only ten months since Chantel had come and the autumn was with us again. The autumn tints and smells still filled me with sorrow but my heart was considerably lightened. That summer had been a wet one and the damp atmosphere had had its effect on Aunt Charlotte; she was still unable to leave her bed. How right Dr. Elgin had been when he said she needed a nurse. The ease with which fragile Chantel was able to lift her up with the help of Mrs. Morton, always astonished me. Aunt Charlotte's disease had moved into an advanced stage and the doctor gave her opium pills to make her sleep. She fought against what she condemned as drugs but finally she gave in.

"One a night," said Dr. Elgin. "At most two. More would be fatal."

The pills were always kept in a cupboard in the anteroom as I called it which adjoined her room. The doctor said it was better not to have the pills near her bedside in case she was tempted to take more than the prescribed dose if her pains were acute, for the drug could become less effective after too frequent use.

"Nurse Loman, you will see to that."

"You can trust me, Doctor," said Chantel.

And of course he did. He talked to me about Aunt Charlotte. How wise I was to have brought in Nurse Loman. My aunt was a very strong woman. There was nothing organically wrong with her. But for her arthritis she would be absolutely healthy. She could go on for years in her present state.

The night after Dr. Elgin had told me that, I had a strange experience. I woke in the night to find myself standing by my bed. I was not sure what had happened to me. That I had had a strange dream I was sure, though I could not remember what. In my mind was the thought of us all growing old, waiting on Aunt Charlotte—Ellen, Mrs. Morton, myself, and Chantel. All I could remember from that dream were the words which were still ringing in my mind: "for years . . ." And I was not sure how I came to be out of bed. At one moment I thought I remembered getting out of bed; and the next I was sure I did not.

It was a frightening experience.

I went to the door of my room and stood there listening to the sounds of the house. Had something happened to disturb me? I could only hear the faint soughing of the wind through the trees outside my window, the sudden creak of a floorboard. Then I was aware of the clocks ticking all over the house.

What had happened? Nothing but that I had been disturbed by a dream.

The weeks passed. The winter was a hard one; the east wind penetrated the house and as Aunt Charlotte said "stiffened up her bones" and made it painful even to move. She was resigned now to being completely bedridden. Her feet were swollen and misshapen and she could not stand on them. She relied completely on Chantel and Mrs. Morton.

I was away from the Queen's House for whole days at a time, visiting sales, though I never went so far that I had to spend the night. A woman could not very easily travel alone. Besides I curtailed my trips as much as possible because it was difficult for business as there was no one to attend to customers while I was away.

I had begun to suspect that Aunt Charlotte had often bought unwisely. The Chinese goods were still hanging fire. Her expert knowledge had often carried her away and she would buy a piece because of its rarity rather than salability—all very well if one were a collector; but our business was buying and selling.

During that long hard winter I kept my journal up to date; and so did Chantel. I learned all that was happening at home, all the little details, made amusing and lighthearted by Chantel; and in more heavy style I wrote about my visits to sales and customers.

And then one morning when I awoke to find a crisscross of frosty pattern on the windows it was to learn that Aunt Charlotte was dead.

Chantel had gone in as usual at seven o'clock to take a cup of tea. She came running to my room. I shall never forget the sight of her standing there—her green eyes enormous, her face unusually pale. Her titian hair falling about her shoulders. "Anna . . . she's gone! I don't understand it. We must send for Dr. Elgin at once. Ellen must go."

So he came, and we were told that she had died from an overdose of her opium tablets which were always kept in the anteroom. How then had she been able to take them? The inference was obvious. Only if someone had given them to her. The Queen's House had become not only a house of death, but a house of suspicion.

We were questioned, all of us. No one had heard anything during the night. My room was immediately above Aunt Charlotte's, Chantel's was on the same floor, Ellen's and Mrs. Morton's were together on the other side of the house.

I cannot remember details of those days now for I did not write in my journal until the inquest. Somehow I could not bring myself to do so. It was a nightmare; I would not believe it was real.

But there was one question which must be answered because the law demanded it. How had Aunt Charlotte taken sleeping pills which were kept in the next room when she could not walk? The inference was: Only if

someone gave them to her. And the inevitable question
was: Who?

Who had something to gain? I was her main beneficiary. The Queen's House and the antique business would be
mine on her death. I was her only surviving relative; it
was a foregone conclusion that everything would be mine.
I had been trained with that object. The suggestion was
there right from the start. Before anyone mentioned it:
Had I become tired of waiting? It hung about the house
like some miasma, horrible. insinuating.

Ellen was struck dumb, but I could see the speculation
in her eyes. Had she got her legacy? Would it satisfy Mr.
Orfey? Mrs. Morton seemed almost relieved. Life in the
Queen's House had not been what Mrs. Buckle would call
a bed of roses. Mrs. Buckle was too simple to hide her
excitement. To be connected with a house in which sudden
death had occurred had raised her prestige enormously.

It was exhausting—the questions, the police, the inquest.

What would have happened to me then but for Chantel? I often wondered. She was like my guardian angel;
she was with me constantly. assuring me that all would be
well. Of course Aunt Charlotte had taken the pills herself. It was just what she would do.

"She never would take her own life," I cried. "Never. It
would have been quite against her principles."

"You don't know what pain can do to people ... pain
that goes on and on and can only grow worse. I've seen it
happen. At first she did not want the opium pills at all and
then she took them and was constantly asking for more."

Oh yes, Chantel saved me. I shall never forget how
valiantly she did battle for me at the inquest. She looked
lovely, yet so discreet in her black nurse's cloak and her
green eyes and reddish hair so strikingly attractive. She
had more than beauty; she had that power to win confidence and I could see that she carried everyone in the
court along with her, as she had in the Queen's House. She
gave her evidence clearly and composedly. It was true
that Aunt Charlotte had been unable to walk across the
room in ordinary circumstances. But she had seen her
achieve the seemingly impossible and not only Aunt Charlotte but another patient she remembered had done the

same. She would explain. A piece of furniture had been put into Miss Brett's room; it was a piece which her niece wanted her to buy and although Miss Brett was so crippled and suffered such pain she kept an alert eye on the business. She had actually left her bed to examine the small cabinet. Nurse Loman had been astonished because she had believed her patient could not walk. But in certain circumstances patients such as Miss Brett could summon up special powers. She believed Dr. Elgin would confirm this and in any case she had found Miss Brett beside the cabinet. It was true she had had to be almost carried back to bed but she had walked to the piece of furniture unaided. Nurse Loman believed that this was what had happened during that night. The pain was intense; the dose she had already taken had given her only a short sleep; so she had decided to take more. Close to the chest on the top of which the opium pills were kept Nurse Loman had found a button from Miss Brett's bedjacket, and she knew that button had not been missing when she had given Miss Brett her pill and said goodnight.

The bedjacket had been produced; the button examined; water had been spilled on the table close to Aunt Charlotte's bed.

The verdict was that Aunt Charlotte suffered great pain and had taken her own life while the balance of her mind was disturbed.

But the matter did not rest there. The will was read. The business and the Queen's House were for me; there was two hundred pounds for Mrs. Morton and—this was a surprise—two hundred for Chantel; one hundred for Ellen and fifty for Mrs. Buckle.

Chantel wrote in her journal: "What a surprise! Although I knew she was a little fond of me. She must have added the codicil that day when the two important-looking gentlemen came to see her. I suppose they were lawyers. But fancy her including *me*. Money is always comforting though. But I do wish it hadn't happened as it did. Poor poor Anna! She's really very vulnerable. As for the others —particularly Ellen—they can't quite hide their jubilation."

Change had certainly come to the Queen's House. Mrs. Morton wanted to leave at once and she did. Ellen said

Mr. Orfey had no objection to her staying until I found
someone else to suit. Chantel asked if she could stay on
for a while although there would be no need for her
services.

"Please stay," I begged, and she did.

We used to sit in the Queen's room—Chantel's favorite
room—and talk about the future. Sometimes she would lie
on the Queen's bed, very gingerly, always aware of its age
and the need to preserve it, and say that she felt like
the Queen. She tried to be lighthearted, but I found that
difficult. I knew that people were talking. I had inherited
so much, they said. And Mrs. Buckle had often talked
about the trouble that always seemed to be brewing between myself and my aunt, although everything did run
more smoothly since Nurse Loman came.

Chantel helped me sort things out. I soon learned
that what I had inherited was mostly debts. What had
happened to Aunt Charlotte? In the last two or three
years she had lost her judgment. No wonder she would
not let me look at the books. I was horrified at the price
she had paid for those Chinese pieces. There were other
pieces too. Beautiful in themselves, but more suitable for
museums than for private buyers. She had borrowed from
the bank at a high rate of interest. I quickly realized that
the business was on the edge of bankruptcy.

Sometimes I would wake in the night and think I heard
Aunt Charlotte's mocking laughter. And then one night I
woke with a horrible thought in my mind. I remembered
the night when I had found myself standing in my room;
and I visualized myself going down in my sleep to Aunt
Charlotte's room and taking six of these opium pills,
dissolving them in water and putting them at her bedside.
She often drank water during the night. There was some
spilt on the bedside table. Suppose . . .

"What's the matter?" demanded Chantel. "You look as
though you haven't slept a wink."

"I'm terribly afraid," I said, and she insisted on my
telling her.

"You didn't write in your journal about that dream you had some time ago."

"No, I thought it was too trivial."

"Nothing's too trivial. And we promised to tell all." She was mildly reproachful.

"Is it important?"

"Yes," she said, "everything is important. That's what I've learned in my profession. But never mind that now. Anna, you must get this suspicion out of your mind."

"I can't. I think I'm suspected. People have changed toward me. I've noticed it about the town."

"Gossips. They must have something to talk about. I found the button from her bedjacket, didn't I?"

"Did you, Chantel?"

"Did I? What do you mean?"

"I wondered whether you were trying to save me."

"Listen," she said, "I'm sure it happened the way it did."

"Did you really see her get out of bed to look at the cabinet?"

"I don't think we should talk about it. People can do these things. I tell you I've seen it. And quite clearly it's what she did."

"Chantel," I said, "I believe you've saved me from something . . . very unpleasant. Perhaps it might have been proved . . . Suppose I walked in my sleep . . ."

"What nonsense. You don't walk in your sleep. You were half awake when you got out of bed. You were upset about her. I expect she had been particularly beastly that day. Listen to me, Anna. You've got to put the whole thing out of your mind. You've got to concentrate on pulling the business together. You've got to forget the past. It's the only way to go on."

"Oh Chantel, the best thing that has happened to me has been your coming here."

"I've enjoyed the job," she said. "You'll be all right. You'd have stood up to them all if it had come to the court. I know you would. But you have to stop working yourself up about the whole thing. It's over. Finished. You've got to start living now. Something wonderful might be happening in a few weeks' time."

"To me?"

"That's the wrong attitude. Wonderful things can happen to us all. That's how I've lived my life. When I've had the most horrid cases I've said to myself: It won't last. Soon it'll be over."

"What should I do without you?" I asked.

"You don't have to . . . yet."

She was right when she said that nothing remained static. She came to me one day and told me that Dr. Elgin had a post for her.

"You'll never guess where. Castle Crediton."

I felt stunned. First she was going to leave me and secondly she was going to the Castle.

"It's good news," she said. "I have to work for my living and just think we shan't be far apart. I'll be able to see you . . . frequently."

"Castle Crediton," I repeated. "Is someone ill there? Lady Crediton?"

"No, the old lady's as strong as a horse. It's Mrs. Stretton I'm going to nurse. The Captain's wife."

"Oh," I said faintly.

"Yes, she's delicate. Our climate I expect. Some lung infection. It wouldn't surprise me if she is going into a decline. There's a child, too. I couldn't resist the job when Dr. Elgin suggested it."

"When do you . . . start?"

"Next week." She leaned over and taking my hand pressed it firmly. "I'll be near at hand. We'll see each other often. And don't forget there are our journals. Have you written in yours recently?"

"I couldn't, Chantel."

"You must start at once. I'll tell you all about Castle Crediton and the strange life of its inhabitants and you must tell me everything that happens here."

"Oh Chantel," I cried, "what should I do without you?"

"To repeat oneself is a sign of encroaching age, I've been told," she said with a smile. "But I must say I found such repetition endearing. Don't be morbid, Anna. You're not alone. I'm your *friend*."

I said: "Everything has changed so abruptly. I have to make plans. The business is rocky, Chantel. I shall have to see so many people—Aunt Charlotte's lawyer and the bank manager, among others."

"It'll keep you busy. Write it all in your journal. I'll do the same. We'll make a pact, we'll tell the truth, the whole truth and nothing but the truth. And we'll both have the comfort of knowing we are not alone. We can live our own lives and that of the other." Her green eyes were enormous. "You must admit, Anna, that that is a very exciting state of affairs."

"We must never lose sight of each other," I said.

She nodded. "And we'll exchange journals so that even when we can't see each other as often as we'd like to, we shall know everything that is happening."

"I shall know everything that is happening to you in Castle Crediton."

"Everything," she declared solemnly. "Anna, have you ever felt you would like to be a fly on the wall to hear and see everything and no one be aware of you there?"

"Who hasn't?"

"Well, that's how it is going to be. You're the fly on my wall." She laughed. How she lightened my spirits! And how I was going to miss her!

Ellen, married to Mr. Orfey, came back to say that he had no objection to her coming in in the mornings to give a hand; Mrs. Buckle continued to come in to dust and polish, but she left at four o'clock, and from then on I was alone in the Queen's House.

It was when the shadows fell that I would find myself brooding on Aunt Charlotte's death.

I would wake up suddenly from a dream in which I walked down to her room and took the pills from the bottle, to hear myself crying out: "No. No. I did not do it." Then I would lie still listening to the clocks and it would seem as though they soothed me. It must have happened as Chantel said. There was no other explanation.

I should not brood on the past. Goodness knows the future was stark enough. How was I going to pay Aunt Charlotte's debts? Many of the pieces which I believed were hers had not been paid for. She had spent far too much of her capital on the Chinese collection; during the last years the business had not been paying its way. Alarming as this was it gave credence to Chantel's theory. Obsessed by ever-increasing pain, always impatient of inactivity, seeing her debts rising and eventual bankruptcy, she had forced herself—and I knew the extent of her will power—to get out of bed and seek oblivion.

I should have to make some decision. I could not allow things to drift. Indeed I should not be allowed to do so. I formed all sorts of plans. To advertise for a partner with money? To sell out and see what remained? Enforced sales often meant cut prices. If I realized enough to pay my debts I should be lucky. There would be nothing left but the house. I could sell that perhaps. That was the answer.

So my mind raced on during the sleepless nights and in the mornings when I looked at my face in the mirror I would murmur to myself: "Old Miss Brett."

Chantel came and left her journal for me while she took mine away. She would return with it the next day.

That night I took it up to bed with me and the thought of reading it brought me out of my melancholy. My life was drab, and even frightening, but Chantel as before was my savior. To look in on what was happening at Castle Crediton would give me the respite I needed. Besides I would always be particularly interested in anything that happened in Redvers Stretton's home.

I felt my spirits lighten a little as I lay back on my pillows and brought the oil lamp—which I had carried up from downstairs—nearer to my bed and started to read Chantel's journal.

THE CASTLE

5

April 28th, 1887. Today I came to Castle Crediton. I couldn't help feeling rather pleased with myself. I had a new patient and I should not be too far from Anna. We should see each other frequently. I was going to make sure of that. The Castle I knew was not a real one. "Fake," Miss Brett had called it, but that meant little to me. It had all the appearance of a castle and I liked driving under the great archway with the gate house overhead. But I never cared for antiquity. I'll ask Anna about it all sometime, if I ever think of it. The stone walls of the castle looked as if they had been there for centuries. I wondered what had been done to give them that appearance. Another thing to ask Anna—if I ever think of it. As for myself I couldn't help thinking how pleasant it must be to own such a place—fake or not. There is an air of opulence about it; and I feel sure that this castle will no doubt be more comfortable to live in than the genuine article. I alighted from the station fly which I had engaged to bring me and my belongings from the Queen's House. I was in a sort of courtyard and there was an iron studded door with a bell beside it, rather like the one at the Queen's House. I pulled this bell and a manservant appeared.

"I'm Nurse Loman," I said.

"Her ladyship is expecting you," he answered. He was very dignified, the perfect butler. I had an idea that everything would be perfect in Castle Crediton—outwardly at least. I went into the hall which I was sure was the one Anna had once mentioned to me. Yes, there were the tapestries she had talked of, and which she had been examining when she had first met her Captain.

"If you will wait for a moment, Nurse Loman, I will inform her ladyship of your arrival."

I nodded and looked about me, impressed by it all. I thought I was going to like living in a castle. In a very short time the servant reappeared and took me up the stairs to her "ladyship." There she was seated in her high-backed chair, a tartar, I thought, if ever I saw one and I was glad that *she* was not to be my patient. I knew from experience that she would be the very worst possible, but she was in perfect health and would scorn illness, thinking, I was sure that it was due to some mental weakness. I can't help comparing myself with Anna. She would have made an assessment of the treasures of the house, and while their obvious worth did not escape me I included them in my summing up of "grand" and concerned myself with the people. Nursing gives one a very clear insight into people; when they are sick and to a certain extent at one's mercy, they betray themselves in a hundred ways. One becomes perceptive, and the study of human beings always seemed more interesting to me than that of inanimate objects. Yet I am inclined to be frivolous—at least when I compare myself with serious Anna.

Lady Crediton was what I call a battleaxe. She looked at me and did not entirely approve of my appearance although I was doing my best to look demure. *Her* appearance was entirely forbidding—or it would have been to anyone less experienced than I was. I thought to myself: Well, Dr. Elgin has recommended me and I'm here and they want a nurse, so at least they'll have to give me a chance to prove my worth. (And I was going to prove it for I found Castle Crediton much to my taste.) The place had appealed to me as soon as I heard of it, and when I learned that there was the possibility of working there, I was elated. Besides, I don't want to be too far from Anna.

"So, Nurse Loman, you have joined our household." She spoke precisely in a rather gruff masculine voice. I could understand the husband seeking consolation elsewhere. She was clearly a very worthy person, almost always right and taking care that those about her realized it. Creditable, but very uncomfortable to live with.

"Yes, Lady Crediton. Dr. Elgin has given me particulars of my patient."

Her ladyship's mouth was a little grim, from which I gathered the patient is no favorite of hers. Or does she despise all patients because they haven't earned her obvious ruddy health?

"I am glad that he has given you some indication of

how we are placed here. Captain and Mrs. Stretton have their own apartments here. The Captain is not in residence at the time, but Mrs. Stretton and her son, with their servants occupy the east wing. But although this is so, Nurse Loman, I myself am ... shall we say the Chatelaine of the Castle, and as such what happens in all parts of it is my concern."

I bowed my head.

"If you have any complaints, any difficulties, anything you wish to be explained—apart from ordinary domestic matters, of course—I must ask you to see me."

"Thank you," I said.

"Your patient is in a way a foreigner; her ways may not always be like ours. You may find certain difficulties. I shall expect you to report anything unusual to me."

It was becoming rather mysterious and I must have looked puzzled for she said: "Dr. Elgin tells me that you are extremely efficient."

"That was kind of him."

"You have been nursing at the Queen's House and were involved in that unfortunate occurrence. I met Miss Brett once when I allowed her to have an escritoire for which I had no use. She gave me the impression that she was a very precise and efficient woman."

"She was," I said.

"It seems very odd, that affair."

"She changed a great deal when she became crippled; she suffered much pain."

Lady Crediton nodded. "It was most unfortunate, Nurse Loman, and I will tell you frankly that I did consider whether I should be wise to employ someone who had been involved in such an unsavory affair."

She was one of those women who would call her own outspokenness frankness and that of other people rudeness. I knew the type. Rich old women very often who had had too much of their own way for too long.

I decided to be affronted. I rose and said: "I have no wish to discountenance you, Lady Crediton. If you feel that having nursed Miss Brett you would rather I did not nurse your ... your patient, I would not wish to remain."

"You're hasty," she said. "Not a good quality for a nurse."

"I must beg to contradict you. I spoke with no haste. However much I considered your remarks I should still say that if you would prefer me to go I should prefer to do so."

"If I had not preferred that you stay I should not have asked you to come here in the first place."

I bowed my head again. First round to me, I thought.

"I merely want to tell you that I deplore the unpleasantness of what happened to Miss Brett and it is impossible to be involved in such unpleasantness without being connected with it."

"If one is involved one must necessarily be connected, Lady Crediton."

Oh yes, I was scoring fast; but I sensed I was only doing so because she was trying to tell me something and did not know how to. She need not have worried. I understood. She did not like "the patient"; there was something strange about "the patient." Something wild perhaps which might involve her in some "unpleasantness." This was growing interesting.

I went on boldly: "One of the qualifications of a person in my position is discretion. I do not think Dr. Elgin would have recommended me to this case if he had not believed I possessed that quality."

"You may find Mrs. Stretton a little ... hysterical. Dr. Elgin will have told you what is wrong with her."

"He mentioned some lung complaint with asthma."

She nodded. And I realized that she accepted me. I thought she liked someone to stand up to her and I had done exactly that. I had her approval as the patient's nurse.

"I daresay," she said, "that you would wish to see your patient."

I said I thought that would be desirable.

"Your bags ..."

"Were brought into the hall."

"They will be taken to your room. Ring the bell please, Nurse Loman."

I did so and we waited in silence for the call to be answered.

"Baines," she said when it was, "pray take Nurse Loman to Mrs. Stretton. Unless you would prefer to go first to your room, Nurse?"

"I think I should like to see my patient first," I said.

She inclined her head and we went out; I could feel her eyes following me.

We went through a maze of corridors and up little flights of circular stairs—stone some of them and worn in the middle—fake I thought. Stone doesn't wear away in the space of fifty years. But I found it fascinating. A house pretending to be what it was not. That made it very human to my mind.

Then we went into the Stretton apartments, high up in one of the towers, I guessed.

"Mrs. Stretton will be resting," said the manservant hesitantly.

I said, "Take me to her."

He knocked at a door; a muffled sulky voice said: "Who's there?"

"It's Nurse Loman who's come, madam," said the servant.

There was no answer so he opened the door and I went in. In my profession we take the initiative. I said to him: "That's all right. Leave me with my patient."

There were venetian blinds at the windows and the slats had been set to let in the minimum of light. She was lying on the bed, thick dark hair hanging loose, in a purple robe with scarlet trimming. She looked like a tropical bird.

"Mrs. Stretton?" I said.

"You are the nurse," she said, speaking slowly. I thought: What nationality? I hazarded some sort of half caste. Perhaps Polynesian, Creole.

"Yes, come to look after you. How dark it is in here. We'll have a little light." I went to the nearest window and drew up the blind.

She put a hand over her eyes.

"That's better," I said firmly. I sat down by the bed. "I want to talk to you."

She looked at me rather sullenly. A sultry beauty she must have been when she was well.

"Dr. Elgin has suggested that you need a nurse."

"That's no good," she said.

"Dr. Elgin thinks so, and we shall see, shan't we?"

We took measure of each other. The high flush in the cheeks, the unnatural brightness of the eyes, bore out what Dr. Elgin had told me of her. She was consumptive and the attacks of asthma must be alarming when they occurred. But I was interested in her more as a person than a sick woman because she was the wife of Anna's Captain and I wondered why he had married her and how it had all come about. I should discover in due course, I had no doubt.

"It's too cold here," she said. "I hate the cold."

"You need fresh air. And we must watch your diet. Dr. Elgin visits you frequently, I suppose."

"Twice a week," she said.

She closed her eyes quiet, sullen, and yet smoldering. I was aware that she could be far from quiet.

"Dr. Elgin is working out a diet chart for you. We shall have to see about getting you well," I said in my bright nurse's voice.

She turned her face away.

"Well," I went on, "now that we've met I'll go to my room. I daresay it is close to yours."

"It's the next to it."

"Ah, good. I can find my way there then without bothering anyone."

I went out of the room and into the next one. I knew it was mine because my bags were there. The shape of it indicated that it was part of the tower. I went to the window which was really a door—of the french window type—opening onto a balcony or rather a parapet. Anachronism, I thought. I must ask Anna. What a view from the parapet—the deep gorge and the river below and on the other side the houses of Langmouth.

I unpacked my bags and as I did so the door was cautiously opened and a small face peered round at me. It was a boy of about seven. He said: "Hello. You're a nurse."

"That's right," I replied. "How do you know?"

"They said so."

"Who are you?"

"I'm Edward."

"How do you do, Edward." I put out my hand and he shook it gravely.

"Nurses come for ill people," he told me.

"And make them well," I added.

His enormous dark eyes regarded me as though I were some goddess.

"You're clever," he said.

"Very," I admitted.

"Can you do twice one are two?"

"Twice two are four. Twice three are six," I told him.

He laughed. "And a, b, c?"

I went through the alphabet with great speed. I had impressed him.

"Are those your clothes?" I told him they were. "Have you medicines for making people die?"

I was taken aback. "Like the furniture lady," he added.

He was sharp; I could see that. I said quickly: "Only for making people well."

"But . . ." he began; then he was alert.

"Master Edward," called a voice.

He looked at me and hunched his shoulders; he put his fingers to his lips.

"Master Edward."

We were both silent, but he had left my door open and his governess came in. She was tall, angular, and wore a most unbecoming gray blouse with a brown skirt—hideous combination; her hair was gray too, so was her skin.

"Oh," she said, "you're the new nurse. I hope Edward has not been annoying you."

"Entertaining me rather."

"He is really far too precocious."

She had rabbity teeth and rabbity eyes. We took an instant dislike to each other.

"Come along, Edward," she said. "You must not disturb your Mamma."

"His Mamma is my patient, I believe," I said.

She nodded.

"I shall soon learn my way around," I added.

"You've just come from the Queen's House." Her eyes were alert. Young Edward looked from one to the other of us.

"My last case was there."

"H'm." She looked at the child, and I thought: How gossip spread! And thought of Anna and the horrible things which had been said about her. They were even inclined to regard me with some sort of suspicion; how much more so they would have regarded Anna!

She sighed. She dared not talk in front of the child. I wished he was not there so that I could discover more, but I had plenty of time.

She took him away and while I unpacked, a parlormaid brought tea to my room. Baines came with her ostensibly to see that she served it in the correct manner but actually to inform me that my meals would be taken in my own room. I realized that this was an edict from Lady Crediton and that he only ventured into this part of the house to deliver such commands.

I was beginning to learn something about the ways of Castle Crediton.

April 30th. This is my third day and I feel as though I have been here for months. I miss Anna. There is no one here with whom I can be friendly. If Miss Beddoes, the governess, were a different type, she might be useful, but she's a bore, always anxious to impress on me that she has come down in the world. A vicar's daughter, she told me. I said: "Snap. So am I." She looked startled. I'm sure she was surprised that one so lacking in decorum should have come out of a vicarage. "What can one do," she demanded. "One has never been brought up to work for a living, and suddenly it is a necessity." "Ah," I replied, "that's where I was more fortunate. I knew from my earliest days that I should have to battle for my bread in a cruel world, so I prepared myself." "Really," she replied with cold disdain. But she does regard me a little more kindly since we both came from similar stables, or as she would say, were "distressed gentlewomen."

She has told me quite a lot about the family, and for that I'm grateful. She whispered that she believes there is a streak of madness in my patient. I would call it hysteria. Mrs. Stretton is a passionate woman deprived of a husband. I think she is obsessed by him. She writes letters to him every day and tears half of them up. Scraps of paper fill her wastepaper basket. He, Miss Beddoes tells me, is *not* very welcome in the house since his "disgrace." What disgrace? I wanted to know. But she couldn't tell me. It is something which is Never Spoken Of. They seem to want to keep him far away. But because of the child they brought Mrs. Stretton over here. "You see," she said, "until Mr. Rex marries, that child is in a way a sort of heir." It's a muddled setup and I haven't quite worked it out, but I intend to. My patient takes up so much time. I cook for her because Dr. Elgin wishes her diet to be watched. She is like a child and I suspect her of getting one of the servants to smuggle chocolates to her. She likes coffee and makes it herself. There is a spirit lamp in her room for the purpose. I think if she were well she would be fat. She is indolent and likes to stay in bed, but Dr. Elgin does want her to rest. She orders the maids to shut the windows after I've opened them. She hates what she calls the "cold," and fresh air is an important part of the treatment.

I discovered this afternoon that Baines' wife, Edith, is Ellen's sister. She came to my room especially to tell me so. She wanted to say that if there was anything she could do to make me comfortable she would be pleased to do it. Great condescension from the butler's wife. She looks after all the maids and they are quite in awe of her. Ellen must have given me a good reference.

May 1st. Two exciting things happened today. I am growing more and more pleased with Castle life. There is something about this place—an atmosphere of tension. I'm never quite sure of what my hysterical patient is going to do, and I'm constantly aware of intrigue. For instance there is what happened to the Captain to make him unwelcome here. I think that if they didn't want him here they might have left his wife where she was. He could have visited her now and then, I suppose. It is some island. She has mentioned it to me as "the Island." I wanted to know where but refrained from asking. She is inclined to retreat if one is too curious.

The first adventure was my meeting with the Crediton heir. None other than Rex himself. I had settled my patient for an afternoon rest and had taken a little walk in the gardens. They are as magnificent as I expected them

to be. There are four gardeners living on the estate with
wives who work at the Castle. The lawns look like squares
of fine green velvet; I never see them without wishing that
I had a dress made out of them; the herbaceous borders
will be dazzling later on I'm sure. Now the big features
are the lovely aubrietia and arabis—in mauve and white
clumps growing on gray stone on the terraces, and of
course Castle Crediton aubrietia and arabis must be twice
as bushy as anyone else's. That is the first thing that
occurs to me in this place: opulence. You know it's the
home of a millionaire and a first or second generation one.
There is a continual straining after tradition, the Creditons want the best ancestry, the best background that
money can buy. It's different from the Henrock's place
where I nursed poor Lady Henrock—and very successfully for she left me five hundred pounds in her will—
just before going to the Queen's House. There had been
Henrocks at Henrock Manor for the last five hundred
years. It was shabby in places but I could see the difference. As I was inspecting the most elaborate of sundials
whom should I see bearing towards me than the heir to
the millions, Rex Crediton himself. Mr. Rex, not Sir Rex;
Sir Edward was only a knight. I am sure that must be
rather a sore point with her ladyship. He is of medium
height and good-looking but not exactly handsome; he
has an air of assurance and yet there is something diffident
about him. His clothes were immaculately tailored; I think
he must get them in Savile Row. There'd never be anything quite like that in Langmouth. He looked surprised
to see me so I thought I would introduce myself.

"Mrs. Stretton's nurse," I told him.

He raised his eyebrows; they are light and sandy, his
lashes are sandy too; he has topaz-colored eyes—yellow-
brown; his nose is aquiline just like Sir Edward's on the
portrait in the gallery; his skin is very pale and his
mustache has a glint of gingery gold in it.

"You are very young for such a responsibility," he said.

"I am fully qualified."

"I am sure you would not have been engaged unless
that had been the case."

"I am sure I should not."

He kept his eyes on my face; I could see that he

approved of my looks even if he was a little dubious about my capabilities. He asked how long I had been at the Castle and whether I was satisfied with my post. I said I was and I hoped there was no objection to my walking in the gardens. He said there was none at all and pray would I would walk there whenever I wished. He would show me the walled garden and the pond; and the copse which had been planted soon after his birth; it was now a little forest of fir trees. There was a path through this which led right to the edge of the cliff. He led me there and examined the iron fence and said the gardeners had strict instructions to keep it in good repair. "It would need to be," I remarked. There was a straight drop right down the gorse to the river. We stood leaning on the fence looking across at the houses on the opposite cliff over the bridge. There was a proud proprietorial look in his eyes and I thought of what Anna had told me about the Creditons bringing prosperity to Langmouth. He looked important then—powerful. He began to talk about Langmouth and the shipping business in such a way that he made me feel excited about it. I could see that it was his life as it must have been his father's. I was interested in the romance of the Lady Line; and I wanted to hear as much about it as he was ready to tell.

He was ready and willing but he talked impersonally about how his father had built up the business, the days of struggle and endurance.

I said it was a wonderfully romantic story—the building of a great business from humble beginnings.

I was surprised that he should talk so freely to me on *such* a short acquaintance and he seemed to be too, for suddenly he changed the subject and talked of trees and garden scenery. We walked back to the sundial together and he stood beside me while we read the inscription on it. "*I count only the sunny hours.*"

"I must try to do the same," I said.

"I hope all your hours will be sunny, Nurse."

His topaz eyes were warm and friendly. I was fully aware that he was not as cold as he liked people to believe; and that he had taken quite a fancy to me.

He went in and left me in the garden. I was sure I

should see him again soon. I walked round the terraces again and into the walled garden and even through the copse to the iron railings beyond which was the gorge. I was amused by the encounter and elated to find I had made an impression on him. He was rather serious, and must probably be thinking me a little frivolous because of the light way I talk, and I laugh quite frequently as I do so. It makes some people like me, but the serious one might well think me too frivolous. He was of the serious kind. I had enjoyed meeting him anyway, because he was after all the pivot around which the household revolved—and not only the household; all the power and the glory was centered on him—his father's heir and now the source from which all blessings would flow when his mother was no more.

I went back to the sundial. This, I said to myself, is certainly one of the hours I shall count.

I looked at the watch I wore—made of turquoise and little rose diamonds, a present from Lady Henrock just before she died, and compared it with the sundial. My patient would soon be waking. I must return to my duties.

I looked up at the turret. This was not the turret in which my patient lived; it was the one at the extreme end of the west wing. I have very long sight and I distinctly saw a face at the window. For a few seconds the face was there and then it was gone.

Who on earth is that? I asked myself. One of the servants? I didn't think so. I had not been near that turret. There was so much of the Castle I had not explored. I turned away thoughtfully; and then some impulse made me turn again and look up. There was the face again. Someone was interested enough to watch me, and rather furtively too, for no sooner had she—I knew it was a woman because I had caught a glimpse of a white cap on white hair—realized that I had seen her than she had dodged quickly back into the shadows.

Intriguing! But was not everything intriguing in Castle Crediton? But I was far more interested in my encounter with the lord of the Castle, the symbol of riches and power, than I could possibly be in a vague face at a window.

May 3rd. A perfect day with a blue sky overhead. I walked in the garden but there was no sign of Rex. I had thought that he might join me there and meet me "by accident" for I believe he is quite interested in me. But of course he would be busy at those tall offices which dominate the town. I had heard from several sources of information that he had stepped into Sir Edward's shoes and with the help of his mother ran the business. I was a little piqued. I had imagined, with a fine conceit, that he had been interested in me. When he did not appear I started to think of the face at the window and pushed Rex out of my mind. The west turret I thought. Suppose I pretended to lose my way? It was easy enough, Heaven knew, in the Castle; and I could quite easily go up to the west wing and look round and if discovered imply that I had lost my way. I know that I am overcurious, but that is because I am so interested in people and it is my interest in them which makes me able to help them. Besides, I had an idea that to help nurse my patient I had to understand her and to do that I needed to discover everything I could about her. As everything in this house concerned her, this must.

Anyway toward late afternoon the sky became overcast, the bright sunshine had disappeared and it was clearly going to rain at any moment. The Castle was gloomy; this was the time in which I could most convincingly lose my way, so I proceeded to lose it. I mounted the spiral staircase to the west turret. Judging that it would be a replica of the quarters in which I lived, I went to a room in which I was sure was the window whence I had seen the face and opened the door. I was right. She was seated in a chair by the window.

"I . . . beg your pardon. Why . . ." I began.

She said: "You are the nurse."

"I've come to the wrong turret," I said.

"I saw you in the garden. You saw me, didn't you?"

"Yes."

"So you came up to see me?"

"The turrets are so much alike."

"So it was a mistake." She went on without waiting for me to reply which was fortunate. "How are you getting on with your patient?"

"I think we get on well as a nurse and patient."

"Is she very sick?"

"She is better some days than others. You know who I am. May I know your name?"

"I'm Valerie Stretton."

"Mrs. Stretton."

"You could call me that," she said. "I live up here now. I have my own quarters. I hardly ever see anyone. There is a staircase in the west turret down to a walled garden. It's completely shut in. That's why."

"You would be Mrs. Stretton's . . ."

"Mother-in-law," she said.

"Oh, the Captain's mother."

"We're a strangely complicated household, Nurse." She laughed; it was slightly defiant laughter. I noted her high color with its tinge of purple in the temple. Heart, possibly, I thought. It was very likely that she might be my patient before long.

"Would you like a cup of tea, Nurse?"

"That is very kind of you. I should be delighted." And I was because it would give me an opportunity of going on talking to her.

Like her daughter-in-law she had a spirit lamp on which she set a kettle to boil.

"You're very comfortable up here, Mrs. Stretton."

She smiled. "I couldn't hope for more comfort. Lady Crediton is very good to me."

"She's a very good woman, I'm sure." She didn't notice the touch of irony in my voice. I must curb my tongue. I love words and they get out of control. I wanted to win her confidence because she was the mother of one of those two boys born almost simultaneously of the same father but by different women and under the same roof, which could have been a situation from one of Gilbert and Sullivan's operas—except of course that they were never improper and this was decidedly so. I must go along and have a look at old Sir Edward's portrait in the gallery. What a character he must have been! What a pity that he was not alive today! I was sure he would have made the Castle even more exciting than it was.

She asked me how I was getting on and if I enjoyed my work. It must be tremendously interesting, but she feared

I must find it trying at times. Another, I thought, who doesn't like my naughty patient.

I said I was used to coping with patients and didn't anticipate that my present one would be any more trying than others I had experienced.

"She should never have come here," Valerie Stretton said vehemently. "She should have stayed where she belonged."

"The climate is not good for her, I admit," I said. "But as this is her husband's home perhaps she prefers to be here, and happiness is one of the best of all healers."

She made the tea. "I blend it myself," she said. "A little Indian mingled with the Earl Grey and of course the secret is to warm the pot and keep it *dry*; and the water must have just come to the boil."

I listened politely to my lesson in tea-making and I wondered how much information I should get from her. Not much I decided. She was not a gossip. I daresay there had been too many secrets in her own life for her to want to chatter lightly about other people's. She must have been extraordinarily pretty when she was young. Her coloring would have been fair; her hair was still abundant though white; her eyes were very blue. Quite a beauty! No wonder Sir Edward had succumbed.

I sipped my tea. "You must know every part of the Castle," I said. "I find its geography so difficult to learn."

"We shouldn't complain of that as it's due to it that I owe the pleasure of this visit."

I wondered what lay behind her words. I came to the conclusion that there was a depth in her which was not apparent. What a strange life hers must have been, living here under the same roof as Lady Crediton.

"Do you get many visitors?"

She shook her head. "It's a lonely life, but I prefer it so."

I thought, she sits and watches the world go by like a nineteenth-century Lady of Shalott.

"Rex visits me often," she said.

"Rex. You mean . . ."

She nodded. "There's only one Rex." Her voice softened slightly. "He was always a good boy. I was nurse to them . . . both."

An even more strange situation. So she was nurse to the two boys—her own and her rival's. What a strange household; they seemed to create unnatural situations. Was that Sir Edward? I decided it was. There was a trace of mischief in the old fellow.

I pictured it. She would favor her own son. Anna's Captain was a spoiled boy: that was why he was careless of other people's feelings, that was why he thought he could amuse himself with Anna and never allow her to suspect that he was already married to a dusky beauty across the seas.

"I daresay you are longing to see Captain Stretton again. When will he return?"

"I've no idea. There was this . . . affair . . ." I waited expectantly but she did not continue. "He's always been away for long periods since he first went to sea. He wanted to go to sea right from a baby almost. He must always be sailing his little boats in the pond."

"I suppose they were both interested in the sea."

"Rex was different. Rex was the clever one. Quieter too. He was the businessman."

The man, I thought, who will multiply his father's millions.

"They are both good boys," she said, suddenly taking on the character of the old nurse. "And now that Redvers is away Rex comes and sees me and makes sure I know that he doesn't forget me."

How complex people are! I had talked to this woman for half an hour and I knew scarcely any more of her than when she was a face at the window. There was a furtiveness about her one moment and a frankness at the next when she seemed simply the nurse who had loved her charges; I imagined she would have wanted to have been fair, and knowing that naturally she would favor her own son she had tried to be equally as fond of Rex. And according to her Rex was a paragon of virtue. That was not entirely true, I was sure. I should not have been as interested in him if he were because he would have been so dull. He was far from that.

"The boys were very different in temperament," she told me. "Red was the adventurous one. He was always talking about the sea and reading romances about it. He imagined himself another Drake. Rex was the quiet one. He had a business head on his shoulders. He was shrewd, quick to seize an advantage right from the start and when they bartered their toys and things Rex always came out best. They were so lovable, both of them ... in their different ways."

How I should have liked to pursue that topic but she was becoming wary. I sensed I should never get anything from her by pressing. My only chance was to lure her to betray herself.

One must never rush confidences. They are so much more revealing if they come out gradually. But she interested me as much as anyone in the house—except perhaps Rex. I was determined that we should become friends.

6

I found Chantel's journal enthralling. Mine was not nearly so interesting. To read what she had written was like talking to her. She was so frank about herself that I felt my writing was stilted in comparison. The references to me and the man she called "my captain" startled me at first but then I remembered that she had said we must be absolutely frank in our journals, otherwise they were useless.

I recalled my own.

"*April 30th.* A man called to look at the Swedish Haupt cabinet. I don't think he was serious. I was caught in the downpour on the way back from the shop and this afternoon to my horror discovered woodworm in the Newport grandfather clock. I got to work on it at once with Mrs. Buckle.

May 1st. I think we've saved the clock. There was a letter from the bank manager who suggests I call. I feel very apprehensive about what he will say."

How very different from Chantel's account of her life! I

sounded so gloomy; she was so lively. I began to ask myself whether it was the different way in which we looked at life.

However the situation *was* melancholy. Every day I discovered that the business was more deeply in debt. After dark when I was alone in the house I would imagine Aunt Charlotte was there laughing at me, implying as she had in life: "You couldn't do without me and I always told you so."

People had changed toward me; I was aware of that. They looked at me furtively in the street when they thought I didn't notice them, and I knew they were wondering: Did she have a hand in killing her aunt? She inherited the business, didn't she, and the house?

If only they knew what anxieties I had inherited.

I tried to remember my father during that time and that he had always told me to look my troubles right in the face and stand up to them, to remember I was a soldier's daughter.

He was right. Nothing was to be gained by pitying oneself, as I knew too well. I would see the bank manager and know the worst, and I would decide whether it was possible for me to carry on. If not? Well, I should have to make some plan, that was all. There must be something a woman of my capabilities could do. I had a fair knowledge of antique furniture, pottery, and porcelain; I was well educated. Surely there was some niche somewhere waiting for me. I shouldn't find it by being sorry for myself. I had to go out and look for it.

At the moment I was in an unhappy period of my life. I was no longer young. Twenty-seven years old—already at the stage when one earns the title of "Old Maid." I had never been sought in marriage. John Carmel might have asked me in due course but he had certainly been quickly frightened off by Aunt Charlotte; and as for Redvers Stretton I had behaved with the utmost naïveté and had myself imagined what did not exist. I had no one but myself to blame. I must make that clear to Chantel when I next saw her. I must try to write as interestingly, as revealingly about my life as she did about hers. It was a measure of our trust in each other, and there was no doubt that writing down one's feelings did give one a certain solace.

I must stop my brief entries about Swedish cabinets and tall clocks. It was my feelings that she was interested in—myself—just as I was interested in her. It was a wonderful thing to have such a friend; I hoped the relationship between us would always be as it was now. I became afraid that she might leave the Castle, or perhaps I might be forced to take a post somewhere far away. I then realized to the full what knowing her had meant to me in these difficult times.

Dear Chantel! How she had stood by me during those dreadful days which had followed Aunt Charlotte's death. Sometimes I was convinced that she had contrived to divert suspicion from me. That was a very bold thing to do; it was what was called tampering with evidence. She was so lighthearted, so loyal in her friendship, it wouldn't occur to her. I must write this down. No I wouldn't because it was something too important to be written down. That was where I was not so frank as she was. When one started to write a journal one realized that there were certain things one kept back ... perhaps because one didn't really admit them to oneself. But when I think of Aunt Charlotte's death I grew cold with horror because in spite of the button which Chantel found and the belief (which I am sure is true) that in certain circumstances people have special powers, I could never believe that Aunt Charlotte would take her own life, however great the pain she was suffering.

And yet it must have happened. How could it have been otherwise? Still everyone in that house benefited from her death—Ellen had her legacy which was more than a legacy because it was the gateway to marriage with Mr. Orfey; and Heaven knew Ellen had been waiting at the gate for a very long time. Mrs. Morton had been waiting too for the happy release from Aunt Charlotte's service. And myself ... I inherited this burden of debts and anxieties, but before Aunt Charlotte's death I had not known they existed.

No, it was as Chantel had made them believe. I might think Aunt Charlotte would never take her life, but what human being knows all about another?

I must stop thinking of Aunt Charlotte's death; I must
face the future as my father would have done. I would go
and see the bank manager; I would learn the worst and
make my decision.

He sat looking at me over the tops of his glasses,
pressing the tips of his fingers together, a look of mock
concern on his face. I daresay he had spoken in similar
strain to people before.

"It's a matter of assets and liabilities, Miss Brett. One
must balance them. And you find yourself in a very
precarious position."

He went on explaining; he showed me figures to back
up his conclusions. I was in a very difficult position indeed
and I had no alternative but to act promptly. He talked of
"voluntary liquidation" which he believed, with care, could
still be accomplished. In a few months' time it might be
too late. I must remember that expenses went on mounting and debts growing.

He was not suggesting that I should rely entirely on his
advice. He was a bank manager merely. But the business
had clearly been going downhill fast. Miss Charlotte Brett
had bought unwisely—there was no doubt about that; she
had often sold at a loss in order to raise money. That was
a very dangerous procedure and could not be repeated too
often. He suggested that I see my solicitor. Miss Brett's
loan to the bank would have to be repaid within the next
three months he feared, and he believed that I should go
into these matters very, very carefully. It might be a wise
plan to cut my losses and sell everything—including the
house. That should settle the debts and leave me a little
capital in hand. He feared it was the best I could hope
for.

He gave me a melancholy handshake and advised me to
go home and think about it.

"I'm sure you are very sensible, Miss Brett, and will
before long have made up your mind."

When I returned to the Queen's House, Mrs. Buckle
was on the point of leaving.

"You look down in the dumps, miss," she said. "I don't
know. I was saying to Buckle it's no life for a young lady,

that's not. That old house, all alone there. I don't reckon it's right. All alone with them valuable things. It gives me the shivers, not that the house itself wouldn't do that at night."

"I'm not afraid of the house, Mrs. Buckle. It's . . ."

But I couldn't explain to her; besides she was a gossip and would be unable to help repeating any confidence.

"Well, it's none of my affair. But I think there's worm in that 'Epplewhite table. Not much. But it was right next to the tall clock and you know what them little devils are."

"I'll have to look into that, Mrs. Buckle."

She nodded. "Well, I'll be getting along. We're short of beeswax. I'll get some on the way in tomorrow. See you then, miss."

She was gone and I was alone.

I went into the garden and thought of that autumn night so long ago now and I wondered foolishly if he ever thought of it. I walked down to the river where the water crowfoot rioted among the lady's-smocks and a swarm of gnats danced above the water. I looked back at the house and thought of what the bank manager had said. Sell everything. Sell the Queen's House. I was not sure how I felt about that. The Queen's House had been my home for so long. It attracted me while it still repelled me, and sometimes when I suddenly realized that it was mine I thought of it furnished as it must have been before it became Aunt Charlotte's storehouse. It would have been a charming happy house then . . . before so many tragic things had happened in it. My mother's death, my father, that brief evening's happiness when I had thought I had met someone who would change my life, the disillusion and then Aunt Charlotte's mysterious death.

I didn't want to sell the house. And yet I believed I should have to.

I walked across the lawns. The apple and cherry trees were covered in pink and white blossom; and there were flowery pyramids on the horsechestnut tree near my window. I had a strong feeling for the Queen's House.

I stepped inside. I stood listening to the clocks. It was still as cluttered as in Aunt Charlotte's day. Not many people came to the house now. Perhaps they felt embarrassed to deal with someone they suspected of being concerned in sudden death.

That night I walked all round the house, through room after room. So much valuable furniture for which I could not find profitable buyers! I should have to sell up and that meant selling to dealers. Anyone knew that they would only buy cheaply.

But I was coming nearer and nearer to a climax.

I seemed to hear my father's voice: "Stand up to your troubles. Face them and then you'll find the way to overcome them."

That was what I was doing and the malicious clocks were telling me, "Sell, sell, sell, sell." Yes, sell and get out; and start afresh. Make a new life . . . entirely.

"There's some people," said Ellen, "that say the Queen's House is haunted."

"What nonsense," I retorted.

"Well, that's what they say. It gives you the creeps."

I looked at her sharply. She had changed since Aunt Charlotte's death. I was certain that at any moment she was going to say that she couldn't continue. After all she had only stayed to "help me out" as she had explained at the time. Mr. Orfey was an exacting husband. With the legacy, he had bought his own horse and cart and was in business on his own—"building up nicely," said Ellen.

But it was not so much Mr. Orfey's growing prosperity that made Ellen chary of the Queen's House It was the memory of Aunt Charlotte. In a way the house was haunted for Ellen as well as for me. Ellen wouldn't go up into Aunt Charlotte's room alone. As she said it gave her "the creeps." I could see that very soon she would be giving her notice.

It was a wet day and the rain had been falling steadily through the night; the skies were overcast and the house was full of shadows even in the afternoon. Mrs. Buckle going up to the attic rooms came hurrying down to say there was a pool of water on the floor of the attic. It was coming through the roof.

The roof had always been a matter for anxiety. Aunt Charlotte had had it patched up now and then but I

remembered the last occasion when we were told it needed major repairs. Aunt Charlotte had said she couldn't
afford it.

I was feeling very melancholy when Chantel arrived.
How pretty she looked in her dark nurse's cloak which set
off her lovely hair to advantage; her cheeks glowed and
her eyes sparkled. "I couldn't resist calling," she told me.
"Miss Beddoes drove me into the high street and I'm
joining her in an hour's time. I was terrified that you'd be
out."

"Oh Chantel, it is good to see you!" I poured out
everything that had happened; my visit to the bank manager, my fears about Ellen and the leaking roof.

"My poor Anna! What shall you do? You must have
that money your aunt left me. I can't imagine why she
should have done such a thing. I'd only been here such a
short time."

"She quickly grew fond of you . . . as anyone would."

"You must satisfy me by taking that money back."

"You know I'd do no such thing."

"Well, at least it's there if you want it. What are you
going to do?"

"The bank tells me I should sell up."

"Can you do that?"

"I can try. There's the house. That should fetch something."

She nodded gravely. "I'm sure you'll do the right thing,
Anna."

"I wish I could be sure."

"Have you written it all in your journal?"

"How could I when you had it?"

"As you have mine. You must give me mine back.
Things must be written when they happen, otherwise they
lose their flavor. One forgets so quickly the essential
feeling of the moment."

"It was wonderful reading it, Chantel. I thought I was
there."

"How I wish you were! What fun that would be. If only
they wanted an antique adviser at the Castle!"

"Did anyone ever want such a thing?"

"It's fascinating, Anna. I'm intrigued by it. It's not only
the place which is so unusual, it's *them*."

"I know. I could sense that. Has anything else happened?"

"I've consolidated my position. I'm getting to know them all so much better. I'm no longer the stranger within their gates."

"And this man . . . Rex?"

"Now why did you pick on him?"

"I fancied he had appealed to you rather specially."

"That's because you're thinking of romance. Now do you think that the heir to all those millions is going to be interested, seriously, in his sister-in-law's nurse?"

"I am sure he must be interested."

"The important word is seriously." She laughed, and I said: "Well, at least *you* are not thinking of him seriously."

"I'm so frivolous, as you know."

"Not always. I shall always remember you, Chantel, at the inquest. You weren't frivolous then."

"I have my serious moments."

"I can't get Aunt Charlotte out of my mind."

"Stop it," she said sternly. "You *must* get her out of your mind. It's all over. It's finished. What you have to think of now is what you are going to do. Is it very bad?"

"Very. The debts are double, treble what I thought. Aunt Charlotte seemed to lose her judgment. She bought the most unsalable things. I shall never get half what she paid for them, and toward the end she let the debts mount up. At one time she was always so meticulous."

"Her illness changed her. It does change people."

"It certainly changed her."

"You ought to get away, Anna. This is no place for you."

"Chantel, it is sweet of you to care so much what becomes of me."

"Why Anna, I look on you as my sister."

"We have not really known each other long."

"Time is not always the foundation on which friendship is built. You can know more of some people in a month than you can of others in years. All that happened here brought us together. I'd like us to stay like that, Anna."

"I want it too. But you have sisters."

She grimaced. "It's odd how one loses touch with one's

family. My sister Selina married and stayed in the village where my father had his living, Katey married a doctor and went up to Scotland."

"And do you never see them?"

"I haven't since I nursed Lady Henrock; you see I came straight to you and there wasn't time to go home; and it's so far away in any case. Right up in Yorkshire."

"I expect they would love to see you."

"They were years older than I. grown up when I was born. I was the afterthought, they used to say. My mother grew sentimental before I was born; she took my name from an old tombstone in the graveyard beside the vicarage. Someone named Chantel was buried there. She departed this life aged twenty-four years. Chantel Spring, her name was. My mother said. If it's a girl I shall call her Chantel Spring. And she did. I'm Chantel Spring Loman. At least that's the story I heard. I never knew my mother. I killed her getting born."

"Killed her! What an expression. You speak as though it were your fault."

"One feels a certain responsibility."

"My dear Chantel, that is quite wrong. You should get that out of your head without delay."

"Look here," she said with a laugh, "I came to give you my advice not ask for yours."

"Well what is yours?"

"Don't worry. Sell up if you have to. And then we'll go on from there."

"You're a comfort to me, Chantel."

Then we talked about the Castle and what had been happening up there. She was certainly excited about the place. She was like a girl in love, I thought, but with the Castle. Unless that was a blind. I was certain that she was very interested in Rex Crediton; but she did not seem in the least bit apprehensive, although she had said he could not possibly be serious about the nurse.

I didn't want her to be hurt, as I had been. It seemed an odd coincidence that she whom I had really begun to think of as the sister I always longed to have, should become too interested in one of those brothers—as I was in the other—too interested, that was, for our comfort.

I felt so much better when she had gone. I was cheered; I felt that whatever was going to happen I could cope with it.

I longed to hear more about the Castle; she took her journal away and said that she must "make it up" as soon as possible. I told her I was longing to read the next installment.

"And you must write yours too, Anna. I want to know everything you do, everything you think, nothing held back. It's the only way to see the truth."

I agreed.

It was some time before I read her journal again. In the meantime I had come to the conclusion that I would have to sell up. I had even considered selling the house. I saw a house agent who told me that this would not be easy. It was an interesting house but no repairs had been done for years. The roof was leaking; there was woodworm in one of the doors and dry rot on the river side. "You're too near the river and the place is damp. Houses like this are very picturesque but they need fortunes spent on them from time to time. Don't forget this one has been standing here for the last four hundred years. It would be folly to put the house up for sale because so much has to be spent on it you would get practically nothing for it."

The best suggestion he could make was that I let the house for a peppercorn rent with the proviso that the tenant must keep it in good repair. This meant that for the privilege of living in the house the tenant would have to see to that leaking roof, that woodworm and dry rot.

"It seems a possible way out," I said.

"Believe me," was the answer. "It's the only way out."

So I made up my mind. I was going to sell up, pay the debts; let the house. I should have little—perhaps nothing; but I should be free of encumbrances.

What I should do then had still to be decided; but these arrangements took so long to settle that I still had months in which to think about my future.

Meanwhile events were taking place at the Castle and of these I learned through Chantel—but chiefly and most vividly through her journal.

7

May 9th. I went to see Anna today and heard what they are advising her. I think it will be good for her to get away from the Queen's House and all its associations—as long as she doesn't go too far and I can't see her now and then. I wish there was a means of getting her to the Castle. What fun it would be if we could talk over things as they happen. Today Edith Baines came to my room to bring some medicine Dr. Elgin had left for my patient and we talked. She is very different from her sister Ellen. Very dignified—mistress of the maids and wife to Mr. Baines! She regards me as an equal which means I am treated to graciousness without condescension which is amusing, and also profitable. I believe Edith knows a great deal about the "secrets" of the Castle. She did confide in me that there would shortly be a bit of a "to-do" in the household. Lady Crediton had summoned her yesterday and told her that she had invited the Derringhams for the first week in June. "So," said Edith, "we shall have some fun and games, and that makes work. Mr. Baines has been told to have the ballroom floor repolished; and I hear she's already been seeing the gardeners."

"The Derringhams?" I said. "They would be important people I imagine since Lady Crediton thinks so highly of them."

"In a way," said Edith, "they're our rivals." Edith always implies she has a share in the Lady Line. "But all very friendly, of course. Sir Henry is a friend of Mr. Rex and of her ladyship. As a matter of fact I think Sir Henry and Lady Crediton have decided that Helena will do very well for Mr. Rex."

"*Do* very well?"

"A match. Link the businesses. That's always a good

thing. My goodness, what a power we'd be—Creditons and Derringhams together."

"It all sounds reasonable," I said.

Edith raised her eyes to the ceiling: "It makes work. And some of those girls are so lazy. You've no idea. At least we'll get Mr. Crediton safely married. After the Captain doing what he did."

"The Captain's a very mysterious person to me."

"That's what comes of . . . well," Edith folded her arms primly. "It's not the same is it? After all who was his mother? She seems like a lady, and there she is waited on hand and foot up in her turret. Jane Goodwin waits on her—thinks the world of her. But I mean to say who was she to start with? Although of course she was a lady's maid." Edith had a close knowledge of the social hierarchy of those who served the rich.

This was cozy. People like Edith were the best sort of informants. They were so righteous; they had such a sense of family. Edith for instance would have been astonished if she were accused of gossiping. Her respect for the family was great but so was her interest in it; and in talking to me she was not discussing it with one of the *lower* servants.

"I should think Mrs. Stretton was very beautiful when she was young," I prompted.

"I fail to see that that excuses her."

"And what of Sir Edward?"

"It should have been hushed up. But . . ." Her eyes had fallen on a speck of dust on my cabinet which seemed of as great concern to her as the conduct of Sir Edward with his wife's lady's maid. I hastily diverted her attention from it. I did not want young Betsy whose task it was to dust my quarters to be scolded on my account. I wanted to be on pleasant terms with everyone.

"Why wasn't it hushed up?" I said quickly.

"My mother told me. She had a post in the household before her marriage and that was why I was taken on in the first place. *Mrs.* Stretton—as she calls herself—is nearly twenty years younger than her ladyship, who was married fifteen years before Mr. Rex was born. It appears that Sir Edward believed her ladyship was barren. She was a wonderful help to him; she understood the business; she entertained when necessary—she was an excellent wife in every way but one. She could not produce a healthy child. And of course what Sir Edward wanted was a son to carry on the business."

"Naturally, he'd want a son."

"Her ladyship had had several failures. Sir Edward was in despair. Then her ladyship was pregnant but no one thought her pregnancy would come to a satisfactory end. It never had before and she was nearly forty. The doctors were dubious and even feared for her life. It became known that Valerie Stretton was about to have a child—and Sir Edward admitted parentage. Sir Edward wanted a son—legitimate if possible—but he wanted a son. There were two chances of getting one and Valerie Stretton seemed the more likely one. He was always a law unto himself. He snapped his fingers at local scandal and no one dared oppose him—not even Lady Crediton who was furious that her lady's maid should be kept in the house. But Sir Edward always had his way—even with her ladyship. The strange thing was that her ladyship was brought to bed only two days after Valerie Stretton had given birth. Sir Edward was wild with joy because his mistress had had a healthy boy; he'd got his son. And a few days later Lady Crediton's boy was born. He'd got two sons, but he wasn't going to lose one of them. Sir Edward, they said, tried for everything and that was why he had got such a great deal. He wanted his wife and his mistress; and what Sir Edward wanted was done. So the two boys were to be brought up in the Castle and Sir Edward doted on both of the boys, though of course he was very strict with them. He was always talking about "my sons." Valerie Stretton's was christened Redvers, but Lady Crediton wanted everyone to know who was the important one, so her baby was christened Rex—the King. Rex would inherit the business; but Master Red would be very well looked after; he'd have a share ... a minor one of course; and Red was all for going away to sea and Rex was all for juggling with money. So they were different in their ways. But Rex is the Crediton. I wonder Sir Edward didn't make Redvers change his name too. I've heard that if anything should happen to Rex ..."

"You mean if he died?" I said.

She looked rather shocked. Death was "anything happening"—I must remember that.

"If anything happened to Rex," she said firmly, "why Redvers would be the heir."

"It's all very interesting," I said.

She admitted it. "My mother was here, you see, before the boys were born. She often talked of what happened. I remember her talking about the day the ship was launched. It was quite a to-do—launching the ships. Sir Edward saw that it was done in the proper way because he used to say it was good for business. He wanted everyone to know that the Lady Line had added to its power."

"Naturally," I said soothingly.

"All the ships as you know are ladies. And Lady Crediton was going to name this one. It was all arranged; she was going to break a bottle of champagne on the side as they do, you know. They had decided to name the ship *The Lucky Lady* or something like that. The day before the launching there had been trouble at the Castle. Her ladyship had discovered Sir Edward's feelings for Valerie Stretton and what was going on. She was most upset. She knew his tendencies, but that it should be in the Castle . . . right under her very nose you might say . . . made her very angry. She wanted to dismiss Valerie Stretton but Sir Edward wouldn't hear of it. Oh yes, there was a rare to-do that day. And the next she went out to name the ship and when they all expected her to say 'I name this ship *The Lucky Lady*' or whatever it was, she said instead, 'I name this ship *The Secret Woman.*' Defiance you see!"

"What a flutter that must have caused."

"The only Woman among the Ladies! But they kept it that way. It shows you, don't you think, the sort of woman she was. Liked her own way and got it. But this was one thing in which she didn't get it. She wanted to send Valerie Stretton away. But oh no, said Sir Edward. She stays. It was funny, too, that her ladyship accepted it and Valerie stayed on as the nurse. They were always cool and distant to each other. But there you are, Sir Edward was no ordinary man."

"He was like an Eastern potentate with his wives and children all under one roof."

"I wouldn't be knowing about that," said Edith. "But there's not much I don't know about the Castle."

May 11th. I thought my patient was dying last evening. She had a terrible attack of asthma and was gasping for her breath. I sent Betsy for Dr. Elgin and when he came he told me that I must be prepared for these attacks. They were dangerous. When she had recovered a little he gave her a sedative and he came to my sitting room (next to my bedroom in the turret) and talked about her.

"It's an unfortunate situation," he said. "She would be better in a climate to which she is more accustomed. The sudden changes here affect her. The damp's no good to her. And she has a touch of consumption, you know. Her temperament doesn't help."

"She seems an unhappy woman, Doctor."

"This marriage is a bit incongruous."

"Why has she come here? As her husband is so rarely here there doesn't seem much point."

"It's the child, of course. Until Mr. Rex Crediton produces an heir, I suppose the boy is important. Moreover they want him brought up in the business more or less. It's entirely due to the child that she is here."

"It seems hard luck on the mother."

"It's an unusual situation. You've probably heard that the boy is Sir Edward's grandson—wrong side of the blanket though it may be. But they want family in the business and the more the merrier; I know it was always a sore point with Sir Edward that he had only two sons. He had visualized a large family of them. It seemed to be the one thing over which he had no control and that irked him. Lady Crediton seems determined to carry out his ideas. So that is why young Edward is here to learn the shipping business with his a, b, c."

"I think Mrs. Stretton is homesick. By the way where is her home?"

"It's an island in the Pacific—not far from the Friendly Isles. Coralle is the name. I believe her father was French and her mother half Polynesian. She's like a fish out of water here."

"The attack last night followed a display of temper."

"That was to be expected. You must try to keep her calm."

I smiled ruefully. "She reminds me of a volcano ready to erupt at any moment. The worst possible temperament for one suffering from her complaint."

"You *must* try to keep her happy, Nurse."

"Her husband might do that ... if he came home. I sense that his absence is the cause of her unhappiness."

"She married a sailor so she should expect absences. Watch her diet closely. Never let her take a heavy meal—small and often is the rule."

"Yes, Doctor."

"Just a glass of milk or cocoa with bread and butter for breakfast. And at eleven milk . . . with perhaps an egg. She could take the egg in the milk. With the midday meal she might take a little wine but not much; and before retiring a glass of milk with a teaspoon of cognac in it."

"I have the diet sheet, Doctor."

"Good. If she were happy she'd be better. These distressing attacks are the result of inner tensions. She'll sleep it off now, and you'll find she'll be calm enough when she wakes."

When the doctor had left I realized how alarmed I had been. I had really thought she was going to die. I can't pretend that I was fond of her; there was something quite unlovable about her; but I thought if she died I should no longer be at the Castle. And that thought made me very concerned. But of course it is the nature of my work. I am at one place for a while and then as Edith would say "something happens" and my services are no longer required. It's a rootless existence; and it has been brought home to me since I came to Langmouth—first when I had to leave Anna and now at the prospect of leaving the Castle. I am growing far too fond of this Castle. I like its thick walls and the fact that it's a fake endears me to it in a way. I think I should have liked Sir Edward. What a pity he died before I came. I have seen his son Rex several times. We seem to meet frequently—more frequently than could be put down to chance. I am enormously interested in him and long to know about his childhood when Valerie Stretton was his nurse, and what he thought of his half brother Redvers. I wish the Captain would come home. I am sure my poor patient would be happier if he did; and it would be interesting to see how they all get on together.

May 12. Last night I was with my patient when she was coming out of her sedation. Her name is Monique. Such a dignified name does not really suit her. I picture her lying on sandy beaches under palm trees gazing out at the coral reefs about the island. She wears coral quite often and it suits her. I picture her meeting the Captain who would have perhaps gone to this Coralle to pick up copra and fish or something like that to take back to Sydney. I imagined her with exotic red flowers in her hair. He was captivated surely and foolishly, for he married her without thinking how she would fit into Castle Crediton society. But this was pure imagination. It probably happened quite differently.

As I sat beside her, she started to mutter; I heard her say: "Red. Why . . . Red . . . You don't love me."

Quite revealing for it shows that he is constantly in her thoughts.

Suddenly she said: "Are you there, Nurse?"

"Yes," I soothed. "Try to rest. It's what the doctor wants."

She closed her eyes obediently. She was really beautiful—rather like a doll with her thick black hair and long dark lashes; her skin looked honey yellow against the white of her nightdress; her brow was low. I thought, she will age quickly. She couldn't have been more than twenty-five now.

She was murmuring to herself and I bent over to listen. "He does not want to come back," she said. "He wishes it had not happened. He wishes to be free."

Well, madam, I thought, I don't wonder at it if you get into tempers like you did a short while ago.

She was wild, passionate, and uncontrolled. What would Lady Crediton think of such a creature? One thing she would be pleased about. If one of the brothers had to make such a *faux pas* at least it wasn't her precious son. I could imagine her fury if the important Rex made a *mésalliance*. What would she do? Had she the power to do anything? No doubt she had an interest in the Company: she would most certainly be a very important share-holder.

There were so many interesting things to be learned in the Castle; more interesting in fact than the matrimonial troubles of this pretty little fish out of water whom I had come to nurse.

May 15th. I heard today that the Captain is on his way home and should arrive in four weeks' time. It was Edward who told me. We have become friends; I must say I find him a bright little fellow and I pity him left to the care of the prim Miss Beddoes. She is the most unimaginative woman imaginable and Edward is really rather a naughty little boy where she is concerned. The other day she brought him in from his walk in the grounds dripping with water. He had decided to take a bath fully dressed in the fountain, he said. She was quite distracted and he only laughed when she scolded him. It is her own fault in a way: she is so lacking in confidence that the shrewd child senses this and makes the most of it. He knows that he has to do what I tell him or go. But I suppose it is easy for me as I am not in control of him. He quite clearly thinks that I am clever and that I am in charge of his Mamma in the same way as poor Miss Beddoes is in charge of him: and to be in authority over a grown-up person makes me very important in his eyes. He comes into his mother's room and watches me give her medicine. I have a little kitchen where I prepare her food and he watches me do that. He likes to have what he calls "tasters" from Mamma's plate. Miss Beddoes frowns on this; she says it is eating between his meals and spoils his appetite; and as in the case of most young people the more this is forbidden the more it is to his taste. He is a lonely little boy in some respects. He is so small; the Castle is so big and his mother has no idea how to treat a child. Sometimes she spoils him and wants to fondle him: at others she loses her temper with him and has no time for him. He is not fond of her, I can see. He despises Miss Beddoes; he is in awe of Lady Crediton; but he is fond of Grandmamma Stretton, and goes to see her every day but Jane won't let him stay long because she said he tires her mistress. It's small wonder that he has become attached to me. I am, I suppose, predictable; my attitude is unchanging. I never fuss over him; in fact I take little notice of him; but we like each other.

So he came in this morning while I was preparing his mother's mid-morning milk and cutting her bread and butter. He sat down watching me, swinging his legs. I knew he had some exciting news to tell and that he was wondering how best to startle me with it. He could not keep it to himself: "My Papa is coming home."

"Well, are you pleased?"

He regarded the tip of his shoe shyly. "Yes," he said. Then: "Are you?"

"I shan't know yet."

"When will you know?"

"When I meet him perhaps."

"And will you like him?"

"I daresay that will depend on whether he likes me."

For some reason that seemed to amuse him; for he laughed aloud, but perhaps that was with pleasure. "He likes ships and the sea and sailors and me . . ."

"That sounds like a song," I said.

I began to sing:

"He likes ships and the sea
And sailors and me."

He looked at me with great admiration.

"I know something else you like," I said.

"What? What?"

"Bread and butter."

I put a slice on a plate and gave it to him.

While he was eating it Miss Beddoes came in looking for him. She knew well enough to come straight to my room when he was missing.

Seeing her he crammed the bread and butter into his mouth.

"Edward!" she cried angrily.

"He'll choke," I said. "That'll do him no good."

"He's no right to come in here . . . eating between meals."

She was criticizing me really, not him. I just ignored her and went on cutting the bread and butter. Edward was taken away. At the door he turned and looked at me. He looked as if he was going to cry so I winked which made him laugh. It always did and he would pull his face into all sorts of contortions to try to wink back. It was flouting authority of course and wrong of me, but it stopped his tears—and after all he was a lonely little fellow.

When I took the tray in Monique was sitting up in bed in a lacy bedjacket looking at herself in a hand-mirror. She had heard the news evidently. What a difference in a woman! She was quite beautiful now.

She frowned at the tray though.

"I don't want that."

"Oh come," I said, "you'll have to be well for when the Captain comes home."

"You know . . ."

"Your son has just informed me."

"Trust you!" she said. "You know everything."

"Not everything," I said modestly. "But at least I know what's good for you."

I smiled my bright nurse's smile. I was pleased that at last he was coming home.

May 18. It seems incredible that I have been here such a short time. I feel I know them all so well. Lady Crediton sent for me yesterday afternoon. She wanted a report on my patient. I told her that Mrs. Stretton seemed to be progressing favorably and there was no doubt that the new diet Dr. Elgin had worked out for her was having a beneficial effect.

"You are quite comfortable, Nurse?" she asked me.

"Very comfortable, thank you, Lady Crediton."

"Master Edward has a cold. I understand that he went fully clothed into the fountain the other day."

I wondered who her informant was. Baines probably—I imagined Edith's reporting to Baines and Baines carrying the news to Lady Crediton. Perhaps our misdeeds were all recorded and presented to our employer.

"He is very healthy and will soon be well. I think a day or so confined to his bedroom and he will be perfectly well again."

"I will speak to Miss Beddoes. She really should have

more control. Do you think Dr. Elgin should look at him when he calls, Nurse?"

I said I thought he might do that but it was not necessary to call him specially.

She inclined her head.

"Mrs. Stretton has had no more unfortunate attacks?"

"No. Her health has improved since the news came that her husband is on his way home."

Lady Crediton's lips hardened. I wondered what she felt about Redvers. I should know when he returned.

"The Captain will not be home until after our house party. I must ask you to take special care of your patient, Nurse. It would be most inconvenient if she were ill at such a time."

"I shall do my best to keep her well."

The interview was over. I felt a little shaken. I am not easily overawed; but there was something snakelike about the woman's eyes. I pictured her smashing the champagne bottle with venom against the side of the ship and saying in a firm voice: "I name this ship *The Secret Woman*." How she must have hated having that woman in the house all those years! And what a power Sir Edward must have been! No wonder the Castle was such an exciting place! What emotions must have circulated within its walls! I wonder Lady Crediton didn't push her rival over one of the parapets or Valerie Stretton didn't put arsenic in her ladyship's food. There must have been ample provocation. And now they still lived under the same roof; Valerie Stretton had lost her protecting lover; and I supposed that all passions were spent. They were merely two old ladies who had reached the age when the past seemed insignificant. Or did people ever feel so?

In any case, I thought, I should not like to offend Lady Crediton. There was no fear of my doing that at the moment. She was clearly quite pleased with me.

I fancied she was less so with Miss Beddoes who even as I left the presence was making her trembling way toward it.

I walked out into the gardens. Rex was there.

He said: "You seem to enjoy our gardens, Nurse Loman. I believe you find them beautiful."

"I find them appropriate," I replied.

He raised his eyebrows and I went on: "Worthy of the Castle itself."

"You are amused by us and our ways, Nurse Loman?"

"Perhaps," I retaliated, "I am too easily amused."

"It is a great gift. Life becomes so much more tolerable when it amuses."

"I have always found it very tolerable."

He laughed. "If we amuse you," he said, "you also amuse me."

"I am glad. I should hate to bore you or make you melancholy."

"I could not imagine that to be possible."

"I feel I should sweep a curtsy and say: 'Thank you, fair sir.' "

"You're different from so many young ladies I meet."

"I daresay. I work for my living."

"You are certainly a most useful member of the community. How pleasant to be both useful and decorative."

"It is certainly pleasant to hear oneself so described."

"Nurse Loman sounds a little stern. It doesn't fit you. I should like to think of you as something other than *Nurse Loman*."

"You are asking my Christian name, I presume. It is Chantel."

"Chantel. How unusual . . . and how delightful."

"And more suited to me than 'Nurse'?"

"Infinitely more."

"Chantel Spring Loman," I told him and he wanted to know how I came by such a name. I told him about my mother's seeing it on the tombstone and he seemed to find that very interesting. He took me along to the greenhouses and he talked to the gardeners about the blooms which would be brought into the house during the period of the house party. He asked my advice and I gave it freely. It was flattering that he passed it on to the gardeners and said "This shall be done."

8

May 21st. There has been drama in the house these last two days. I think it had begun before I realized it. I noticed that Jane Goodwin, Valerie Stretton's maid, was worried. I asked her if she were feeling well.

"I'm quite all right, Nurse," she said.

"I thought you looked . . . anxious."

"Oh no, no," she said, and hurried away. So I knew that something was wrong. I kept thinking about what went on in the west turret and wondering how Valerie felt about her son's return. Was she eager to see him? She must be. From all accounts he was such a fascinating fellow. His wife was madly in love with him and my dear cool Anna had been ready to fall in love with him, so surely his mother should be happy by his return. I had quickly summed up Jane as being one of those women made to serve others. I doubted she had ever had a life of her own; the center of her existence would be her mistress and friend, in this case Valerie Stretton. So if Jane were anxious I guessed something was amiss with Valerie.

It was about nine o'clock in the evening. I had given Monique her food and was reading when Jane knocked at my door.

"Oh Nurse," she said, "do come quickly. It's Mrs. Stretton."

I hurried to the west turret to find Valerie Stretton lying on her bed and distorted with pain. I thought I knew what was wrong and that it was what I had suspected. I turned to Jane and said: "I want Dr. Elgin at once."

Jane ran off. There was nothing I could do. I believed it was an attack of angina and had thought "Heart" as soon as I set eyes on her.

I bent over her. "It'll soon pass. It's passing now, I believe."

She did not speak but I think she was comforted to

have me there. What startled me was the manner in which she was dressed. She wore high boots; the mud on them had stained the counterpane and her hat had half-fallen from her head. What I noticed particularly was the heavy veil which would have concealed her face. She had been out. I would not have believed that possible if I had not seen her boots and the hat. Why had she gone out dressed like that at that time of the evening?

The pain was passing. Such an attack would last about half an hour, and I knew that this was not a major attack.

But it was a warning.

Without disturbing her I removed her boots; they were very muddy. I took her hat off, but I did not take her coat from her as I did not wish to move her until the doctor had been.

When he came the attack was over. He examined her and I gently undressed her. She was too exhausted to tell him much but I described what I had seen and he looked grave.

She was to rest, he said; he wanted her to sleep.

He came into my sitting room afterward.

"Very grave, is it, Doctor?"

He nodded.

"Angina pectoris undoubtedly. I'm glad you're here, Nurse. That's if you're prepared to take on another patient."

"I certainly am."

"I just want you to watch her very carefully. There must be the minimum of exertion; fatigue and anxiety must be avoided, excitement too. And of course her diet must be watched. She must eat sparingly. You've probably nursed this sort of case before."

"Yes, the one before Miss Brett was a heart."

"Good. Now, there may not be another attack for weeks, months . . . or even longer. On the other hand she could have another within the hour. Give her a little brandy if there is any sign of another attack. I'll send up some nitrite of amyl. You know how to use it?"

"Five drops on a handkerchief inhaled?"

He nodded. "Was she alone when this happened?"

"No. Jane Goodwin was with her. She had just come in, though."

"Ah, she had walked too far. She must be careful in future. She should always have close at hand a piece of cotton wool soaked with nitrite of amyl. There's a special bottle I can give you; it has a particularly tight stopper. Put the five drops on the cotton wool and the wool into the bottle; then if she feels an attack coming on and is alone she can have it all ready for use. I want her to rest for a while—and either you or Jane Goodwin will be at hand. Jane seems a sensible young woman."

I said I was sure she was.

"All right, I'll go and see Lady Crediton and tell her the state of affairs. She should be grateful that you're installed in the house, Nurse."

Lady Crediton, if not exactly grateful, because she would never be that to someone she paid, at least found it most convenient (her word) that I should be there.

"Dr. Elgin tells me that you will keep an eye on Mrs. Stretton, Senior," she said, making it seem the lightest of duties. "I understand that she has a bad heart." Her nose was lifted with disapproval, as though she was saying: "How typical of such a woman to have a bad heart at such a time!"

I thought she was as hard as the nails which were driven into the Company's "ladies" (if they do drive nails in. My knowledge of shipbuilding is nonexistent). I could see her fierce and implacable; and I wondered afresh how such a woman could ever have tolerated that situation which Sir Edward had put her into. It only went to show what a man of iron *he* must have been. And then suddenly it occurred to me that it was the Shipping Line she loved. It was Big Business, the acquisition of money. Sir Edward and she had been partners not only in marriage but in business; and if the marriage failed her, she was determined that the business never would.

May 24th. There is that feeling in the air which suggests that we are moving toward some climax. I believe it is the house party which will begin on the first of June. Such activities there are throughout the Castle! Baines importantly struts (there's no other word for it) around, investigating the wine cellar, instructing the maids and informing the footmen what will be expected of them. This visit of the Derringhams is going to be important. I fancy that Rex is a little uneasy. Perhaps he doesn't relish the fair Helena Derringham. Ironical that she should be called Helena. Though Helen would have been more apt. I said something to him about the face that launched a thousand ships and he smiled a little perfunctorily, as though it were too serious a matter (or perhaps too melancholy a one) over which to joke. I gather that the matchmaking is Lady Crediton's doing. She will expect Rex to marry where *she* wishes. Poor Rex! I feel this will be something of a test for him. He has met Helena at dances when she came out two years ago, and I gather he was not exactly stunned by her charms. But of course her ladyship has a controlling interest in the business. This slipped out, too. Sir Edward left everything in her hands. He must have had a great respect for her business acumen—and I'm sure he was not a man to be mistaken. I understood that it could be very uncomfortable for Rex if he did not fall in with his Mamma's wishes. She could leave her share away from Rex if he displeased her. To the Captain? I wondered. No, that was something she would never do, I am sure. She bitterly resents Red having any shares at all; but he has a small holding; Sir Edward had left that to him and of course he would always be one of the Company's Captains. I was surprised that Rex should confide in me. But we had a rather special friendship—rather like the one I had with young Edward, perhaps. They found me different from the people they usually met. Besides, the people at the Castle do behave rather unconventionally.

May 25th. My original patient is much better. She blossoms. It is the thought of the husband's return rather than my nursing, I'm sure. But it's always so with that type of patient. I have difficulty though in making her rest and keep to her diet. Oddly enough when she's excited she wants to eat more; she goes through her wardrobe and tries on her dresses—all in gay colors. She favors a flowered robe, loose and shapeless and split almost up to the knee. She looks as Edith said disapprovingly, "foreign." Yesterday afternoon she flew into a temper because she couldn't find the sash she wanted. I thought she was going to have an attack—but we avoided that. My other patient is much more sick and I have been spending a great deal of time with her. Jane welcomes me because I think she feels I know how to treat her mistress. I asked Valerie Stretton yesterday if she had walked very far on the day she had had the attack.

"Yes, quite far," she said cautiously.

"Farther than usual?"

"Yes, much farther."

"You usually walk in the grounds, don't you?"

"Yes, I do, but . . ."

She was plucking at the bed coverlet and I thought I had better change the subject because this was exciting her too much. But was it merely fatigue, I asked myself, which had brought on the attack or was it due to some anxiety?

I discovered that she had had vague warnings before in the form of slight pains in the arms and chest. They had passed within a few minutes though and she had thought of them vaguely as some sort of rheumatism.

I said: "The thing is to avoid too much exercise. You must never overtire yourself. But I think anxiety would probably be more dangerous than anything else."

Again that look of fear.

When I left her it was with the certainty that she had something on her mind. I wondered what, and being myself I knew I should not be happy until I found out.

June 6th. I have not had time to write in my journal for nearly a fortnight, and that is not surprising. Such excitement we have had in the Castle and it is due of course to the Derringhams' visit. They arrived on the 1st—a lovely summer's day and the roses were looking quite magnificent. The gardeners had been in a fever of excitement and the lawns and the flower beds were certainly at their best. The scent of pinks filled the air and the fountain-lawn marquee had been set up for the garden party which was to be the first what Edith would call "to-do." I was longing for a glimpse of the fair Helena and when I saw her I knew why Rex was melancholy. I am sure she was a young woman who was full of virtues, but she was not exactly an attractive one. She was awkward, with large hands and feet, and walked like a woman who spends a great deal of time in the saddle—which I'm sure she did. In fact her face was rather the shape of a horse's; her laughter had an equine quality too; she neighed, one might say. She talked in a loud and piercing voice; she was a character. I wondered whether Lady Crediton had looked rather like her in her youth and then it occurred to me that Sir Edward might have felt the same reluctance as I was sure Rex was feeling now. But Sir Edward would do his duty. And there was no doubt that Lady Crediton heartily approved of Miss Derringham. How could she help it when she considered the Derringham million or so—and Sir Henry had no son. Moreover he doted on his daughter. I was glad that some people admired her for I had a notion that Rex was not being the attentive squire his mother and Helena's father expected him to be.

I was at the window watching the guests on the lawn. It was a perfect day. Even the weather had to toe the line for Lady Crediton, it seemed. The grass was even more soft and velvety than usual, and the colored dresses, the big shady hats and parasols made an enchanting picture accentuated by the dark clothes of the men. I longed to be down there among them. I pictured the dress I should wear—green as the grass and my hair should be piled high. Perhaps I would have a froth of flowers and veiling on it but nothing more, and a parasol that was a mass of green and white frills like the one I most admired down there. If I had the clothes I would go down and mingle with the guests and I would be as beautiful and amusing as any of them—and no one would know that I was merely the nurse.

"Stop it, Cinderella Loman," I said to myself. "It's no use your looking round for a fairy godmother with a magic wand and pumpkin. You ought to have learned by now that *you* have to be your own fairy godmother."

Monique had gone to the party. She insisted. She looked strange among those elegantly dressed women. Monique would never be elegant, only colorful. I imagined that Lady Crediton would not wish her to be there. How tiresome of her, she would think, to be well enough to attend the garden party when on almost all other occasions she was so ill that Dr. Elgin had suggested they employ a nurse!

Rex was being attentive to her, which was kind of him. He was quite fond of Redvers so I supposed he thought he should be kind to his wife.

I went along to see my other patient and I found her sitting at her turret window looking down on the scene.

"How are you today?" I asked, sitting beside her.

"I'm very well, thank you, Nurse."

It wasn't true, of course.

"It's colorful," I said. "Some of the ladies' dresses are really beautiful."

"I see Miss Derringham . . . in blue there."

I had a good look at her. It was the wrong shade of blue—too light; it made her fresh color look crude.

"There are hopes, I believe, that an announcement will be made during the visit," I said, because I could never curb my curiosity enough to resist bringing up the subjects I wanted to talk about.

"It's almost a certainty," she said.

"You think Miss Derringham will accept?"

"But of course." She looked surprised that I could suggest anyone could possibly refuse Rex. I remembered that she had been his nurse and would have loved him as a small boy.

"It will be an excellent thing to link the two companies which is what will happen naturally. It will certainly be one of the biggest companies in the Kingdom then."

"Very good," I said.

"She'll be lucky. Rex was always a good boy. He deserves his good fortune. He's worked hard. Sir Edward would be proud of him."

"So you are hoping this marriage will take place."

She seemed surprised that I should imply there was an element of doubt.

"Yes, it will make up for Red's marriage. That is a disaster."

"Well, perhaps not entirely so. Young Edward is a charming child."

She smiled indulgently. "He's going to be just like his father."

It was very pleasant talking to her but I got the impression that she would give little away. There was a definite air of wariness about her. I suppose it was natural considering her past. I remember my sister Selina's calling me the Inquisitor because she said I was completely ruthless when I was trying to prise information out of people who didn't want to give it. I must curb my inquisitiveness. But, I assured myself, it was necessary for me to know what was in my patient's mind; I had to save her from exerting herself, worrying about anything—and how could I do that unless I knew what she was troubled about.

Then Jane came in with a letter for her mistress.

Valerie took the letter and as her eyes fell on the envelope I saw her face turn a grayish color. I went on talking to her, pretending not to notice, but I was fully aware that she was paying little attention to what I was saying.

She was a woman under strain. Something was bothering her. I wished I knew what.

She quite clearly wanted to be alone and I could not ignore the hint she gave me; so I left her.

Ten minutes later Jane was calling me. I went back to Valerie and gave her the nitrite of amyl. It worked like a miracle and we staved off the attack while it was merely an iron vise on her arms and was over before it reached the chest and the complete agony.

I said there was no need to call Dr. Elgin; he would be looking in the next day. And I thought to myself: It was something in that letter that upset her.

The next day a most unpleasant incident occurred. I disliked the Beddoes woman right from the start, and it seems she felt similarly about me. Valerie was feeling so much better that she was taking a short walk in the garden with Jane, and I was in her room making her bed with the special bedrest Dr. Elgin had suggested to prop her up when her breathing was difficult.

The drawer of her table was half-open and I saw a photograph album in it. I couldn't resist taking it out and looking at it.

There were several photographs in it—mostly of the boys. Underneath each was lovingly inscribed: Redvers aged two; Rex two and a half. There was a picture of them together and again with her. She was very, very pretty in those days, but she looked a little harassed. She was obviously trying to make Redvers look where the photographers wanted him to. Rex stood leaning against her knee. It was rather charming. I was sure she loved them both dearly; I could tell by the way she spoke of them and I imagined her trying not to show favoritism to her own son; they were both Sir Edward's children anyway.

I put the album back and as I did so I saw an envelope. I immediately thought of what had upset her and wondered if this was the letter; I couldn't be sure because it was an ordinary white envelope like so many. I picked it up. I was holding it in my hand when I was aware that someone was in the room watching me.

That sly rather whining voice said: "I'm looking for Edward. Is he here?"

I swung round holding the letter and I was furious with myself because I knew I looked guilty. The fact was I hadn't looked inside the envelope. I had only picked it up and I could see by her expression that she thought she had caught me red-handed.

I put the envelope back on the table as nonchalantly as I could and I said calmly that I thought Edward was in the garden. He was probably walking with his grandmother and Jane.

I felt furious with her.

I shall never forget the night of the fancy dress ball. I was very daring, but then I always had been. It was Monique oddly enough who goaded me to it. I fancied she was becoming rather fond of me; perhaps she recognized in me something of a rebel like herself. I encouraged her to confide in me because my policy was that the more I knew about my patients the better. She had started to talk to me about the house where she had lived with her mother on the Island of Coralle. It sounded like a queer, shabby old mansion near the sugar plantation which her father had owned. He was dead and they had sold it now but her mother still lived in the house. As she talked she gave me an impression of lazy steamy heat. She told me how as a child she used to go down to watch the big ships come in and how the natives used to dance and sing to welcome them and to say goodbye. The great days were when the ships arrived and the stalls were set up on the waterfront with the beads and images, grass skirts and slippers, and baskets which they had made in readiness to sell to the visitors to the island. Her eyes sparkled as she talked and I said: "You miss it all." She admitted she did. And talking she began to cough; I thought then: She would be better back there.

She was childish in lots of ways and her moods changed so rapidly that one could never be sure in one moment of abandoned laughter whether she would be on the edge of melancholy in the next. There was no contact whatever between her and Lady Crediton; she was much happier with Valerie, but then Valerie was a much more comfortable person.

She would have liked to go to the fancy dress ball but she had had an asthmatical attack that morning and even she knew it would be folly.

"How would you dress?" I asked her. She said she thought she would go as what she was, a Coralle islander. She had some lovely coral beads and she would wear flowers in her hair which would be loose about her shoulders.

"You would look magnificent, I'm sure," I told her. "But everyone would know who you were."

She agreed, and said: "How would you go . . . if you could go?"

"It would depend on what I could find to wear."

She showed me the masks that were being worn. Edward had taken them from the big alabaster bowl in the hall and brought them to her. He had come in wearing one crying "Guess who this is, Mamma." "I did not have to guess," she added.

"Nor would anyone have to if you went as you suggest," I reminded her. "You would be betrayed at once and the whole point is to disguise your identity."

"I should like to see you dressed up, Nurse. You could go as a nurse perhaps."

"It would be the same thing as your going with your coral beads and flowing hair. I should be recognized immediately and drummed out as an imposter."

She laughed immoderately. "You make me laugh, Nurse."

"Well, it's better than making you cry."

I was taken with the idea of dressing up. "I wonder

how I *could* go?" I asked. "Wouldn't it be fun if I could so completely disguise myself that that were possible."

She held out one of the masks to me and I put it on.

"Now you look wicked."

"Wicked?"

"Like a temptress."

"Rather different from my usual role." I looked at myself in the glass and a great excitement possessed me.

She sat up in bed and said: "Yes, Nurse. Yes?"

"If you had a dress that I could wear . . ."

"You would go as an island girl?"

I opened the door of her wardrobe; I knew that she had some exotic clothes. She had bought them on the way home from Coralle at some of the eastern ports at which they had stopped. There was a robe of green and gold. I slipped out of my working dress and put it on. She clapped her hands.

"It suits you, Nurse."

I pulled the pins out of my hair and it fell about my shoulders.

"Nurse, you *are* beautiful," she cried. "Your hair is red in places."

I shook it out. "I don't look so much like the nurse now, do I?"

"They will not recognize you."

I looked at her startled. I knew that I was going down there; but I was surprised that she did.

I looked round the room.

"Take anything . . . anything," she cried. I found a pair of golden slippers. "I bought those on my way over," she added.

They were loose but that did not matter. They matched the green and gold robe perfectly.

"But what am I supposed to represent?" I picked up a piece of thin cardboard which Edward used for his drawing lessons—he had brought his latest picture in to show her—and twisted it into the shape of a steeple hat. "I have an idea," I said. I took a needle and thread and in a moment I had my steeple hat. Then I took one of her sashes—a gold colored chiffon—and I draped it about the hat and let it flow down in cascades.

She was sitting up in bed rocking on her heels.

"Put on the mask, Nurse. No one will know you."

But I had not quite finished. I had seen a silver chain girdle which she often wore about her negligée so I put it round my waist and picking up a bunch of keys which were lying on the dressing table I attached them to the girdle.

"Behold the Chatelaine of the Castle!" I said.

"The Chatelaine?" she asked. "What is this?"

"The lady of the house. The one who guards the keys."

"Ah, that becomes you."

I put on the mask.

"Will you dare?" she said.

There was a recklessness in me. Selina had noticed it and warned me about it. Of course I was going.

What a night it was—one I am sure I shall never forget. I was down there, among them; it was so easy for me to slip in. I felt a wild excitement grip me. Selina had said that I ought to be an actress; and I certainly acted that night. It was scarcely acting—I really felt that I was the Chatelaine of the Castle, that I was the hostess and these were my guests; I was quickly seized by a partner. I danced, resisted his attempts to discover my identity and joined in the game of mild flirtation which seemed to be the purpose of the affair.

I wondered how Rex was getting on with Helena Derringham. I could be certain that if he saw through her disguise he would do his best to avoid her.

It was almost inevitable that he should discover me in time. I was dancing with a portly Restoration nobleman when I was seized and wrested from him. Laughing I looked into the masked face and knew that my troubadour was Rex.

I thought: If I know him will he know me? But I flattered myself that I was more completely disguised. Besides, I was expecting to see him; he certainly was not expecting to see me.

"I'm sorry for the rough treatment," he said.

"I think a serenade first of all would have been more appropriate."

"An irresistible urge possessed me," he said. "It was the color of your hair. It's most unusual."

"I shall expect you to make a ballad about it."

"I won't disappoint you. But I thought we should be together—after all we belong."

"Belong?" I said.

"Just about the same period. The medieval lady ... the Chatelaine of the Castle and the humble troubadour who waits outside to sing of his devotion."

"This troubadour seems to have found his way into the Castle."

He said: "You might have come as a nurse."

"Why?" I asked.

"You would have played the part to perfection."

"You might have come as the shipping lord. How would that be, I wonder? A nautical uniform with a string of little ships hanging round your neck."

"I see," he said, "that there is no need to introduce ourselves. Did you really think I shouldn't know you? No one else has hair that color."

"So it was my hair which betrayed me! And what are you going to do? Dismiss me ... in due course?"

"I reserve judgment."

"Then perhaps you will allow me to retire gracefully. Tomorrow morning I shall expect to receive a summons from her ladyship. 'Nurse, I have just heard of your most *inconvenient* conduct. Pray leave at once.' "

"And what of your patients if you deserted them in that cruel way?"

"I should never desert them."

"I should hope not," he said.

"Well, now you have caught me red-handed, as they say, there is nothing more to be said."

"I think there is a great deal to be said. I do apologize for not sending you an invitation. You know that had those matters been left to me . . ."

I pretended to be relieved, but I had known all along that he was pleased I was here.

So we danced and we bantered together, and he stayed with me. It was pleasant and I know he thought so, too. But if he had forgotten Miss Derringham, I had not. In my impulsive way I asked if he knew what she was wearing. He said he had not inquired. And is there to be an announcement? I wanted to know. He replied that it certainly wouldn't be tonight. The Derringhams were leaving on the seventh and on the night of the sixth there was to be a very grand ball. This would be more ceremonious than tonight.

"Opportunities will *not* be given to intruders?" I asked.

"I'm afraid not."

"The announcement will be made, toasts will be drunk; there'll be feasting probably in the servants' hall; and those neither below stairs nor quite above—such as the nurse and the long suffering Miss Beddoes—perhaps even may be allowed to enter into the general rejoicing."

"I daresay."

"May I say now, that I wish you all the happiness you deserve."

"How do you know that I deserve any?"

"I don't. I wish that if you deserve it you may have it."

He was laughing. He said: "I enjoy so much being with you."

"Then perhaps my sins are forgiven?"

"It depends on what you have committed."

"Well—tonight for instance. I am the uninvited guest. The Chatelaine with false keys ... and not even an invitation card."

"I told you I am pleased you came."

"Did you tell me that?"

"If I did not I tell you now."

"Ah, Sir Troubadour," I said, "let us dance. And have you seen the time? I suppose they will unmask at midnight. I must disappear before the witching hour."

"So the Chatelaine has turned into Cinderella?"

"To be turned at midnight into the humble serving wench."

"I have never yet been aware of your humility—although I admit you have many more interesting qualities."

"Who cares? I have always suspected the humble. Come, sir. You are not dancing. This music inspires me so and I have not much longer."

And we danced and I knew that he was reluctant for me to leave. But I left a full twenty minutes before midnight. I had no intention of being discovered by Lady Crediton. Besides, I remembered Monique would no doubt be waiting to hear what had happened. I could never be sure what she would do. She might suddenly decide to see for herself. I pictured her coming down and looking for me and perhaps betraying me.

She was awake when I got up to her room and inclined to be sullen. Where had I been all this time? She had felt so breathless; she had thought she was going to have an attack. Wasn't it my place to be with *her*? She had thought I would just go down and come straight back.

"What would have been the good of that?" I demanded. "I had to show you that I could deceive them all."

She was immediately restored to good humor. I described the dancers, the plump Restoration knight who had flirted with me; I imitated him and invented dialogue between us. I danced about the room in my costume, reluctant to take it off.

"Oh, Nurse," she said, "you're not in the least like a nurse."

"Not tonight," I said. "I'm the Chatelaine of the Castle. Tomorrow I shall be the stern nurse. You'll see."

She became hysterical laughing at me; and I became rather alarmed. I gave her an opium pill and taking off my costume, I put on my nursing dress and sat by her bed until she slept.

Then I went to my room. I looked out of the window. I could hear the strains of music still. They would have unmasked; and were dancing again.

Poor Rex, I thought maliciously. He wouldn't be able to evade Miss Derringham now.

June 7th. There is a strange flat feeling throughout the Castle. The Derringhams are leaving. Last night was the great finale, the great ceremonial ball. Everyone is talking about it. Edith came into my room on a pretext of inspecting Betsy's work but actually to talk to me.

"It's very surprising," she said. "There was no announcement. Mr. Baines had made all the arrangements. We were going to celebrate in the servants' hall naturally. They would expect it. And there was simply no announcement."

"How very odd!" I said.

"Her ladyship is furious. She hasn't spoken to Mr. Rex yet. But she will. As for Sir Henry he is very annoyed. He did not give Mr. Baines the usual appreciation and he has always been *most* generous. Mr. Baines had promised me a new gown because he was sure that after the announcement Sir Henry would be more generous than usual."

"What a shame! And what does it mean?"

Edith came close to me. "It means that Mr. Rex did *not* come up to scratch as the saying goes. He just let the ball go by without asking Miss Derringham. It is most odd because everyone was expecting it."

"It just goes to show," I said, "that no one should ever be too sure of anything."

With that Edith heartily agreed.

June 9th. Lady Crediton is clearly very upset. There have been "scenes" between her and Rex. The acrimonious exchanges between mother and son could not go entirely unheard by one or other of the servants and I gathered that there must have been some lively conversation behind the green baize door and at that table presided over with the utmost decorum by Baines at one end and Edith at the other. Edith of course learned a great deal and she was not averse to imparting it to me. I was very interested and rather sorry that my special status in the household prevented my joining those very entertaining meals when the conversation must have been so lively—I am sure it made up for the celebration they missed.

"My word," said Edith, "her ladyship is in a nice paddy. She reminds him what he owes to her. You see Sir Edward had a very high opinion of her and she still has a business head on her shoulders. She's the one who always has to have the last say in all business matters. And if she couldn't cut him off with a shilling—as the saying goes— she could divert a big proportion of the shares. That was her word, 'divert.' Mr. Baines heard it distinctly."

"To whom I wonder would she divert. To Captain Stretton?"

"Never! She could tie things up in some sort of trust . . . perhaps for Mr. Rex's children if he had any. But she could make it so that he didn't have all that much say in things after she'd gone. No more than he has now. Her ladyship is in a fine paddy, I can tell you."

"And Mr. Rex?"

"He keeps saying he wants time. He doesn't want to rush into anything and all that."

"So he hasn't definitely decided *against* the marriage."

"No. It's just that he hasn't committed himself. He'll come to it."

"Can you be sure of that?"

"Oh yes, it's what her ladyship wants and she always gets what she wants."

"She didn't . . . once."

Edith looked surprised and I pretended to be embarrassed. "Well, it's common knowledge," I went on. "I was thinking of how put out she must have been about the Captain and Mrs. Stretton . . . but she had to accept that."

"Ah, that was Sir Edward's will. There was no going against that. But there's no Sir Edward now, is there? And her ladyship has taken his place. You mark my words, Mr. Rex will come to it sooner or later. A pity he had to hang about like this . . . when you think of all those preparations Mr. Baines made for the staff celebration."

"Very unfair to Mr. Baines," I commented; and wondered whether I had gone too far; but Edith was incapable of recognizing irony. It certainly had been *inconvenient* for Mr. Baines.

June 13. I have heard today—through Edith—that Sir Henry is taking Miss Derringham on a long sea voyage. It will be very beneficial to the health of them both.

"They are going to Australia," said Edith. "They've a branch there. So have we, of course. After all, many of our main voyages are to Australia and back. So naturally we've our branch there. Sir Henry's not the sort to go for the pleasure alone. But of course they're going because of the disappointment."

"What does her ladyship think of that?"

"She's furious. Do you know it wouldn't surprise me if she punished Mr. Rex."

"Send him to bed without his supper?"

"Oh, Nurse, you are a one for jokes. But she was talking about solicitors and all that."

"But I thought it was only a postponement and that he just wanted Time."

"Suppose she meets Another out there?"

"But surely there isn't another shipping line like ours!"

"There is certainly not," said Edith stanchly. "But Sir Henry has fingers in lots of pies. He's a man with wide business interests. He might have someone else in mind for Miss Derringham."

"Then what shall *we* do?"

Edith laughed. "You can bet her ladyship's got the trump card up her sleeve."

Yes, I thought; and I wondered what would happen when she used it.

9

June 18th. The Captain has come home. What a stir there is in the house. He is not as important as Rex, of course, but somehow he makes his presence felt. For the last few days Monique has been impossible to control—alternating between excitement and depression. "You'll *love* the Captain, Nurse," she told me.

"I think that is an exaggeration," I replied deciding to be the cool nurse.

"Nonsense! All women do."

"Is he so devastatingly attractive?"

"He's the most attractive man in the world."

"It's a mercy we don't all think alike on such matters."

"People think alike about him."

"Wifely prejudice," I retorted, "and very admirable, of course."

She tried on her dresses, exhausting herself; then she was depressed. I found her crying quietly one afternoon before he came back. It was not unusual that she should cry but that she should do it quietly was.

"He doesn't want me," she gasped between sobs.

"What nonsense," I said nonsensically. "You're his wife. And pray calm yourself. You want to be well for his return. Now come along. What shall you wear for the great occasion? These beautiful corals. How lovely they are!" I slipped them round my neck. I loved beautiful things and they became me as much as they did her. "These," I said, "and that long blue dress. It's most becoming." She had stopped crying to watch me. I took it out of the wardrobe and tried it against myself. "There," I said, "don't you think that's lovely. Don't you see how right for a dutiful wife?" I composed my features in a humble and devoted expression which made her smile. I was finding that I could often lure her from a stormy mood to a sunny one by one of my little acts.

She talked about him then. "We did not know each other so very well when we married. He had come to the Island . . . only twice."

I pictured the big gleaming ship and the irresistible Captain in his uniform; the beautiful girl and the tropical island.

"He was brought to the house by a friend of my mother's," she said. "He dined with us and afterward we walked in the gardens among the fan-shaped palms and the fireflies."

"And he fell in love with you."

"Yes," she said, "for a time."

Her lips were beginning to tremble so I started to play the amorous captain and the dusky beauty in the garden where the fireflies flitted about the fan-shaped palms.

Oh yes, poor Monique was certainly difficult during those days.

And when he was in the house it changed, because without meaning to he made his presence felt. And when I saw him I realized the attraction. He was certainly good looking—taller than Rex, more blond, lacking that reddish tinge which was Rex's; but their features were similar. The Captain laughed more readily, talked more loudly; and I should imagine was less guarded than Rex. He was the adventurer type—the sea rover; Rex's adventures would be confined to business deals. Rex seemed pale in comparison with the Captain whose skin was deeply tanned; his deep blue eyes were more startling than Rex's topaz-colored ones.

I couldn't help being excited by his arrival. But I did wonder whether his coming had added any happiness to the house. I daresay his mother was delighted to see him;

and I wondered whether I ought to have a word with him regarding the seriousness of her illness; but perhaps that was for Dr. Elgin to do. Lady Crediton was cool toward him for obvious reasons and I heard from Edith that this seemed to amuse him rather than upset him. He was that sort of man. I was sorry for poor Monique because it became very clear to me that she was not happy. You're fickle, Captain, I thought; the exotic little flower once plucked no longer charms you.

And I was thinking a great deal about Anna. I always do; but particularly now that the Captain was home. But it was long ago that he went to visit her and caused such trouble with old Miss Brett. I could understand the fascination he had had for Anna, though.

June 20th. The Captain came to my room this morning, nonchalant, at ease, very much the man of the world.

"Nurse Loman," he said, "I wanted to speak to you."

"Certainly Captain Stretton. Do sit down."

"About your patients," he went on.

Ah yes, he would be concerned about his wife and his mother.

"They are both a little better at the moment," I said. "Perhaps it is due to their pleasure in your return."

"Do you find any change in my wife since you've been here? Has her complaint . . . worsened?"

"No." I watched him covertly and wondered what his feelings were for Monique. I suppose there is nothing more nauseating than to be pursued passionately by someone one does not want. I believed this to be the case with him. And I wondered: Is he hoping that a benevolent fate will give him his freedom? "No," I went on. "Her condition is much the same as when I arrived. It depends a great deal on the weather. During the summer she will be a little better, especially if it is not too damp."

"She was better in her own land," he said.

"That's almost inevitable."

"And . . . your other patient?"

"Dr. Elgin will be able to give you more details than I but I think she is very ill."

"These heart attacks . . . ?"

"They're really a symptom of imperfections in the heart."

"And dangerous," he said. "Which means that at any time she could die."

"I think that is what Dr. Elgin would tell you."

There was a brief silence and then he said, "Before you came here you were on another case."

"I was at the Queen's House. You probably know the place," I added craftily.

"Yes, I know it," he admitted. "There was a Miss . . ."

"Brett. There were two Miss Bretts. My patient was the elder and her niece lived with her."

He was rather easy to read, this Captain. He was not as subtle as Rex. He wanted to ask about Anna; and I felt a little more friendly toward him. At least he remembered her.

"And she died?"

"Yes, she died. Rather suddenly."

He nodded. "It must have been rather alarming for Miss . . . er, Miss Brett."

"It was decidedly unpleasant for us both."

"She took an overdose of pills, I heard."

"Yes. That was proved at the inquest," I said quickly and I discovered that when I had mentioned the matter in the past I had spoken as though I defied anyone to deny it. That was what I did now.

"And Miss Brett is still at the Queen's House?"

I said: "Yes, she is."

He stared beyond me; and I wondered whether he was thinking of calling on Anna. Surely not. That would cause quite a scandal now that he had his wife actually living at the Castle. But one thing I did know; he was not indifferent to her.

Young Edward came in, looking for his father, I believed. He had little time for me now; there was no one for him but his father. His eyes were round with adoration. He had shown me the model of a ship his father had brought him. He took it to bed with him and clutched it all night, Miss Beddoes said; moreover he had nearly driven her frantic by sailing it in the pond, and had all but drowned himself; she had caught cold getting him out. He carried the boat under his arm now, and saluted the Captain.

"All present and correct?" asked the Captain.

"Aye aye, sir. Gale blowing up, sir."

"Batten down the hatches," said the Captain with a serious face.

"Aye aye, sir."

I watched them. The Captain could charm a child as easily as he could women. He was that sort of a man.

June 21st. Monique spat blood this morning and the sight of it so frightened her that she had one of the worst asthmatical attacks as yet. I believe there had been a scene between her and the Captain on the previous night. He occupied a room close to hers in the turret—and because I was not far off and Monique never controlled her voice, I often heard it raised in anger or protest. When Dr. Elgin came he was very grave. He said he thought her condition would worsen with winter. The English winter climate would be no use to her. He really thought she should get out before the autumn was over. After he had seen both of the patients he had a long session with Lady Crediton.

June 25th. We have had a death in the house. Jane Goodwin awakened me at four o'clock this morning and begged me to go to her mistress; I scrambled into my slippers and dressing gown but by the time I reached Valerie Stretton she was dead. I was horrified. I had known of course of her precarious condition but when one comes face to face with death and realizes that one will never see the person again, one feels shaken. I know I should be used to this by now—and I am to some extent. But I have never been so shocked by a patient's death before. I had become so interested in this woman's story and I was getting to know her. I believed that she had something on her mind and I wanted to discover what, that I might understand her case. There was that occasion when she had had her first attack and I knew she had been out because of the mud on her boots. I felt there was some drama in her life which was still going on, and I had wanted to understand it. And now she was dead.

June 27th. A house of mourning is a sad place. Lady Crediton finds it most inconvenient, Edith tells me. After all these years her rival is dead. I wonder what she really feels. What passionate emotions erupt within these walls. The Captain is grieved. She was after all his mother. Monique is alarmed. She is afraid of her own death. Edward is bewildered. "Where is my grandmamma?" he asked me. "Where has she gone?" I tell him she has gone to heaven. "In a big ship?" he asked. I said he should ask his Papa, and he nodded as much as to say Papa would surely know. I wonder what the Captain told him. He had a way with children . . . children and women.

The west turret is the turret of death. Lady Crediton does not wish the funeral gloom to penetrate to the rest of the Castle. In Valerie's old room the blinds are drawn; the coffin stands on its trestles. I went in to see her for the last time; she lies there with a white frilled cap hiding her hair and her face looks so young that it seems one of Death's roles is that of a laundress to iron the lines out. I can't help thinking of her coming to the Castle all those years ago, and of her love for Sir Edward and his for her. All that violent passion and now he is dead and she is dead. But their passion lives on for there is the Captain, virile, so vital, so alive to give proof to it. And there is young Edward too, and the children he will have, and their children, and on forever, so that that love affair will have left its mark for generations to come. I feel frustrated that I had not been able to discover what had frightened this poor woman and what may well have hastened her death. I went back and back again to that darkened room to take a look at her. Poor Valerie, what was her secret, whom did she go to meet? That was the question. That person whom she had gone to meet, the person who had written the letter to her. That was the one I should like to discover. I should like to say: "You hastened her to her death."

June 28th. Last evening at dusk, I went along to that chamber of death and as I put my hand on the door handle I heard a sound from within. I felt a strange sensation in my spine. I am not superstitious and my profession has made me familiar with death. I have laid out people for their burials; I have seen them die. But as I stood outside that door I did feel this strange sensation, and I was afraid to go into that room. Lots of foolish images flashed into my mind. I imagined she would open her eyes and look at me and say: "Leave me and my secrets alone. Who are you to pry?" And I was shivering. But this foolishness passed and I heard that sound again. It was a stifled sob from a living throat. I opened the door and I looked in. The coffin loomed up in the gloom and there was a shape . . . beside it. For a moment I thought that Valerie had left her coffin. But only for a moment. Commonsense returned, and as soon as it did I saw that it was Monique standing there. She was crying quietly.

I said sharply: "Mrs. Stretton, what are you doing here?"

"I came to say goodbye to her before . . ."

"It's no place for you." I was brisk, efficient, as much for my own benefit as for hers. I could not imagine how I could have been so foolish. I had almost had an attack of the vapors.

"Oh, it is terrible . . . terrible . . ." she sobbed.

I went to her and shook her firmly by the wrist. "Come back to your room. What possessed you to come here! You will be ill if you act so foolishly."

"My turn next," she said in a whisper.

"What nonsense!"

"Is it nonsense, Nurse? You know how ill I am."

"You can be cured."

"Can I, Nurse? Do you really believe that?"

"With the right treatment, yes."

"Oh, Nurse . . . Nurse . . . you always make me laugh."

"Don't laugh now. You come back to your room with me. I'll give you some warm milk and a little cognac, eh? That will make you feel well."

She allowed me to lead her from that room and I have to admit that I was glad to get outside. For some odd reason I couldn't get out of my mind that something in that room was watching us . . . that it was probing into our innermost thoughts.

She felt it too for she said as the door closed behind us: "I was frightened in there . . . yet I had to go."

"I know," I soothed. "Come along now."

I got her to her room where she began to cough a little.

Oh dear! That fatal telltale stain! I would have to report it to Dr. Elgin.

I said nothing of it to her.

I tut-tutted as I got her into bed. "Your feet are like slabs of ice. I'm going to get you a hot-water bottle. But first the hot milk and the cognac. You should not have gone there, you know."

She was crying quietly now, and the quietness was more alarming than her noisy outbursts.

"It would be better if I were the one lying in that coffin."

"You'll have a coffin when the time comes like the rest of us."

She smiled through her grief. "Oh, Nurse, you do me good."

"The cognac will do you even more good, you see."

"At times you're the stern nurse and at others ... at others you're quite something else."

"We all have two sides to our natures, they say. Now let's see the sensible one of yours."

This made her laugh again, but she was soon in tears.

"Nobody wants me, Nurse. They'd be glad ... all of them."

"I won't listen to such nonsense."

"It's not nonsense. They'd be glad, I tell you, if I was the one in that coffin. *He'd* be glad."

"Drink up this nice milk," I said. "The bottle will be ready in a little while. And let's think about this nice feather bed. It's more comfortable than a coffin, I do assure you."

And she was smiling at me through her tears.

June 30th. The day of the funeral. Gloom in the house. In the servants' hall they will be talking of the love affair between the dead woman and that legend which is Sir Edward. There may be some of the older servants who will remember. I wonder if there are. I would like to talk to them about her. Jane Goodwin is heartbroken. I wonder what she will do now? I expect she will stay on at the Castle. Baines will be asked to find some job for her. Poor Jane, she was closely associated with Valerie Stretton for years. Valerie must have confided in her. She must know something. The Captain is the chief mourner. Monique was too ill to go; and little Edward did not either. Rex went. He is very fond of the Captain and the Captain of Rex. The tolling bells are very depressing. Jane lies in her room engulfed in desolation; Monique cries that it should have been her because that is what *some people* want. And I went down to draw the blinds in the death chamber and while I was there who should come down but Miss Beddoes. For some reason she dislikes me. It is mutual. She looked a little disappointed when she saw that I was merely pulling up the blinds. I wondered what she expected. In my room in the turret I can hear the bells of the nearby church tolling, telling the world that Valerie Stretton has passed away.

July 4th. Edith came to my room with news.

"It's almost certain that Mr. Rex is going away," she said.

"Going away?" I echoed, by which I really meant: Tell me more.

"He's going to Australia," Edith smiled slyly. "Well, we know who he'll meet there."

"The Derringhams have a branch there," I said, "and so have we."

"Well you see how it's working out, don't you?"

"Brilliant strategy," I said.

"What's that?" she asked but did not wait for an explanation. She was sure that what she had to say was more interesting than anything I could. "Mr. Baines heard her ladyship talking to Mr. Rex. You must see what's happening over there," she said. "Your father always believed in keeping in touch."

"Keeping in touch with the Derringhams?"

"Well, this could put everything right. After all he's had the time he wanted now, hasn't he?"

"I should think so."

"Mr. Baines thinks it is almost certain that Mr. Rex will leave for Australia fairly soon. Changes never come singly. Mrs. Stretton's passing away . . . and now Mr. Rex."

I agreed that there would certainly be changes.

July 5th. Dr. Elgin questioned me very closely about my patient.

"She is certainly not improving, Nurse."

"She is always so much worse on the damp days."

"That is natural, of course. The condition of the lungs has worsened."

"Also the asthma, I think, Doctor."

"I was going to suggest that you try the nitrite of amyl if there should be a bad attack. But perhaps in her case this would not be advisable. Himrod's Cure has been known to be effective. Not that I like patent medicines, but there is nothing harmful in this one. You know it, Nurse?"

"Yes," I said. "One burns the powder and the patient inhales the fumes. It was effective with one of my patients. I also found burning paper which had been dipped into a solution of saltpeter effective."

"H'm," he said. "We have to remember the lung complication. I will give you a mixture of iodide of potassium and sal volatile with tincture of belladonna. We'll see how that goes. This can be given every six hours."

"Yes, Doctor. And I shall hope that the weather stays warm and dry. So much depends on it."

"Exactly. To tell the truth, Nurse, in my opinion they should never have brought her over here."

"Perhaps it would be advisable for her to return."

"There is no doubt in my mind of the wisdom of that."

And with those words he went down to report to Lady Crediton.

July 8th. In the gardens today I met Rex.

He said: "Snatching a little recreation, Nurse?"

"It is necessary now and then," I replied.

"And walking is a good substitute for dancing?"

"I would hardly say that."

"And you prefer your Chatelaine's robes?"

"Infinitely."

"Well, those are equally becoming, but perhaps yours is the kind of beauty which needs no enhancing."

"All beauty needs the right setting. I have heard that you will shortly be leaving us. Is that true?"

"It's almost a certainty."

"And you are going to Australia. Is that so?"

"How well informed you are."

"There is a very good news service in the Castle."

"Ah," he said, "servants!"

"I am sure you will enjoy your trip. When does it start?"

"Not until the end of the year."

"So you will be going into the Australian summer and leaving us to face the rigors of winter."

He looked at me very intently and I was rather piqued because he did not seem to be in the least regretful. I had thought he had felt some special friendship for me. But no, I thought, it is just a mild flirtation. How could it be otherwise?

"And," I went on, "I expect Sir Henry Derringham and his daughter who, I am informed, are already there, will give you a very warm welcome."

"I daresay."

Then he said: "There is talk of Mrs. Stretton's returning to her parents' home."

"Oh?"

"Indeed, yes. The doctor had a talk with my mother. I think she feels that it would be wise in every way for Mrs. Stretton to go back to a climate she is used to."

"I see," I said.

"Your patient's future would affect yours, of course," he said.

"Of course."

"My mother will be speaking to you of this. When she does, it will naturally come as a complete surprise."

"Naturally."

We walked to the pond and stood for a while watching the ancient carp swimming to and fro.

He talked about Australia; he had been there some years ago. The harbor was magnificent, he said. He had always felt that he would like to return.

July 9th. I am expecting Lady Crediton to send for me. I am wondering what she will say when she does. Will she suggest that I might accompany my patient? Or will she give me a month's notice ... perhaps longer, for she will wish me to stay until Monique leaves. But Monique will need attention on the voyage. Australia. I had never thought of leaving England, but if I had been asked I should have said I always wanted to travel. Now I thought of leaving home and it was not my childhood's home that I was thinking of, but Anna at the Queen's House. While I have been writing this journal I have been thinking of Anna; and in a way I have been writing it for her, because I know how interested she is in everything that goes on at the Castle. I now share her interest. It has made me feel very close to her, and the first thing that occurs to me when I think of going away is leaving her. Of course I don't have to leave her. I could leave the Castle instead. But it has become so much a part of my life. How could I leave it?

So every time there is a tap on my door I expect one of the servants to come in and say I am summoned to her ladyship. I feel very disturbed.

July 10th. There has been great consternation in the Castle today. Young Edward was lost. Miss Beddoes was quite distracted. She had lost him just after he had had his midday meal. He had left the table and had gone to the nursery. I suspect she was having a nap and when she awoke he was no longer there. She didn't concern herself very much but went into the gardens to look for him. When he hadn't come back at four when he usually had a glass of milk and piece of cake, she began to be worried. She ran to his mother, which was a foolish thing to do, because Monique immediately panicked. She began to scream that her little boy was lost. In a very short time we were all searching. The Captain went off with Miss Beddoes and Baines and I went with Rex, Jane, and Edith. We went into the gardens because we were sure he must have gone out, and I think we all made our way through the copse to the iron railing at the cliff edge. It was sound enough but was there room for a small boy to squeeze between those rails? I looked fearfully at Rex. He said: "He couldn't. Someone would have seen." I didn't think that was necessarily so. While we were standing there I heard Monique's voice and I realized that she had come out to this spot too. Her hair was flowing round her shoulders; she wore a silk dressing gown of scarlet and gold, and her eyes were wild.

"I knew it," she cried. "I knew he came here. He has

fallen over there. I know it. I will go with him. I'm not wanted here."

I went to her at once and said: "This is ridiculous. He is somewhere else, playing somewhere."

"Leave me alone. You're deceiving me, all of you. You don't want me here. You'd be glad if I were the one . . ."

It was one of her hysterical fits and I knew how dangerous they could be.

I said: "I must get her back to the house."

She threw me off so that I went sprawling and would have fallen had not Rex caught me. I had already been made aware of the extreme strength she seemed to have in her rages.

"Now," she cried, "he has gone and I'll go with him. No one will stop me."

I cried: "You will be ill. You must go back at once."

But she was running toward the rail.

Rex got there before her. He tried to hold her back and I had a horrible fear that both of them would go hurtling over.

The Captain appeared suddenly with Miss Beddoes and Baines. He saw what was happening, ran to his wife, and catching her he dragged her away from the rail. "You'd be glad . . . glad . . ." she cried, and began to cough.

I went over to them, and the Captain gave me a wry look.

"I'll carry her back," he said, and he lifted her as though she were a baby.

I went with them up to her room. I felt the shocked silence behind us; momentarily everyone had forgotten the lost child.

I could see the attack would soon be at height and I wanted her safely in her room where I could treat her. I told the Captain that I thought he should send for Dr. Elgin and I gave her the mixture the doctor had prescribed for her.

I thought she was going to die. It was the worst attack she had had since my arrival.

Dr. Elgin came but by that time her breathing had improved; she was limp with exhaustion but I knew that she was not going to die that time.

Just before the doctor came I was able to tell her that Edward had been found.

I was unprepared for the second scene of that day. I myself found Edward. It was just after I had given his mother her medicine and made her as comfortable as it was possible for anyone to be in her condition that I went to my room to get a handkerchief. I had given mine to Monique. There was a huge cupboard in my room—so big that it was more like a little off-room; one could walk about it, and there curled up on a cushion building bridges with my coat hangers was Edward.

I said: "They're searching for you. Come out and show yourself, for Heaven's sake."

I took his hand and called to Betsy who came running.

She gasped when she saw the child.

"He was in my cupboard all the time," I said. "Let everyone know he is safe as quickly as possible."

I went back to my patient to be told a few minutes later that the doctor had arrived.

It had been an exhausting day. Monique was settled for the night. Dr. Elgin had given her opium and said that she would sleep through till the morning. She needed the rest. So I went to my room and decided on an early night. I had a great deal to think about. I had slipped off my dress and put on my nightgown and was brushing my hair when the door was flung open. I was astonished to see Miss Beddoes. Her face was distorted; she had obviously been crying; her pince-nez were quivering and her skin was blotchy. I had rarely seen such hatred and it was directed against me.

"You'll say you didn't do it," she cried, "but I know you did! I know you. You're wicked. You've always hated me."

"Miss Beddoes," I said, "I beg you calm yourself."

"I am calm," she cried.

"Forgive me but you are far from calm."

"Don't try your nurse's tricks on me. Don't soothe me with your soft voice. I believe . . ."

"And I believe that your good sense has deserted you."

"It deserted me when I first saw you or I should have been prepared for you."

"Miss Beddoes, I beg of you be calm. Sit down and tell me what has happened."

"What you arranged should happen."

"I have no notion of what you are talking about—so what could I have arranged?"

"That I should go. You've been worming your way into young Edward's confidence ever since you came."

"But . . ."

"Oh you'll deny it. You're a liar, Nurse Loman. I know that. You want me out of the way. You don't like me, so you think that you can brush me aside, just like a fly."

"Do believe me when I say I don't understand. I can't defend myself until I know the accusation."

She sat down on a chair—a frightened woman.

I said gently: "Please tell me."

"I'm to go," she said. "Lady Crediton sent for me. She said she doesn't think I have the right methods for controlling Edward. I'm to pack and leave because she doesn't like people being here under notice. She's given me a month's wages in lieu of notice."

"Oh . . . no!"

"Why do you sound surprised? It's what you wanted."

"Miss Beddoes, I . . . I have never thought of anything like this."

"Weren't you always implying that I couldn't look after the boy?"

"I never did."

"He was always in here."

"His mother is nearby."

"It was you he came to see."

"I liked him. He is a bright boy. It was nothing more than that."

She stood up and came close to me. "You hid him this afternoon. You hid him in that cupboard. Yes you did. I know it."

"Miss Beddoes, I did no such thing. Why should I?"

"Because you knew they were dissatisfied with me. You thought that would be the last straw, and it was."

"I can only say that you are wrong. I should be angry with you, but I'm sorry, Miss Beddoes. I'm desperately sorry. Are you all right . . . for money . . ."

Her face twisted. Oh God, I thought, help lonely women. Surely those brought up in genteel poverty suffer most.

"I have my month's wages," she said.

I went to the table and unlocked a drawer. I took out two five-pound notes.

"Take these," I said.

"I'd rather die," she retorted dramatically.

"Please, I beg of you."

"Why should you beg of me?"

"Because you suspect me of something. I'm not sure what. You think I helped to bring this about. It's quite untrue but because you have suspected me you owe it to me to take this money."

She stared from it to me, and I could see the look in her eyes; she was calculating how long it would last. As for myself I was picturing her in some lonely lodging writing for posts that sounded good on paper. I thought of arrogant and demanding mistresses—peevish old ladies who needed a companion; mischievous thoughtless school-boys like Edward. I felt the tears coming to my eyes.

She saw them too and they were more effective than any words I could have uttered.

"I thought . . . I thought . . ." she said.

"That I had hidden the child? But what could I have possibly done that for? Don't you see it's all so far-fetched. Oh, I understand. You're terribly upset. I daresay Lady Crediton was . . . beastly."

She nodded.

"Please, will you take this money? It's not much. I wish I could give you more."

She sat down then, staring before her, and I put the money into the pocket of her dress.

"I'm going to make you a good cup of tea," I said. "A nice sweet cup of tea. You'll be surprised how much better you'll feel."

I put the kettle on. I was by no means as calm as I appeared; my hands were shaking a little.

While I was waiting for the kettle to boil, I told her that if I heard of any suitable posts I would get in touch with her. In my profession I went around quite a bit. I would not forget it.

She sipped the tea and when she had drunk it, she said: "I owe you an apology."

"Forget this," I said. "I understand. You have had a shock. You'll feel better in the morning."

"I shall leave in the morning," she said.

"Where shall you go?"

"I know a very reasonable lodging house in the town. I shall soon find something."

"I know you will," I said.

And when she left I was sure she looked upon me as a friend. As for myself, I was certainly disturbed, but I had meant it when I said that if ever I heard of a post which would be suitable for her I should let her know.

July 11th. Lady Crediton sent for me today. I had forgotten how awe-inspiring she could be for it was so rarely that I was received into the presence. She sat upright, her back as straight as that of her ornate chair which was like a throne. Her snowy white cap might have been a crown, she wore it so regally.

"Ah, Nurse Loman, pray be seated."

I sat.

"I sent for you because I have a proposition to put before you. I have had several talks with Dr. Elgin and he informs me that your patient's health is *not* improving."

She looked sternly at me as though this was somehow due to my incompetence, but I was no Miss Beddoes to be intimidated.

I said: "Dr. Elgin has no doubt told you of the reason for this."

"He believes that our climate is not good for her, and it is because of this that I have come to this decision. Mrs. Stretton is going to pay a visit to her native shores. If this improves her health we shall know that it was indeed the climate here which was detrimental to it."

"I see."

"Now, Nurse. Two alternatives present themselves. She will need a nurse in attendance. We have no doubt of that. Dr. Elgin has a good opinion of your efficiency. Therefore I am offering you a choice. You may accompany her and continue to nurse her if you wish; or if you decide that you do not wish to stay with her you will be brought back to England at my expense. If however you do *not* wish to accompany her, there is nothing to be done but terminate your engagement here."

I was silent for a while. I had been expecting this of course, but I kept thinking of Anna.

"Well?" she said.

"Your ladyship will understand that it is rather a big decision to make."

She grudgingly conceded this.

"I admit that it would be a little inconvenient if you were to decide to leave your patient. She has become accustomed to you . . . and you to her."

She waited. The use of her favorite word "inconvenient" implied that she expected me to save her from that undesirable state.

"I do agree that I understand her," I said. "But it is still a big decision for me to make." Then I said suddenly: "Lady Crediton, may I put a proposition to you?"

She looked startled, and before she could refuse I hurried on: "I have been wondering about the little boy, Edward. He will presumably be with his mother?"

"Y—yes," she admitted grudgingly. "For a short time perhaps. He is young and would come back here in due course, I daresay."

"But he would go with her?"

She looked at me with astonishment. This was not the usual manner in which she conducted interviews with her employees.

"Miss Beddoes has gone," I said. "I could not undertake to look after the child and my patient, but I daresay your ladyship had thought of employing a governess or nurse for the child."

She was still amazed. She did not discuss the domestic affairs of the Castle with people whom, she considered, they did not concern.

I went on quickly: "It is just possible that a friend of mine might agree to take on the post of looking after Edward. If she did . . . then I should be delighted to accompany Mrs. Stretton."

A look of relief came into her face, and she was too taken aback to hide it. She very much wanted me to go with Monique; and she had realized that after all she would be needing a governess for Edward.

✤✤✤✤✤✤✤✤✤✤✤✤✤✤✤✤✤✤✤✤✤✤✤✤✤✤✤✤✤✤✤

THE SERENE LADY

10

When Chantel came to see me that day I was aware of how excited she was as soon as I heard the iron gate click and, looking from a top window, saw her coming across the lawn. She looked almost breathtakingly beautiful. She was so dainty and with her cape flying out about her, her feet scarcely seeming to touch the ground, she was like an illustration from *The Golden Fairy Book* from which my mother used to read to me.

I ran down to the door. I did not have to wend my way now that so much of the furniture had gone. We embraced. She was laughing excitedly.

"News, news!" she cried. She came into the hall and looked round it. "Why, it's changed. It *looks* like a hall."

"It's more how it was meant to look," I said.

"Thank goodness some of those wicked old clocks have gone. Tick tock, tick tock. I wonder they didn't get on your nerves."

"They've gone alas, for what is called 'a song'."

"Never mind. They've gone. Now listen, Anna. Something has happened."

"I can see that."

"What I want you to do is to read my journal and then you'll get the picture. While you do that I'm going into the town to shop."

"But you've only just come."

"Listen. Until you've read that you won't see the picture clearly. Do be sensible, Anna. I'll be back in an hour. Not longer. So get down and read now."

She was off again, leaving me standing there in the depleted hall, the book in my hand.

So I sat down and read; and when I came to the rather abrupt ending of her account with her in Lady Crediton's presence making her suggestion, I knew what this implied.

I found myself staring at the few pieces that were left, and I thought irrelevantly that no one would ever buy the truly exquisite jewel cabinet, with its pewter and ivory on an ebony ground and its carved figures representing spring, summer, autumn, and winter. Who wanted such a jewel cabinet now, however beautiful? What had possessed Aunt Charlotte to spend a large sum of money to acquire something for which there were very few buyers in the world? And upstairs was the Chinese collection. Still, in the last weeks I had begun to see the daylight of solvency. I would be able to pay the debts I had inherited. It seemed that I might have a clear start.

A clear start. That was exactly what Chantel was offering me.

I could scarcely wait for her return. I asked Ellen to make a pot of tea before she left. She was not working every day now. Mr. Orfey had put his foot down. His business was improving and he wanted his wife at home to help him. It was only as a special favor that she came at all.

Ellen said she would make the tea and added that her sister often spoke very highly of Nurse Loman.

"Of course they think highly of her."

"Edith says she's not only a good nurse but sensible, and even her ladyship has no cause for complaint."

I was pleased; and all the time I was thinking of leaving England, of saying goodbye to the strange solitude of the Queen's House. Often people talked of leading a new life. It was a recognized cliché. But this would truly be a new life, a complete breakaway. Chantel was the only link with all that had happened.

But I was jumping to conclusions. Perhaps I had read Chantel's implications incorrectly. Perhaps I was indulging in a wild dream as I had on at least one other occasion.

Ellen set the tea on a lacquered tray; she had used the Spode set. There was that delicate Georgian silver tea strainer. Oh well, it couldn't make much difference now and this was after all a special occasion.

Ellen hung about for another glimpse of Chantel and when she had gone and we were alone in the house, Chantel began to talk.

"As soon as I heard there was a possibility of my being asked to go I thought of you, Anna. And I hated the thought of leaving you in this lonely Queen's House with your future all unsettled. I thought I can't do it. And then

it all turned out so fortuitously . . . like the benign hand of
fate. Poor old Beddoes being sent off like that. Of course
she was quite incompetent and it would have happened
sooner or later. Well then this magnificent idea came to me
and I presented it to her ladyship."

"In your journal you don't say what she said."

"That's because I have a true sense of the dramatic.
Don't you realize that as you read? Now if I told you, the
impact would have been lost. This was far too important.
I wanted to bring the news to you myself."

"Well, what did she say?"

"My dear, two-feet-on-the-ground-Anna, she did not
dismiss it."

"It doesn't sound as though she were very eager to
employ me."

"Eager to employ? Lady Crediton is never eager to
employ. It is for those whom she employs to be that. She
is aloof from us all. She is a being from another sphere.
She only feels convenience and inconvenience and she
expects those about her to see that she is in a perpetual
state of the former."

She laughed, and I felt it was good to be with her
again.

"Well, tell me what happened."

"Now where did I leave off? I had implied that I would
agree to travel with Mrs. Stretton if my friend could come
as nurse or governess or whatever it was to the boy. And I
saw at once that she thought this a *convenient* solution. I
had so taken her off her guard by my presumption that
she had not the time to compose her features into their
usual mold of stern aloofness. She was pleased. It gave me
the advantage.

"I said, 'The friend to whom I refer is Miss Anna
Brett.'

" 'Brett', she said. 'The name is familiar.'

" 'I daresay,' I replied. 'Miss Brett is the owner of the
antique business.'

" 'Wasn't there something *unsavory* happened there?'

" 'Her aunt died.'

" 'In rather odd circumstances?'

" 'It was explained at the inquest. I nursed her.'

" 'Of course,' she said. 'But what qualifications would this ... person ... have?'

" 'Miss Brett is the highly educated daughter of an Army officer. Of course it might be difficult to *persuade* her to come.'

"She gave a snort of a laugh. As much as to say whoever had to be persuaded to work for her!

" 'And what of this ... antique business?' she asked triumphantly. 'Surely this young woman would not wish to give up a flourishing business to become a governess?'

" 'Lady Crediton,' I said, 'Miss Brett had a hard time nursing her aunt.'

" 'I thought you did that?'

" 'I was referring to the time before I came. Illness in the house is very ... inconvenient ... in a small house, I mean. And the strain is great. Moreover the business is too much for one to run. She is selling it and I know would like a change.'

"She had decided right from the start that she wanted you and the objections were purely habit. She merely did not want me to think that she was eager. And the outcome is that you are to present yourself for an interview tomorrow afternoon. When I return I shall tell her whether or not you are coming for the interview. I made her understand that I would have to persuade you—and that my accompanying Mrs. Stretton might well depend on your acceptance."

"Oh, Chantel ... it can't!"

"Well I daresay I should have to go in any case. You see, it is my job and I feel that I'm beginning to understand poor Monique."

Poor Monique! His wife! The woman to whom he had been married when he came here and led me to believe ... But he didn't. It was my foolish imaginings. But how could I look after *his* child?

"It sounds rather crazy," I said. "I had thought of advertising to help an antique dealer."

"Now how many antique dealers are looking for assistants? I know you're knowledgeable but your sex would go against you, and it would be a chance in ten thousand if you found one."

"It's true," I said. "But I need time to think."

"There is a tide in the affairs of men
   Which, taken at the flood, leads on to fortune."

I laughed. "And you think this is such a tide?"

"I know that you shouldn't stay here. You've changed Anna. You've grown . . . morbid. Who wouldn't, living in such a place . . . after all that happened?"

"I have to let the house," I said. "I can't sell. I never should. So much needs to be done for it. The house agent has found a man and his wife who are passionately interested in old buildings. They would have the house and look after it and do the repairs, but I should get no rent for three years during which time they undertake to do all that is necessary."

"Well that settles it."

"Chantel! How can it!"

"You without a roof over your head. Your tenants will do the repairs and live in the house. Of course it's the answer."

"I have to think about it."

"You have to make an appointment to see Lady Crediton tomorrow. Don't look alarmed. It wouldn't be final even then. Come and see her. See the Castle for yourself. And think of *us*, Anna. And think too how lonely you would be if I went away and you joined that miserable antique dealer whom you haven't found yet and probably never will."

"How do you know the antique dealer will be miserable?"

"Comparatively so . . . compared with the excitement I'm offering you. I'll have to go. I'll tell Lady C. that you will come along and see her tomorrow afternoon."

She talked of the Castle for some little time before she left. I was caught up in her excitement about the place. She had made me see it so clearly through her journal.

How quiet it was at night in the Queen's House. The moon shone through my window filling the room with its pale light, showing the shapes in my room of those pieces of furniture which had not yet been sold.

"Tick tock, tick tock!" said the grandmother clock on

the wall. Victorian. Who would want it? They had never been so popular as grandfathers.

I heard the creak of a stair, which when I was young used to make me think some ghost was walking, but it was only the shrinking of the wood. Silence all about me—and the house, now denuded of the clutter of furniture, gaining a new dignity. Who could admire the paneled walls when they were hidden by tallboys and cabinets? Who could appreciate the fine proportions of the rooms when pieces of furniture were put there as I used to say "for the time being."

Lately I had been picturing the house furnished as I should have liked to furnish it. In the hall I would have a Tudor chest like the one I had seen in an old house and had tried to buy but was outbidden. Fourteenth century with St. George and the Dragon carved on the front; a carved refectory table; high wooden chairs.

But what was the use of dreaming? I could not afford to live in the Queen's House although it was mine, for if I did it would soon start falling into ruin. For its own sake I must leave it.

And this offer? To go right away, even out of the country. In the past I had dreamed of sailing on a ship to go to India to my parents. I remembered those days when I had walked down to the quay with Ellen and looked at the ships and dreamed of stowing away.

And now ... the opportunity had come. I should be a fool to miss it.

I thought of what life would be like if I did. The utter loneliness. Trying to find a post. As Chantel asked: How many antique dealers were looking for an assistant at this moment?

And I could enjoy this excitement. Yes, I was excited. That was why I couldn't sleep.

I put on my dressing gown. I went to the foot of the stairs. It was here that Aunt Charlotte had fallen on that night. It was here that I had stood with Captain Stretton. He was beside me holding the candle high, and we had gone downstairs together. I could recapture the excitement of that time, because I had believed that I was on the brink of a wonderful adventure. I had gone on believing that until that day when I had learned that he was married ... had actually been married when he came here and laughed with me and made me feel—as I had not since my mother died—that I was of some importance to someone.

Down the stairs to the room where we had eaten together.

I could not bear to think of it now.

And I was proposing to go away to look after his child!

Where would he be? I had not asked Chantel. He was at the Castle now, I knew. I suppose he would go away soon but if I looked after his child there would be times when I saw him.

What was I doing walking about the house at night holding a candle in a beautiful gilded candlestick—the same one which he had held that night, for we had never sold it.

I was becoming eccentric. Young Miss Brett was becoming Odd Miss Brett; very soon she would be odd, *old* Miss Brett. And if I did not take this opportunity I would blame myself for the rest of my dull life.

And if I did, if I agreed to go and look after *his* child, what then?

I dressed myself with care. Neat, I thought, not rich nor gaudy. "The apparel oft proclaims the man" ... or the woman for that matter.

I was thinking of Lady Crediton whom I had seen only once in the presence of Aunt Charlotte. That had been a long time ago. I was determined that she should not get the better of me.

Being apprehensive I seemed to acquire a cool indifference; not even those who knew me very well realized that it was assumed. Even Chantel believed me to be in command of myself, mistress of the situation. That was what Lady Crediton must believe.

I had ordered the local fly to take me to the Castle so that I should not appear windblown or flustered on arrival. In my brown costume, which Chantel had pointed out was not the color which most became me, with a rather sedate brown hat trimmed with straw-colored chiffon and my plain brown gloves, I thought I looked the perfect governess—as though I could accept authority while in my own sphere I could command it.

But why should I be concerned. If Lady Crediton decided against me, that would settle the matter, and I should not have to make the decision.

Did I want to accept? Of course I did, for even though I knew that if I did I should see the Captain again and that I could be bitterly hurt, I found the prospect irresistible.

There were two roads open to me. I could go on in my drab way or I could seek strange new adventures. But I said to myself: I could find disaster along either road. Who could say?

So . . . let Lady Crediton decide for me.

I was in that hall again. There were the tapestries. I could almost hear his voice. What an impression he had made! Surely after all these years I should have forgotten him.

"Her ladyship will see you now, Miss Brett." That was the dignified Baines, spoken of with awe by Ellen, the rather comic Baines of Chantel's journal.

I followed him up the stairs as I had on that other occasion. I felt as though I were going back in time and when he opened that door I should see Aunt Charlotte sitting there, bargaining for the escritoire.

She had changed little; she sat in the same high-backed chair; she was as autocratic as ever; but she was more interested in me than she had been on that other occasion.

"Pray be seated," she said.

I sat down.

"I hear from Nurse Loman that you wish for the post of governess which is vacant."

"I should like to hear more of it, Lady Crediton."

She looked faintly surprised. "I understood from Nurse Loman that you were free to take the post."

"I should be in a month or so, if it suited me."

It was the way to treat her, as Chantel had said. And while she talked of my duties, my salary, one side of me was studying the room and assessing values in my usual way while the other was alert wondering what the outcome would be and trying to discover what I really wanted.

My lack of eagerness must have been an asset. Lady Crediton was so used to humility in those who worked in her household that any sign of independence disconcerted her and made her believe that any who showed it must have special qualities.

At length she said: "I shall be pleased, Miss Brett, if you agree to take this post and should like to see you here as soon as possible. I would be willing to make the same arrangement that I have with Nurse Loman. You would accompany the child to his mother's home and if you did not wish to stay you would be brought back to England *at my expense*. As the child's governess has already gone, we need her replacement as soon as possible."

"I understand that, Lady Crediton, and I will let you know my decision within a day or so."

"Your decision?"

"I have a business to clear up. I am sure it will take me the best part of a month."

"Very well, but you can decide now. Suppose I agree to wait a month?"

"In that case . . ."

"The matter is settled. But, Miss Brett, I shall expect you to come as soon as possible. It is so . . . inconvenient for a child to be without a governess. I shall not take up references, since you have been recommended by Nurse Loman."

I was dismissed; I came out of the room slightly dazed.

She had decided for me, but of course I should not have let her do that unless I had wanted her to.

Why deceive myself? As soon as Chantel had made this proposition, I knew that I was going to accept it.

It was mid-October before I left the Queen's House. Everything was settled. I had cleared out to a dealer the remaining pieces at a great sacrifice. Only the famous bed remained which was the house's heirloom and would never be moved. The new tenants were to arrive the day after I went to the Castle, and the keys of the house were with the house agent.

I walked through those empty rooms, seeing them as I never had seen them before. How lovely they were with the lofty carved ceilings which one had scarcely noticed before; the exciting little alcoves which had usually been occupied to invisibility; the buttery and stillroom restored to their original meaning. I was sure the new tenants would love the house. I had met them twice and the excitement in their eyes over the old beams, the herring-bone decorations on the panels, the sloping floors and so on had made me realize that they would cherish the house.

My bags were packed; the station fly would be at the door any moment now. I took one more look round the house and the bell was tinkling. The fly had come.

So I walked out of the old life into the new.

This was my third visit to the Castle, but how different it was from the two previous ones. Then I had been paying calls; now I had come in order to be part of its life.

I was received by Baines and very soon handed over to Edith. This was a concession and due to the fact that not only was I Chantel's friend but Ellen had worked for me and, I presumed, given me a good reference.

"We hope you'll be very comfortable here, Miss Brett," said Edith. "If there is anything which doesn't please you you must let me know." She had borrowed dignity from Baines. I thanked her and said that I was sure I should be comfortable during my stay in the Castle.

For that was what it was. We should be sailing in a month or so.

My room was in the turret which Chantel had described to me. The Stretton turret. Here lived the sick, hysterical Monique, Chantel and my charge.

I looked round the room. It was large and comfortably carpeted. The bed was a fourposter, small, uncurtained, early Georgian. There was a small chest, rather heavy—Germanic; with two chairs of the same period as the bed and one armchair. There was an alcove rather like the *ruelle* one finds in French châteaux and there were a table with a mirror, a hip bath, and toilet necessities. I should be more comfortable here than I had been in the Queen's House.

No sooner had Edith left me to unpack than Chantel

came in. She sat on my bed and laughed at me. "So you're really here, Anna. It's wonderful how everything works out as I want it."

"Do you think I shall be all right? After all, I have never had anything to do with small children. Edward will probably loathe me."

"In any case he won't despise you as he did poor old Beddoes. Respect is what you have to get from children. Affection follows."

"Respect? Why should this infant respect me?"

"Because he will see in you an omniscient, omnipotent being."

"You make me sound like a deity."

"That's exactly how I feel. At this moment I am proud of myself. I feel there is nothing I can't accomplish."

"Why? Because you have succeeded in putting a friend into a vacant post?"

"Oh, Anna, please. Not so prosaic. Let me enjoy my power for a while. Power over Lady Crediton, who sees herself if ever anyone did as the reigning sovereign."

"At least *she* has to come down to earth."

"Anna, it *is* good to have you here! And think—we are going to the other side of the world ... together. Doesn't that excite you?"

I admitted that it did.

The door opened and Edward peeped in.

"Come along in, my child," cried Chantel, "and meet your new governess."

He came—eyes alight with expectation. Oh yes, he was the Captain's son all right. He had the same eyes which turned up slightly at the corners. My emotions were startling. I thought how happy I would have been if he were my son.

"How do you do," I said politely, extending a hand.

He took it gravely. "How do *you* do, Miss ... Miss."

"Brett," said Chantel.

"Miss Brett," he repeated.

He was somewhat precocious. I suppose his had been a rather unusual life so far. He would have lived on this island to which we were going and then suddenly he was brought to England and the Castle.

"Are you going to teach me?" he asked.

"I am."

"I am rather clever," he informed me.

Chantel laughed. "Edward, that is for others to decide."

"But *I* have decided."

"You hear that, Anna, he has decided that he is rather clever. That will make your task quite easy."

"We shall see," I said.

He regarded me warily.

"I am going on a ship," he said. "A big ship."

"So are we," Chantel reminded him.

"Shall I do lessons on the ship?"

"But of course," I put in. "Otherwise there wouldn't be any point in my coming."

"I shall go on the bridge," he said, "if we're shipwrecked."

"For Heaven's sake don't say such a thing," cried Chantel. She turned to me. "Now you have met Master Edward, let me take you and introduce you to his Mamma. She will be most interested to meet you."

"Will she?" asked Edward.

"Of course, she will want to see the governess of her darling child."

"I'm not her darling child . . . today. I am some days though."

That bore out what Chantel had told me of his mother.

I had met his child, now I was to meet his wife.

Chantel took me to her. She was lying in bed and I felt a twinge of emotion which I could not quite analyze. She was so beautiful. She lay back on lace-edged pillows and she wore a white silk and lace bedjacket over her nightdress. There was a faint flush in her cheeks and her dark eyes were luminous. She breathed heavily and with some difficulty.

"This is Miss Brett, Edward's new governess."

"You are a friend of Nurse Loman's." She made it a statement rather than a question.

I agreed that I was.

"You are not much like her." I could see that was not meant to be a compliment. She looked at Chantel and the corners of her mouth turned up slightly.

"I'm afraid not," I said.

"Miss Brett is more serious than I," said Chantel. "She will make an ideal governess."

"And you had a furniture shop," she said.

"You could call it that."

"You couldn't," declared Chantel indignantly. "It was an antique business, which is very different. Only highly skilled people who know a great deal about old furniture can manage an antique shop successfully."

"And Miss Brett managed this successfully?"

It was a sly thrust. If I had managed successfully in such a highly skilled endeavor why should I be taking the post of governess?

"Very successfully," said Chantel. "And now that you have met Miss Brett I am going to suggest you have your tea; and after that a little rest." She turned to me. "Mrs. Stretton had an attack yesterday . . . not a bad one . . . but still an attack. I always insist on her being very quiet after them."

Yes, Chantel was in charge.

Edward, who had been watching the scene quietly, said that he would sit by his Mamma and tell her about the big ship they were going to sail on. But she turned her face away and Chantel said: "Come and tell me instead, Edward, while I cut your Mamma's bread and butter."

So I went back to my room to finish my unpacking and I felt somewhat lightheaded, as though I had strayed into some dream, completely out of touch with reality.

I stood at the turret window and looked out. I could see right across the grounds to the gorge and beyond it to where the houses of Langmouth looked like dolls' houses in a toy town from this distance. And I thought am I really here—I, Anna Brett, in the Castle at last—governess to *his* son, living in close contact with *his* wife.

And then I thought: Was I wise to come?

Wise? By the state of my feelings I knew that I had been most unwise.

11

I settled down to my duties immediately. I found my pupil as he himself had informed me bright and eager to learn. He was wayward as most children are and while he was quite good at the lessons which appealed to him—such as geography and history—he set up a resistance against those which he did not like such as arithmetic and drawing.

"You will never be a sailor unless you learn everything," I told him and this impressed him.

I had discovered that he could always be lured to do something if he was told it was what sailors did. I knew why.

Of course the Castle fascinated me. It was a fake, as Aunt Charlotte had said, but what a glorious fake. In building the Castle, the architects had certainly had the Normans in mind and here was displayed the massiveness of that kind of architecture. Arches were rounded, the walls very thick, the buttresses massive. The staircases which led to the turrets were typically Norman—narrow where built into the wall and widening out. One had to watch one's step on these but I did this automatically because I never ceased to marvel at the skill in giving them such an appearance of antiquity. The Creditons had done what one would expect of them—they had combined antiquity with comfort.

I learned from Chantel that we were sailing on *Serene Lady*. "And I trust," said Chantel, "that she will live up to her name. I should hate to be seasick." We were carrying a cargo of machine tools to Australia and after a short stay there we should go on to the islands with another cargo, she supposed.

"There will only be twelve or fourteen passengers, so I heard, but I'm not at all sure. Don't you feel excited?"

I did, of course. When I had seen Monique and the boy I had wondered about the wisdom of my coming, but I knew that if I had the opportunity to make the decision again I would do exactly the same. It was a challenge.

Chantel guessed my thoughts. "If you had stayed in England and gone on with your drab plans you would have settled down to a life of regrets. There's nothing more boring, Anna, for you and for those about you. You would have set up an image of your Captain and enshrined it in your memory. Why? Because nothing exciting would have happened to you. When you experience something like that, the only way to get it out of your mind is to impose images over it. And one day something so wonderful will happen that it will completely obliterate it. That's life."

I often said to myself: "What should I do without Chantel?"

During my second week at the Castle I came face to face with the Captain.

I had walked in the grounds as far as the cliff edge and stood by the rail looking over at the sheer drop when I was aware of someone coming up behind me.

I turned and there he was.

"Miss Brett," he said; and held out his hand.

He had changed a little. There were more lines about his eyes; there was a grimness about his lips which had not been there before.

"Why . . . Captain Stretton."

"You look surprised. I do live here, you know."

"But I thought you were away."

"I've been up to the London office, getting briefed for my voyage. But I'm back here now, as you see."

"Yes," I said, seeking to cover my embarrassment. "I see."

"I was very sorry to hear about your aunt . . . and all the trouble."

"Fortunately Nurse Loman was with me."

"And now she has brought you here."

"She told me that the post of governess to your . . . son . . . was vacant. I applied and was given it."

"I'm glad," he said.

I tried to speak lightly. "You have not really tested my qualifications yet."

"I am sure they are ... admirable. And our acquaintance was far too brief."

"I do not see how it could have been otherwise."

"I was going to sea, I remember. I shall never forget that night. How pleasant it was ... until your aunt returned. Then the warm cozy atmosphere was gone and we had to face her disapproval."

"That night was the beginning of her illness. She came to my room after to speak to me."

"By which you mean to reprimand?"

I nodded. "Going back to her room she fell over a piece of furniture."

"Her furniture?"

"Yes, but she fell down the stairs and that was the beginning of her being crippled."

"You must have had a trying time."

I did not answer, and he went on: "I thought of you often. I wished I had been able to call again and ask what happened. And then I heard that she had died."

"Everyone was talking of it at the time."

"After I left you I went off on *The Secret Woman*. You remember the name of the ship."

I did not tell him that I still had the figurehead which I had taken him up to my bedroom to see.

"That was disastrous too," he said.

"Oh."

But he had changed the subject. "So now you are here to teach young Edward. He's a bright boy, I believe."

"I believe he is so."

"And you are sailing shortly on *Serene Lady*."

"Yes. For me it is something of an adventure."

"It is years since you have been at sea," he said. "At least I suppose you have not sailed since you came home from India."

"I'm surprised that you remember that."

"You would be even more surprised if you knew how much I remembered."

He was looking at me intently. I was suddenly happier than I had been since I had last seen him. It was foolish but I couldn't help it. I thought: It is the way he has. He looks at women as though he finds them interesting, making them feel they are important in his eyes. It's just a habit charming people acquire. Perhaps it is the very essence of charm. But it doesn't mean anything.

"Well, that is flattering," I said lightly.

"At the same time I must convince you that it is the truth."

"I should need a little convincing," I said.

"Why?"

"You are a sailor. You are accustomed to adventures. That evening at the Queen's House for me was an adventure. For you it was a casual encounter. You see, my aunt's return and her fall made it high drama for me."

"Well, I was part of the drama, too."

"No. You had already left the stage before the drama began."

"But the play's not over is it? Because here are two of the characters engaging in their dialogue in another scene."

I laughed. "No, it ended with Aunt Charlotte's death. 'The drama of the Queen's House.'"

"But there'll be a sequel, perhaps it will be the comedy of *Serene Lady*."

"Why should it be a comedy?"

"Because I always liked them better than tragedies. It's much more fun to laugh than cry."

"Oh, I agree. But sometimes it seems to me that there is more in life to cry about than to laugh at."

"My dear Miss Brett, you are misled. I shall make it my duty to change your view."

"How . . . when?" I asked.

"On *Serene Lady*, perhaps."

"But you . . ."

He was looking at me intently.

"But surely you had heard? She's my ship. I shall be in charge of her during our voyage."

"So . . . you . . ."

"Don't tell me you're disappointed. I thought you would be pleased. I assure you I am a most capable master. You need have no fears that we'll founder."

I gripped the rail behind me. I was thinking I should never have come. I should have found that post which would never again have brought me into contact with him.

I was not indifferent to him; I could never be, and he was aware of this. He did not mention his wife any more than he had on that other night. I wanted to talk of her. I wanted to know of the relationship between them. But what concern was it of mine?

I should never have come. I knew it now.

There followed weeks of feverish energy. Chantel was in a state of great excitement.

"Who would have believed this possible when we were in the Queen's House, Anna?"

"I admit it's strange that we should both be here, and about to leave the country."

"And who brought it about, eh?"

"You did. And did you know that Edward's father is the Captain of our ship?"

She was silent for a while. Then she said: "Well, we have to have a captain, don't we? We can't sail without one."

"So you did know," I said.

"In due course. But does it matter, Anna?"

"I knew that I would sail with his wife and son but not with him."

"Does it bother you?"

I must be frank with Chantel. "Yes," I said, "it does."

"He still has power to stir your emotions in spite of the fact that you know him for what he is."

"What is he?"

"A philanderer. A maritime Casanova. Oh, nothing serious. He likes women. That's why women like him. It's a false theory that we like misogamists. We don't. The men who are attractive to women are those who are attracted *by* women. It's simply a matter of flattery."

"That may be, but . . ."

"Anna, you're perfectly *safe*. You know him now. You know when he says charming things and gives you languishing looks it's all part of a game. It's not an unpleasant game. It's known as Flirtation. Quite enjoyable as long as you know how to keep it under control."

"As you do . . . with Rex."

"Yes, if you like."

"You mean you know Rex will never marry you, that he is going to propose to Miss Derringham, but you can be quite happy being what you would no doubt call flirtatious friends?"

"I can be quite happy with my relationship with Rex," she said firmly. "As you must be about yours with our gallant Captain."

"I can see," I said, "that I must learn from your philosophy of life."

"It has served me very well so far," she admitted.

Teaching was easier than I had believed. Perhaps it was because I had such a bright and interested pupil. We studied maps together and I traced our journey with him. His eyes—so like his father's, except that they were brown—would light up with excitement. The map was not a sheet of paper with different colored portions; it was a world.

"Here," he would say, putting a finger into an expanse of blue, "is Mamma's island."

"You see it is not very far from the continent of Australia."

"When she gets there she'll be happy," he told me.

"Let us hope that we shall all be happy there."

"But . . ." His eyes were puzzled, and he struggled to express his thoughts. "We are now. It's only Mamma who has to be happy. It's because it's her island, you see."

"I see."

"The Captain will love her again there," he announced gravely. He always spoke of his father as the Captain with reverence and awe. I wondered how much he heard of their quarrels and what construction he put on them.

Monique never made any attempts to restrain herself, and I was near enough to her room often to hear her voice raised in anger. Sometimes she seemed to be pleading. I wondered how he was with her. Was he unhappy? He did not seem so. But then he probably treated his marriage too lightly to be especially bothered because it was not a success. As Chantel had said of him: He liked all women too well to be too much involved with one. That must be a comfort to him, and yet what sorrow for the woman who loved him, as I believed Monique did.

I should never have come. I was not sufficiently aloof. It was no use my trying to adopt Chantel's philosophy. It could never be mine. I was already too deeply involved.

And Chantel, was she as in command of her feelings as she would have me believe?

When I saw her walking in the gardens with Rex it would have been easy to believe that they were lovers. There was something about their pleasure in each other's company, the way they talked and laughed together. Is she as invulnerable as she pretends? I wondered; and I was concerned that she might be hurt as I had been.

Such uneasy weeks they were. I think the happiest hours were those when I was alone with Edward. We had taken to each other. I think I must have been an improvement on the not very satisfactory Miss Beddoes, and it is always easier to follow a failure than a success. Lessons had become centered round the coming trip. That was easily explained in geography, but I found myself telling of the colonization of Australia and the arrival of the First Fleet. In arithmetic he found it easier to concentrate when the sums were concerned with cargo. A magic word in itself.

Whenever we went out our walks always took us to those heights where we could look down on the docks and see the shipping spread out before us.

Edward would dance about with excitement.

"Look at her. She's a wool clipper. She's going to sail to Australia. Perhaps we'll get there before her. I think we shall . . . because we are sailing with the Captain."

Once we took the binoculars with us and there we saw her. We could make out her name painted on her side in bold black letters: *Serene Lady*.

"That's our ship, Edward," I told him.

"It's the Captain's ship," he replied soberly.

"They're getting her ready for her journey," I added.

The time was close at hand when we should leave England.

It was a thrilling moment when, Edward's hand in mine, I climbed the gangway and stepped onto the deck of *Serene Lady*. I felt reckless and yes, happy. I couldn't help it. The excitement of the adventure was with me, and I knew that had I stayed behind and known that on this ship Redvers Stretton sailed—and Chantel with him—I should have been as depressed and unhappy as I ever was in my life.

I thought *The Serene Lady* beautiful. I had been as excited as Edward when I had seen her through the binoculars; but to step on board to see for myself her polished brass and gleaming decks and to think that she was Captain Stretton's ship thrilled me deeply. She was one of the new steamers which Chantel told me "we" (quoting Edith) were adding to "our" fleet. "Perhaps nothing can be quite so romantic as the sailing barques, brigs, and cutters, but they're fast becoming old fashioned and we have to be up-to-date."

Serene Lady was not a big ship, but she carried a sizable cargo and twelve passengers into the bargain, among whom were to be Rex, Chantel, Edward, his mother, and myself.

Chantel was with me when I went on board. Her green eyes sparkling like gems, the breeze catching at her titian hair, she looked lovely and I wondered afresh whether the obvious interest she had in Rex made her as vulnerable as I feared I was.

The cabins were fitted with carpets, beds, fixed dressing tables, which could be used as desks, armchairs, and built-in cupboards.

While we were examining them Chantel came in. I must go and see hers which was only a few doors away. Hers was part of a suite and Monique's adjoined it. She showed us this. There were flowers on the dressing table and the curtains at the porthole were of silk not chintz as in ours.

Edward sat on the bed and started to bounce up and down on it.

"It's very grand," I said.

"Well, what did you expect for the Captain's wife?" demanded Chantel. "Mind you, she won't always sleep here. Only when I have to keep my eyes on her. I daresay she will want to share the Captain's quarters." She pointed up. "Near the bridge," she added.

"I'm going on the bridge," said Edward.

"If you're not careful, my lad," said Chantel, "you'll be ill with excitement before you have a chance to suffer from the sea."

But there was no calming Edward. He wanted to explore; so I took him up to the top deck and we watched the final preparation's being made for our departure.

On that wintry afternoon when a big red sun showed itself through the mist, to the sound of sirens we began to move out into the Channel and began our journey to the other side of the world.

The lady remained serene through the Bay of Biscay. When I awoke in my cabin on the first morning I had difficulty in recalling where I was; and as I looked round I really could not believe that I was on board the Captain's ship en route for exotic places. My trouble was, as Chantel had pointed out on several occasions, that I *expected* life to be dull and uneventful. Hardly uneventful, I had pointed out grimly, recalling Aunt Charlotte's death. "Well," she had temporized, "you always imagine that exciting romantic things won't happen to you. Therefore they don't. We get what we work for in this world, remember . . . or some part of it. Take what you want. That's my motto."

"There's an old saying, Spanish I think, that says 'Take what you want,' said God. 'Take it and pay for it.' "

"Who's complaining of the cost?"

"People don't always know what it will be until the bill is presented."

"My dear, precise, prosaic old Anna! There you are, you see. Immediately you think of pleasure you start calculating the cost when anyone knows that that is likely to put a damper on the proceedings."

I lay there on that first morning recalling that conversation, but when I got up and felt the slight roll of the ship beneath my feet, when I parted the chintz curtains and looked through the porthole at the gray-blue sea, I felt a lightening of my spirits that was more than excitement, and I said to myself: I'll be like Chantel. I'll start to enjoy life and I won't think of the cost until the bill is presented.

And that determination stayed with me. I was indeed intoxicated by the novelty of being at sea, living close to my friend Chantel, and knowing that Red Stretton was on board and that at any moment I might meet him face to face.

She was a good ship because she was his ship. There was to me a feeling of security because he was in charge. The fact was that if I did not look into the future and ask myself what would happen at the end of the voyage, I could be content during those golden days when we sailed past the coast of Spain and Portugal to call at the Rock of Gibraltar before entering the Mediterranean Sea.

There were eight passengers on board besides our own party, including a boy of about Edward's age. This was reckoned to be good luck because the two boys would be companions for each other.

The boy was Johnny Malloy, the son of Mrs. Vivian Malloy, who was going to Australia to join her husband who had already made a home for her there; she was accompanied by Mrs. Blakey, her widowed sister, who was helping her to look after young Johnny.

Then there were Gareth and Claire Glenning. Claire was a gentle, almost timid woman in her early forties, I imagined, and her husband was a few years older, very courtly and gallant and overanxious for his wife's comfort. The other party consisted of an elderly couple, Mr. and Mrs. Greenall, who were going out to Australia to visit a married daughter and her family, and with them traveled Mrs. Greenall's sister, Miss Ella Rundle, a rather prim woman who was constantly finding fault with everything.

During the first days or so at sea these people were just figures to me, but it was not long before they began to develop definite personalities. Chantel and I used to discuss them. I would go into her cabin, when Monique was not in the next one, and we would invent life stories for them which the more outrageous they were the more they amused us. I was beginning to get as lighthearted as

Chantel. I told her I was taking over her philosophy of life.

A great deal of my time was devoted to Edward. I was obsessed by the fear that he might fall overboard and I would not let him out of my sight during those first days. To make matters more difficult, in the beginning of their acquaintance he and Johnny took a dislike to each other, until, realizing that there was no one else with whom they could play, there was at first an armed neutrality then a truce followed by a reluctant acceptance of each other which was to flower into friendship. But during those early days the sights and scenes of the ship were so new that it was difficult to absorb them and it was some time before I could accept them as normal.

I took breakfast, luncheon and tea with Edward, and Johnny and Mrs. Blakey joined us at table. Mrs. Blakey, although the sister of Mrs. Malloy, was treated as a poor relation. She told me that dear Vivian, her sister, had paid her passage and was going to give her a home in the new world. She wanted to show her gratitude by doing all she could. It seemed to me that she did this by acting as nursery governess to Johnny Malloy.

I learned quite a lot of her life history. The runaway match with the young actor of whom her family did not approve, and who, at the time of their marriage, had already been on the point of going into a decline; his death and destitution, the forgiveness and return into the family. Beneficent Vivian would take her to Australia, give her a new start and for that she would be expected to show a little gratitude.

Poor Lucy Blakey, I was sorry for her. I knew what it meant to have been helped when in need, to be expected to pay by service. Surely the most exorbitant of costs.

We became quite friendly over our meals or when we walked the decks with our charges and sat watching them while they played quoits and deck tennis.

In the evenings the children had supper and went to bed at half-past seven; and for dinner, which took place at eight o'clock, Mrs. Blakey and I joined the rest of the company. There was a place for me at the Purser's table; Mrs. Blakey sat at the First Officer's.

The Purser's table was at one end of the dining salon, the

Captain's table at the other, so I did catch a glimpse of Redvers now and then, though he did not appear in the dining salon every evening. Sometimes he took his dinner in his own quarters but during our first three evenings I only saw him once. He looked handsome in his uniform, which made his blond hair look more fair than ever. At his table were Monique, Claire and Gareth Blenning, and Mr. and Mrs. Greenall.

Chantel was at the Ship's Doctor's table with Rex. I quickly realized that even though the Captain was on the ship I should very likely see little of him, and it dawned on me then that I was not the one in danger so much as Chantel. I wondered what her true feelings for Rex were and whether beneath her air of casual pleasure she was hurt and bewildered. Rex paid attention to her in his way—and it was a different way from that of the Captain. More serious, one might say, for Rex gave me the impression that he was not the man to be lightly flirtatious.

I had started to think a great deal about Rex. I had the impression that he was a man who showed little of his feelings to the world. It was only occasionally that I caught the look in his eyes when he glanced at Chantel; it was almost fierce, possessive. But how could this be when he was, as we knew full well, on his way to Australia to renew his courtship—if it had ever begun—of Miss Derringham?

And Chantel? I could not understand her either. I had often seen her in animated conversation with Rex and she seemed at such times to sparkle and be even more gay than usual. And yet she never seemed in the least perturbed when Miss Derringham's name was mentioned.

I said to her: "Chantel, I should love to see your journal again. It would be interesting to compare our views of ship life."

She laughed. "I don't keep it now . . . as I did."

"Do you never write in it?"

"Never. Well, hardly ever."

"Why not?"

"Because life is so exciting."

"But isn't that a reason why you should capture it, write it down, so that in the future you can live it all again?"

"Dear Anna," she said, "I think I wrote all that when I

was at the Castle for you. I wanted you to share in it all, and that was the only way. Now it's not necessary. You're here. You're living it first hand. You don't need my journal."

We were sitting in her cabin, I on the armchair, she stretched out on her bed.

"I wonder," I said, "what will be the end of it."

"Now that depends on ourselves."

"As you've remarked before."

"The fault, as somebody said, is not in our stars but in ourselves."

"Shakespeare."

"Trust you to know. But it's true. Besides the element of doubt makes it all so fascinating, doesn't it? If you knew exactly what was going to happen what would be the point of living it?"

"How is . . . Mrs. Stretton?" I asked.

Chantel shrugged her shoulders. "She won't make old bones," she said.

I shivered.

"Why, what's the matter?" she asked.

"It's your way of expressing it."

"Very apt you must admit, very much to the point. Her lungs are badly affected."

"Perhaps her native air . . ."

Chantel shrugged her shoulders. "I was talking to Dr. Gregory this afternoon" (he was the ship's doctor, a tall pale young man already attracted by Chantel I had noticed on more than one occasion). "He said that he thought the disease had too big a hold on her. Even the balmy airs of Coralle may not be of any use now."

"Does the Captain know?"

"You can bet the Captain knows. Perhaps that's why he behaves in such a jaunty way."

"Chantel!"

"Anna! But we mustn't be hypocritical, must we? The gallant Captain must be fully aware that he made a bad mistake, the sort that very often has to be paid for during a whole lifetime. It looks as though the payment demanded may not be of such long duration."

"Chantel, I wish . . ."

"That I would not be flippant about death. Why not? It

helps you not to be afraid of it, for yourself or for other people. Don't forget I'm on better acquaintance with that grim creature than most. I meet him frequently in my profession. It makes me feel less respectful toward him. And don't grieve for the Captain. Who knows, there might be what is called a happy release."

I stood up. I did not want to sit in Chantel's cabin discussing the death of his wife.

She jumped off the bed and slipped her arm through mine.

"I'm always flippant when I'm most serious. You should know that, Anna. But don't worry about my patient. You can be sure I shall give her the very best attention. And if the inevitable should happen . . ."

Her face was close to mine; how her green eyes glittered.

And I thought: She is thinking that if she died the Captain would be free . . . free for me.

How fond I was of her. But I wanted to explain I could not wish for the death of anyone whatever the advantages were to me.

12

Our first port of call was Gibraltar; I awoke one morning, looked through my porthole and there it was—the great rock rising high out of the water.

I had passed by here before. Years and years ago it seemed, as a child, a little older than Edward; and I remembered how excited I had felt, and how safe because my parents were in the next cabin. I often wondered what Edward felt for his mother; I knew that he considered his father to be some sort of god. Was that because he was a captain and sailed ships round the world, or because of the man himself?

I thought of Chantel's verdict on Monique; and I wondered about the future, and of Chantel herself—with that aura of fascination which surrounded her. It was not only

Rex and the ship's doctor who were attracted by her; I had seen the glances that came her way. It was not only her beauty—and undoubtedly she had that—it was her vitality, a certain passion within herself; I felt that life with her would always be exciting. I suppose that was how others felt and wanted to share it.

We should be docked for a few hours at Gibraltar and there would be an opportunity to take a trip ashore. Chantel had said that she would have liked to make up a party—say myself and the ship's doctor and perhaps the First Officer. The Glennings were going off to visit friends ashore. And who wanted to be with the really rather decrepit Mr. and Mrs. Greenall—and even less did one desire the company of Miss Rundle!

I pointed out that I was here to look after Edward and he would wish to go ashore so I must go with him; and as Mrs. Blakey would be taking Johnny and the two boys wanted to go together I should go with her and Mrs. Malloy.

Chantel grimaced. "What a shame! Poor Anna!" she said lightly.

We had hired a carriage with a driver who would show us the sights. The boys were bouncing on their seats with excitement and poor Lucy Blakey could not restrain Johnny one bit—or perhaps she feared to in the presence of Mrs. Malloy. I felt no such restrictions. I told Johnny to sit still and to the amazement of his mother and aunt he obeyed me; I thought it was an excellent moment to give them a little combined geography and history lesson. Chantel would have laughed at me if she had been there. How I wished she had been.

It was a beautiful day and the sunshine seemed brilliant after the misty dampness of Langmouth.

"It has belonged to us since 1704," I told Edward.

"To the Creditons?" he asked.

Mrs. Malloy and Mrs. Blakey joined in my laughter. "No, Edward, to Britain."

Edward was a little puzzled; I was sure he believed that his formidable grandmother owned Britain.

"It is called Gibraltar," I went on, "after an Arab called Gebel Tarik who came here long, long ago."

"Before we did?" asked Johnny.

"Long before we did and he built a castle for himself and he gave the place its name. You see Gebel Tarik became Gibraltar. If you say it quickly you'll see."

The boys started shouting together: "Gebel Tarik. Gibraltaric . . . Gibraltar."

"You will see the castle soon," I told them and that silenced them, but when they saw the old Moorish Castle they pointed excitedly to it shouting "Gebel Tarik"; and I said to Mrs. Blakey: "That is something they will remember forever."

"It's an excellent way of teaching children," said Mrs. Malloy graciously. I think she was a little piqued not to have been invited to join one of the other parties and I was sure she was thinking that the two nursery governesses should have been left to manage the children on their own. Poor Lucy Blakey! If one had to be an underling it was so much better to be so outside one's own family. How much more independent I was now than when I was with Aunt Charlotte.

The highlight of our little trip was of course the sight of the apes. Several carriages had made the climb to the upper part of the Rock and were pulled up there. The Greenalls were there with Miss Rundle and they called a greeting.

We had difficulty in keeping the boys away from the apes, who were very spry and mischievous. Our driver had warned us not to get too near or they might steal our gloves or even our hats. It was a great pleasure to see the delight of the two boys; they chuckled and whispered together and I was a little afraid that one might urge the other on to some recklessness.

And then as we stood there watching the antics of the little creatures one of them came running down from higher up the slope with a green scarf in its mouth. There had been a shout of laughter and looking back whence he had come I saw Chantel with Rex. They were standing close together; his arm was through hers; they were laughing and I realized of course that it was her scarf which had been snatched.

So she and he had come exploring together. The pleasure of the outing was spoiled for me. I thought: She is going to be hurt, deeply hurt, because Lady Crediton will never allow it; and he is on his way to propose to Miss Derringham.

We drove back to the docks and I tried not to show that my mood had changed.

The boys were chattering about the apes. "Did you see that one . . ."

"Oh, I liked the other little one better." I wondered whether Mrs. Malloy had seen them, or Mrs. Blakey; and what they were thinking.

I said in my most prim governess voice, "There is a story that the apes came to Gibraltar through a passage under the sea from Barbary which is their native country."

"Can we go through the passage?" asked Edward.

"It's only a legend," I said. "And there are bound to be legends about such things. Gibraltar is the only place in Europe where they are to be found. And they say that if ever they disappeared from the Rock it would cease to belong to us."

The boys looked alarmed—whether or not it was due to the thought of the apes' disappearance or the loss of the Rock I was not sure. I was not even thinking of them. My thoughts were occupied by Chantel and Rex; and I wondered how much she hid from me.

After Gibraltar we ran into choppy seas. The ship's decks became deserted and most people kept to their cabins. To my joy I discovered that I was a good sailor. Even Edward had to keep to his bed, and this gave me a few hours of complete freedom. The wind was fierce and it was almost impossible to stand up, so I made my way with difficulty to one of the lower decks and lay stretched out on a chaise-longue type chair wrapped in a rug and watched the seas tossing the ship hither and thither as though she were made of cork.

Serene Lady, I thought. She was serene, unperturbed by the storm. Serenity! What a gift. I wished it were mine and I supposed that I gave the impression that it was; but that was only because I managed to hide my true feelings. Everyone on the ship I supposed did that. I began to wonder about them and to ask myself how different they really were from the personalities they showed to the world. In all of us, I suppose, there was a secret man or woman in hiding.

Philosophical thoughts, and suited to a solitary lying on a deserted deck, when the rest of the ship's passengers—or most of them—were laid low with the effects of the weather at sea.

"Hello!" Someone was reeling along toward me. I saw it was Dick Callum, the purser.

"Brave woman," he shouted above the roar of the sea.

"I have heard that the fresh air is the best thing possible on occasions like this."

"Maybe, but we don't want you washed overboard."

"It's a little sheltered here. I feel quite safe."

"Yes, you're safe enough there and the gale's not so strong as it was half an hour ago. How do you feel?"

"Fairly well, thank you."

"Fairly well suggests not completely well. I'll tell you what, I'm going to get you a small brandy. That should make you feel absolutely well."

"Please . . . I don't . . ."

"But this is medicinal," he said. "Purser's orders. And I'm taking no refusal."

He staggered away and was gone so long that I thought he had forgotten me, but eventually he emerged carrying with great balancing skill two glasses on a small tray.

He gave the tray to me to hold and then pulling up another of the chairs stretched out beside me.

I sipped the brandy and he was right; the faint queasiness I had felt began to disappear.

"One does not see much of you in ordinary weather," he said with a smile. "It takes a gale to bring you out. You're like the lady in the weather vane who only comes out for stormy weather."

"I'm out," I said, "but I have my duties."

"As I have mine."

"And on occasions like this?"

"A few hours off duty. Believe me we are in no danger of shipwreck. This is a high wind, and there's a swell on. That's all. We sailors don't call this weather."

There was something very attractive about him, something which seemed familiar to me; I could not quite place it.

"I almost feel," I said, "that we've met before but that's impossible, unless of course you came into the shop at Langmouth and looked at some furniture . . . briefly."

He shook his head. "And if I had met you I don't think I should have forgotten."

I laughed at that. I didn't believe it. I was no outstanding beauty, and my personality, rather aloof I always thought it, was not particularly memorable.

"Perhaps," he said, "it was in another life."

"Reincarnation. You believe in it?"

"A sailor is always ready to believe anything, they say. We're a superstitious crowd. How's the brandy?"

"Very warming, uplifting. I feel better for it. Thank you very much."

"I know," he said, "that you came out with the family. Were you at the Castle long before you sailed?"

"A very short time. I went there with the express purpose of making this voyage."

"Quite a household, eh? And of course, we who owe our livelihood to the family are very respectful toward it."

"You don't sound particularly respectful at the moment."

"Well, we're off duty . . . both of us."

"So it is only on duty that we must remember our gratitude to them?"

"Gratitude!" He laughed. Was he a trifle bitter? "Should I be? I do my job. I'm paid for it. Perhaps the Company should be grateful to me."

"Perhaps it is."

"It's not often that we carry the Crown Prince and heir apparent on board."

"You are referring to Mr. Rex Crediton."

"I am indeed. I fancy he misses little. He will no doubt carry a report of all to headquarters and woe betide us if we fail in our duty."

"He doesn't strike me as being that kind of person at all. He always seems . . . pleasant."

"A chip off the old block. The only thing that mattered to old Sir Edward, I always heard, was the business. He inspired Lady Crediton with the same ambitions. You see, she was ready to accept the Captain and his mother. I hear that lady died only a short while ago."

"Yes, I heard that, too."

"A strange household, eh?"

"Very unusual."

"Of course our gallant Captain is a little piqued."

"Why?"

"He'd like to be in Rex's shoes."

"Has he . . . told you so?"

"I'm not in his confidence. But I sympathize with him, in a way. The two of them brought up together and one the legitimate son and the other not legitimate. It would gradually dawn on him. There you have it. Rex the heir to millions and our gallant Captain . . . merely a captain with perhaps a small holding in the business."

"He doesn't seem to be the least bit resentful."

"So . . . you know him well?"

"N-no."

"Did you know him before you came on the ship? You must have. You can't have seen much of him since we set out. He'll be busy until after Port Said. So you did know him before the voyage started?"

"Well, I had met him."

My voice had changed. I noticed it myself and could only hope that he did not.

"I see. And the nurse is a great friend of yours?"

"Oh yes, it was through her I came."

"For a moment," he said with a laugh, "I thought that it was our Captain who had brought you here to look after his son."

"It was Nurse Loman," I said quickly. "She nursed my aunt, and when this . . . post was vacant she recommended me."

"And Her Majesty Lady C. accepted that recommendation."

"She did and here I am."

"Well, it'll be an interesting voyage. Having the two of them on board makes it that."

"You have sailed with Captain Stretton before?"

"Several times. I was with him on *The Secret Woman*."

"Oh!"

"You sound surprised."

"No . . . only I had heard of *The Secret Woman* and . . ."

"What did you hear of it?"

"Just that it was a ship ... and that Lady Crediton had launched it."

He laughed. "Yes. It should have been a Lady. Perhaps that was the trouble. It's what you get for taking a woman to sea."

"What do you mean by that?"

"She should have been a Lady. Perhaps that would have made all the difference. Sailors' superstition again."

"Tell me what happened on *The Secret Woman*."

"That is a mystery which I could not begin to tell you. Perhaps if you were to ask the Captain ... he might know more."

"A mystery?"

"A great mystery. There are many who think that only Captain Stretton knows the answer to the riddle."

"And he won't tell?"

Dick Callum laughed. "He scarcely could."

"It all sounds very mysterious."

"It was ... and some say very beneficially mysterious to the Captain. I always felt I understood him, though. He had to grow up and see his half brother proclaimed as the Crown Prince."

"Crown Prince ..."

"Well, the Crediton fortune with all its ramifications is an empire in itself. And Rex is to inherit it. Yes, I always felt a certain understanding for the Captain. After all, he is a Crediton. I doubt whether he might not think reputation well lost for a fortune."

"But what has this to do with the mystery of *The Secret Woman?*"

"Everything, I should imagine."

"Now you have whetted my curiosity."

"Miss Brett, I am but an employee of the Company; moreover I owe allegiance to my Captain. I have been indiscreet. My only excuse is that the circumstances were extraordinary. A high wind in the treacherous Mediterranean which is not as benign as it is made out to be; a brave lady on deck; the warming comfort of brandy. Please forget what I have said and forgive me if I have spoken too freely. It must have been, my dear Miss Brett, because you were such a sympathetic companion. Now, I beg of you, forget my foolish observations. We are on *The Serene Lady* who very shortly will arrive at Naples. And when we leave Naples I'll prophesy that we shall have left the gales behind us. We shall sail on into sunshine; and everything will be very merry on board under the influence of our very excellent Captain."

"What a speech!"

"I have what my mother called the gift of the gab. A not very elegant phrase, but then she was not very elegant. However she was devoted to me and she gave me what she could, and as a result I received some education. Enough to insure that I was taken into the great Crediton Empire and allowed to serve my masters."

"You sound not altogether pleased about that."

"About my mother's sacrifices?"

"No, entering the Empire, as you call it."

"Oh but I am, I am the Empire's grateful and humble servant."

"Now you talk like Uriah Heep."

"God forbid, and as you gather I am not particularly humble."

"I had observed it."

"You have great powers of observation, Miss Brett."

"It would be pleasant to think so."

"What did you think of Gibraltar?"

He had successfully changed the subject and while I felt slightly relieved at this, I was a little disappointed.

I talked of Gibraltar; and as I talked I thought of the ape with Chantel's scarf and the sight of her arm in arm with Rex.

The powerful Empire, I thought. And those who attempted to thwart it—what happened to them?

We talked lightly for some time, and I felt I had a new friend. He was solicitous for my comfort and suggested that I might be getting cold. I thought it was time I returned to the cabin to see how Edward was, so I thanked him for the brandy and his company and made my way very cautiously, for we were still rocking, back to my cabin.

Dick Callum was right. Although it was cold in Naples where our stay was very short, as soon as we sailed out we moved toward the warmth. I often saw Dick Callum, who made a point of looking after me. I realized that he was an important member of the crew, being in charge of a large proportion of the staff, whereas the Captain was concerned with the navigation and this of course meant rare appearances. I felt this to be good, and when I had imagined myself going on this voyage I had thought that it would be like living in the same house with him. How different it was.

"The Captain comes down from the heights only rarely," Dick Callum told me.

Chantel came to my cabin and I often went to hers, and I mentioned to her that I had seen her on the occasion when she had lost her scarf; she did not show the slightest embarrassment.

"Right at the last minute," she said, "Rex Crediton asked me to accompany him, so I did. You're looking shocked. You think I should have had a chaperon. My dear Anna, this is not England. We are allowed a little license surely in foreign parts? As a matter of fact poor Dr. Gregory had been bullied into taking Miss Rundle and that was something we could not endure. Escape was the only possible alternative. So . . . we lost them. Poor Dr. Gregory, he came back looking exhausted and . . . murderous."

"Not very kind of you," I commented.

"No, but wise."

"Was it?" I asked, hoping this would lead to confidences, but it didn't.

She turned the tables on me which was a favorite trick of hers. "You seem to be getting on well with Mr. Callum."

"He has been most kind."

"So I've noticed."

"It's natural that we should notice each other," I told her.

She laughed suddenly. "You are enjoying this, Anna. It's different from the old Queen's House, eh? Imagine being there now, and thinking of me here . . . and all that might have been."

"I admit that I am finding this very interesting. But . . ."

"Oh stop it, Anna. You are not going into dismal prophecy, are you? You should always be gay. You never know what is round the corner. Every cloud has a silver lining, they say, and they wouldn't have kept on saying it if it hadn't been true."

"They also say that it never rains but it pours."

"You're determined to be gloomy. Well, I intend to enjoy life."

"Chantel, what happens when we arrive in Sydney?"

"I long to see it. I hear it's quite fantastically beautiful. I shall ask if I may go up to the bridge when we come into the harbor so that I can see it perfectly."

"Lots of people will leave the ship then ... including your Mr. Rex Crediton."

"But *your* Captain will remain."

"*My* Captain!"

"*My* Mr. Rex Crediton!"

"Oh Chantel, there are times when I am a little uneasy."

"My poor Anna. I must teach you to enjoy life. Did you know we are going to have a fancy dress dance? It's customary you know. We have to think up some costumes."

"You can't go as the Chatelaine this time."

"Well I'm not in a castle. Who ever heard of a chatelaine on a ship? I shall be a dancing girl, I think. Hair flowing ... or perhaps a yasmak. That would be fun and appropriate, because there will be an Eastern atmosphere to the whole affair."

How excited she could become about dressing up. I found this almost childlike quality appealing. I was growing more and more fond of her, but the more I did, the more uneasy I felt as to her relationship with Rex. I wondered what would happen when he left us at Sydney and we went on. She would know that as we sailed into the Pacific he was staying behind to be fêted and honored, and to work for the Company of course, while he paid attention to Helena Derringham and brought about that happy state of affairs so desired by Lady Crediton and Sir Henry Derringham: the amalgamation of the two companies.

I feared greatly for her.

One morning we woke to find that we were at the gateway of the East. The sun was streaming onto the decks and there was a great deal of noise and excitement everywhere.

Before Edward was dressed and had had his breakfast with me in my cabin Mrs. Blakey brought Johnny along. Chantel joined us. She was dressed in a simple white dress and jacket and she looked lovely, her hair not completely hidden by the shady white hat she wore. It always startled me to see her out of her nurse's uniform, lovely as she looked in that.

"I suppose," she said, "that you two will have to take out the children. You poor things! I'm glad that when we're in port I have a very good chance of a few hours off duty."

"The Captain is looking after his wife, I suppose," said Mrs. Blakey.

"He is taking her visiting—agents and their families and so on, I believe. If she's well enough."

"She seems a little improved."

"It's the sunshine, this dry warmth is so good for her. We are going for a tour of the town."

"We?" I asked.

"A party of us." She was vague. Rex? I wondered. She said quickly: "You two ought to come to some arrangement. It doesn't need two of you to look after the boys. You could take it in turns. You see what I mean, Anna, you could look after two as well as one, and leave Mrs. Blakey free sometimes. And vice versa."

Mrs. Blakey thought it was an excellent idea, and I agreed that it was.

"We must think about it," I said.

"Anna is the most conscientious woman in the world," laughed Chantel.

The ship was lying some distance from the port and when we took the boys on deck they were greatly excited by the sight of young Arabs no bigger than themselves who were swimming out to the ship and begging for coins. When these were thrown into the sea they dived for them, right down to the harbor bed. The water was so clear that we could see the coins and the dark wriggling bodies as they went under.

Edward and Johnny shrieked with pleasure, and wanted to throw pennies into the water; we had some difficulty in preventing their jumping in themselves. But I was caught up in the excitement just as they were.

Miss Rundle strolled along and stood with us, watching.

"It's begging," she said, "nothing more."

Her nose twitched in the unpleasant way it had, but the sun was too warm, the excitement too great for us to take much notice.

And then another voice spoke behind us.

I felt the color rise in my cheeks and I couldn't help being aware of Miss Rundle's observant eyes.

"Good morning, Captain." Mrs. Blakey spoke first.

"Good morning," I said.

Edward stood still, overawed, and I knew that the sight of his father pleased him even more than that of little Arabs diving for pennies.

"Good morning, Captain," said Miss Rundle. "We don't often have the pleasure of seeing you."

"How good of you to refer to it as a pleasure. But you see I'm in charge of the ship and it's been taking up most of my time and attention. Later when we get a run at sea I might be able to avail myself of the *pleasure* of your company."

She was pleased by his remark; she tittered a little.

"Well, Captain, we shall look forward to that."

I thought: He can charm even her.

"And is my son enjoying the trip?" he asked.

"Aye, aye, sir," said Edward, and we all laughed.

Johnny said: "You're a real captain, are you, sir?"

"Absolutely real," replied Redvers. "Guaranteed not to disappear in a puff of smoke. So don't be afraid when you see Gulli-Gulli tonight."

"Gulli-Gulli?" cried Edward on a shrill note of excitement.

"Mystery man," said the Captain. "You wait and see."

"When? Why?" cried the children simultaneously.

"Tonight. I daresay you will be allowed to sit up for him." He turned to us and smiled and my heart beat faster and I fervently hoped I didn't betray my feelings.

"What time does this mystery man appear?" asked Mrs. Blakey.

"Half-past eight. We shan't linger over dinner."

"*Please,*" cried Edward, and then, "Gulli-Gulli. Gulli-Gulli."

"Well, I think this once, don't you?" I said to Mrs. Blakey.

She agreed.

The Captain said: "I wanted to see you." He was looking straight at me and smiling and I knew I was not hiding my feelings adequately. It was ridiculous, it was unwise; it was wrong to feel like this about another woman's husband. My only excuse was that it had happened before I knew.

He went on: "You'll be doing a little sightseeing, I suppose. I wanted to tell you not to go unaccompanied. I've arranged for a conveyance for you both and the boys. The First Officer will go with you."

"Thank you," I said.

He bowed and left us. Edward's eyes followed him adoringly; I wondered if mine did the same.

Miss Rundle sniffed slightly. "He has quite a reputation," she said.

I glanced at the children and she shrugged her shoulders. I felt very angry with the woman.

It was two hours before we left the ship and set off in the company of the First Officer, who took us to the mosque where we heard the call to prayer from the high tower and went into the bazaars. I bought some white and gold slippers with pointed toes which curled up at the tips and a piece of turquoise colored silk with which I thought I might make a dress.

There were spangled scarves in lovely bright colors to be bought very cheaply and I thought one might help me to dress up for the fancy dress dance. Mrs. Blakey bought perfume of which there was a great deal for sale. It was very strong, and smelled of musk. For the boys we bought a red tarbush apiece and these they delightedly wore. We agreed though that they should have a rest in the afternoon as they were to have a late night and we returned to the ship all of us rather exhausted by the sudden change of temperature.

Chantel did not return until an hour or so before dinner.

I had gone to her cabin earlier to find it empty. I wondered where she was. I went back to my cabin and when she did come she asked me to come into her cabin to see her purchases. She had bought several bottles of the

Egyptian perfume, a necklace and bracelet and swinging earrings made of gold and lapis lazuli.

"They are lovely," I cried. "They must have cost a great deal."

She laughed at me. And I thought: Rex has given them to her.

"Well," she said, "you must remember that things are cheaper here than at home."

She sat on her bed trying the various perfumes; the cabin was full of the smell of musk and flowers—not our English spring flowers with their light refreshing scents but the heavy exotic essences of the East.

"I shall go as Queen Nefertiti, I think."

"A Queen's a step up from a Chatelaine," I commented.

"Nurse Loman must always be at the top. Who was Nefertiti?"

"A Queen of Egypt. I think her husband had one of her eyes put out because she was so beautiful he thought other men might covet her."

"A pure example of masculine beastliness. I shall be Nefertiti. I'm sure she kept both eyes to the end—and she was more beautiful anyway. So ... Nefertiti is my choice for the moment."

"And Rex Crediton?" I asked.

"Oh, he's going as a grave robber. He'll be attired in a burnoose and have the requisite tools or whatever they used to open the graves of departed Kings and rob them of their treasures."

"So you have been exchanging ideas?"

"Well, it's not a masked ball this time. There's no need for secrecy. Do try this scent, Anna. H'm. It's strange, don't you agree? The haunting perfume of the East. But I must get ready for dinner. Look at the time."

I left her thinking that although she talked a great deal she told me very little—and the one thing I wanted to know was how deeply she was involved with Rex Crediton. I should, of course, have been worrying about my own reactions to the Captain. But I should never betray my feelings, I assured myself. No one will ever know.

The Egyptian conjuror known as the Gulli-Gulli man who came aboard at Port Said to entertain us with his tricks was a great success—particularly with Edward and

Johnny. Chairs were arranged in a circle round a space in
the middle of the lounge and the two boys sat cross-legged
on the floor in the front.

The burnoose gave the conjuror the added touch of
mystery in their eyes and his wide sleeves must have been
a great asset in his work. He did wonders with rings and
paper; but the chief trick was the sudden production of
living baby chicks which he produced from the strangest
places, including the pockets of the boys. He used both
boys to hold his rings and papers or whatever he was
working with and I doubt whether either of them had ever
enjoyed anything so much.

When he put his hands into Johnny's coat and brought
out the two baby chicks, they leaped about in their excitement; and when he did the same to Edward they were
rolling about with laughter and delight. With the conclusion of each trick the conjuror uttered the cry of "Gulli-
Gulli"; and the boys joined in, clapping their heartfelt
approval.

That night, exhausted as Edward was, it was long before he slept. The Gulli-Gulli man had left the ship and
we had begun our progress down the Canal.

It was a lovely night—there was a moon and the sight
of those sandy shores and the occasional palm tree
through my porthole window was so alluring that I could
not resist slipping out of my cabin and going onto the top
deck.

It was deserted and as I leaned over the rail I wondered
what Aunt Charlotte would say if she could see me now.
My lips curled into a smile as I thought of her disapproval.

"Hello."

I turned and he was standing there. The moonlight on
his bronzed face seemed to make it glow. He was wearing
the white dinner jacket and I could understand why Edward thought of him as a kind of super being.

"Hello," I said rather uncertainly.

"I haven't had much opportunity of speaking to you
alone since we left England," he replied.

"Of course not. You have the ship to look after. The
passengers are another matter."

"They are my concern too."

"Everything on this ship is, I know. But *we* can be safely left to ourselves."

"That is what we hope," he said. "Are you enjoying the trip?"

"I should say like Edward 'Aye aye, sir.' "

"He's a bright little fellow," he said.

"Very. And you are his ideal."

"Didn't I say he was bright?" He was flippant but somehow I sensed a seriousness in his mood. Then he said an astonishing thing: "I notice that you have become rather friendly with Dick Callum."

"Oh yes, he has been very helpful."

"He has more opportunities of mingling with the guests than I have. It's the nature of our work—although when we're in port he can be busy."

"One just thinks of a ship sailing comfortably along, I'm afraid. One forgets that it is all due to the expert work of the Captain and his crew."

He touched my hand lightly and briefly as it lay on the rail. "Do you miss the Queen's House?"

"In a way."

"I'm afraid we can't offer you Louis Quinze settees on board."

I laughed. "I should have been very surprised to have found them here; and in any case they would be most unsuitable. That's the whole point about choosing furniture. The surroundings are as important as the pieces themselves." I surprised myself by saying vehemently: "I'm glad to have got away from the Queen's House."

With that remark our mood changed.

He was suddenly serious. "I can understand it. I thought of you often."

"Did you?"

"Because of that evening. It was a very pleasant evening for me. And for you?"

"And for me."

"And then it changed suddenly, didn't it? It was only when your aunt appeared that I realized what an exceptional evening it had been. There she stood like an avenging angel with the sword of flame. Get out of Eden, you miserable sinners."

I laughed. "That's carrying the simile too far, I think."

"And then she died."

"That was much later."

"And there were rumors. I'm sorry, perhaps I shouldn't have mentioned them. Perhaps it upsets you when people talk of them."

"Not you," I said. I no longer cared how I betrayed myself. I was happy now as I had been on that evening in the Queen's House. He—and he alone—had that power to make me throw all caution to the winds.

"She died, and there was some doubt how," he went on. "And for a while that must have been very unpleasant for you."

"Yes," I said. "You see it seemed so incredible that she should take her life. It was so unlike her. And then of course she was incapacitated. But for Chantel . . . Nurse Loman . . . I don't know what would have happened. I think it might have been . . . horrifying."

"People do strange things. One can never be sure of their motives. If she did not kill herself who else would have done it?"

"I've often thought of that. There was Ellen who desperately wanted to get married and was afraid Mr. Orfey never would marry her if she didn't bring Aunt Charlotte's legacy to him and she wouldn't have that until she died, of course."

"That seems a good enough motive."

"But it's so trivial and I could never see Ellen as a murderess. I could much more easily imagine Mrs. Morton as one. She was something of a mystery. There was a daughter who was ill and she longed to be with her. I knew that she was only staying with Aunt Charlotte in the hope of what she would get on her death. I never really knew Mrs. Morton in spite of all the years in the Queen's House. Then of course there was myself—the main beneficiary who was not on the best of terms with her and who would inherit everything."

"Which I gather was not very much."

"I was not to know that. It was only after she died that I realized how hopelessly in debt we were."

"I believe you were very unhappy at that time."

"It was . . . horrible. People in the streets looked at me furtively, whispered about me."

"I know," he said.

"You *know*."

"I know what it means to be under a cloud." I stared at the land, grayish in moonlight, at the indigo sky and the myriads of stars; the air seemed scented with the faint smell of musk.

"Have you heard any rumors ... concerning me?" he asked.

"What rumors? I don't understand."

"I thought perhaps you might. From Callum for instance. Has anyone mentioned *The Secret Woman?*"

"I may have heard the name of the ship but he has told me nothing about it."

"You may well hear something," he said, "and if you did I should like you to hear it from me."

"It was the ship on which you sailed after ..."

"Yes, after that evening when you entertained me at the Queen's House. I want to tell you about that voyage. It was a disaster and is a mystery to this day."

"Tell me then."

"Callum was my purser on *The Secret Woman* as he is on this ship. Several members of the crew who were with me then are with me now. She was different from *Serene Lady*. She was a sailing ship."

"She was also a woman." I said.

"Odd. It seemed to make a difference. She was a beauty. What we call a barquentine made for the China trade. I was taking her out to Sydney via the Cape and then I was going on to the islands. We had a few passengers on board as we have on this one and one of these was a jewel merchant, John Fillimore. He was taking out a fine collection of diamonds and was going to look at Australian opals. He was a garrulous man who liked to talk of the deals he had made and wanted everyone to know how astute he was. And he died."

"You mean ..."

"I mean that he died. Dr. Gregory diagnosed a seizure. We had dined one evening and afterward had gone to the bar and he had taken I think a brandy or two. He drank rather much. Then he went to his cabin. Next morning when his steward went in he found him dead."

"Dr. Gregory was on *The Secret Woman* too."

"Yes, he was ship's doctor then as now. It's a feature of our line that we always carry a doctor. Generally, it is only done when the number of passengers is considerably larger. We buried John Fillimore at sea but the diamonds were missing."

"Did he keep them in his cabin?"

"That was where he was foolish. They were worth a fortune, he said. We had pointed out to him that he would be wise to put them in our safe, but he wouldn't hear of it. Not, he said, while we were in port. Someone could blow the safe and make off with the diamonds. He wasn't trusting that. He was highly suspicious and I think those suspicions were directed at some members of the crew. I remember one night when several of us were talking together——Callum and Gregory were there I believe——he said that knowing he was to sail with such a precious cargo many practiced jewel thieves might have joined the crew for the sole purpose of robbing him. He was very conscious of his valuable stock. That night he told us gruesome stories of how his house as well as his business premises had been burgled; he said he was taking no risks with his diamonds. He never kept them in one place for more than a few days at a time. I thought he had them attached to his waist on a leather belt which he wore next to his skin. One night he was the worse for drink and had to be helped to his cabin and to bed. He was horrified the next day that someone might have seen the bag of diamonds. We used to joke about it. We all said we would be glad when we reached Sydney so that we could be rid of our highly dangerous cargo. And then he died and we buried him at sea. And the diamonds had disappeared. His cabin was turned inside out to search for them. They were nowhere to be found. If some of us hadn't seen them we should not have believed that they existed. When we reached land the matter was reported. The whole ship was searched, but the diamonds were never found. It was the belief of everyone that they were somewhere on the ship."

"And you never discovered?"

"They were never found," he repeated. "But you can imagine what rumors there were. John Fillimore had died although he was only in his late thirties and had shown no signs of illness before. That was mysterious in itself but nothing, of course, compared with the missing jewels. And there is one man who is supposed to be aware more than anyone of what goes on in his ship. You know who that is."

"The Captain?" I said.

"Exactly. I had seen the diamonds. I had held them in my hands. I had, as some will tell you, gloated over them."

"Had you?"

"I could never feel enthusiastic enough over a diamond to gloat."

"They represented a lot of money."

"That is the point. Some people believe that for money any crime may be committed."

"It's unfortunately true."

"But I must tell you the rest of the story. We left Sydney for the islands."

"Coralle?"

"Yes, Coralle. We were staying there two days and nights. There's no real harbor there and the ship lay in the bay."

"And your wife was there."

"Yes, she lived there with her mother in a rather broken-down old mansion. You'll see it when you get there. It was a feast day on the island. There were special native dances; bonfires, and all day long drums could be heard summoning people to the main town for the celebrations which were to begin at dusk. It was a colorful occasion and of course everyone wanted to be there. Since the death of John Fillimore and the suspicions which were rife there had been an uneasy atmosphere in the ship. There's something uncanny about a ship. It seems to be a living thing—but perhaps that's a sailor's view. Yet *The Secret Woman* seemed to have changed. She was alert and uneasy. I was aware of it. There was a spirit of mutiny on board. One could not lay one's finger on it, it was just something that a sailor feels. I almost felt that I was master of the Flying Dutchman. You know the story. I suppose every sailor does."

"It was a ghost ship that was seen off the Cape of Good Hope in stormy weather, I believe."

"Yes, doomed to sail the seas forever because a murder had been committed on board; there was precious metal on board and the crew was struck with plague and not allowed to enter any port. Well, there was that doomed feeling on *The Secret Woman*. Some said a murder had been committed, in fact it was generally believed and if we hadn't precious metal we had the Fillimore diamonds. In the legend the crew was smitten with plague, but there was a plague of a sort on *The Secret Woman*. It was in their minds; and it seemed that every man on board knew that we were moving towards some climax. There was a subtle disobedience. No one exactly refused to obey orders ... but how can I explain it? I was the Captain and I knew and I wished to God I had never seen John Fillimore and his diamonds. So we came into Coralle. Every man wanted to be ashore for the feast but naturally some would have to stay on board, so it was arranged that a skeleton crew would be on duty there—not more than half a dozen men—until midnight when the rest would return to the ship. I had seen the feasting before; it did not interest me. I was uneasy that night as though I knew that my ship was in danger. From the house I could see it lying there in the bay and I had a premonition that all was not well with my ship. So uneasy was I that I decided to row out and see for myself. I went down to the shore. I took one of the small rowing boats, but I had only just pulled away from the shore when there was a loud explosion and the ship broke into pieces which were flying all over the sea. People were rushing down to the shore. There was no moon, only the light of a thousand stars. I could only turn the boat and row back to the shore because I could hear the warning rumble and suspected a further explosion. I heard someone shout: 'It's the Captain.'

"And the explosion was actually on *The Secret Woman?*"

He nodded. "It was the end of her. She was a mass of floating wreckage. Before morning was out she had sunk in the bay and on the water pieces of her floated dejectedly. I had lost my ship. You can guess what that means to a sailor. She had been entrusted to my care and I had allowed this to happen to her. I was dishonored, shamed."

"But it was no fault of yours."

"I don't know what happened on the ship that night, but it was very mysterious. The strange thing was that the rest of the skeleton crew which should have been on duty were on the island. There had been some mistake about the duty sheet. An unheard of thing. But at the inquiry we never got to the bottom of it. It was one of the most mysterious parts of the whole affair."

"It sounds," I said, "as though there was a plot and that several people were involved in it. As though it had been arranged that there should be no one there."

"Captain's orders was how some people put it. I was in charge of the ship and she was left for those few hours, deserted, lying in the bay while every member of the crew, including myself, was ashore."

"So you have no idea who had destroyed the ship?"

"I wish to God I had."

"It's a long time since it happened."

"It is something which is never forgotten." He was silent for a while then he said: "After that night when I came to the Queen's House everything seemed to have changed. Before life had been a sort of joke. After that it ceased to be so."

After the disaster? I wondered. After the visit to the Queen's House?

"Before I was a careless boy. I was lucky, Rex used to say. I would get myself into difficult situations and trust to my unfailing luck to extricate me. But it had deserted me. I had learned that one could act carelessly, lightheartedly, and because of this suffer regret perhaps for the rest of one's life. One could curse oneself for a fool—which I do constantly, I assure you. But that's a futile occupation."

"If you could solve the mystery, if you could discover who destroyed the ship, then you would cease to feel this regret."

"That," he said, "is not all." He was silent for a while and I knew that he was referring to his disastrous marriage. Was I, as I had on another occasion, reading something into his words which was not intended?

He went on: "You see, here I am. A man in irons. Held fast by my own reckless actions."

"But how could you have prevented this disaster?"

He did not speak; and instinctively I knew that he was not then thinking of *The Secret Woman*. I wondered how he had come to marry Monique. Perhaps I should discover later when I saw that "broken-down old mansion" as he called it, when I saw her in her native setting. He had acted rashly, that much he was telling me. And I could well believe. Carried away by chivalry or necessity? Surely he must have known that Monique was not the wife for him.

Did I feel *I* was? I asked myself cynically. And I answered myself boldly: Yes, I did. I would be the perfect wife for him. He was gay; I was serious. He was charming; I was not. I was making myself fit the case. I was a fool.

I pretended to be thinking of the ship.

I said: "You don't give up hope of ever discovering what happened?"

"Strangely enough, I don't. Perhaps that's due to my nature. I was always an optimist. Rex was constantly telling me so. When I think of it I ask myself how could I possibly discover. What evidence is there? The ship is lost forever and the secret must be on the ship. If no one stole the diamonds they must have been there in which case they've probably been swallowed by fishes."

"Perhaps someone did steal them?"

"Who? Callum? Gregory? One of the crew? It would not be easy to get away with such a haul. They were watched, I know. I daresay I was. Any display of sudden riches would have been investigated. No, it remains a mystery—with suspect number one the Captain. But I have told you myself. You understand why I wanted to do that."

"Yes, I do. As I wanted to talk to you of my Aunt Charlotte's death in case you should think ..."

"I never should."

"Nor I."

"Ah, you see, that evening at the Queen's House taught us something of each other."

"Perhaps it did."

"And now we are here. Fate, as some would say, has thrown us together."

"I don't like that," I said, trying to speak lightly. "Not thrown anyway. It makes us sound like flotsam."

"Which we certainly are not."

We were silent for a while; I thought he was going to talk about his marriage. I half hoped, half feared he would, because I had become certain during this encounter that there was some special quality in our relationship. Desperately I wanted it to develop although I knew this was unwise. He had talked of his recklessness and that was the last quality I would apply to myself. But perhaps if my yearnings were deeply involved I was as capable of folly as anyone else.

No, I must never forget that he was married. I must never allow myself to be in a situation like this again. The warm evening air, that dark mysterious sky, the dim outlines on the nearby land—they were the backcloth of romance. He was a romantic. It was said of someone— George IV I think—that he loved all women too well to love one constantly. I kept telling myself that this might be said of Red Stretton. Hadn't I seen even Miss Rundle brighten at the caress in his voice?

I must be strong, sensible. Who was I to fret over Chantel's seeming recklessness with Rex, since I was equally so with his half brother.

I shivered and he said: "Are you cold?"

"No. Who could be on such a night? But it's getting late. I think I should go to my cabin."

He escorted me there. I went ahead of him down the narrow alley and at my door we paused.

"Good night," he said, and his eyes were bright and eager. He was so like he had been on that magic night in the Queen's House.

He took my hand and kissed it quickly.

A door opened and shut. Miss Rundle's! Had she heard our voices? Had she seen us?

Reckless? I thought. I was as reckless as anyone else in love. There! I had admitted it.

13

We had spent a hot and windy afternoon in Aden and had left that rather forbidding yellow volcanic coast and were once more at sea.

Now and then I saw the Captain and he always made a point of stopping to talk to me. People were beginning to notice. Miss Rundle I was sure had spread the news that she had seen him escort me to my cabin late one night and there kiss my hand. I was aware of her special interest in me, and the cold speculation in her rabbity eyes behind the gold pince nez.

Mrs. Blakey and I had accepted Chantel's advice and took it in turns to take charge of the boys, which gave us more freedom. We were all feeling as though we knew each other very well indeed. The Glennings were popular; they always seemed so eager to be friendly. Their great passion was chess, and every afternoon they would find a shady side of the ship and sit there poring over the board with great concentration. Rex sometimes played a game with them, and often Gareth Glenning would take on both his wife and Rex, and I believe beat them. Rex seemed to be very friendly with them; so did Chantel. The four of them were often together.

Miss Rundle was thoroughly unpopular; her sharp nose, often a little pink at the tip even in the tropics, smelled out trouble and her glinting eyes seemed to see in everything that happened something that was shocking. She watched Rex and Chantel as eagerly—and as hopefully—as she watched my relationship with the Captain. Mrs. Greenall was quite different and it was difficult to believe that they were sisters. She talked constantly of her grandchildren whom she was going to visit and bored us all with the same stories told over and over again. Her husband was a quiet man who would listen while she talked, nodding his head as though in corroboration of the wonders performed by their grandchildren and looking sharply at us as though to make sure we appreciated their cleverness. Mrs. Malloy had formed a friendship with the Chief Officer which contented her as much as it did Miss Rundle who would inquire of any who happened to be at hand whether they did not think it rather shocking that Mrs. Malloy should appear to forget that she was going out to join her husband.

The only passenger who did not arouse Miss Rundle's criticism was perhaps Mrs. Blakey who was so inoffensive, so eager to please not only her sister who was magnanimously giving her a home in Australia, but everyone on board.

In the evenings we sometimes played whist and the men—the Glennings, Rex and the First Officer—often had a game of poker.

So passed those lazy days and nights; and the time had come for the fancy dress dance.

The theme was the Arabian Nights; Redvers had told me that these fancy dress occasions were the highlight of the entertaining during the voyage. "We want to keep our passengers happy," he explained, "so we try to give them plenty to relieve the monotony of long days at sea when the next port of call seems far away. They can think about their costumes for days; and then after the ball they can discuss that for a while. It's necessary to have a happy ship."

For me the highlights of the voyage were those brief interludes when I met him by chance and we would stand for a while chatting. I let myself fancy that he tried to prolong those occasions even as I did; and that they meant something to him.

Monique's health had undoubtedly improved during the voyage. Chantel said it was the weather and the Captain —though the former was warmer than the latter.

"Do you know," she said to me one day, "sometimes I think he hates her."

"Surely not," I had said, turning away.

"It's the most disastrous of marriages. She tells me things sometimes when she's drowsy with her drug. I have to drug her a little now and then. Doctor's orders. She said the other night: 'But I caught him. I got him in the net. He can wriggle but he'll never get free while I live.'"

I shivered.

"My poor prudish Anna. It is shocking. But you yourself are a little shocking too. At least according to Miss Rundle. She is whispering about you no less than about me."

"That woman would see things which are not there."

"I'm sure she would . . . as clearly as she would see things that were there. I think we should beware of Madam Rundle, Anna, both of us."

"Chantel," I said, "how does . . . Rex . . . feel about Australia?"

"Oh, he feels it's a country of opportunity. The branch there is flourishing as the green bay tree and of course it will flourish even more after he has been out there for a while."

"I meant . . . about leaving the ship."

She opened her cool green eyes very wide and said: "You mean about saying goodbye to *Serene Lady?*"

"I mean about saying goodbye to you."

She smiled. "It will make him a little sad, I fancy."

"And you?"

"Perhaps myself too."

"But . . . you don't seem to *care.*"

"We have known all the time that he will leave the ship at Sydney. Why should we suddenly behave as though it's a surprise?"

"You don't wear your heart on your sleeve."

"A particularly ridiculous cliché, Anna, and I hardly expect you to be guilty of using it. Heart on sleeve indeed! How could it be fed by the veins and arteries if it were in such an impossible position?"

"Nurses are cold blooded."

"Our blood, my dear Anna, is at normal temperature."

"Stop being clinical. Chantel, *are* you all right?"

"I have told you before. I shall always be all right."

That was the only satisfaction I could get. But when we left Sydney, when he had really gone, would she be able to preserve this magnificent indifference?

It was the night of the ball. I had wrapped the silk I had bought in Port Said about me. I put on the white and gold slippers with the pointed turned-up toes and draped the spangled scarf over my face in the form of a yasmak.

"You look . . . beautiful," Edward told me when I went into his cabin.

"Oh Edward, only in your eyes."

"In everybody's eyes," he declared stoutly.

He had not been very well that day, having eaten too much that was rich the day before; the fact that he was content to lie in his bed for most of the day showed how wan he must be feeling. John had been in his cabin to keep him company and they had been painting in their books together.

As Edward had had little to eat all day I wanted him to have some milk before he settled down for the night. He said he would, so milk and biscuits were sent up to the cabin. As soon as he saw them he didn't fancy them, and said he would have them later on when he was hungry.

When I was dressed I went along to Chantel's cabin to show her my costume to see what she thought of it. She wasn't there, so I sat down to wait. I knew she must come soon or she would not have much time to get ready. On her bed lay a pair of Turkish trousers of green gauze and slippers such as I had bought in Port Said.

I had not been waiting long when she came in.

"Heavens, you're all ready."

I wondered whether she had been with Rex. I wished she would confide in me.

"I'll be back," I said, "when you're dressed."

"No, don't go. I want you to help dress me. It's difficult to get into those things."

"So I'm to be your lady's maid?"

"Like poor Valerie Stretton!"

I wished she hadn't said that. I thought everywhere one looks something seems to be shrouded in mystery; and suddenly I remembered Chantel's journal and how she had described Red's mother coming in with her muddy boots and being so ill. Life was like a stream, often clear on top with murky undercurrents only visible when you peered too closely.

"What made you think of her?" I asked.

"I don't know. She just came into my mind. Aren't these trousers fun? I bought them in Port Said."

"Just for this occasion?"

"I thought they would startle Miss Rundle and were worthwhile if only for that."

She put them on. They were amazingly attractive with the slippers. Her eyes were more glittering than ever tonight. But that was her costume. She draped matching green material about her shoulders and dexterously formed it into a bodice. She looked magnificent.

"You should have a sparkling circlet about your head," I said.

"No. In any case I haven't one. I shall wear it loose. I think that will be more effective."

It was quite startling.

I said: "Chantel, I think you are the loveliest woman I ever saw."

She put her arms about me and kissed me then. I thought I saw tears in her eyes.

Then she said soberly: "Perhaps you don't see the real me."

"No one knows you as well as I do," I said firmly. "No one. And no one could look as lovely if they were not ... good."

"What rubbish you talk! Perhaps you'd like me to go as a saint. Unfortunately I don't know any Arab saints, do you?"

"You'll be much more effective as the slave girl or whatever you're supposed to be."

"And I hope give delighted offense to Miss Rundle. At least we shall be colorful against all those burnooses. Is that the right plural, my learned friend?"

"I'm sure I don't know, but will they be there in the plural?"

"You can be sure of it. I've made inquiries. Rex has one. Gareth Glenning has and Mr. Greenall coyly admitted to me that he had too. Mrs. G. said it was fun and would be something to tell the grandchildren. I wonder if they will talk of Grandpapa's doings as much as he does of theirs? Ivor Gregory told me that there's a stock of them—burnooses I mean—on the ship and that some of the crew will be wearing them. He even admits to having one himself. After all what else is there for a man to wear?"

"It'll be like going into a souk."

"Well, isn't that the general idea? There! I'm complete. I think I must have a yasmak too, don't you? You see you and I are not dissimilar although I wear the trousers."

"We're quite different, really. Yours is far more true to life as well as being far more lovely."

"My dear, dear Anna, always setting yourself at a disadvantage. Do you know that the world takes you at your own valuation? I can see I shall have to give you a few lessons in life."

"I get them every day. And are you sure that you would be such a good teacher?"

"I need notice of that cryptic remark," she said. "And time marches on."

"I am just going back to the cabin to tuck up Edward for the night."

She came with me. Edward was sitting on the lower bunk turning over the pages of his painting book.

He gave a little shriek of pleasure when he saw Chantel.

"You're wearing trousers," he accused.

"I'm a lady of the East so naturally I do."

"I'd like to paint them," he said.

"You shall make a picture of me in the morning," she promised.

I noticed how sleepy he was.

I said: "Edward, let me tuck you in before I go down."

"He hasn't finished his milk and biscuits yet," said Chantel.

"In a minute," said Edward.

"Drink it up," suggested Chantel, "and then poor Anna can go down with a good conscience."

"Hasn't she got a good one now?"

"Of course she has. People like Anna always have good consciences."

"Do *you?*"

"Now that's another matter." She took up the glass of milk and sipped it. "Delicious," she said.

He held out his hand for it and started to drink.

"Have a biscuit with it," I said; but he did not want to eat.

He finished the milk and Chantel said: "Wouldn't you like to be tucked in and kissed goodnight by a Turkish slave?"

"Yes," he said.

"Well get in and I'll oblige."

He giggled: Chantel could charm him and I believe that he was as fond of her as he was of me ... in a different way of course. I represented a certain solidity; she amused him, and who does not like to be amused?

She tucked him in and kissed him.

"You *are* sleepy tonight," she said.

And he yawned again.

I was glad that he was so ready for sleep; and Chantel and I left the cabin together.

The lounge had been decorated for the occasion; some-one—the First Officer, Mrs. Malloy whispered to me—had stuck Arabic signs on the walls, and the place was in semidarkness. All the men seemed to have chosen the burnoose; and the lounge certainly did have the appearance of a Middle East street. One of the officers played the piano for dancing. Mrs. Malloy danced with the First Officer and Chantel with the doctor. There would be a shortage of women so I supposed everyone would find a partner—even Miss Rundle.

I looked for Redvers, but he was not there. I should have known him anywhere even if he were in fancy dress, which he would not be. He had told me that the Captain could not dress up; he had to be ready for duty at any moment. I was surprised that the doctor and the First Officer should have appeared as they did.

But it was not the Captain who was inviting me to dance but Dick Callum.

I was not an expert dancer and apologized to him.

"You're too modest," he told me.

"I see you are in regulation dress," I told him, indicating his burnoose.

"We're an unimaginative lot, we men," he said. "There are only two beggars howling for baksheesh and two fellaheens, and a few sporting the tarbush. The rest of us merely put on this robe and leave it at that."

"They're so easy to come by, I suppose. Did you buy yours in Port Said?"

He shook his head. "Whenever we make this trip we have our Arabian Nights Fantasy. There seems to be a stock of the things on board."

"I daresay you get a little blasé doing this sort of thing regularly."

"It's always a pleasure to be with those who are not. It's hot in here. Would you like to sit down for a while?"

I said I would and we slipped out onto the deck.

"I've been wanting to talk to you," he said. "There's something I wanted to say, but I hardly know how to."

"You're not usually at a loss for words."

"That's true. But this is . . . delicate."

"Now you are making me very curious."

"You'll probably hate me."

"I can't imagine myself doing that in any circumstances."

"What a comforting person you are. I'm not surprised the Captain's son adores you."

"I think that's an exaggeration. He has a mild respect

for me. It doesn't go beyond that. But tell me what it is you want to say."

"You promise to forgive me before I begin."

"Oh dear, you're making me feel it's something terrifying."

"I don't think it is . . . yet. Well, here goes. It's about the Captain."

"Oh."

"I have offended you."

"How could you when I don't know what you are going to say?"

"Can you guess?"

I could but I said: "No."

"You see, I've sailed with him, often. You know the saying about sailors having wives in every port. Sometimes it's true."

"Are you accusing the Captain of bigamy?"

"I believe he has only gone through the ceremony once."

"Then . . . what?"

"Anna—may I call you Anna? We know each other well enough, don't we?"

I inclined my head.

"Then, Anna, he has a reputation of being something of a philanderer. On every voyage he selects a passenger to whom he pays special attention. On this voyage he has selected you."

"I had met him before, you know. We were not entirely strangers."

"I'm sorry if I've offended you. It's only out of my concern."

"I'm not very young. I can take care of myself."

He seemed relieved. "I should have known you recognized him for what he is."

"What . . . is he?"

"A man of casual affairs."

"Really?"

"He never thought he would get caught as he did. But they were too much even for him—the girl's mother and her old nurse. She was going to have a child and they called forth all their black magic. They'd put a curse on him and every ship he commanded unless he married her."

"Are you telling me that he would marry for such a reason?"

"He had to. Sailors are the most superstitious men on earth. None of them would have sailed with a master who had been cursed. They would have known it, too. He had no alternative. So he married the girl."

"It seems a little far-fetched."

"Life often is not as simple as it seems."

"But to marry because of a curse!"

"He owed her marriage in any case."

"Perhaps that was the reason he married her."

Dick laughed. "But you see, don't you, why I am concerned for you?"

"You have been jumping to conclusions. Perhaps they have been suggested by Miss Rundle?"

"That old gossip. I wouldn't accept anything she told me. But this is different. This concerns you, and anything that concerns you is of great importance to me."

I was startled, but my thoughts were too occupied with Redvers for me to give much attention to Dick Callum's hints.

"You are kind," I said, "to concern yourself over me."

"It's not a matter of kindness but of inability to do otherwise."

"Thank you. But do please stop worrying about me. I can't really see why you should be anxious because now and then I have had a word with the Captain."

"As long as you understand ... I fear, I'm making a mess of this. If you ever needed my help would you let me give it?"

"You talk as though I should be doing you a favor by letting you, when it is I who should thank you. I'd willingly accept your help if I needed it."

He put his hand over mine and squeezed it.

"Thank you," he said. "It's a promise. I'll keep you to it." I thought he was about to say more, so I said quickly: "Shall we go and dance?"

We were dancing when we heard the shrieks from the lower deck. The piano stopped abruptly. It was a child's voice. I immediately thought of Edward and then I knew at once that it was not Edward but Johnny Malloy.

We ran down to the lower deck. Others had already arrived before us. Johnny was shouting at the top of his voice: "It was the Gulli-Gulli man. I saw him. I saw him."

My first thought was: The child has had a nightmare. But then I saw something else. Lying on the deck, fast asleep, was Edward.

Ivor Gregory had come out and picked up Edward. Johnny went on shouting: "I saw him I tell you. He was carrying Edward. And I followed him and I shouted 'Gulli-Gulli, wait for me.' And Gulli-Gulli put Edward down and ran away."

It sounded crazy. I went to the doctor who looked at me steadily and said: "I'll get him back to his cabin."

I nodded and went with him. I saw Mrs. Malloy running to Johnny demanding to know what he was doing out there and what all the fuss was about.

Dr. Gregory laid Edward gently on his bed and bent over him; he lifted his eyelids and looked at his eyes.

I said: "He's not ill, is he?"

The doctor shook his head and looked puzzled.

"What on earth could have happened?" I demanded.

He didn't answer. He said: "I think I'll take the child along to the sick bay. I'll keep him there for a bit."

"Then he *is* ill?"

"No . . . no. But I'll take him."

"I don't understand what could possibly have happened."

He had thrown off his burnoose when he laid down the child; when he went out I noticed it lying on the floor.

I picked it up. There was a faint odor of musk about it, the perfume several people had bought in the bazaar. It was so strong and pungent that it seemed to cling to anything that came near it.

I dropped the thing and went out on deck. Johnny had been taken to his cabin by his mother and Mrs. Blakey. Everyone was talking about the incident. What on earth had happened? How had the sleeping child got out there? And what was this wild story about a Gulli-Gulli man carrying him along the deck and putting him down when Johnny called?

"It's some prank," said Chantel. "We were having fun, so they thought they would, too."

"But how did the child get out?" asked Rex, who was standing close to Chantel.

"He came out and feigned sleep. That's easily explained."

"The doctor didn't seem to think he was awake," I put in.

"That's nonsense," said Chantel. "He wouldn't have walked out in his sleep would he? But perhaps he did. I've had patients who did the oddest things when asleep."

Miss Rundle was well to the fore. "All this talk about the Gulli-Gulli man. Pure fabrication! They should be whipped both of them."

Claire Glenning said softly: "I imagine it was just a bit of fun. We don't want to make too much of it."

"Still, it gave some of us a fright," put in Chantel. "I suppose that's what they wanted to do."

"A storm in a teacup," said Gareth Glenning.

"All the same," Miss Rundle announced, "children have to be taught discipline."

"What do you want to do?" asked Rex. "Clap them into irons?"

Rex had set the tone as he so often did. Quiet as he was, no one ever forgot that he was that Rex Crediton, industrialist, financier, millionaire—or he would be on the death of his mother. His gravity, dignity and almost self-effacing manner implied that he did not have to call attention to his personality. It was enough that he was Rex, if not yet ruler he would be in due course—of the great Crediton kingdom.

"On with the dance!" he said, and he was looking at Chantel.

So we went back to the lounge and we danced, but it was impossible to forget that strange scene on the lower deck and though we did not continue to talk of it, I was sure it was still in our minds.

I left early; and when I reached my cabin it was to find a note from Dr. Gregory on my dressing table. He was keeping the child in the sick bay for the night.

Early the next morning one of the stewards came to tell me that the doctor would like to see me.

I went along to his quarters in some alarm.

"Where's Edward?" I asked.

"He's in bed still. He's been a little sick . . . nothing to worry about. He'll be perfectly well by midday."

"You're keeping him here?"

"Only until he gets up. He's all right . . . now."

"But what happened?"

"Miss Brett, this is rather grave. The child was drugged last night."

"Drugged!"

The doctor nodded. "That story Johnny told . . . he wasn't imagining it. Someone must have gone to the cabin and carried the child out."

"But whatever for?"

"I don't understand it. I've questioned Johnny. He said that he couldn't go to sleep because he was thinking about all the dancing and the costumes. He had drawn a picture of his mother and he wanted to show it to Edward, so he put on his dressing gown and slippers and came out to look for him. He lost his way and was trying to find his bearings when he saw what he calls the Gulli-Gulli man hurrying along carrying Edward."

"The Gulli-Gulli man. But he came on at Port Said and left."

"He means he saw someone in a burnoose."

"Who?"

"Almost every man on board was wearing one last night, Miss Brett."

"But who could have been carrying Edward?"

"That's what I should like to know. And who drugged the child beforehand?"

I had turned pale. The doctor's eyes were on my face as though he thought that I was responsible.

"I can't believe it," I said.

"It seems incredible."

"How could he have been drugged?"

"Easily. Sleeping tablets dissolve in water . . . milk . . ."

"Milk!" I echoed.

"Two ordinary sleeping tablets would have sent a child into deep unconsciousness. Did you have any sleeping pills, Miss Brett?"

"No. I daresay his mother has. But she would not . . ."

"It would be the easiest thing in the world for anyone who wanted to get hold of sleeping tablets to do so. The mystery is . . . with what object?"

"To drug the child so that he did not give the alarm

when he was picked up, to carry him out to the deck. For what purpose? To throw him overboard?"

"Miss Brett!"

"But what else?" I asked.

"Such an idea seems quite preposterous," he said.

We were silent for a while. And I thought: Yes, of course it is preposterous. Am I suggesting that someone was trying to murder Edward?

I heard myself say in a voice that was high pitched and unnatural: "What are you going to do?"

"I think the less this is talked of the better. It will be exaggerated. Heaven knows what will be said. At the moment most of them believe that it was a game the boys were playing."

"But Johnny will insist he saw someone whom he called the Gulli-Gulli man."

"They will believe he imagined it."

"But they know that Edward was unconscious."

"They'll think he was pretending."

I shook my head. "It's horrible," I said.

He agreed with me. Then he started to ask me questions. I remembered how the milk had come up, how he had not wanted it, how I had gone out to Chantel's cabin, and how she had come back with me, and had even tasted the milk when she had cajoled him to drink it.

"I'll ask her if she tasted anything odd."

"She would have said if she had."

"You can't throw any light on this mysterious matter?"

I said I couldn't.

I went back to my cabin feeling very uneasy.

I wanted to talk to Redvers. I knew that Dr. Gregory would report to him, and I wondered what his reaction would be when he knew that someone had tried to murder his son. Murder was a strong word. But for what other purpose could the child have been drugged?

The doctor did not want anyone to know of it. Perhaps he would keep it secret from most of the ship's passengers, but I as his governess must know, and Redvers as his father must know; besides as Captain of the ship he must know everything that happened on board.

I would go up to his cabin now and talk to him. I must.

There was a knock on my door and Chantel's voice said: "May I come in?"

"How's our nocturnal adventurer this morning?" she asked.

"He's in the sick bay."

"Good heavens!"

"He's all right. Chantel, the doctor doesn't want this to get about but he was drugged last night."

"Drugged! How?"

"*Why* is perhaps more important. Oh, Chantel, I'm afraid."

"Surely no one meant the boy any harm?"

"But why drug him and carry him out? If it hadn't been for Johnny what do you think might have happened?"

"What?" she asked breathlessly.

"I think someone was trying to kill Edward. He could have been thrown overboard. No one would have heard anything. The child was unconscious. Perhaps a slipper left by the rail. It would have been presumed he had wandered out and fallen overboard. Don't you *see?*"

"Now that you put it like that, yes. The easiest place to commit a murder must be at sea. But whatever for? What possible motive?"

"I can't think of one."

"This will get Miss Rundle working overtime."

"Dr. Gregory thinks it should be kept quiet. It would upset Edward terribly if he thought he was in danger. He knows nothing about it. He must not know."

"And Johnny?"

"We'll find some way of dealing with him. After all he had no right to be wandering about at night so he's in disgrace for that. Thank God he did."

"Anna, aren't you dramatizing all this? It could well have been a joke that misfired."

"What joke?"

"I don't know. It was after all a special night and we all felt very merry in our Eastern costumes. Perhaps one of our disguised Arabs had too much to drink or had some plan that went wrong."

"But the boy was drugged, Chantel. I'm going to see the Captain."

"What, now?"

"Yes. I think he may be in his cabin at this hour. I want

to talk to him. I shall have to take special precautions for the rest of the voyage."

"Dear Anna, you're taking this too seriously."

"He is my charge. Wouldn't you feel the same responsibility if *your* patient were involved?"

She admitted this and I left her looking dubious. As I climbed to the bridge and the Captain's quarters I did not stop to think that I might be behaving in an unconventional manner. I could only think of someone's drugging the child and carrying him out, and what might have happened but for Johnny Malloy.

I reached the top of the stairs and was at the Captain's door. I knocked and to my relief it was his voice that bade me enter.

He was seated at a table with papers before him.

He stood up and said: "Anna!" as I entered.

His cabin was large and filled with sunshine. There were pictures of ships on the walls and on a cabinet a model of one in bronze.

"I had to come," I said.

"About the child?" he asked; and I knew that he had already heard.

"I don't understand it," I told him. "And I feel very uneasy."

"I talked with the doctor earlier this morning. Edward had been given a sleeping tablet."

"I can't understand it at all. I hope you don't think that I . . ."

"My dear Anna, of course I don't. I trust you absolutely with him. But can you throw any light on this? Have you any idea?"

"None. Chantel . . . Nurse Loman thinks it was some joker."

He looked relieved. "Is it possible?"

"It's so pointless. Why drug the child? It must have been solely because whoever did it did not want him to know who was carrying him. It seems a great length to go to for a joke. A terrible suspicion has come to me. What if someone were trying to murder Edward?"

"Murder the child? For what reason?"

"I thought . . . you might know. Could there possibly be any reason?"

He looked astounded. "I can think of none. And Edward?"

"He doesn't know anything about it. And he mustn't. I don't know what effect it would have on him. I must be more vigilant. I should have been in the cabin, not at the dance. I should have watched over him by night as well as day."

"You are not blaming yourself, Anna? You mustn't do that. He was asleep in his cabin. Who would have dreamed that any harm could come to him there?"

"Yet someone put the sleeping tablet into his milk. Who could have done that?"

"Several people might have done it. Someone in the galleys ... someone when it was being brought up. It might have been treated before it was handed to you."

"But why ... *why?*"

"It may not be as you think. He may have found the tablets in his mother's room and thought they were sweets."

"He hadn't been there. He had been a bit seedy all day and had slept most of the time."

"He might have got them at any time. That's the most plausible answer. He found the tablets in his mother's room, put them in his pockets thinking they were sweets, and ate them that night."

"And the man whom Johnny saw carrying him?"

"He might have come out on his own before the tablets had had their effect. It's possible that the two boys were on deck for some time and Edward suddenly began to feel sleepy. Seeing him lying there fast asleep Johnny didn't know what to do so he invented the Gulli-Gulli man story to get them out of a scrape."

"It's the most likely explanation so far, and the most comfortable one. I had to talk to you. I had to."

"I know," he said.

"I shouldn't have come here ... disturbing you. It's most unethical I'm sure."

He laughed: "My only answer to that is that I'm delighted to see you at any time."

The door had opened so silently that we were not aware of this until a strident laugh rang through the cabin.

"So I have caught you!"

It was Monique. She looked wild, with her hair half up,

half down; she was clutching a red silk kimono about her on which was painted a golden dragon. I could hear the faint gasp as she struggled for her breath.

"Come and sit down, Monique," said Redvers.

"And join in your *tête-à-tête?* Make it all cozy, eh? No, I will *not* sit down. I will tell you this. I will not have it. I will not. Ever since she came into the Castle she has been trying to take you from me. What will she do next, I wonder? I am watching her. I will have her know that you are married ... married to me. She may not like it ... you may not like it ... but it is true, and nothing will alter that."

"Monique," he said gently, "Monique."

"You are my husband. I am your wife. Nothing will change it while I live. Nothing will change it."

I said: "I will call Nurse Loman."

Redvers nodded and going to Monique tried to lead her into his bedroom, but she thrashed about wildly and began to shout more loudly, but the more she shouted the more difficult it was for her to breathe.

I ran down to the cabin. Chantel was just coming out.

"Oh Chantel, there's a fearful scene. I think Mrs. Stretton is going to be very ill."

"Where is she?" asked Chantel.

"In the Captain's cabin."

"Heaven help us," she groaned, and seizing the case in which she kept her things she hurried off.

I wanted to follow her, but I knew that was unwise. It was the sight of me that had started the trouble.

I went back to my cabin and sat down uneasily, wondering what would happen next.

14

Monique was very ill, so ill that the nocturnal episode involving the two boys was forgotten. Chantel was constantly up in the Captain's quarters attending to her. It was the general opinion that the Captain's wife was on the point of death.

Edward had completely recovered. We told him nothing about his adventure. He merely believed that he had eaten something that had not agreed with him and that it had made him very sleepy as well as sick. He was very excited to have been in the sick bay which gave him a decided advantage over Johnny. As for Johnny he was reprimanded very severely by his mother—of whom he was in great awe and told that his wisest plan was to forget the whole affair. It was some sort of joke connected with the Arabian Nights' party and as he had no right to have been there, it could mean that the decision to let him go unpunished might have to be reconsidered. His best plan was, therefore, to forget all about it as quickly as possible.

Besides Edward had a further importance. His mother was very ill.

The atmosphere of the ship had changed. People had changed towards me.

It was inevitable that the fact of Monique's becoming so ill when she had discovered me in the Captain's cabin should be common knowledge. Miss Rundle had seized on the information like a jackdaw on a glittering stone. She embellished and garnished in her usual manner and served it up with the special Rundle flair for making the most of juicy titbits.

The discovery of a woman in his cabin had brought on the attack. Poor woman, she had a great deal to put up with. The tales she had heard of that Captain! Miss Rundle didn't know what the world was coming to. Even among such a small company of passengers there was Nurse Loman far too often in the company of Mr. Rex Crediton and she wondered if the scheming creature hoped to catch him. (What a hope! Miss Rundle had it on good authority that he was all but engaged to the daughter of another shipping magnate.) There was Mrs. Malloy constantly in the company of the First Officer and she with a husband in Australia and he with a wife and two children in Southampton. (This was gospel truth because when Mr. Greenall had shown him a picture of the grandchildren in England, which he was taking out to show the grandchildren in Australia, the First Officer had been *trapped* into confessing that he was the father of two children himself.) But all this paled against the scandal of that "governess creature" being discovered in the Captain's cabin by his wife, which had so upset her (poor thing and no wonder!) that she was brought to the point of death. No, she didn't know what the world was coming to, and with such a Captain what could one expect?

It was certainly unpleasant.

Chantel tried to comfort me. When she came down from the Captain's quarters she invited me into her cabin. Edward was with Johnny in the charge of Mrs. Blakey; but I was never happy at such times. I felt that I should watch over him always and although Mrs. Blakey was conscientious, I never liked him out of my sight. On the other hand I was afraid of showing my fear and communicating it to him.

"She's not as ill as she appears to be," said Chantel. "These attacks terrify people who see them, and they're awful for the patient. It's the gasping for breath. But she'll be all right in a day or so."

"I do hope so."

"My poor Anna." She began to laugh. "You must admit the thought of you as the *femme fatale* is amusing. But the Captain, I do believe, is as Edith would have said 'a little gone on you.'"

"Chantel!"

"It's true. There's a look in his eyes when he speaks to you. And you too, my dear. Well, of course you did build up an image of him all those years ago. You're a romantic, Anna. I'll tell you something else. Dick Callum is rather taken with you too."

"He's been very kind to me."

"But of course you prefer the romantic Captain. Well, he's not free, but he might be one day. She could go off any day in one of those attacks, and then there's the lung trouble."

"Oh Chantel, please don't talk like that."

"I never thought, Anna, that you would be one to shy away from the truth."

"This is all so . . . so . . . disturbing."

Her face was almost mischievous suddenly. "Do you wish you had never come? Do you wish you had gone to that antique dealer to be of assistance for a small remuneration. You'd never have found him . . . or her . . . in any case. It's fate. The way it all worked out. My coming to the Queen's House, my going to the Castle, and bring-

ing you in. Fate . . . with a little assistance from Nurse
Loman."

"I didn't say I wished I hadn't come."

> *"A crowded hour of glorious life*
> *Is worth an age without*

. . . something. I forget which but Wordsworth knew."

"Attributed to Scott, but it's by no means certain that
he was the author, and it was a name which doesn't really
apply, does it?"

"Trust you to know. But the sentiment is the same. I'd
rather have my brief gaudy hour (and there's another one
for you) than live out my drab unexciting days without
danger and without fun either."

"It depends," I said.

"At least I've given you something to cogitate about
and have taken your mind from that beastly Miss Rundle.
But don't fret. In a few days our Captain's wife will be on
her feet again. I shall bring her down here as soon as I
can so that I can keep my eyes on her and give the poor
Captain a rest from her. She's a fearful trial to him, I
believe. But at sea the high drama of one day is forgotten
the next. Look how we've all recovered from the Edward-
Johnny incident. It's scarcely ever mentioned now."

So once more she had comforted me.

I said suddenly: "Whatever happens, Chantel, I hope
that we shall always be together."

"I'll arrange it," she said. "Fate may take a hand—but
you can safely leave it to me."

Chantel was right. In a few days Monique was as well
as she had been when she first came on board. She
returned to her cabin next to Chantel and everyone ceased
to talk of her imminent death.

Occasionally she sat on deck. Chantel would bring her
out and sit with her. Edward would be with them sometimes, to be petted or ignored according to her mood. This
he accepted philosophically.

She ignored me, although at times I would find those
beautiful dark eyes fixed on me, and it seemed with
amusement. I wondered whether she would dismiss me

when we reached her home. I mentioned this to Chantel but she said this would not be the case. It was for us to decide whether we should return home or stay. Hadn't Lady Crediton said so? I was too good with Edward for Monique to want to get rid of me, and there was no malice in Monique. She made scenes because she liked them, and she would be especially grateful to those who gave her cause to do so and I, because of the Captain's penchant, was in this category.

This seemed to be the case, for one day she asked me to sit beside her on deck and she said, "I hope you don't take the Captain seriously. He likes women you know. He's gallant to them all."

I didn't know what to reply to that so I stammered that I thought there had been a misunderstanding.

"It was the same when we came over to England. There was a young woman on the ship. She was rather like you. Rather quiet ... what is the word ... homely. He likes that. It makes him feel so good to be kind to those who must rather specially appreciate his kindness."

"I'm sure," I said with some asperity, "we are all very grateful to him, the more so for being unused to such attention."

She laughed. Chantel told me afterward that she had said she liked me. I had such an odd way of talking which amused her. She understood why the Captain had selected me for his attentions this voyage.

"You see," said Chantel, "you should not let the gossips worry you. Monique is not like a conventional English woman. I doubt whether Island morals are like those of a Victorian drawing room. She gets angry because she's passionately in love with her Captain and his indifference maddens her at times. But she likes to see him admired by others."

"I find it all rather bewildering."

"It's your habit of taking everything too seriously."

"Serious matters should surely be taken seriously."

"I am not sure."

"Chantel, there's not much time left. Everything has changed suddenly. There seems to be an atmosphere of ... doom. I've felt it since that night when Edward was taken from his cabin."

"Doom!" she cried.

"Well, I can't forget what happened. I can't get out of my mind the fact that someone was trying to kill him."

"There must be another explanation."

"The Captain thinks that he found his mother's sleeping tablets and thought they were sweets."

"Very likely. He's an inquisitive young man—always probing here and there. 'What's this?' 'What's that?' And Mamma's room is an Aladdin's cave to him."

"If he and Johnny went out on deck perhaps to peep at the dancing from some place, and he fell asleep and Johnny invented his Gulli-Gulli man . . ."

"Of course. That's the explanation. It fits perfectly. When you come to consider it, it's the only explanation."

"I wish I could be sure."

"I feel perfectly sure. So much for your doom. I'm surprised at you, Anna. And you the practical, sensible one!"

"All the same I intend to watch over that child every minute he's in my care. I shall lock the cabin door at night."

"And where is he now?"

"In Mrs. Blakey's care, with Johnny. She feels the same because you see Johnny should never have been allowed to get out. We now lock the cabin doors in the evenings when they're in bed."

"That will put a stop to their nightly prowls. Well, we shall soon be saying goodbye to Johnny and his mother and aunt."

I looked at her sharply. And Rex too, I thought. Did she really care for him? Sometimes I thought she hid things from me.

How could she contemplate losing him when we docked in Sydney and be so indifferent? He would be greeted by the Derringhams and caught up in a whirl of business and social activities. Poor Chantel, her position was as hopeless as my own. But it need not have been. If Rex defied his mother, if he asked Chantel to marry him, they could be happy. He was *free*.

But I sensed a weakness in him. He was attractive it was true; he had the sort of easygoing charm which Red possessed to a much greater extent. To me he seemed like a pale shadow of his half brother.

But Rex had defied his mother when he had failed to

propose to Helena Derringham. How far, I wondered, would he carry that defiance? I wished Chantel would confide in me concerning her feelings for him. But of course I had not confided my true feelings to her. The fact was that I refused to consider them. How could I admit that I desperately loved a man who was married to another woman? I dared not.

We must keep our secrets even from each other.

The heat was intense in Bombay. Monique's breathing became difficult and Chantel had to cancel her trip ashore. The Captain had business in Bombay and was entertained by some of the company's agents; he took Edward with him.

Mrs. Malloy told me that the First Officer and the purser had suggested she and I accompany them on a tour of exploration. Mrs. Blakey was taking care of Johnny and was going with the Greenalls and Miss Rundle.

I accepted the invitation and we rode out in an open carriage, Mrs. Malloy and I shaded from the hot sun by big hats and parasols.

It was a strange experience for me and my thoughts traveled back to the day long ago when I had lived here with my parents. When we saw the women washing their clothes in the river, and wandered through the markets looking at the ivory and brass, the silk and the carpets, I was taken right back to the days of childhood. We passed the cemetery on Malabar Hill and I looked for the vultures.

I told Dick Callum of my memories and he was very interested. Mrs. Malloy and the First Officer listened politely; they were more interested in each other.

We stopped by the roadside near a teahouse and we wandered off separately, Dick Callum and myself, and Mrs. Malloy and the First Officer. Outside the teahouse traders had their wares spread out—beautiful silk shawls, exquisite lace mats and tablecloths, ebony elephants with gleaming white tusks.

They called to us in their soft voices to buy and we paused and looked. I bought a tablecloth which I thought I would send home to Ellen and a little elephant for Mrs. Buckle.

I admired a beautiful white silk shawl with the beautiful blue and silver embroidery. Dick Callum bought it.

"It seems such a shame to disappoint them," he said.

It was cooler in the teahouse; and a wizened old man came to the tables with lovely peacock feather fans for sale. Dick bought one for me.

As we sipped the tea which was most refreshing he said: "What is going to happen when we reach Coralle?"

"It's some time yet."

"Two weeks or so out from Sydney."

"But we haven't reached Sydney yet."

"Shall you stay there?"

"I feel my fate is in the balance. Lady Crediton made the position clear. If I am not approved of, or if I wish to return I shall be brought to England at the Company's expense. The same applies to Nurse Loman."

"You are very great friends, you two."

"I can't imagine being without her now, although a few years ago I hadn't met her. But we have become so close, like sisters, and sometimes I feel I've known her all my life."

"She's a very attractive young woman."

"I don't think I have ever seen a more attractive one."

"I have," he said, looking at me earnestly.

"I can't believe it." I spoke lightly.

"Would you like me to go on?"

"I don't think you should because I shan't believe you."

"But if I think so . . ."

"Then you are misled."

"I can't imagine what it will be like on *Serene Lady* once we have left you behind. Sailors do have friends ashore."

"Then we'll be friends."

"That's a comfort. I want to ask you something. Will you marry me?"

I picked up my peacock feather fan. I was suddenly so hot. "You . . . you can't mean that?"

"But I do."

"You . . . but . . . you hardly know me."

"I have known you since we left England."

"That is not really very long."

"But on a ship one gets to know people quickly. It is

like living in one house. It's different from being ashore. In any case, does it matter?"

"It matters very much. One should thoroughly *know* the person one marries."

"Does one ever thoroughly know another person? In any case, I know enough to have made up my mind."

"Then you have been . . . rather hasty."

"I am never hasty. I have thought, Anna is the one for me. She is handsome, clever, kind, and good. She is reliable. I think that is the quality I prize most."

This was my first proposal although I was twenty-eight years old. It was not as I had dreamed—in those long ago days when I had imagined someone's proposing to me. This was a calm assessment of my virtues, the greatest of which was my reliability.

"I have spoken too soon," he said.

"Perhaps you should not have spoken at all."

"Do you mean the answer is 'no,' then?"

"The answer must be no," I said.

"Just now. I accept that. It could change."

"I like you very much," I said. "You have been very kind to me. I am sure you are as . . . reliable as you think I am; but I don't believe that to be a strong enough foundation for marriage."

"There are other reasons. I'm in love with you, of course. I can't express myself as well as some. I'm not like our gallant Captain who would I am sure make the most impassioned speeches . . . and act accordingly . . . and not mean half he said."

I looked at him sharply. "Why do you dislike him so much?" I demanded.

"Perhaps because I sense you like him too much. Anna, stop thinking of him. Don't let him treat you as he has others."

"Others?" I said hoarsely.

"My God, you don't imagine you're the only one. Look at his wife. The way he treats her."

"He . . . he is also courteous to her."

"Courteous! He was born courteous. It's part of the charm. Charm! It's given him a place in the Castle. A place in the company. He's got charm . . . as his mother had before him. That's why she became Sir Edward's mistress. And our Captain can go his carefree way. He can be caught up in such a scandal that would have ruined any other man, but his charm . . . his eternal charm comes to his rescue."

"I don't know what you're talking about."

"You've heard of *The Secret Woman*. Or if you haven't you should. There was a fortune on that ship. One hundred thousand pounds, they say . . . all in diamonds. And what happened to them? What happened to the merchant? He died on board. He was buried at sea. I was there when they lowered his coffin into the water. The Captain took the service. Poor John Fillimore, who died so suddenly. And his diamonds? What happened to them? Nobody knew. But the ship was blown up in Coralle Bay."

I had stood up. "I don't want to listen to this."

"Sit down," he commanded, and I obeyed him. I was fascinated by the change in him; he was vehement in his hatred of the Captain; he really believed that Redvers had murdered John Fillimore and stolen his diamonds.

"I *must* talk to you, Anna," he went on, "and the reason is that I love you. I have to save you. You're in danger."

"Danger?"

"I know the signs. I've sailed with him before. He has a way with women which I don't possess. I don't deny it. He will deceive you as he did that poor wife of his although he didn't escape entirely. He's a buccaneer if ever there was one. Two hundred years ago piracy would have been his trade. He'd be sailing under the Jolly Roger. No highjacking on the high seas for him now; but when he sees a fortune of a hundred thousand pounds within his grasp he can't let it go."

"Do you realize that you are talking about your Captain?"

"On board I obey his orders, but I am not on board now. I am talking to the woman I am going to marry and I want to speak the truth to her. Where are those diamonds? It's clear to me. It's clear to many, but it can't be proved of course. They are hidden away in the safe deposit of some foreign port. They are his fortune salted away for when it will be safe to realize it. It's not easy to dispose of diamonds you know. They're recognizable, so he has to be careful. But he'll manage it. His fortune is waiting for him. He has to have a fortune of his own, doesn't he?"

"This is the wildest conjecture."

"I have evidence to support it."

"Then I suggest you lay it before the Captain."

"My dear, dear Anna, you don't know our Captain. He would have the answer. He always has the answers. Didn't he conveniently dispose of the ship . . . the scene of the crime. The Captain who lost his ship! How many captains would have lived that down? Anyone else would have been dismissed, disgraced and living on a far distant island somewhere in the Pacific, like Coralle itself. But of course he would have his fortune in diamonds so he would still be a rich man."

"You have surprised me twice today," I said. "First by your declaration of love for me and secondly by your declaration of hatred toward the Captain. And I notice that you are more vehement in your expression of hate than of love."

He leaned toward me; his anger had brought hot color to his face; even the whites of his eyes were faintly tinged with red.

"Don't you understand," he said, "the two are one. It is because I love you so deeply that I hate him so much. It is because he is too interested in you . . . and you in him."

"You misjudge me," I said. "I am surprised since you claim to know me so well."

"I know that you would never act . . . dishonorably."

"So I have another virtue to set beside my reliability."

"Anna, forgive me. I have allowed my feelings to get the better of me."

"Let's go. Our hour must be up."

"Just like that! Have you no word for me?"

"I don't care to hear you make accusations for which you have no proof."

"I'll get proof," he said. "By God, I'll get proof."

I had stood up. "You'll change," he went on. "You'll understand and when you do I shall speak to you again. At least tell me that you won't object to that."

"I should object very much to losing your friendship," I said.

"What a fool I am! I shouldn't have spoken yet. Never

mind, everything is as it was before. I don't give up easily, you know."

"I'm sure you don't."

"If you need my help at any time ... I shall be at hand."

"That is comforting to know."

"And you don't dislike me?"

"I don't suppose a woman ever really disliked a man for telling her he loved her."

"Anna. I wish I could tell you everything that is in my mind."

"You have told me quite a bit to be getting on with," I reminded him.

We walked slowly back past the vendors squatting beside their goods. The other two were already in the carriage.

"We thought we'd lost you," said Mrs. Malloy.

When we reached the dock and had mounted the gangway Dick pressed the white silk shawl into my hands. "I bought it for you," he said.

"But I thought you had bought it for someone else."

"For whom did you think?"

"Well, perhaps your mother."

A faint shadow darkened his face. He said, "My mother is dead." I wished I hadn't said that because I knew that the thought of her had given him pain. And then it occurred to me that I really did not know very much about him. He loved me; he hated the Captain. What other violent emotions were there in his life?

We were slipping slowly away from the dock when Chantel came into my cabin. She grimaced. "To think that I've had to be the stay-at-home."

"How's the patient?"

"A little better. It was the heat which was too much for her. She'll soon recover when we're at sea again."

"Chantel," I said, "it won't be long now before we reach Australia."

"I'm beginning to wonder what our island is going to be like. Imagine it! Or can't you? I think of palm trees and coral reefs and Robinson Crusoe. I wonder what we shall do when the ship has sailed away and left us there."

"We shall have to wait and find out."

She looked at me sharply. "Something happened to-day."

"What?" I asked.

"I mean to you. You went out with Dick Callum didn't you?"

"Yes and Mrs. Malloy and the First Officer."

"Well?"

I hesitated. "He asked me to marry him."

She stared at me. And then she said quickly: "And what did you say? 'Sir, this is too sudden'?"

"Something like that."

She seemed to breathe more freely.

"I gather you don't like him much," I said.

"Oh, I'm indifferent. But, Anna, I don't think he's good enough."

"Really. Not good enough for *me!*"

"Underrating yourself as usual. So you refused him, which refusal he took like a gentleman and asked leave to renew the invitation at a later date."

"How did you know?"

"Regulation pattern. Mr. Callum would conform to it. I'm sure. He's not for you, Anna."

I felt a great desire to defend him.

"Why not?"

"Good heavens you're not coyly considering, are you?"

"I'm not likely to get another invitation and many people believe it's better to be married to someone one does not love than never to be married at all."

"You give in too easily. I prophesy that one day you will marry the man of your choice."

She narrowed her eyes and looked wise; and I knew what she was thinking.

I said: "Well, I refused him and we're still good friends. He gave me this."

I unwrapped the shawl and showed her.

She took it from me and put it round her shoulders. It suited her to perfection; but then everything suited her.

"So not being able to accept his proposal you accepted his shawl."

"It seemed churlish not to."

"He'll renew his proposal," she said. "But you'll not accept him, Anna. It's never wise to accept second best."

She had seen the fan and her eyes widened with horror. "A fan . . . a peacock feather fan! Where did you get it?"

"I bought it near Malabar Hill."

"It's unlucky," she said. "Didn't you know? Peacock's feathers are cursed."

"Chantel, what a lot of nonsense."

"Nevertheless," she said, "I don't like it. It's tempting fate."

She picked up the fan and ran out with it. I ran after her. I caught her up at the rail; but she had already dropped the fan overboard.

15

There were hot days and nights when we crossed the Indian Ocean. We were too lazy to do very much but lie stretched out on our chairs on the port side of the ship. Only the two boys seemed to have any energy. I saw Redvers now and then; after the scene in his cabin he had appeared to avoid me for a few days, and then he ceased to do so. While we crossed this quiet tropical sea he had more leisure; and as Edward liked to be with him as much as possible, that meant that I often was too.

Edward would say: "Come on, we're going up to the bridge. The Captain said I might."

"I'll take you up," I told him, "and leave you."

"I know the way," scorned Edward, "but the Captain said I could bring you too."

So we were there among the navigating instruments, and during the lapses when Edward was so absorbed in some instrument that he would cease to ask his shrill questions, we would exchange a word or two.

"I'm sorry about that outburst," he said to me on our first encounter after the scene. "It must have been most embarrassing for you."

"For you too," I replied.

"Not such a novelty for me." It was the first time I had detected a note of bitterness in his voice.

"I was terrified that it would have some disastrous effect."

"One of these days . . ." he said. His eyes, which seemed to have become even more blue since we were at sea, were fixed on the curve of the world where the sea met the duller-blue cloudless sky. "Yes, one of these days there will be."

Then he looked at me: his blue eyes piercing, interrogative. I felt my heart leap up. Was this another proposal, the proposal of a man who had a wife already living? Was he asking me "Wait"?

I shivered. I hated the thought of waiting on Death. When people had said to me "When your aunt dies you will be comfortably off," it had shocked me. It was horrible to wait for death to remove others from your path. I was reminded of the vultures on Malabar Hill.

I feared that the slightest response from me would have released a flood of words which were better left unsaid, but as Chantel would have pointed out to me, the thoughts existed whether they were spoken or not.

Edward came up and saluted.

"Captain, what's that thing with the handle?"

The moment had passed. "Better show me, Bo'sun." He had christened Edward Bo'sun much to Edward's delight; Edward made Johnny address him as such.

I felt deeply touched to see them together. I would never believe he could kill a man for a fortune. He was innocent. And yet . . . he had come to the Queen's House and had not told me he was married. And now was he really suggesting that I should wait?

What a dangerous situation could arise when someone else stood in the way of something which was passionately desired. A common enough situation to have earned a cliché title—the eternal triangle. And to think that I should have been at one point of this.

I had left the sheltered life and come out into the danger zone, I, homely Anna (as Monique called me). I might have been safe in England, adviser to an antique dealer, companion to an old lady, governess to a child. Those were the alternatives.

Edward was absorbed.

"He'll be a sailor one day," said Redvers coming back to me.

"That would not surprise me, although children change and often ambitions of their early days lose their appeal as they grow older."

"What was your ambition as a child?"

"I think it was merely to be like my mother."

"She must have been a successful parent."

"As you are with Edward."

He drew his brows together. "I wouldn't give myself full marks. I see so little of him."

"I did not see a great deal of my mother."

"Perhaps children idealize a parent when they don't see too much of him . . . or her."

"Perhaps. To me my mother was the ideal of grace and beauty, because I never saw her anything but gay. I suppose she was sad sometimes, but not when I was there. She laughed a great deal. My father adored her. She was quite different from him. It brought it back so vividly when we were in Bombay."

"Did you enjoy your trip ashore?"

I hesitated. Then I said, "I went with Dick Callum, Mrs. Malloy and the First Officer."

"A pleasant little party."

"He has sailed with you many times, I gather."

"Callum? Yes. He's a good conscientious fellow."

I wanted to say: "He hates you. I believe he would do you some harm if he could." But how could I?

"I believe he thinks that I arranged the whole thing on *The Secret Woman* and that I have the jewels in safe keeping."

"You know he thinks that?"

"My dear Anna, everyone thought it. It was the obvious conclusion."

I was startled and delighted by the way in which he said "My dear Anna" because it made me feel as though I really was.

"But you accept that?"

"I can't blame them for thinking the obvious."

"But doesn't it . . . upset you?"

"It has had its effect on me. It makes me determined to solve the mystery, to say 'There, you were wrong!'"

"Only that?"

"And to prove I'm an honest man, of course."

"And you can only do that by discovering the diamonds?"

"I believe *them* to be at the bottom of the sea. What I want to discover is who destroyed my ship."

"These people think that you did."

"That's why I want to prove I did not."

"But how?"

"By discovering who did."

"Have you any hope of doing this?"

"I always hope. Every time I go to Coralle I believe that I am going to find the answer to the riddle."

"But the ship is lost and the diamonds with her. How can you?"

"Someone somewhere in the world, and very likely on the island, knows the answer. One day I shall find out."

"And you think the answer is on Coralle?"

"I feel it must be."

I turned to him suddenly. "I shall try to find it. When *Serene Lady* has sailed away and left us there I shall do everything that is in my power to prove your innocence."

He smiled. "So you believe in it?"

"I think," I said very slowly, "that you could make me believe anything you wished."

"What a strange statement ... as though you believe against your will."

"No, no. My will would force me to believe, because I want to."

"Anna ..."

"Yes."

His face was close to mine. I loved him; and I knew that he loved me. Or did I know it? Was this an example of my will forcing my mind to believe?

"I was thinking of you all the time in Bombay. I wished that I could have been with you. And Callum ... He's not a bad sort but ..."

I put out a hand and he took it. Then he put into words the thought that had been in his mind. "Anna, don't do anything rash. Wait."

"What for?" demanded Edward who had come over to us suddenly. "And why are you holding hands?"

"That reminds me," I said. "We must go and wash our hands before lunch."

I had to hurry away. I was afraid of my emotions.

On the boat deck Gareth Glenning and Rex Crediton were playing chess. Chantel was in the cabin in close attendance on Monique who had been ill during the night. Mrs. Greenall had cornered Mrs. Malloy and I could hear her talking about her grandchildren.

"Naughty of course. But boys will be boys and he's only six years old. Why I said to him, by the time we get back to England you'll be quite a little man."

Mrs. Malloy grunted sleepily.

Edward and Johnny were playing table tennis on the green baize table at the end of the deck with a net round it to save the balls and through which I could keep a comfortable eye on them.

I had a book in my lap but I was not reading. My thoughts were in too much of a turmoil. I kept hearing one word in my ears, "Wait."

He never spoke of his marriage to me; he never mentioned what he suffered through it. It was from Chantel that I was able to understand what a miserable failure it was. Chantel listened to Monique's confidences; she lived close to them; she had spent some time in the Captain's quarters when Monique had been there.

"I wonder he doesn't murder her," she said. "Or she him. She works herself up. Once when I was up there she picked up a knife and came at him. It wasn't serious of course. She could hardly find the energy to breathe let alone drive a knife into that solid manly breast." Chantel might joke about it, I could not.

"You see," said Chantel, "he was trapped into marrying her. What he thought was a light love affair turned into something more. He had to marry her. There was some old nurse who threatened to put a curse on him if he didn't. She told me this. You can't have a captain with a curse."

I didn't tell her that I had heard this before.

"Master Edward may or may not have been on the way. Dear, dear, the sins ye do by two and two you pay for one by one. At least you do if you're found out. As for poor Monique, she continues to adore her Captain. She writes letters to him. I am continually taking them up to his cabin. She won't trust them with anyone but me. Passionate, passionate Monique. Well, perhaps he might be nice to her. She can't last for long."

I said it was a very tragic situation.

"Less so than if she was a strong and healthy woman, though."

I couldn't bear it when Chantel talked like that. There were times when I thought we should have been wise to have stayed in England, both of us.

And here I was on the boat deck listening to the *plop-plop* of balls on a green table and the sudden shrill cries of joy and protest from the boys, glancing at the printed page, reading a paragraph and afterward not knowing what I had read, looking up and watching the porpoises frolicking or the flying fishes rising and swooping over the water.

A warm soft wind was blowing and perhaps this was what brought the voices to me so clearly.

They were coming from the chess table. It was Rex speaking with more intensity than I had ever heard from him before.

"You . . . *devil*."

He could only be addressing Gareth Glenning; and anyone less like a devil it would be hard to conceive.

I suppose he has put him in check, I thought idly. But how vehement he had sounded and then I heard Gareth's laugh. It was unpleasantly mocking.

I must have been half asleep and full of fancies. They were merely playing their favorite chess together and I suppose Gareth was winning.

Soon, I thought, we shall be in Sydney and then it will be quite different. So many will have left us. Rex, the Glennings, Mrs. Malloy and all the passengers. The only ones who will remain were myself, Edward, Chantel, and Monique. And once we reached Coralle there would be change again, but I should not be there to see that.

A ship had appeared on the horizon, her sails full blown in the strong winds. The boys came running out to look at her.

"Yankee Clipper!" cried Edward.

"China Clipper," contradicted Johnny.

They argued together, forgetful of their table tennis. They stood watching the ship while Edward boasted of his superior knowledge gleaned from the Captain.

Miss Rundle strolled along, her big hat tied under her chin by a chiffon scarf to protect a complexion which Chantel had once said was hardly worth the trouble.

"Hello, Miss Brett." The very way she spoke my name was a reproach. "Have you any objection to my sitting beside you?"

I had, but I could scarcely say so.

"Oh dear." Her eyes rested on Mrs. Malloy and Mrs. Greenall. "*She* is not going to like saying goodbye to her officer."

"I think it's just a shipboard friendship."

"I think you are very charitable, Miss Brett."

Which was more than I could say for her.

"But then . . ."

She paused with a snigger; but she had really said enough.

"And you will be staying on after we have said goodbye."

"Only for a short time until we reach Coralle."

"You'll have the crew . . . and the Captain . . . to yourselves. But *you'll* have to share them with the others. How is *poor* Mrs. Stretton?"

"She is keeping to her cabin, Nurse Loman tells me."

"Poor creature! What she has to put up with, I shouldn't like to imagine."

"Shouldn't you?" I asked with some irony.

"Dear me no. With a man like that. The way he smiled at me when he said good day . . ."

"Really?"

"He's a born philanderer. Yes, I'm very sorry for her . . . and anyone else whom he seems to fascinate. Of course people should have more sense, and more decency. But I don't know. People amaze me. There is your friend Nurse Loman . . . and er . . . ." She looked round at Rex. "What does she think she will get out of it?"

"I don't think everyone is wondering what they are going to get out of their friendships. Well, they'd hardly be friendships if they were."

"Oh you're very clever at talk. I suppose a governess would be. Those boys . . . How they shout! Shouldn't they be kept in order? My goodness when I was young . . ."

"The old order changeth and gives place to the new," I said, and thought of Chantel who liked to quote and usually misquoted, as I was probably doing now.

"H'm," she said.

"It *is* a Yankee Clipper," Edward was shrieking. "I'm going to ask the Captain."

He came running along the deck, Johnny in his wake.

"Edward," I called, "where are you going?"

"To see the Captain. I want to look through that thing he has up there. It's wonderful. You can see things far away ever so clearly."

"When did you see it?" jeered Johnny.

"I've seen it once . . . and twice. I have seen it, haven't I, Anna? I saw it when we were up there. You know that time when the Captain was holding your hand and telling you to wait. That was the time. There was a great big ship then. I asked the Captain and he said it was a Yankee Clipper."

Miss Rundle could scarcely contain her excitement.

I said: "You can't go now. What of your game of tennis? Go and finish that."

"But . . ."

"You can describe it to the Captain when you see it. Perhaps he'll show you pictures and you can identify it."

"He's got lots of pictures up there, hasn't he, Anna?"

I said: "Yes and I daresay he'll show them to you both sometime. But you must remember that he has the ship to look after. So go and finish your game and see them later."

So we sat on the deck. The ship had sunk below the horizon, and the porpoises were leaping with joy. Rex and Gareth were still intent on the chess board; Mrs. Malloy and Mrs. Greenall were dozing, and Miss Rundle departed. I knew she was looking for someone to whom she could whisper her latest discovery.

The Captain had held my hand and asked me to wait.

It was fortunate, I believed, that we should soon reach Fremantle. The excitement of coming into port always seemed to smother everything else among the passengers. Even Miss Rundle could not be greatly excited about scandal concerning people to whom she would soon say goodbye forever.

I had no doubt that she had spread Edward's revelation, but it no longer seemed as important as it was three or four weeks earlier. Mrs. Malloy was less absorbed by the First Officer; that friendship was dying a natural death. She was fussily preparing everything for her landing at Melbourne. Mr. and Mrs. Greenall were in a state of fervid excitement and asking each other twenty times a day whether the grandchildren were to be brought to Circular Quay to meet them.

"Not the youngest, surely," she told me repeatedly. "Not at his age surely."

Chantel and Rex were in each other's company at every possible moment; I was afraid for them. I came upon them once leaning on the rail talking earnestly. I was worried about Chantel. Her indifference was not really natural. Edward and Johnny were the only ones who behaved normally. They would part at Melbourne but in their minds that was, as they would say, ages away. A day in their lives was a long time.

And one morning I awoke and there we were.

On the quay people stood welcoming the boat wearing long white gloves and big hats trimmed with flowers and ribbons. Somewhere a band was playing *Rule Britannia*. Redvers had told me that there was a welcome and send-off from Australian ports for ships from England which was "Home" even for those who had never even seen it. On the big passenger ships, of course, people came to meet visitors, but we were essentially cargo. Still we had our welcome and the bands played patriotic tunes.

The children were excited and as I had given them lessons in the history of the countries before we reached them their interest was heightened. They were looking forward to seeing their first kangeroos and koala bears, so Mrs. Blakey and I took them ashore for the few hours we were in port. It was very hot but the boys seemed unaware of this. They kept shrieking their delight; and I must say I was enchanted as we drove along beside the Swan River where the red flowering gum and the yellow wattles made a great splash of color. But our stay was necessarily short and all the time we had to keep our eyes on our watches. During the trip I caught sight of Chantel and Rex riding together in one of the open carriages and I fervently hoped that Miss Rundle would not see them.

Poor Chantel. Soon she would have to say goodbye to

Rex. Could she keep up her flippancy, her feigned indifference? I wondered.

And ahead of us—not so far ahead of us—lay our parting with the ship. Soon we should reach Coralle and she and I, with Edward and Monique, would be left behind. Whenever I thought of that a great apprehension came to me. I tried to dismiss it, but it wasn't easy.

I saw Dick Callum when we came aboard. He was coming out of his office, busy as he often was during our stays in port.

"How I wish I could have taken you for a trip ashore," he said.

"Mrs. Blakey and I took the boys."

"Pressure of business prevented me ... perhaps a little unnaturally."

"What does that mean?"

"Some in high places might not have wished me to be free."

"It sounds very mysterious," I said and left him. I was really rather delighted that the Captain may not have wished me to be in Dick Callum's company.

They were just about to take the gangway up when Chantel and Rex came hurrying on board.

She saw me at the rail and she came to me. Rex did not join us but went past.

"That was a near thing," I said. "You might have missed the boat."

"You can trust me never to miss the boat," she said meaningly.

I looked at her flushed, lovely face. I had to admit that she did not look like a girl on the point of saying goodbye forever to her lover.

At Melbourne Mr. Malloy, a tall bronzed man who was making a success of his property some miles out of town, came aboard to collect his family.

There was a change in them all. Johnny looked very sober in his sailor's suit and round sailor's hat with *H.M.S. Success* on it. Mrs. Malloy was dressed in a big straw hat with flowers and ribbons more suited to London than to the outback of Australia; but in her gray coat and skirt and pearl gloves and gray boots, she looked very attractive. Mrs. Blakey also wore her best clothes.

They seemed like strangers, no longer interested in their shipmates, no longer a part of us.

Mr. Malloy carried them off and they invited Edward to go and see them sometime in the vaguely cordial way people do when they know the invitation will never be accepted. Then they were gone, out of our lives forever.

It was going to make a difference to me. Edward would miss his friend, and I would miss Mrs. Blakey's help.

Miss Rundle was at my side. "And where is the First Officer, eh?" she whispered. "Making himself scarce, which is only to be expected."

Chantel joined us.

"And we shall soon be saying goodbye," she said blithely, smiling meaningfully at Miss Rundle.

"Some of us are going to miss each other."

"Alas!" sighed Chantel.

"I am sure you and Mr. Crediton must be a little sad at parting."

"And you too," said Chantel.

"Miss Rundle," I said, "is an observer of human nature."

"Let's hope she finds herself in company as rewarding as this which is now so sadly breaking up." Miss Rundle looked startled and Chantel went on: "We must not forget that we are merely 'ships that pass in the night.' Finish it for me, Anna."

"And speak to each other in passing;
Only a signal shown, and A distant voice in the darkness."

"Beautiful, isn't it?" said Chantel. "And so true. 'Ships that pass in the night.' And then ... go on and on ... never seeing each other again. It's fascinating."

Miss Rundle sniffed. She was not enjoying the conversation. She said that Mrs. Greenall was waiting for her in her cabin.

She left us standing there.

I said to Chantel: "The next port of call will be Sydney itself."

"Yes, and then Coralle."

"Chantel, how are you going to like it?"

"I'd have to be clairvoyant to answer that question."

"I mean parting with Rex Crediton at Sydney. It's no use your pretending. Yours is a special friendship."

"Who's pretending?"

"If you're in love with him, if he's in love with you, what's to prevent your marrying?"

"You ask that question as though you know the answer."

"I do," I said. "Nothing. That's unless he is so weak that he's afraid of his mother."

"Dear Anna," she said, "I believe you are very fond of your undeserving friend. But don't worry about her. She'll be all right. She always has been. She always will be. Didn't I tell you I never miss the boat."

She was confident.

They must have an agreement of some sort, I thought.

Perhaps we were all growing reckless. I saw little of Chantel. It might have been that Monique wanted to give her as much time as possible with Rex before they parted. Perhaps she took a sly interest in their romance. They seemed to have struck up a close friendship with the Glennings. Or perhaps this was just to provide chaperones. In any case the four of them were often together.

The night before we were due to arrive at Sydney I met Redvers on the deserted boat deck. It was a warm night and the breeze which was ever present during the day often dropped at night.

To be alone with him was something for which I longed yet feared.

"Anna," he said as he came toward me. I was leaning on the rail looking down into the dark water and I turned and faced him.

"Here we are on this ship," he said, "and I scarcely ever see you."

"It won't be long now before I leave the ship."

"Has it been a good journey?"

"I have never known anything like it. I shall never forget it."

"Nor I."

"You have had so many voyages."

"Only one with you on board."

"Where shall you go after you leave us on Coralle?"

"I shall be carrying cargoes for two months or so and then I shall call back at the Island before the journey home."

"So . . . we shall meet again."

"Yes," he said. "We usually put into the Island for a couple of nights. I have been thinking . . ."

"Yes."

"Wondering," he went on, "what you will make of the Island."

"I don't quite know what to expect. I've no doubt that the island of my imagination is quite different from the reality."

"It's half cultivated, half savage. That's what makes it so strange. Civilization exists rather . . . uneasily. I have been thinking a great deal about your staying there."

"My staying there?"

"Monique must stay. It is necessary for her health. And Edward should of course stay with his mother. But I wonder about you, and Nurse Loman of course. I think when I return you may well ask to be taken home."

"Would there be cabins for us on your ship?"

"I shall see that it is possible."

"That is comforting," I said. "Very comforting."

"So we may have another voyage together?"

I shivered.

"You're cold?"

"Who could be cold on a night like this."

"Then it was a shiver of apprehension. Anna, why are you afraid?"

"I don't know if I should call my feeling fear."

"I should not speak to you like this, should I? But should we pretend to be what we are not, to deny the truth?"

"Perhaps it would be better to."

"Could it be right at any time to deny the truth?"

"In some circumstances I am sure it is."

"Well," he said, "I shall not be governed by such ethics. Anna, you remember that night when I came to the Queen's House?"

"I remember it well."

"Something happened then. That house . . . I've never forgotten it. The clocks ticking, the furniture all over the place, and we were there at that table with those candles burning in the sticks."

"Very valuable sticks. Eighteenth-century Chinese."

"We seemed isolated, just the two of us, and that girl flitting back and forth waiting on us. It was like being alone in the world and nothing else being of any importance. Did you feel it? I know you did. I couldn't have felt it so intensely if you had not."

"Yes," I said, "for me too it was a memorable evening."

"Anything else that had happened before seemed of no significance."

"You mean your marriage?"

"*Nothing* else seemed of any significance. There were just the two of us, and those clocks ticking away, they seemed to do something with time. Does that sound stupid? I had never been so happy in my life. So elated and yet contented, excited and yet serene."

"That was before the disaster of *The Secret Woman*."

"But I was already married and that was a greater disaster. Oh yes I shall speak frankly to you. I make no excuses for myself. I just want you to understand. The Island fascinated me when I first saw it, fascinated me as it now repels me. When you see it, perhaps you'll understand. And Monique, she was so much a part of the Island. I was entertained there by her mother. It's a queer place, Anna. I shall be uneasy thinking of you there."

"Chantel will be with me."

"I'm glad of that. I don't think I should allow you to be there alone."

"Is it so terrifying?"

"You will find it strange, difficult to understand perhaps."

"And you can leave Edward there happily."

"Edward will be all right. He is after all one of them."

"Tell me about them."

"You will see for yourself. Her mother and the old nurse, and the servants. Perhaps it is my imagination. I was fascinated at first and I thought Monique beautiful. I should have got away. I should have known, but of course I didn't until it was too late. And then marriage became a necessity and after that I was committed."

"You left Monique on the island and sailed away?"

"It was a similar trip to this one. And when I came out again that was with *The Secret Woman*. And then next time when I called at the Island I brought Monique back to England. And now . . . I shall leave *you* there."

He was silent for a while and then he went on: "I wonder what will happen this time."

"I hope nothing disastrous. But it's comforting to know that if we want to return you will take us. I shall tell Chantel this."

"I think she will certainly want to come back. I could see you there, Anna, in certain circumstances, but not Nurse Loman."

"At least we shall be interested to see the Island."

"It's beautiful. Lush foliage, surf breaking on sandy beaches; palm trees swaying slightly in the soft breezes, and the clear sea blue as sapphires and green as emerald lapping the golden sands."

"And when you get back to England what shall you do?"

"Stay a few days before I set out again."

"For the same voyage?"

"So much depends on what cargoes we have to carry. One thing I shall do is go to Queen's House and say 'I have come on behalf of Miss Brett, the owner, who has asked me to call and see how you are getting on here.' I shall stand in the garden as I did on that damp autumn night. And I shall stand in the hall and think of that night which changed everything in my life, and changed me too."

"Did it?"

"Oh yes, it did. Indeed it did. I wanted something different from life after that."

"What had you wanted before?"

"Adventure! Change! Danger! Excitement! But after that night I grew up. I wanted to be with one person. Before, I had always believed that I would never want to be with one person for more than a limited span. I was seeking perpetual excitement. I needed continual stimulation which only novelty could give. I grew up that night. I knew what life was about. I saw myself living there, in that house. The lawn with a table under a brightly colored sunshade and a woman sitting under it with a china teapot pouring tea into blue china cups. And perhaps a dog lying there—a golden retriever—and children, laughing and playing. I saw it all clearly as something that I wanted and I never had wanted before. I shouldn't speak of this, should I? But there is something in the air tonight. Here we are sailing close to the Australian coast. Can you see the lights over there? We are very close to land. And it's summertime and . . . there is nothing so soothing as tropical nights at sea, because then you believe that anything could happen. But perhaps there are other places, like the garden of the Queen's House. And sometimes I tell myself that that night there I saw a vision and one day that table with sunshade will be there, and I'll be there."

I said: "It can't be. It was already too late when you came. I don't think you should be talking in this way and I don't think I should be listening."

"But I am and you are."

"Which shows how wrong we are."

"We are human," he said.

"But it's no good. It's no use saying what might have been, when something has happened to prevent it."

"Anna . . ."

I knew what he meant. It was Wait. It could so easily happen. And these are dangerous thoughts. We were separated and while Monique lived his dream—and mine—could never come true.

I wanted to explain to him that we must not think of this because to think of it was to desire it with a passion that could only be sinful.

I thought I must not be with him alone again. He was a man of deep and urgent needs. I knew that. He had not lived the life of a monk and I feared for him . . . and myself.

It was too late. I must make this clear to him.

We were in danger of wishing the way was clear for us.

"It's getting late," I said. "I must go in."

He was silent for a few seconds and when he spoke his voice was as calm as my own.

"We shall sail into the harbor tomorrow. You should come up to the bridge for the best view. You must see the entire harbor in one view. I can assure you it is well worth while. Monique will be up there if she is well enough and Nurse Loman must come. Edward will want to be there too."

"Thank you. I'll enjoy that."

"Goodnight," he said.

"Goodnight."

And as I turned away I thought I heard him say "My love."

16

It was a glorious morning; the sun beat down on the decks as slowly we sailed into the harbor—grand, impressive, and beautiful beyond my imaginings. The description I had read of it "the finest harbor in the world in which a thousand sail of the line may ride in the most perfect security" was surely true. It was indeed a sight to take the breath away—the many coves and inlets, the magnificent Heads through which we must pass; the trees, the flowers, the birds, and the gloriously blue sea.

Even Edward was silent and I wondered whether he was thinking as I was—for I had taken the opportunity to give him a history lesson—of the arrival of the First Fleet a hundred years ago. It must have looked a little different then. There would have been no houses, no town, only miles of uncultivated land, and beautifully plumaged birds swooping over a dazzling sea.

Chantel stood with us, subdued too by that magnificent spectacle; or was it partly due to the fact that she must now say goodbye to Rex? We did not see Redvers who was of course on duty; there were just the three of us alone up there.

It was two hours later when we had come into Circular Quay; there was the usual bustle. Edward and I went to our cabin, Chantel went to hers. My thoughts were of Chantel. I thought: Now I shall know the true state of her feelings, for surely if she loves him she will not be able to hide it from me.

Monique was a little better. The excitement of arriving at Sydney had done her good. She had dressed and Chantel had told me she was with the Captain. Certain people would come aboard and be entertained here, she believed, and the Captain's wife, since she was on board, would be expected to do certain honors.

A steward came down and asked that Edward be taken up to the Captain's cabin.

I took him up and when I arrived and knocked at the door it was opened by Rex.

He smiled at me and said: "Oh, here's Edward. Thank you, Miss Brett."

I caught a glimpse of Redvers and an elderly man with a youngish woman—in her mid-twenties, I guessed.

I went back to my cabin. Chantel was there, studying her face in my looking glass.

"Visitors?" she asked.

"An elderly man and a youngish woman."

"You know who they are, don't you?"

"I've never seen them before."

"They are Sir Henry and Helena Derringham."

"Oh."

"Well, what did you expect. Of course they came aboard to welcome *Serene Lady* to Sydney. Rex was there I suppose."

"Yes."

She was looking at me in the glass; but still she betrayed nothing.

We spent two days in Circular Quay. This gave me an opportunity to see Sydney. The Greenalls with Miss Rundle had left; so had the Glennings. It seemed so different without them and the usual routine of days at sea. There was a great deal of the bustle that went with the loading and unloading of cargo. Chantel and I went shopping— she for herself and Monique, I for Edward and myself. We could not talk of what I wanted to in Edward's company; nor was I sure that Chantel would have talked to me alone. I felt such a deep sympathy for her, the more so because of my own position; then I felt angry with Rex because their future lay in his hands, and because he was so weak he had come to Sydney to make the proposal to Helena Derringham which he had failed to make in London.

There was one consolation. Surely such a weak man was not worthy of Chantel?

In the afternoon of the second day I sat on the deck with a book. I had been out in the morning and was rather tired. Edward was with his parents. I did not know where Chantel was.

Dick Callum came and sat beside me.

He said: "May I have the pleasure of taking you out to dine tonight?"

I hesitated.

"Oh come, you mustn't say no. I shall be most hurt if you do."

His smile was very pleasant and after all what had he done except honor me with his admiration and bear a certain animosity to Redvers, which in the circumstances some people would say was natural.

So I accepted. He could not stay with me now. He was on duty and the purser's office as I knew was at its busiest when we were in port.

That evening he took me out to Rose Bay. It was a delightful restaurant, each table candlelit with blue and gold candles: there was an orchestra which played romantic music and a violinist who came to our table and played especially for me.

Dick was doing everything possible to please me, and it would have been ungrateful not to appreciate this.

He apologized for his outburst on the previous occasion.

"I admit," he said, "that I am jealous of the Captain."

"Then," I said, "this is the first step to conquering this emotion which . . ."

"Yes. I know. It hurts me more than it hurts him."

"Do I sound so tutorial?"

"Charmingly so. And it is true, of course. I suppose it's a form of admiration. He's a first-class captain. And that is important. The Captain sets the pattern for the whole of the ship. It's a pity . . ." He hesitated and I urged him to go on.

"It's no good harking back, but it is a pity about The Secret Woman. That sort of thing sticks. There's not a member of the crew who doesn't know something about that shady incident, and very likely puts a certain construction on it. At least it makes them fear a man if they don't respect him."

"So the crew fears and does not respect the Captain."

"I didn't mean to put it so definite as that, but when an incident occurs like that, when a captain loses his ship in mysterious circumstances, he never escapes from the stigma. As I said to you before, if it had happened to anyone not connected with the Creditons, he would have lost his master's ticket. But we don't want to talk of that, do we. We have said all that can be said. What do you think of Sydney?"

"Interesting, beautiful beyond my expectations."

He nodded. "And what are you going to think of the Island?"

"That's something I can't say as yet surely?"

"Anna, I don't like leaving you there."

"It's kind of you to be so concerned. But why do you feel this anxiety?"

"Perhaps it's because of what happened there. The ship ... being blown up in the bay there."

"I thought we had decided not to discuss the incident."

"I'm not discussing the incident really. I'm thinking of the Island. It's uncanny. Suppose the Captain was not concerned? Suppose someone there put a curse on the ship?"

"Oh really, you do not believe that sort of thing do you?"

"Many people don't believe in ghosts in the bright daylight do they? But they change their minds when the darkness falls. How many scoffers would spend the night alone in a house reputed to be haunted? Well, I don't believe in curses and spells here in Sydney, here in this restaurant with you sitting opposite me and the violins playing Mendelssohn's *Song Without Words*. But on the Island it might be a different matter, and we are getting very near to the Island."

"Who would put a spell on a ship?"

"Perhaps it went back long ago. Perhaps it wasn't one of the islanders. There is a story about that ship. It was to be named *Lucky Lady* or something like that. I never heard what. But Lady Crediton named it ... somewhat unexpectedly. Imagine her feelings when she named that ship. She was thinking of that woman, the Captain's mother. She said 'I name this ship *The Secret Woman* and may God bless all who sail on her.' Suppose she did not say bless, but curse. Suppose she was the one who laid the curse on the ship?"

"You are talking like some old soothsayer. Not at all like the Purser of *The Serene Lady*."

"We all have our moments of superstition, Anna. Even you will have yours, if you have never had them already. Wait until she gets to the Island, until you feel the atmosphere of the place. We shall be coming back there after a while."

"Two months," I said.

"And then, Anna, I shall ask you again what I asked you before, for who knows what may happen in two months?"

Then we talked of other things; he told me of his ambitions. He wanted a home in England, somewhere to come back to in between voyages. He had seen the Queen's House. It was well-known in Langmouth. I realized it had become so after Aunt Charlotte's death.

I think he was picturing coming home to the Queen's House. He was trying to build up a picture for me to see. A life together—a life of serenity and perhaps happiness.

I let him talk. I hadn't the heart to say I could never marry him.

And that night as I slept in the ship lying still in the dock I dreamed of Aunt Charlotte. She came to my room in the Queen's House. I opened my eyes and saw her standing there, and her face was hazy and benevolent as it had rarely been in life; she was like a dream figure but the cluttered furniture of the room was lifelike.

"Don't be a fool," she said. "Take what you can get. Don't go stretching out for the impossible. And how is it possible, eh? Not without disaster. Not without tragedy. You were involved in sudden death once before, my girl."

Then in my dream I heard mocking laughter. It was Monique's.

My pounding heart awoke me and I lay thinking of the future, the Queen's House, and children, my children playing on the lawn. Then I slept again and strangely the dream continued. I went to the gate and there were two men standing there. And I was not sure which one I came in with.

A fantastic dream. Symbolic?

We were sailing at midday. The Glennings had come on board the previous day. They were staying for a few weeks in a hotel on Bondi Beach and asked me if I would like to bring Edward for a little outing. Edward, who was present, declared his desire to go so I accepted the invitation. They had always been very pleasant to me although I had had little to do with them.

They took us out driving and we went beyond the town and to where in the far distance we could see the hazy Blue Mountains. I was a little uneasy for I feared we should not be back on the ship in time, and I wondered what would happen if it sailed without us.

Gareth Glenning, understanding my anxiety, soothed me. "Don't worry, Miss Brett, we'll get back in good time."

"If you didn't," said Edward, his eyes round with horror, "would the Captain sail without us?"

"Ship's time waits for no one," I said. "But we've time."

"We are going to miss you all," said Claire. "So much. But we're seeing Mr. Crediton in Sydney."

"A pity you have to go on and leave us," added Gareth. "Still you have Nurse Loman with you."

"The Captain is sailing with us," said Edward proudly.

"Where the ship is he has to be," I added.

"We're getting near to the docks. I can see masts," said Edward. "Look."

"Nurse Loman is a very lively companion," went on Claire. "We are going to miss her very much."

"So will Uncle Rex," said Edward. "Everybody says so."

The Glennings smiled in rather an embarrassed way. I believed they were sorry for Chantel; and they had seen more of her in Rex's company than I had.

I said, changing the subject: "We shall find it much cooler when we're at sea again." But Claire brought the conversation back to Chantel. She must have had an adventurous career. She had nursed a Lady Henrock, they believed, before she came to my aunt.

"She has talked of her."

"A very unusual young woman."

Naturally they were impressed by Chantel. Anyone would be. She was far more interesting than I was. I had always known that. It occurred to me that the Glennings had brought me out to talk about her. I wondered whether they knew of a case and were hoping to engage her after ... I must stop being obsessed by the thought that Monique would not live long.

"We shall think of you on the Island," said Gareth. "We've heard quite a lot about it."

"From Mr. Crediton? I didn't know he'd ever been there."

"I don't believe he has," replied Gareth. "But it's talked of on the ship. There seems to be some ... bogey about it."

"Oh Gareth, you shouldn't say that," said Claire, mildly reproving. "Miss Brett is going to live there."

"Just a lot of talk," said Gareth.

"I've heard the rumors. In any case if we don't like it we can leave."

Now we were at the docks. It was half an hour before we sailed, not a lot of spare time because the gangways would be taken up within ten minutes. I took a last farewell of the Glennings, and Edward and I went to our cabin. He was chattering about cranes and cargoes. He wanted to see us leave the dock, so I took him on deck and we remained there while the last duties were performed. We waved to the people on the dockside and the band there played and Edward skipped about with excitement until he remembered that he was leaving Australia and that Johnny was somewhere in that vast continent; then he became a little thoughtful.

He said to me in a hushed whisper: "The Captain's guiding her, you know. He's up there telling them all what to do."

And that seemed to comfort him.

I wanted to see Chantel—I thought I must know how she was taking her parting from Rex and this would be the time to discover.

She was not in her cabin. So I went uneasily to mine.

I said to Edward: "Let's go for a walk on deck."

We walked, but there was no sign of Chantel.

I might have known, I thought. She's gone. They've run away together. That was why she was so calm. She's been planning this.

Edward did not know what a turmoil my thoughts were in. He was wondering what there would be for lunch.

I tried to answer his questions as though nothing had happened. I was thinking: I am going to that island alone. It was brought home to me afresh—although I had always been aware of it—how much I relied on her, her gaiety, her crazy outlook on life, her absence of sentimentality.

Of course, I thought, he would never let her go.

In a short time we should be right out into the Pacific sea and no longer see the comforting land.

And then the Island, the strange alien Island with its atmosphere of doom and curses, the Island about which everyone was warning me, without Chantel.

I left Edward in the cabin and went again to Chantel's. Its emptiness depressed me—more than that it frightened me.

I was not as bold or as strong as I believed myself to be. I should never have come on this journey but for Chantel. I went back to my cabin. Edward began to chatter about Johnny. He still wondered what he was having for his luncheon.

I couldn't settle. Half an hour had passed.

Soon luncheon would be served and it would be discovered that Chantel was missing.

Had she gone out and miscalculated the time? After all, it was what I had feared might happen to us. Oh no, I thought, Chantel would never do that. Chantel would never miscalculate.

But why hadn't she told me?

I couldn't rest. I went back to her cabin.

I threw open the door and walked in and as I did so I was caught in a firm grip and a hand was placed over my eyes. In that second I was terrified that something fearful was going to happen to me. It is amazing how many thoughts can come crowding into the mind in such a short time. I thought of Edward's being carried out onto the deck. I thought of myself overpowered, thrown into the sea. The easiest place to commit a murder would be at sea, Chantel had said. There would be so little difficulty in disposing of the body.

Then I heard a chuckle. I tore the hand from my eyes and swung round.

Chantel was laughing at me.

My joy and relief was obvious.

"Confess!" she said. "You thought I had deserted."

"Oh Chantel, why ever did you do this?"

"I was only teasing," she said.

"I've been . . . horrified."

"Flattering," she said complacently.

"But to give me such a fright."

"Poor Anna. You really are devoted to me, I believe."

I sat down in her armchair and looked up at her—lovely, laughing and mocking.

"I'm a little worried about you, Anna," she said. "You care for people so intensely."

I was recovering myself. "One either cares for people or one doesn't."

"There are degrees."

I knew what she meant. She was saying: Don't worry about me. I liked Rex but I knew it wouldn't come to marriage from the start. She was calm, judicial. I wished that I could be as philosophical.

"In fact," I said, "I was thinking of myself. My emotions were entirely selfish. The idea of being on the Island alone quite frightened me."

"That Island's a weird place by all accounts. Never mind. I'll be there, Anna. 'Whither thou goest, I shall go. Thy people shall be my people.' Has it ever occurred to you, Anna, that there are quotations to fit almost any situation?"

"I daresay that's true. Chantel, you are . . . not unhappy?"

"Why? Do I look so sad?"

"Sometimes I think you hide a great deal."

"I was under the impression that I spoke rashly without giving due thought to my utterances. At least that was your opinion of me."

"I was thinking of Rex."

"Rex is in Australia. We are on the high seas. Isn't it time we stopped thinking of him?"

"I can if you can."

"My dear, dear Anna." She put her arms round me suddenly and hugged me.

Now we were out on the wide Pacific. The sun beat down on the ship and the afternoons were too hot for us to do anything but lie stretched out on the decks. Even Edward was languid.

The atmosphere had changed. We had four new passengers who were going out to one of the Pacific ports but we saw little of them; there was not what Chantel called the "house party" feeling.

Even the crew had changed. They talked about Coralle in whispers, almost looking furtively over their shoulders as they did so. The island of mystery, where a captain—their captain—had lost his ship. It was almost as though they expected something fearful to happen there.

I saw more of Chantel than I had at any other time during the voyage. She was sorry for the fright she had given me.

"Sheer egoism," she commented. "I wanted you to know how necessary I was to your comfort."

"You didn't have to point that out," I told her.

"Worrying about my affairs," she scolded, "when your own are far more exciting."

I was silent, and she went on: "Monique has changed. She's, how shall I say . . . truculent. Soon she'll be on her home ground. She'll have allies."

"You sound as though we're going to war."

"It might be something like that. She hates the Captain often. Then she loves him. Typical of her nature of course. Unreasoning, thinking with her emotions rather than her brain, which is not thinking at all. The setting for high tragedy. Steamy heat. It will be steamy, won't it? Tropical nights. Stars, hundreds of them. The Southern Cross which always sounds so much more emotional than the Plow, don't you think? Great waving palms, banana trees and orange groves, and the sugar plantations. Just the right background for . . . drama."

"And who will be the actors in your drama?"

"Monique the central character with the Captain in male lead."

"He won't be there. He'll stay for three days and nights and then he will sail away for two months."

"How tiresome of him. Well there will be Mamma and the old nurse. There'll be you and myself. I shall just be a small part player."

"Oh stop it, Chantel. You're trying to be dramatic."

"I'm sure it would have been if he had been there. I

wish we could think of some way of detaining him. Blowing up his ship in the bay or something."

I shivered.

"Poor Anna, you take everything too seriously, me included. What would be the good of blowing up the ship? He would have to get back to Sydney, I don't doubt without delay and await instructions. No, blowing up the ship won't do."

"Even supposing you could do it."

"My dear Anna, haven't you learned yet that I am capable of anything?"

She was flippant, and her flippancy was as helpful as her sympathy had been at the time of Aunt Charlotte's death. But I was the one who should have been comforting her. After all she had lost a lover—for I am sure he was that—not because anything really separated them, but because he had not the courage to marry her.

I could not help being delighted that she was still with me, which was selfish of me. How much happier she would have been if she had eloped with Rex and was in Sydney with him now.

I was amazed and full of admiration for her ability to hide her unhappiness—for unhappy she must be.

She gave no sign of this. She flirted with Ivor Gregory; she kept up her assiduous care of Monique; and during the long drowsy afternoons she and I were often on deck together.

And in due course we came to the Island.

CORALLE

17

It was a deeply emotional moment when I stepped ashore on the island of Coralle. I shall never forget the impression of noise, color, and heat. There had been a heavy downpour of rain which lasted only a few minutes before the sun came out and set the steam rising from the earth. The heat seemed terrific and in my cream-colored blouse and navy blue skirt I felt suffocated.

I was aware of the scent of flowers; they were everywhere. Trees and bushes were covered with scarlet, mauve and white blossoms. There were a few houses near the water—huts rather, and they appeared to be made of mud and wattle and were on props so that they were a foot or so from the ground. Several of the inhabitants had come to see the ship. There were girls in long flower-patterned cotton dresses slit up to the knee on one side to show bare brown legs, who wore red, white or mauve flowers in their hair and necklaces of the garlands. There were men in light-colored trousers, torn and tattered mostly, and shirts as colorful as the women's dresses; some of the children wore almost nothing at all. They watched with big brown wondering eyes.

There was music coming from some of the houses, strange haunting music played on tinkling instruments.

The sand was golden and the moist green palms were very different from those dusty ones which we had seen in the East.

And as I stood there in that torrid heat I remembered that in a few days' time *Serene Lady* would sail away and I should be left here ... a prisoner until it returned. Here was a life of which I knew almost nothing. What was waiting for me I could not conjecture; but I fancied as I had when I first entered the Queen's House some premonition was warning me. Beware!

I looked at Chantel standing beside me on that golden shore and was thankful for her presence as I had been many times before, and for a few brief moments I allowed myself to imagine how I should have felt if she had deserted me at Sydney and I were now standing here without her. The thought of that raised my spirits. At least we should be together.

Monique had come ashore with us. She might have been expected to come with her husband but the Captain was not yet ready to leave the ship and naturally Monique was eager to see her mother. I was surprised that she had not come to meet the ship. There was no one but an old coachman who stood there in tattered trousers, open grimy shirt, grinning and saying: "So you come home, Missy Monique."

"Jacques!" she cried. "I'm here. And this is my little Edward—grown since you last saw him but still my baby."

Edward scowled and was about to protest at being called a baby but I gripped his shoulder and I suppose he too was feeling bewildered, for he was silent.

Jacques was studying us curiously and Monique said: "It's the nurse and Edward's governess."

Jacques said nothing; and at that moment a young girl came up and threw garlands of flowers about our necks. Nothing could have looked more incongruous than those red highly scented flowers on my plain tailored blouse and skirt. But Chantel looked charming in a mauve garland. She grimaced at me, and I wondered if she were feeling as apprehensive as I was.

"We shall have to get ourselves suitably attired," she whispered.

We climbed into the open carriage. There was just room for the four of us. I noticed that the woodwork of the carriage was scratched, the upholstery dusty and the two horses which drew it were thin and ungroomed.

"Soon home, Missy Monique," said Jacques.

"It can't be too soon for me," said Chantel, "and I'm sure I speak for Missy Monique. This heat is going to take a bit of getting used to."

Jacques whipped up the horses and we rattled along; children stood back to gaze at us with wide solemn eyes as we turned away from the sea and took an unmade road on either side of which glistening green foliage grew in abundance. Enormous blue butterflies flitted about us and a gorgeously colored dragonfly settled on the side of the carriage for a second or two.

Edward directed our attention to it with delight.

"You will have to be careful," said Monique with a certain gleeful malevolence. "Mosquitoes and other deadly insects will be thirsting for your fresh English blood."

" 'Fe, fi, fo, fum,' " cried Edward.

" 'I smell the blood of an Englishman.' "

"That's right," said Monique. "You see it's thick for a cold climate and therefore more tasty."

Edward studied his hand intently and Chantel said: "I shall be here to take care of all bites and stings. Remember I'm the nurse."

We had turned again and were now riding parallel with the sea. Before us was a sight of great beauty—the Island in its natural state, unlike the waterfront, which was spoiled by the little mud and wattle huts, and all that went with a not very affluent human habitation. Now we could see the curve of the bay, the coral reef, the luscious palms which grew close to the water; the pellucid sea clear blue, with here and there what looked like pools of peridot green.

"It's safe for bathing where the water's green," said Monique. "The sharks never go into green water, so they say. It's true is it not, Jacques?"

"That's true, Missy Monique," said Jacques.

"Sharks," cried Edward. "They bite off your legs and eat them. Why do they like legs?"

"I am sure they find arms equally delectable," said Chantel.

Edward was staring in fascination at the blue water. But I noticed that he moved closer to me. Did he feel this repulsion which was gradually creeping over me? I felt touched that it was to me he should instinctively move for comfort.

Monique had leaned forward, her eyes glistening. "Oh, you are going to find it very exciting here."

There was a note of hysteria in her voice. Chantel had noticed it. She took her arm and held her gently back in her seat—the efficient nurse, mindful of her duties even when trundling over an unmade road into what even she must believe might well be a very trying situation.

We turned up a path and went through a pair of wrought iron gates into a wilderness of growth through which there was a path so narrow that the branches scraped against the sides of the carriage as we rode. We rounded a bend and there was the house. It was long, of three stories, and made of some kind of stucco, but little of this was visible because the walls were covered with climbing plants. There was a porch and an open balcony on the lower floor, and balconies at several of the upper windows and where the stucco was visible it was dilapidated and breaking away.

There was a stretch of grass before it which might have been called a lawn if it had not been so overgrown. On it were two large trees which must have darkened the house considerably. But my attention was caught by the woman who was standing on the porch. She was fat as I imagined the natives of the island would be as they grew older. She was tall too and wearing the flower-patterned robe which seemed to be the island costume; her heavy black hair—turning gray—was skewered up on the top of her head by pins with enormous heads; around her neck were rows of beads made of cowrie shells; and her dangling earrings were made from these too.

She screamed: "Jacques! You've brought her, then. You've brought Missy Monique."

"I'm here, Suka," said Monique.

And she scrambled out of the carriage and threw herself into the arms of big Suka.

Chantel and I alighted and I helped Edward out.

"And here is my baby," said Monique.

Suka's enormous black eyes, slightly bloodshot, were on Edward. She had picked him up and cried: "My baby's baby."

"I'm not a baby," said Edward. "I've sailed the sea with Captain Stretton."

"There now," said Suka.

Chantel and I might not have existed, and as I saw a certain mischievous look in Monique's eyes I knew that this was how she intended it to be. She was the mistress here. We were the servants. I wondered what Chantel was thinking. I soon realized.

She said: "We should introduce ourselves. Miss Anna Brett and Nurse Loman."

"The governess and the nurse," said Monique.

Suka nodded and the great black eyes were turned on

us momentarily. Her expression implied that she did not think much of us.

"Come in to your *Maman*," said Suka to Monique. "She waits for you."

"Should we come?" asked Chantel sarcastically. "Or go by way of the back door."

"You should come," said Monique smirking.

As we stepped up onto the porch, I saw a creature like a lizard dart between the piles and it occurred to me that the houses were built a foot or so from the ground as a protection against insects.

We stepped into the hall. The difference in temperature was apparent. It must have fallen twenty degrees. In our present state we could only be glad of this. How dark it was. It was a second or so before my eyes grew accustomed to the gloom. At the one window the green shutters were closed—again I supposed to keep out unwelcome insects—but this was the reason for the dimness of the hall. There were mats in brilliant colors—native work I imagined—on a floor which at home it would have been thought necessary to polish. It was rough and some of the floorboards were broken.

At the far end of the hall was a bead curtain in place of a door and on a table was a bronze figure with an incredibly ugly face, naked but for a loin cloth and beside it a stick in bronze or copper. I gathered it was a dinner gong.

We were taken up a flight of stairs which were carpeted with a strip of red, leaving the side of the stairs bare. They had not been painted or polished for a long time I guessed, and the carpet was dusty.

We reached a landing and there was a door which Suka threw open.

"Missy Monique is here," she announced; and she went into the room.

Again we were faced with that gloom, but my eyes had grown accustomed to it. Edward was gripping my hand and I held his firmly.

It was a strange room, full of heavy furniture. There were brass ornaments, a small brass table, heavy chairs, and pictures on the wall. Here too the green shutters kept out the heat and the insects.

Seated in a chair was Madame de Laudé, Monique's mother.

"My dear Monique!" she said.

Monique ran to her and knelt at her feet burying her face in her lap. I realized that she was an invalid and that was presumably why she had not come to greet her daughter.

"*Maman* . . . I am here. At last I am home."

"And let me look at you, my little one. Ah, it is well you have come home. And Edward?"

She held out a thin hand with the blue veins standing out on it; it was adorned with rings and on her wrists were several bracelets.

Edward went forward uncertainly and was embraced in his turn.

"It is so long," she said. "So long."

She had raised her eyes and was looking at Chantel and me.

"You are the nurse and the governess. Which is which, please?"

"I am Nurse Loman," said Chantel. "This is Miss Anna Brett."

"I have heard that you have taken good care of my daughter and grandson. Welcome to Carrément House. I hope you will be happy here. You are a little fatigued. I will have mint tea sent to your rooms. It will refresh you and after I will see you both." She reached out and picked up a brass figure of a girl in a long robe which hid a bell. She moved it in a languid gesture and immediately a young woman arrived. She was not more than fifteen I imagined, but fifteen was mature on the Island. Her feet were bare and she wore the long colored gown, not very clean, which most of the women seemed to wear.

"Pero," she said, "take Nurse Loman and Miss Brett to their rooms and then make mint tea for them. I will see you later," she said to us. She smiled almost apologetically. "At first I wish to be with my daughter and grandson."

As we followed Pero, Edward ran after us and gripped my skirt.

"Edward will stay," said Madame de Laudé.

Edward was about to protest so I gave him a little push away from me.

"Come along, Edward," said Monique. "We want you to stay."

He obeyed but reluctantly.

Along the creaky corridor we went; up a flight of stairs with banisters beautifully carved but inlaid with dust.

Our rooms were on the same corridor, for which we were thankful. We both felt that we did not want to be far apart in this house. Mine was large with a wooden floor that looked as though it had been attacked by woodworm or some such pest. There were the inevitable shuttered windows—two in this case; the bed was covered with a brilliantly colored counterpane; the carved armchair, its seat upholstered with gold damask, was definitely Louis XV. There was a delightful console table—gilt rococo with a central carved motif. Its marble top rested on a frieze decorated with ivy leaves. It was enchanting—and genuine. The other chairs were crude, made of unpolished wood and looked as though they had been nailed together by some unskilled carpenter.

I wondered how anyone could have allowed the armchair and the console table to remain in this room with the rest of the furniture.

Chantel having inspected her room came back to mine.

"Well?" she said.

"It's very peculiar."

"I do so agree. Anna, what do you make of it? It's such an odd place. So this is her home! It looks to me as if it will fall about our heads one stormy night. What do you think of the house?"

"That a good spring clean would not come amiss."

"It hasn't had that for years. If it did it would probably fall apart. How are we going to endure two months in this place?"

"I can only face it because you're here," I shivered. "When I think that you might have left us at Sydney. At least that was what I thought when you didn't appear to have returned."

"I was on board all the time, so your fears were without foundation. But we're here now and we have to stay here for two months."

"Of course," I said, "we are passing judgment rather hastily."

"And that is not your way, I know. I am the impulsive

one." She went to the window and opened the shutter. Framed in the window was a view so lovely that it looked like a painting on the wall—deep blue sea, palm trees, golden sands, and the exquisite curve of the bay.

Chantel looked down at her hands; they were grimy where she had touched the window.

"Are there no servants here?" she said.

"We've seen Jacques and Pero."

"Not forgetting Nurse who came out to greet her Missy Monique on arrival."

"Jacques has his horses and carriage to care for. He probably does the garden."

Chantel snorted. "What I've seen doesn't exactly suggest he overworks in that direction. Unless he has such green fingers that everything he touches sprouts up several feet overnight."

"That's the sun and the humid climate, I daresay."

"Well, suppose he does work outside. There's still Pero in the house and what's that other creature doing all day when she has no Missy Monique to croon over."

"The climate would not be conducive to hard labor."

"I must say I agree with that. I feel quite limp."

"That mint tea should revive us if it ever comes."

It did come almost immediately. The girl brought it in very timidly on a metal tray on which flowers in red and Prussian blue had been rather crudely painted. The tea was in tall glasses in which were long spoons with stems shaped like a hoof. I recognized them as valuable. Aunt Charlotte had bought some like it and they were known as *Pied de Biche*.

What struck me afresh was the strange contrasts in the house. Valuable pieces of period furniture were side by side with things which were not only worthless but tasteless and crude.

"I hope this tea is to your liking," said Pero.

She was shy and young and gave covert glances at us—particularly at Chantel who was well worth looking at by any standards.

I thought we might learn something from the girl and I knew Chantel was thinking the same.

Chantel said to her: "You have been expecting us?"

"Yes," she said. She spoke rather halting English. "We know, we hear that the ship will be coming and bringing the two ladies ... one for Missy Monique; one for Master Edward."

"They don't mind our coming?" I asked. "I mean did they think there might be people here who could do what we are doing?"

The girl's face was solemn. "Oh, but the lady over the water ... she send you. You are hers. Madame is very poor. She cannot pay. But the lady over the water is very rich and Missy Monique will be rich because she is married to the Captain." She closed her mouth firmly and was clearly wondering whether she had said too much.

We sipped the tea. It was tepid; but the flavor of mint was refreshing.

We heard steps in the corridor and old Jacques appeared at the door. He looked severely at Pero who vanished, then he indicated the bags.

"Those are mine," I said. "Thank you."

He brought them in without a word and then took Chantel's to her room.

Chantel sat on my bed. I sat on the damask Louis XV chair—reverently I must admit—and we looked at each other.

"This is a strange household we've come to," said Chantel.

"Didn't you expect it to be?"

"Not quite so strange. They seem to resent us."

"The old nurse would, I suppose. After all you're looking after her darling Missy and I've got Edward. She would consider them hers."

"She looks as if she'll cast a spell over us at any minute."

"Perhaps she'll make wax images of us and stick in pins."

We laughed; we could joke while we were together, but we were both feeling the effect of this strange house.

Chantel went along to unpack and I did the same. I found water and a hip bath in a cupboard which was fitted with a basin and ewer. I washed and changed into a light linen dress and felt much better.

As I was doing my hair there was a light tap on the door. I opened it and there was Pero.

Madame de Laudé would like to see me, she told me. She would also like to see Nurse Loman. But not together. If I were ready she would take me down to her now, as Nurse Loman was not yet ready.

I hastily pinned up my hair and followed her downstairs. I sensed she was extremely in awe of her mistress.

Madame de Laudé said: "Pray sit down, Miss Brett. I'm afraid I dismissed you rather hastily. It is so long since I had seen my daughter and my grandchild. They are now with their old nurse so you need not concern yourself on Edward's account."

I inclined my head.

"This must be very strange to you, coming from England."

I admitted it was rather different.

"I have never been to England although I am English. My husband was French. I have lived in this house since my marriage. Before that I lived on the other side of the island. When my husband was alive we were rich, very rich by island standards, but he has been dead for twenty years, and I have become ill. You may wonder why I tell you this, for you have come here to teach Edward and you may think it is not your concern, but I think you should know how matters are here."

"It is kind of you to put me in the picture, as it were."

She inclined her head. "You are not employed by me. You know this. It is Lady Crediton who employs you."

"Yes, I did know that."

"I could not afford to employ you. Things have changed here. Once it was very different. Then we entertained, lavishly, people who came to the Island from France, from England. My husband was a great gentleman, and the sugar plantation flourished. But now that is gone and we are poor. We have to be very careful. We do not waste in this house. We can do nothing. We are very, very poor."

I thought this was a very strange way to talk to one in my position, but I realized that she was warning me that I must not expect much service. Doubtless I would have to wait on myself, clean my own room. I liked frank speaking and I asked if this was what she meant.

She smiled. It was. I was not in the least put out. I had intended to clean my room in any case and now I could do it without any fear of giving offense.

"It is a large house. There are thirty rooms. It is square

in shape, or it was when my husband first built it, but then he built on. That is why he called it Carrément. Square you see. Thirty rooms and only three servants. It is not enough. There is Jacques, Suka, and Pero. And Pero is young and not experienced, and island people are not energetic. It is the climate. Who can blame them? Oh, the climate! It is not good for much. It ruins the house. It breeds the insects. The weeds and bushes are everywhere. The climate, it is always the climate, they say. I have lived my life in it and I am used to it. But for some it is trying."

"I understand, Madame."

"I am glad. Now I must see Nurse Loman. Oh, we shall take our meals together. It's less trouble that way, and it's cheaper to prepare a dish for us all. Jacques and Suka cook and Pero waits. You know the household now. We eat at eight o'clock. The Captain will join us tonight. He will wish to spend as long as possible with his wife and son."

I wondered if she noticed my heightened color.

"And now," she said, "if Nurse Loman is ready I will see her."

I went to Chantel's room. There were one or two pieces of good furniture in her room, both French.

I said: "I have just had an illuminating interview with Madame. Your turn now. We have certainly come to a strange household."

13

Darkness came quickly on the island. There was no twilight. It was daylight, and then a moment or so later it was night.

At a quarter to eight Chantel came to my room. She had changed into a black lace dress which suited her coloring to perfection. She clicked her tongue when she saw me. I was wearing a black dress too.

"That won't do, Anna," she said. "I always hated that dress. To tell you the truth—it's drab."

"I'm not expecting to go down to a banquet."

Her eyes were dreamy. "Anna," she said, "the Captain is dining here tonight. Perhaps he will dine here tomorrow night, and then he'll go away. He'll remember you as you are tonight so don't let it be in that unbecoming old thing."

"Chantel, please . . ."

She laughed and started to unhook my dress.

"You seem to forget that he has a wife," I said.

"*She* won't let me forget it. The Captain must have a pleasant memory to take away with him."

"No, it would be better . . ."

"If you were to make yourself ugly? How unromantic you are!"

"Should one be romantic about someone else's husband?"

"One should always be romantic, and there is something very romantic about love that cannot be fulfilled."

"Chantel, please, don't joke about this."

"I'm not. If you only knew how much I want you to be happy. And you're going to be even if it is not with the Captain and it isn't going to be with the Captain, Anna."

Her eyes flashed and she looked like a prophetess. I said, "I wish you would stop talking about this."

"I'm going to talk about it," she said. "He's not for you. He's not good enough for you, Anna, as I've told you before. All the same I do think you should put on something pretty tonight." She had taken out a blue silk dress and held it up to her. "There. It's one of your best. Please, Anna."

I slipped out of the dress and put on the blue one. Whatever I said I wanted to look my best tonight.

I looked at myself in the mirror in the blue dress. With the color in my cheeks I was not unattractive, I decided.

Chantel was watching me intently and I said, to change the subject· "Pero brought these candles in. She said they never light them until it's impossible to see without them. Candles are very expensive on the island."

"Surely they can't be as poor as all that. I think our Madame has a mania for saving money. You look pretty now, Anna."

"It's this expensive candlelight. It hides the faults. Everyone knows it softens the features and brightens the eyes."

"I'm surprised that we are to eat at the family table—being only nurse and governess."

"It's cheaper if we eat together, she told me."

"She told me that too."

Chantel began to laugh.

"Oh, Anna, what sort of a madhouse have we come to?"

"We shall have to wait and see."

She went to the window and opened the shutter.

"Come here. You can see the ship."

There it lay in the bay, as *The Secret Woman* must have done.

"It gives you a feeling of security," I said.

"How will you feel, Anna, when it is no longer there?"

I shivered. "That," I said, "remains to be seen."

"Never mind, it's only for two months."

"Are you sure?"

She smiled at me. "I'm positive. I shall not stay here for longer."

"You've already made up your mind?"

"I just know it in my bones," she said. "I shall not stay here for more than two months."

"Prophetic!"

"If you like."

"I should not want to stay here alone."

" 'Whither thou goest I shall go.' And on that biblical note let's go down to dinner."

Chantel opened the door so that the light from the oil lamp in the corridor could show us the way. I closed the shutter and blew out the candles. The room looked eerie in darkness.

But through the shutters I could see the ship in the bay and I guessed that Redvers was below. I was glad he was here for our first night.

There was a candelabrum on the table which was strikingly beautiful. In spite of the strangeness of everything I noticed it immediately; a young goddess supported the *torchère* on which the candles stood. Priceless, I thought. And French like most of the valuables in the house. It was worthy to have stood on one of the tables in Versailles. The light from the candles threw flickering shadows round the room. We were a large party tonight. I wondered what it would be like when there were only four of us.

At the head of the table sat Madame de Laudé. Red was on her right; at the other end was Monique, breathing fairly easily; on *her* right was Ivor Gregory and her left Dick Callum; Chantel and I faced each other.

Pero and Jacques waited on us; I imagined Suka was in the kitchen.

There was fish which I could not identify; it was probably caught in the bay, a dish of beans and vegetables followed and after that delicious fresh pineapple. We drank a French red wine which although I was no connoisseur I guessed to be good.

Conversation ran smoothly. We talked of the voyage and of our fellow passengers. Every now and then I would be aware of Red's eyes upon me, and turning would find Dick Callum watching me too, while Chantel flirted daintily with Ivor Gregory. Monique talked a great deal, and her mother watched her indulgently I thought.

Madame de Laudé was very dignified and I believed that in the past she had entertained frequently. I could imagine this room filled with guests and all the lovely pieces of furniture like that magnificent candelabrum being used for these occasions.

"Do you think, Captain," she said, "that Nurse Loman and Miss Brett will be happy here?"

"I hope they will," he replied uncertainly.

"They will find it very different after England. It *is* very different, is it not?"

"It's a little warmer here," said Redvers lightly.

"I was very anxious for them to come when I knew that Lady Crediton had engaged them. I have heard how very useful they have been ... during the voyage. I hope they will want to stay."

"They have been very useful," said Monique. "Nurse Loman bullied me outrageously."

Chantel retorted, "Madame Laudé will know it was done for your own good."

Monique pouted. "She made me keep to my diet and sniff that beastly stuff."

"Doctor's orders," said Chantel. "Confirmed by Dr. Gregory here."

"I think, Madame," said Dr. Gregory, "that Mrs. Stretton was lucky to have so efficient a nurse to look after her."

"Nurse Loman looked after me, and Miss Brett looked after Edward. Edward was constantly seeking his Papa's company, and that meant that Miss Brett was too."

I heard myself say in an aloof voice, "It was only rarely that Edward was allowed on the bridge, naturally, and then he was most eager to learn everything possible."

Monique looked from me to Chantel. I believed that she was bent on mischief; I wondered what she had already told her mother.

"It seems to be the general impression that when there are passengers on board it's the Captain's duty to entertain them," said Red. "This, alas, is not so, for I am sure it would be very pleasant. The Captain's job is to navigate the ship. That's so, isn't it Callum?"

Dick Callum said indeed it was. And the ship's officers first care had to be the ship.

"But there is some social life?" asked Madame.

"There are occasions when we are free to mingle, but they are not as frequent as we could wish."

"So the Captain's wife is often left alone," said Monique. "It is sad, is it not?"

"And do you think the voyage has been beneficial to my daughter, Doctor?"

"I think it has," said Ivor Gregory.

"Before you leave the island you must have a word with our doctor here. He is very old . . . failing, alas. But the best we have. We will have a young man—one of our islanders—coming out soon. He is in England now at one of the hospitals in London where he is learning to qualify."

"I'll go along to see him tomorrow," said Ivor, "and give him Mrs. Stretton's dossier."

"Dossier!" cried Monique. "It sounds as if I am a prisoner who has done wrong."

There was polite laughter and Madame said the coffee would be served in the *salon*. Would we like to adjourn there?

The *salon* was a long room with French windows open-

ing onto a balcony. Through the french windows I could
see the unkempt lawn; there was a rocking chair on the
balcony, a table and two straw basket chairs. The shabby
parquet of the floor showed between the brilliantly colored
native-made mats. The table caught my eye immediately. I
thought it was a Georges Jacob. It was beautiful with an
ebony veneer and dentil ornament round the edges. I
could not resist running my fingers over that ebony sur-
face. There was dust on it. It seemed sacrilege to treat
such a piece so. There were a few chairs of a slightly
earlier period with spirally fluted legs; the brocade with
which they were upholstered was stained, but that could
easily be remedied; the beautiful framework and margue-
rite decorations proclaimed them to be valuable.

Pero had brought in the coffee and placed it on the
Jacob table. The cheap tray looked incongruous there, but
the coffeepot and cream jug, the sugar basin and tongs
were decidedly English Georgian.

Madame de Laudé sat on the brocade upholstery of
one of the chairs and asked how we liked our coffee. As
she poured graciously I kept thinking how different it must
have been in this house when her husband was alive. And
now she was battling with poverty, saving on candles when
she was surrounded by pieces of furniture which in aggre-
gate must be worth a small fortune.

The lamps had been lighted. There were only two of
them, one at each end of the room, and they were far
from adequate. The room was gloomy. I thought how I
would like to rearrange the furniture and what use I
would make of that lovely candelabrum in the dining
room. I would have others of the same period about the
room.

Monique was mischievous that night. She was talking
about Rex Crediton. Madame de Laudé was eager to
hear of him, for she betrayed a great desire for news of
all the Creditons. Was she hoping that through her marriage Monique was going to rescue her from penury?

"I should have liked to have met your half brother,
Captain," she said.

"His business took him to Sydney," Redvers explained.
"He's a very busy man."

"He was very busy during the voyage." Monique looked

at Chantel and laughed. "Now he will be busy courting Miss Derringham."

"A young lady he met on the ship?" asked Madame de Laudé.

"Oh no. She was in Australia. I think that was why he went out. They are very rich, the Derringhams. Are they as rich as the Creditons, Redvers?"

"As I am not a member of the Derringham company I don't see their balance sheets," said Red coolly.

"They have many ships, just like the Creditons. And Lady Crediton thinks it will be so good for them to link up ... in marriage."

"Lady Crediton is a very wise woman I know," said Madame de Laudé. "And when these two marry and there is a ... how do you say ...?"

"An amalgamation," said Dick.

"Then they will be very rich indeed."

Her eyes glistened. The thought of riches softened her. She talked of money as though she were speaking of a lover.

"It is very romantic," she said. "And romance is always charming."

"One could call it golden, in this case," said Dick, his lips curling slightly.

"He knew how to amuse himself during the voyage." Monique's eyes had come to rest with seeming innocence on Chantel, who sat very still. Poor Chantel! I felt sad for her.

"He is a man who likes to amuse himself?" asked Madame.

"What man does not?" asked Monique laughing in Redvers' direction.

"There is no sin in amusement, surely," said Redvers. "In fact it's more intelligent to be amused than bored, to be interested rather than indifferent. I can tell you, Madame, that my half brother is an extremely intelligent man. He has his wits about him, very necessary in his position."

"You are fond of him I know," said Madame de Laudé.

"My dear Madame, we were brought up together. We are brothers. We never bothered about the 'half.' We were in the nursery together. He is now a man of affairs.

There's very little about the Lady Line that Rex doesn't know."

"Oh yes, he knows a great deal about the Lady Line," said Monique laughing immoderately. Chantel watched her anxiously; she was always alert when Monique laughed too much. It could end in a struggle for her breath.

Chantel had risen. For a moment I thought she was going to betray her emotions which I was sure existed. I could not believe in her indifference to Rex.

She was looking at Dr. Gregory. "Should I give Mrs. Stretton ten drops of belladonna?"

"I should," said Ivor.

"I'll get it now."

"What for?" demanded Monique.

"You are getting breathless," said Chantel.

"Just a precaution," added the doctor.

"You are going to your room?" asked Madame de Laudé. "You will need to be lighted up." She picked up a figure from a small table and rang it. It was surprising what a noise it made.

Pero came running in, looking frightened. "Light Nurse to her room."

When the doctor and Chantel had left, Monique said: "I am treated like a child."

"My darling," said Madame, "they are concerned for you."

"You know it is better to ward off an attack than to deal with it when it comes," said Redvers.

"I don't believe I am going to have an attack. I don't believe it. It was to stop me because I was talking about him. She never thought he'd go to Sydney and marry Miss Derringham. She thought she was irresistible." She began to laugh.

Redvers said sternly, "Stop it. Don't say another word about matters of which you know nothing."

He had spoken in such an authoritative tone that we were all a little startled. It was as though a new man had stepped out from behind the mask of urbane charm. Monique sat back gripping the arms of her chair.

Dick Callum said: "I have already gathered that this has been a record year for coconuts, and we shall be taking a good cargo of copra back to Sydney."

It was the cue to turn the conversation; to try to restore normality, to change the sultry atmosphere to one of pleasant conviviality.

"Sugar is not in such a fortunate position." Madame shook her head mournfully. "But we are forgetting our duty. It is long since we entertained. You would like a brandy, a liqueur? I can promise you a very good cognac. My husband left a good wine cellar; and we don't have much opportunity to make use of it. Fortunately its contents don't deteriorate with age."

Chantel and the doctor returned, Chantel carrying a glass which she proffered to Monique who pouted and turned away.

"Come along," said Chantel, very much the efficient nurse, and Monique took the glass like a sulky child and drank the contents.

She sat back in her chair scowling. Her mother watched her anxiously. I saw Redvers looking at her, and on his face was an expression of hatred mingled with weary exasperation. It alarmed me.

After that the talk became desultory, with several conversations going on at the same time. Dick Callum, who was near me, said that we must see each other (by which he must have meant alone) before *The Serene Lady* sailed. I replied that I thought there would be no opportunity for this.

"You must make one," he said. "Please."

Chantel was discussing Monique's treatment with Ivor Gregory.

"I think the tincture of belladonna is a good substitute for nitrite of amyl," she was saying.

"It's effective, but as it's taken internally you must be more watchful. Make sure that she doesn't have more than the ten drops. During an attack the dose could be repeated ... say every two or three hours. Have you a supply?"

"Yes, for two months."

They talked earnestly of Monique's state, very much the professional nurse and doctor.

It was nearly midnight when Dick and the doctor returned to the ship. Redvers was staying at the house.

Pero was summoned to show Chantel and me to our bedrooms. She went before us carrying an oil lamp. I suppose it had been worked out that this was cheaper than lighting a candle.

They both came into my room and Pero lighted candles on my dressing table. I said goodnight and the door shut on me.

Sleep was elusive. I had carried one of the candles to my bed and when I was in blew it out. There was a moon so I was not in utter darkness. I lay and my eyes growing accustomed to the gloom I could see the objects in my room quite clearly. Faint light filtered through the shutters. One must keep them closed because of strange insects which flew in. I thought of Chantel who might well be lying sleepless along the corridor. It was a comforting thought.

I heard the creak of a board and was reminded of the Queen's House where boards had creaked in the quiet of the night without visible reason.

I went through all the events which had brought me here; and I realized that there had been a point in my life when it had been in my power to make a choice. I could have said: I will not come. I could have stayed in England. And then everything would have been different. I saw then that everything else which had happened to me—my life at the Queen's House, my relationship with Aunt Charlotte—had been unavoidable. And then had come the moment of decision, and I had chosen this path. The thought excited me, and at the same time alarmed me. I could say to myself, Whatever happens it was your own choice.

The sound of voices! Raised angry voices! Monique's and Red's. Somewhere in this house they were quarrelling. I got out of bed and stood listening. I went to the door and stood there for a while. Then I opened it. The voices were more audible although I could not hear what was being said. Monique's raised, passionate and angry; Red's low, placating? Authoritative? I thought of his expression as I had seen it earlier. Threatening? I wondered.

I stepped into the corridor and opened the door of Edward's room. The moonlight showed me his face for he had thrown back the sheet. He was asleep.

I shut the door and went and stood outside my own room.

The voices continued. And as I stood there a shiver ran through me; for at the end of the corridor something moved. Someone was standing there watching me.

I stared at the shape. I tried to speak but although I opened my mouth the words were not there.

The shape moved—large, bulky. It was Suka.

"You wanted something, Miss Brett?"

"N-no. I couldn't sleep. I went to see if Edward was all right."

"Edward will be all right." She spoke as though I had been impertinent to suggest otherwise.

"Goodnight," I said.

She nodded. I went back into my room and shut the door. I was still shaken from the shock of seeing her there and knowing that I had been watched when I had been unaware of it.

What was she doing there? Could it be that the door at which she was crouching had been that leading to the room which Monique and Redvers occupied? Had she been listening at their door, ready to run to the aid of her Missy Monique if she should be needed?

I went back to bed. How strange that I should be so cold in this humid heat. All the same I lay there for a long time shivering. It seemed like hours before I slept.

I was awakened the next morning by Pero who had brought breakfast to my room. It was mint tea, toast and butter with a very sweet preserve of which I did not know the origin, a piece of watermelon and two little sugar bananas.

"Very tired," said Pero with a smile. "You did not sleep well?"

"It's being in a strange bed."

She smiled; she looked young and innocent. It was amazing how differently one could feel in daylight. The room looked shabby but no longer eerie with the sun filtering through the shutters. Edward came in while I was eating. He sat on the bed and said gloomily: "I don't want to stay here, Miss Brett. I want to go sailing on with *The Serene Lady*. Do you think the Captain would take me?"

I shook my head.

He sighed. "That's a pity," he said. "I don't think I'm going to like it here. Are you?"

"Let's wait and see," I suggested.

"But the Captain is sailing tomorrow."

"He's coming back."

That comforted him as it comforted me.

Redvers had gone back to the ship to attend to business. Chantel was already with Monique who was not so well. Suka remained in the bedroom, staring at her, Chantel told me afterward, like a basilisk or the Medusa. "What she thought I was doing to her precious Missy, I don't know. I told her to go," she added. "But Missy said she was to stay and was going to have hysterics if she didn't so I had to put up with her."

Edward was a far less exacting charge. If he could not be with the Captain he wanted to be with me.

I said we would go and explore and asked Pero where we should have our lessons.

She pointed upward, very eager to please. There was the old schoolroom, she told me, where Missy Monique used to have her lessons. She would show me.

I took up the books I had brought with me and we went to a large room at the top of the house. The windows were not shuttered and there was a good view of the bay. I could see the ship lying there but I didn't point this out to Edward for I knew it would only upset him.

There was a big table with a wooden form beside it. Edward was amused by the form and sat astride on it, whipping an imaginary horse and shouting, "Gee up!" and "Whoa!" at intervals while I looked round. There was a bookcase in which there were one or two readers and textbooks. I opened the glass doors. I thought they might be of use to us.

While I was studying them Suka came in. Edward eyed her suspiciously. I guessed she had tried to play the nurse with him and he did not like it.

"So you are here already," she said. "You'd not waste time, Miss Brett."

"We haven't begun lessons yet. We're spying out the land."

"Spying out the land," sang out Edward. "Gee up!"

Suka smiled at him tenderly, but he did not see her.

When she went to sit on the form beside him he got up and started running round the room. "I'm *The Serene Lady*," he said. He gave piercing shrieks like a siren. "All present and correct, sir."

I laughed at him. Suka smiled—not at me but him; when she turned to me her eyes glittered and she made me shiver again as I had when I had seen her on the landing last night.

There was a rocking chair near the bookcase like the one I had noticed on the porch. She sat on it and started to rock to and fro. I found the squeak of the rockers—they needed oiling—irritating and her presence embarrassing. I wondered whether she was going to follow me round. I was determined that she should not remain while we were having our lessons. At the moment though I could not tell her to go: and as she said nothing and I found her silence unbearable I said: "We have a real schoolroom, I see."

"That is what you did not expect? You think we do not have schoolrooms on Coralle?"

"Of course I didn't think that! But this looks as if it has been used for generations."

"How could that be? There was no house here until Monsieur built it."

"And Mrs. Stretton was the only pupil?"

"Her name was Miss Barker."

"Whose?"

"The governess."

She rocked on her chair smiling to herself; she muttered something under her breath. It sounded uncomplimentary to Miss Barker.

"She came from England?" I asked.

She nodded. "There was a family that came here. He came to see whether he would stay altogether. There was a girl and a boy and they had a governess. And Monsieur he said that it was time Missy Monique had lessons. So the governess came here and she taught them in this room. Miss Monique and the little girl and little boy."

"That was pleasant company for her."

"They used to fight. The girl was jealous of her."

"That was a pity."

"The boy loved her. It was natural."

I felt dubious. I imagined Monique—a spoiled, willful and unpleasant child.

"And so the governess taught them all," I said. "It was convenient."

"Not for long. They went back. They did not like the island. Miss Barker stayed."

"What happened to her?"

Suka smiled. "She died," she said.

"How sad."

She nodded. "Oh, not at first. She taught Missy here and she loved her. She was not a good governess, not strict. She wanted Missy to love her."

"Indulgent," I said.

She rocked to and fro. "And she died. She is buried on the hill. We have a Christian cemetery."

Her great eyes roved over me and I thought she was measuring me for my coffin.

What an uncomfortable woman!

19

That afternoon there was great excitement on the shore. I was resting in my room because of the heat. Everyone in the house—and on the island—seemed to follow this habit. In any case it was too hot to do anything but lie behind shutters in the middle of the day.

I heard shouting, but I took little notice; and it was Chantel who came in to tell me what had happened.

"Our gallant Captain is the hero of the occasion," she said.

"What occasion?"

"While you were slumbering it's been a matter of life and death out there in the bay."

"The Captain . . ."

"Has been behaving with his usual eclat."

"Chantel, do be serious."

"He's saved Dick Callum's life."

"What . . . the Captain!"

"You look surprised. Surely you expect heroic deeds from him."

"Tell me what happened. Is he ... ?"

"Completely unconcerned by the adventure. He looks as though he saves lives every day."

"But you're not telling me what happened."

"How impatient you are! In brief, Dick Callum took a swim. He had been warned that the waters were shark infested, but he waved aside all warnings. He went in; the sharks were interested. Then he was overcome by cramp. He yelled. The Captain was at hand and 'accoutr·d as he was plunged in' (Shakespeare). He saved him. Snatched him from the very jaws of the murderous shark."

"He did that?"

"Of course he did. You wouldn't expect him to do otherwise."

"Where are they?"

"Dick is on board and Dr. Gregory is in attendance. He's suffering from shock and is being kept to his bed for a day or so. At the moment he's sleeping. Greg has given him an opium pill. It's what he needs."

I was smiling and she laughed.

"You look positively beatific. Ah, it is just as well he sails away tomorrow."

She was looking at me wistfully.

"Chantel," I said seriously, "you and I should never have come here."

"Speak for yourself," she mocked me. "And don't deceive yourself. You wouldn't have missed this for ... a flourishing antique business."

That evening was different from the previous one. Dick stayed on board in his bed; Monique kept to her room. Last night's outburst had had its effect on her and Chantel had been giving her the drops of belladonna as prescribed by the doctor, watching her carefully, she told me, because like most effective drugs it was highly dangerous if given to excess.

Dr. Gregory came to dinner; Redvers was there with Chantel, Madame and myself. It seemed a much more civilized occasion without Monique. Pero and Jacques

waited on us discreetly; Madame seemed more relaxed
and played the role of grande dame with dignity.

We had excellent wine from the cellar which her husband had left her; the food was simple. There was more
fish—the main dish this time served with a sauce which
contained mangoes. There was a soup which I believed
was mainly constituted of what had been left over from
yesterday's meal; we finished with passion fruit and sugar
bananas. After that we took coffee in the *salon*, as before.

The conversation was largely about the incident that
afternoon. Madame told stories of some adventures with
sharks; how a man had been walking along close to the
sea when one had nipped off his arm.

"They are very dangerous in these waters. You were
very brave, Captain, to venture when one was near."

"He wasn't very close. I had time to get Dick in."

"It will be a lesson to him," I said.

"He's a strong swimmer. He would have been safe
enough if he hadn't been suddenly attacked by cramp."

"A dreadful experience," said Chantel. "To be swimming strongly and suddenly to find oneself powerless."

"Poor Dick Callum!" said Red. "I've never known him
so shaken. He seemed ashamed of himself ... as if it
couldn't happen to any of us."

We talked of the Island then. Madame said she was
sorry the ship would not be there for the great celebration. It was the day of the year for the islanders, and
visitors always enjoyed it as much as the natives.

Chantel asked what happened during the celebration.

"Feasting and ritual dancing. You will be impressed by
the flame dancers, will they not, Captain?"

"They are very skilled," agreed Red. "They would need
to be to perform this very dangerous dance."

"That's what makes it effective, I suppose," said Chantel. "The danger."

"I suspect," said the doctor, "that they are wearing
some fireproof substance on their bodies. They could not
possibly use their flaming torches as they do without."

"Their skill lies in their speed," said Red.

Madame turned to us, explaining: "There is a family on
the island who have done this flame torch dance for
generations. They wish it to be known that they have the
protection of the old fire goddess. It is that which makes

everyone so eager to see them perform. They would not dream of telling anyone the secret."

"Does the old man still dance?" asked Red.

"No, it is the two sons now. They in their turn have sons to whom they are teaching the art. There's a legend which they make sure is kept going. Their ancestors came from the Fire Country and that is why they are on good terms with fire which will not harm them. That's the story. But as you say it is some substance they smear on their skin and their clothes I daresay; and of course their marvelous agility."

"Do they still live in that house along the coast?" asked Red.

"They would never move." Madame turned again to Chantel and me. "You will not see the house unless you explore thoroughly. It is hidden by trees. This family has lived there, so they tell us, since they came from the Fire Country. They have refused to accept new ideas which have come to the island. I think they would like to see the island go back to what it was a hundred, two hundred years ago."

"And where is this Fire Country?" asked Chantel.

"In their imagination?" I suggested.

"That is so."

"What is it supposed to be? A kind of sun?" said Chantel. "It could only be somewhere in the sky?"

"You are too analytical," said Red with a laugh. "Just accept it. These people are expert performers. It may be that they need their myth to enable them to do this highly inflammable act. If so, let them have it, I say. The dance is very good entertainment."

"You see," said Madame, once more addressing Chantel and me, "there is some entertainment on the Island."

The doctor went back to the ship at ten o'clock, and Chantel and I retired to our rooms.

I had not been in mine more than a few moments when I heard the sound of pebbles hitting the shutters. I opened them and looked out.

Redvers was below.

"I must see you," he said. "Can you come down here?"

I said I would shortly be with him.

I blew out my candles and went out into the corridor.

The oil lamp stood on a table, the wick turned low for reasons of economy. I found my way, rather uncertainly, down to the hall and went out onto the porch from where I saw Redvers standing in the shadow of the house.

"I had to speak to you," he said. "There won't be another opportunity. Let's walk away from the house."

He had taken my arm; I felt his hands burning my flesh as we went silently across the grass. There was not a breath of wind; it was a beautiful night and although the heat of the day still seemed to hang in the air, it was not stiflingly hot. The stars were brilliant; the Southern Cross— as remote as our own Plow—dominated the sky, fireflies flitted past and then I heard the drone of an unknown insect. There was a soft perpetual hum coming from the bushes.

"It's no good, Anna," he said. "I have to talk to you frankly. Tomorrow I shall leave you. I had to talk to you tonight."

"What is there to say?"

"What I have not yet said but what you must know. I love you, Anna."

"Please . . ." I began faintly.

But he went on: "I can't go on with this pretense. You must know this is different from anything that has happened before."

"It has come too late."

"That mustn't be."

"But it is. This is her home. She is in that house now. She is your wife."

"God help me, Anna, sometimes I hate her."

"No good can come of this. You must know that."

"You doubt me. You have heard scandal . . . gossip. And even now I am talking to you in a way which you believe to be wrong."

"I should go in."

"But you will stay a while. I've *got* to talk to you. Anna, when I come back, you will be here and . . ."

"Nothing will have changed," I said.

And I thought of Monique gasping for breath and of Chantel's saying: "She won't make old bones." I couldn't bear it. I didn't want such thoughts to come into my mind.

"There are times when she so maddens me that I . . ."

But I could not bear him to say it. I cried: "No . . .
no."

"But yes," he said. "Tonight is different. Tonight is like
that other night. The night at the Queen's House. I feel as
though we are alone in the world as I did then. I could
forget everything all around us. There were just the two
of us then, and now it is the same."

"But Aunt Charlotte came and showed us that it was an
illusion. Of what use are illusions? They are nothing but
dreams and we have to wake up and face reality."

"One day, Anna . . ."

"I don't want you to say this. I should never have come
here. I should have stayed in England. It would have been
the best way."

"I stayed away but I did not forget. I've been haunted
by you ever since that night in the Queen's House. Oh
God, how did I let this happen to me."

"You loved her once."

"I never did."

"You married her."

"I want to tell you how it happened."

"Don't. It does no good."

"But you must know. You must understand."

"I understand that you no longer love her."

"Sometimes I think she has become mad, Anna. Sometimes I think she always was."

"In her way she loves you."

He passed a hand over his brow.

"I hate her," he said. "I hate her for what she is, and I
hate her because she stands between you and me."

"I cannot bear it when you talk like this."

"Only tonight, Anna. I must tell you the truth tonight. I
want you to know how it happened. We had met, you and
I. You were a child and I was drawn to you then, but how
could I understand? It was only later when I came to the
Queen's House that I understood. Then I said, 'I must go
away. I must never see her again because this emotion
which is between us is something I have never known
before and I believe I should be unable to resist it.' I'm
not a hero, my darling. I want you. I want you more than
anything . . . to sail with you, to be with you every minute
of the day and night, never separated. We should be part
of each other. That's what I know. I knew it in the

Queen's House, but I know it a thousand times more certainly now. Anna, there is no one else for me in this world and there is no one for you. Do *you* know this?"

"I know that it is so with me," I said.

"My dearest Anna, you are so honest, so true, so different from anyone I have known before. When I come back, I shall take you home with me. That won't be the end. We shall be together, we must be together . . ."

"And Monique?"

"She will stay here. She belongs here on this evil island."

"You call it evil?"

"It has been so for me. There has been nothing but misfortune here. That night of the flame dance . . . it is like a nightmare. I dream of it often. The hot night, the brilliant stars, the moonlight. It's always the night of the full moon. The drums are going all day to call people to this side of the Island. You'll understand when you've seen it for yourself. I thought it was exciting. I was carried away by the excitement. I didn't recognize the evil then. It was not until the misfortunes came. Here I married. Here I lost my ship. Here I experienced the great disasters of my life. No, I shouldn't talk of this, but tonight is different. This is our night when we tell the truth and come out from behind conventional nothings to say what really matters: the truth. I must make you see it. I can't bear that you should not. I'm not making excuses. Everything that happened was my own fault. Imagine it. Those drums, the strangeness of everything, the feeling that everything in life is working up to some tremendous crescendo. We sat round in a great circle; we drank the native drink. It's called Gali and it's served in coconut shells which have been treated for the occasion. It's highly intoxicating. They call it Fire Water. The Flame Men brew it in that house of theirs. They are at the very heart of the festival. They don't want the European way of life thrust on the islanders. I think this is the purpose behind the feasting and dancing. I am trying to excuse myself, you see. The excitement, the intoxication . . . and Monique was there, one of them and yet not one of them. She joined in the dances. She was not ill then. I went back with her to Carrément . . . eventually."

"There is no need to tell me," I said.

"But I want you to understand. It was like a trap and I walked into it. We sailed away for a short trip the next day and when we came back two months later . . ."

"I understand. Marriage was inevitable. And that old nurse saw that it took place."

"Madame de Laudé, the old nurse, Monique herself . . . they were determined. I was still under the spell of the Island. I was a fool. Oh God, Anna, if you knew what a fool. I still am, because I am telling you this, I am showing myself to you in the worst possible light. These matters which an honorable man would keep to himself . . . Anna, you must go on loving me. It is only when I remind myself that you do that I can feel the slightest happiness. Sometimes when she is in one of her mad passions . . ."

"Please don't say it," I cried fearfully. "Don't even think it."

I was terribly afraid. He had called the Island evil. I could believe that some evil was hovering close to us now. I thought: I shall remember this garden with its thick foliage, hot humid air, the subdued hum of insects as I remembered that other garden on the other side of the world, damp, misty with the almost imperceptible odor of chrysanthemums and Michaelmas daisies and the damp earth.

A revelation had come to me. I loved him; I had known that for a long time, but I had loved him as the strong and conquering hero, now I knew him in his weakness, and because of that weakness I loved the more. It frightened me though, because he carried such a heavy burden of tragedy. Could there be any worse fate than to be married to a woman whom one loathed and to have been placed in those circumstances by one's own youthful folly? When a man such as Redvers, a man of deep strong passions, loved another woman, the situation was not only tragic: it was dangerous.

I was deeply aware of those passions—as yet held in check; and I thought of Monique, reckless, violent and maddened by jealousy. And even at such a time I could be struck by the incongruity of finding myself, plain homely Anna, in the center of such a whirlpool of passion. Was I as capable of folly as any of them?

He had gripped my hands and I was overcome with

tenderness and the need to protect him ... to protect us all, myself and Monique as well.

I heard myself say coolly, for I felt in that moment that I could be an impartial observer, "Let us consider this calmly. We are not the first man and woman to find ourselves in this situation. I often think that if that night at the Queen's House had happened *before* you went to the Island, everything might have been different for us. Time is so important in shaping our lives. I used to think that when I listened to all the clocks ticking away in the Queen's House."

And even now, I thought, I am talking for something to say. I am playing for time. I want to soothe him, to make him understand that we must not meet like this again.

He had drawn me closer to him and I said desperately: "No. We are being reckless. We must be careful."

"Anna, it will not always be so."

Somewhere in the distance I heard the call of a bird. It sounded like mocking laughter.

"I must go in," I said. "What if we were seen together?"

"Anna," he said, "don't go."

He held me fast. His lips were close to mine. And again came that mocking cry.

I knew in that instant that it was for me to decide the future; I must be the one to show restraint. Perhaps I should be grateful to Aunt Charlotte's rigorous upbringing and the scorn she had always poured on those who broke the moral laws. And it was as though she were there in the garden—not sour and scornful as she had often been, but lifeless as I had seen her lying in her coffin—dead; and the suspicion of murder was hanging over me.

This present situation was far more dangerous than that which had existed in the Queen's House; and yet there I had been suspected of murder. What would happen if one morning I awoke to the news that Monique was dead. What if there was a suspicion of murder? What if there was proof?

I felt that somewhere someone was warning me.

"I must go," I said, and released myself and started to walk rapidly away.

"Anna." I heard the poignant longing in his voice and I dared do nothing but hurry away.

I went into the house; and of course Suka was there. I
believed she had been watching from the balcony.

"You like the night air, Miss Brett?" she asked.

"It is pleasant after the heat of the day."

"Anna. Anna, my dearest . . ."

It was Red. He had stepped onto the porch before he
saw Suka.

"You too find the night air very pleasant after the heat
of the day, Captain?" said Suka.

He answered her coolly. "It is the only time to
walk comfortably." All sign of the passionate lover was
gone. With a hasty goodnight, I made my way to my
room.

There I sat in the armchair and put my hand over my
fast beating heart.

I was elated and fearful. I was loved . . . but dangerous-
ly. I was no adventuress who looked for danger. I wanted
to be serenely happy. But I had fallen in love with the
wrong man for that. How different it would have been if I
could have loved Dick Callum.

I thought of Suka. I wondered whether she would tell
Monique what she had seen. She hated me. I sensed her
hatred; and it would go deep.

It was no use going to bed. I should not sleep. The
candles guttered in their sticks. I wondered whether I
should be told I was burning too many candles. No matter
what violent passions circulated about the inhabitants of
this house, they must always be watchful of economy.

I would go to bed because then I could blow out the
candles. How incongruous, to think of this at such a time.
My life would flicker away like those candles. In frustra-
tion I should return to England, but not in *The Serene
Lady*. I might get a governess post with people who were
traveling back. After all Miss Barker—was that her
name?—had found a post on the Island.

I washed in the cold water which was kept in the ewer;
I plaited my hair and blew out the candles. I took one last
look at the ship in the bay.

This time tomorrow it would be gone.

The next morning I went down to the ship to see Dick
Callum as I had promised. Edward would have wanted to

accompany me had he known but he was with his mother and I left him with her. Cargoes of copra, watermelon and sugar bananas were being taken out to the ship; and there was a great deal of traffic to and fro. I was rowed out in one of the little boats and scrambled up the gangway which had been dropped from the deck into the sea.

Dick was waiting for me. He was up but he looked a little shaken, and I was not surprised.

His eyes lit up with pleasure when he saw me.

"I knew you'd come," he said, "but I was contemplating whether I should come ashore to see you."

"Congratulations!" I said.

"So you've heard?"

"I was horrified. You should have been more careful."

"It's a lesson. I'll not bathe recklessly in shark infested waters again."

"Then perhaps it was not in vain."

"It would have been the end of me but for Captain Stretton."

I couldn't help glowing with pride.

"It might have been the end of us both," he went on. "The speed with which he came at me and hauled me back was something to be seen."

"And how are you feeling now?"

"Still shaken and . . . ashamed."

"It might have happened to anyone."

"Let's sit down," he said. "I should really be on duty, but Gregory says I should relax till we sail. I want to talk to you, Anna. So it's a good opportunity. I'm going to miss you. I hope you'll miss me."

"I shall be desolate to look from my window and see that the ship is no longer in the bay."

"And I shall be thinking of you in that house, that strange house."

I was silent and he studied me closely. "It *is* a strange place. You've discovered that. Broken down, shabby, very uncomfortable I should imagine."

"I hardly expected it to be another Castle Crediton."

"You'll be homesick, won't you?"

"I don't know. Life had not been very happy at home. My aunt had died."

"Yes, I know. Anna, I'm trying to pluck up courage to

say something to you. I want to tell someone, and you are the most important person to me. I want you to know."

I turned to him. "Then tell me."

"You know I want to marry you, but it is not of that I'm trying to speak. First though I want you to know that I'll be waiting. You're going to have two months here. Perhaps at that time you will change your mind."

"About what?"

"Marriage."

"I don't understand."

"You may not be in love with me, but you do not dislike me."

"Of course I don't."

"And there may come a time when you say to yourself that a happy life can be built by two people who are determined to build it. Great passion is not always the rock on which to build the future. It changes; it's like shifting sands ... but mutual affection, good sense that's steady as a rock."

"I know."

"And perhaps one day ..."

"Who can say? One cannot look into the future."

"And now we are good friends."

"The best of friends."

"That is why I must tell you this."

"Please do, for I am sure it is something which is on your mind and you'll feel happier for talking."

"I hated the Captain."

"I know."

"You sensed it then?"

"You betrayed it. It was in the very way you talked of him. You were so ... vehement."

"And now he has saved my life. Because of the way I hated him I would rather anyone else had saved me."

"But it was the Captain."

"He is a brave man, Anna. A great romantic figure, eh? He has his faults but they are *romantic* faults, you think. He is the great adventurer, the buccaneer. I hated him because he had what I wanted most. Envy. That is what I felt for him. It's one of the seven deadly sins—I think the deadliest."

"Why did you envy him so much?"

"Because," he said, "I might so easily have had what is his."

"You mean you might have been a sea captain?"

"I mean I might have been brought up at the Castle; I might have shared my childhood with Rex; I might have been treated as a son of the house as the Captain has been."

"Are you telling me . . ."

"He is my half brother. I am three years older than he is. My mother was a seamstress who came to the Castle to work for Lady Crediton. She was very pretty and she caught Sir Edward's eye, as others had before her. When I was born Sir Edward gave my mother an allowance so that she did not have to visit the Castle. My education was taken care of and in due course I was given my training and joined the Company. But I was never acknowledged as Sir Edward's son, as the Captain was."

"Does the Captain know?"

"No. I shall tell him."

"I think he will understand your feelings. I am sure he will."

"They can't be the same from now on. You can't hate a man who has saved your life."

"I'm glad . . . for you and for him. You'll both be better without that senseless hatred."

"And don't forget, whatever happens in the next two months, I'll be back. How I wish that you were sailing with us! I don't like to think of you in that house."

"But it was solely to be with Edward that I came."

"Two months," he said, "is not very long, but a great deal can happen in that time."

"A great deal can happen in a day, as you've just discovered," I reminded him. "Not long ago you hated the Captain, now your admiration is greater than your dislike. Tell him so. I am sure he will understand."

"You think very highly of him, don't you?" he said wistfully.

I did not answer. I was afraid to speak of my feelings to anyone.

When I left him to come ashore Redvers was waiting for me at the gangway.

"There won't be another opportunity to speak to you alone, Anna," he said. "I've written to you."

He thrust a letter into my hand.

We stood close looking at each other but it was impossible to talk there. So I said: "Goodbye, Captain. A safe and happy voyage."

And then I started down the gangway.

I could not wait to read the letter. It was short, but his love for me was in every line. It was my first love letter.

My dearest Anna,

I should say I am sorry for last night but I'm not. I meant it ... every word. There is no happiness for me without you. I love you, Anna. Anna ... wait. I know it will not always be as it is now. Think of me as I will be thinking of you. I love you.

Redvers.

I should have destroyed it. I should have remembered that it came from one who was not free to write in that way to me, but instead I folded it and tucked it inside my bodice; and the feel of paper scratching my skin filled me with elation.

I was loved.

Chantel came to my room. She looked startled at the sight of me.

"Something's happened," she said. "You've grown beautiful."

"What nonsense."

She took me by the shoulders and dragged me to the mirror. She stood there holding me by the shoulders, and then she laughed and spun round. The letter had ridden up and was showing at the top of my blouse. She snatched it, laughing at me mischievously.

"Give it back to me, Chantel," I cried in panic. Even Chantel must not see that.

She allowed me to snatch it from her. She was smiling. Then she was suddenly grave.

"Oh, Anna," she said. "Take care."

That afternoon the ship sailed away.

Edward was in tears. We stood in the garden watching it for I had thought it unwise for him to go down to the beach.

I said: "We can see it as well from the garden."

So we stood watching. The tears fell slowly down his cheeks as he wept silently and this was far more moving than when he cried noisily.

He put his hand in mine and I pressed it firmly.

I whispered: "Two months is not very long. Then we shall be standing here watching it come back."

The thought cheered him a little.

"You can mark the days as they go by on your calendar," I told him. He had been given one last Christmas and always meticulously tore off each month as it passed. "You'll be surprised how quickly time can pass."

Monique came into the garden; her eyes were red and swollen. I thought: She really does love him. And the thought was like a death knell, but loving him or hating him she was bound to him.

She saw me standing there with Edward and she cried dramatically: "My baby! My baby! We are alone now!"

She held out her hand but Edward turned away and stared stonily in front of him. Suka had come out in the stealthy way she had.

"Come in, Missy," she said. "There's nothing to be gained by tears."

Monique immediately began to wail. She came over and took Edward's hand but he snatched it away and buried his face in my skirt, which was unlike him. He hated to behave like a baby.

"He doesn't want me," said Monique bitterly. "He'd rather have Miss Brett." She laughed hysterically. "And he's not the only one."

Suka put her arm about her.

"Come in, my pet Missy. Come in."

Monique's eyes were dilated, her cheeks suffused with blood.

I said, "I'll call Nurse Loman."

Suka looked at me scornfully and led Monique into the house.

The glance she cast in my direction was venomous.

How she hates me! I thought. Far more than Monique does. I believed it was true that Monique rather liked me because I gave her a reason for making scenes.

I was very uneasy.

20

Monique was ill a few days after the departure of the ship, and Chantel was constantly with her.

I told Edward that we would get down to our lessons without delay and that would help to pass the time. He was fascinated by geography and history, and I made a point of dealing with those places through which we had passed and which were more than marks on a map to him. He pored over the blue of the Pacific and found our island a black spot in the vast expanse of blue among other black spots. The names enchanted him; he went about saying them in a singsong voice: "Tongatapu, Nuku'alofa, the Friendly Isles. Kao: Fonuafoou." He was going to visit them all when he was a sailor. We had worked out the approximate time of the ship's return and he had painted red lines about the date. He had been amused by the phrase "a red letter day." This was going to be one. He had made certain of it by coloring it in red.

He did not like the house; he did not like the food. He liked best to be with me or with Chantel. His mother embarrassed him with her too ardent caresses, and he seemed relieved when she ignored him. He did not like Suka who tried so blatantly to win his affection, but Pero amused him and he liked to tease her; also he liked old Jacques and would climb in and out of the carriage and help groom the horses. He was a little in awe of his grandmother but at least he respected her.

He liked the Island, but I was afraid to allow him to swim for fear of sharks. And I was glad of Dick's adventure, since he had come safely through it, because in addition to its changing his attitude toward Redvers, I was able to assure Edward of the danger.

We walked a little, usually after the heat of the day. We would go down to the group of shops which were like huts and watch the girls in their long colored skirts making shell necklaces, bracelets and earrings. They sat under a thatch—"a house with no sides" Edward called it—and worked till it was dark; and they were there in the early morning. It was at midday and just before and after that the Island was deserted.

Along by the waterfront were the storing places for the copra and fruit which was to be shipped abroad and by which trade the islanders lived.

"It's not much like Langmouth," Edward commented. "And we're going home one day."

There were moments when I felt that we had slipped into a normal routine. There were others when the atmosphere of the house seemed unbearable. This would be at night when I lay in bed unable to sleep, thinking of *Serene Lady*, wondering where she was now and whether Redvers was lying in his cabin, thinking of me. Then I would take out his letter and read it. I could not find a safe place for it. There were no keys to the cupboards and drawers. So I put it in between my clothes and whenever I came back to my room after being away, I assured myself that it was still there.

Boards creaked uncomfortably by night. In the corridor the oil lamp was replaced by a rush light after midnight. I would hear Suka come along the corridor, flap flap in the raffia shoes she always wore—just a straw sole and a bar across and on the bar were colored strands of straw. They looked very untidy and hers had usually been worn too long. I would hear her pause, and I used to imagine that she came to my door and stood there and that if I leaped out of bed and opened the door I would catch her.

Why? It was pointless. But I could never be near her without feeling those great eyes on me . . . watching.

I used to look at Edward's red-lined date and I was sure that he did not long for that day with more intensity than I did, although I wondered what hope it could bring me beyond the joy of seeing Redvers again.

It would be easier, I told myself, when Chantel was less occupied, but she told me that she was afraid to move far away from Monique. The foolish creature was working herself into illness—which was very easily done with her complaint.

The Island doctor came. He was very old and only waiting for the new man to come out before he retired. He talked to Chantel but she told me that he was years

behind the times. And could you wonder? He had been on
the Island for the last thirty years.

About three days after the ship left Monique sent Edward to bring me to her; and as soon as I saw her I knew
she was in a dangerous mood.

She said slyly: "You must be lonely, Miss Brett."

"No," I replied cautiously.

"You'd miss the ship?"

I did not speak. "How strange!" she went on. "The two
of them liked you, didn't they? Dick Callum as well. You
don't look like a *femme fatale* ... I'd say Nurse Loman
was more that, and she didn't get Mr. Crediton, did she?"

I said, "Did you wish to talk of Edward's progress?"

That made her laugh. "Edward's progress! He doesn't
want me either. No. You are not content with the Captain. You want everything. You would not even leave me
Edward."

Edward looked alarmed and I said: "Edward, I think
we should be working on those maps."

Edward rose with alacrity, as eager to get away as I
was. But she began to scream at us. She was a frightening
sight. She changed suddenly; her eyes were wild, her face
scarlet; her hair had escaped from its restrictive ribbon
and as she threw herself about in a frenzy the words of
abuse fell out ... fortunately she was incoherent. I should
not have liked Edward to have known of what she was
accusing me.

Chantel came in. She signed to me to go and I hurried
away.

I said to myself: I shouldn't stay. It's an impossible
situation. I should get away before the ship returns. But
how?

I pictured the ship's coming in. How could I sail away
with Redvers and leave her there? Chantel had said definitely with a gleam of determination in her eyes that she
would not stay on the Island. When the ship came back
she would go with it. And I must go with her too.

But how could I? And where to? Could I sail back to
England with Redvers? I knew that would be madness.

I washed my hands and changed my dress. The doctor

came. Chantel had sent for him. It was a bad attack this time.

As I let down my hair and was combing it, my door slowly opened. I saw Suka in the looking glass, standing there. She looked murderous and I thought she had come to do me some harm.

How she hated me!

She said: "Miss Monique is very ill."

I nodded. We faced each other, she standing there, her hands hanging limply at her side, myself with my hair loose and the hairbrush in my hand.

Then she said quietly: "If she die ... you have killed her."

"That's nonsense," I said sharply.

She shrugged her shoulders and turned away. But I called her back:

"Listen," I said, "I will not allow you to say such things. She brought the attack on herself. I had nothing to do with it. And if I hear you say such a thing again I shall take action."

My firm and resolute voice for some reason seemed to frighten her for she recoiled and lowered her eyes.

I said: "Please go, and do not come into my room uninvited again."

She shut the door and I heard the raffia slippers shuffling along the corridor.

I looked at myself in the glass. There was color in my cheeks and my eyes were blazing. I certainly looked ready to go into battle. I looked again. Now that she had gone my expression had changed.

There was fear in my eyes. I had been accused of murder once before. It was strange that that should happen to me twice.

It was like some eerie pattern repeating itself.

There were shadows in the room but deeper shadows in the house.

Two months, I thought. But there were the long days and nights between.

All about me was a sense of doom.

I was afraid.

I dined alone with Madame. Chantel did not wish to

leave Monique and had had something sent up to her on a tray.

Madame was restrained.

She said: "It is hardly worth cooking for the two of us. So we will have a little cold collation."

The cold collation was the remains of the fish we had yesterday—always fish. It was caught by the local fisherman and was the cheapest food available, that and the fruits, some of which grew in the garden.

It did not concern me. I had little appetite.

The only thing that was lavish at her table was the wine. There must have been a good stock in the cellar.

The candelabrum which I had admired was on the table as a center decoration but the candles in it were not lighted. There was enough light from the oil lamp, Madame said.

Candles were expensive on the Island, I remembered; I was beginning to consider the cost of everything. One could not be in that house without doing so.

I tried to turn my thoughts from alarming conjectures and give my full attention to Madame de Laudé. How different she was from her daughter. Dignified, poised; her only eccentricity was this economy which was sometimes carried to absurdity. One of the ghosts which haunted this house was that of Poverty.

She smiled at me across the table.

"You are very calm, Miss Brett," she said. "I like that."

"I am glad I seem so," I replied. If she could have read my thoughts she would have changed her mind.

"I fear my daughter is very ill. She brings on these attacks to some extent herself."

"That's true, I'm afraid."

"It is why she needs a nurse in constant attendance."

She could not have a better, I said.

"Nurse Loman is efficient as well as being decorative."

I agreed wholeheartedly with that.

"You are very fond of her ... and she of you. It is pleasant to have friends."

"She has been very good indeed to me."

"And you to her perhaps?"

"No. I don't think I have had the opportunity of doing much for her. I should welcome it."

She smiled. "I am glad you are here. Edward needs you

and my daughter needs Nurse Loman. I wonder whether
you will stay . . ."

Her eyes were wistful.

"One can never look too far into the future," I said
evasively.

"You must find life so different from what you have
been used to."

"It is very different indeed."

"You find us . . . primitive here?"

"I did not expect a great metropolis."

"And you are homesick perhaps?"

I thought of the gorge and the houses on either side of it
and Castle Crediton dominating the scene; I thought of the
old cobbled streets of Langmouth and the new part of
the town which had expanded through the good graces
of Sir Edward Crediton who while he had engaged in his
sensual adventures had become a millionaire and brought
prosperity to everyone. Even the lady's maid had lived in
the house like a lady and the seamstress had been set up in
establishment of her own and her son had been brought
into the Company.

I felt a great longing to be there—to smell the cold
clean air coming from the sea, to watch the activity at the
docks, to see the sails of the cutters and the clippers side
by side with the new modern steamers like *Serene Lady*.

"I suppose one is always homesick for one's native land
when one is away from it."

She asked questions about Langmouth and it was not
long before she brought Castle Crediton into the conversation. She was avid for details and her admiration for Lady
Crediton was unbounded.

There was no point in sitting over our meal. We had
both eaten very little. I looked regretfully at the remains
of the fish and expected to see it the next day.

We went into the *salon* and Pero brought in the coffee.
It was clearly an evening for confidences.

"My daughter is a great anxiety to me," she said. "I was
hoping that when she lived in England she would change,
grow more restrained."

"I could not imagine her being so wherever she lived."

"But in the Castle . . . with Lady Crediton . . . and the
graciousness of everything . . ."

"The Castle," I said, "is indeed a Castle, although it was

built by Sir Edward. You would think it was of Norman origin and this of course means that it is vast. People could live in it without seeing each other for weeks. Lady Crediton kept to her own quarters. It was not like living in a family, you understand."

"But she invited my daughter. She wanted Edward to be brought up there."

"Yes, and I think she continues to want that. But Mrs. Stretton was ill and the doctor thought the English climate aggravated her disease. That was why they wanted her to come back here for a while. We shall see what effect it has on her."

"I liked to think of her there. Comfortable and secure. Here . . . As you see we are very poor."

I did not wish her to go on in this strain because her poverty was something which obsessed her and like all obsessions was boring to other people. Moreover I did not believe she was as poor as she professed to be. I looked round the room at the furniture I had noticed before. Since I had been in the house I was constantly finding pieces of interest.

I said to her: "But Madame de Laudé, you have many valuable articles here."

"Valuable?" she asked.

"The chair on which you are sitting is French eighteenth century. It would fetch a high price in the market."

"The market?"

"The antique market. I must explain to you. I am not a governess by profession. My aunt had an antique business and trained me to help her. I learned something of furniture, objets d'art, porcelain and so on. My aunt died and I was unable to continue the business. It was rather distressing and my friend Nurse Loman suggested that I needed a change and that I should take this post."

"That's interesting. Tell me about my furniture."

"Some of it is very valuable. The majority of it is French and the French were noted throughout the world for their artistry. No other country has ever produced more beautiful furniture. Now that chiffonier over there. I know it is a Riesener. I have already looked and discovered the cypher. You may think I am inquisitive, but I have a passionate interest in these things."

"Indeed not," she said. "I am glad of your interest. So pray go on."

"Its lines are so beautifully straight. Can you see it? The marquetry is exquisite and those short pedestal legs are perfect. It's an example of how effectively simplicity and grandeur can be combined. I have rarely seen such a piece outside museums."

"You mean it is worth . . . *money!*"

"Quite a sum, I should say."

"But who would buy it here?"

"Madame, dealers would come right across the world for such pieces as you have."

"You surprise me. I did not know."

"I thought you did not. The furniture should be cared for . . . examined. You must make sure that it is not attracting pests. It should be polished, kept free of dust. It should be examined from time to time. But I run on."

"No, no. Polish! It is not easily obtained here, and is very expensive."

Like candles, I thought, and I was exasperated.

"Madame," I said, "I am convinced that there is a small fortune in furniture and other rare pieces in this house."

"What can I do about it?"

"It could be made known that it existed. That chiffonier I was talking about. I remember an inquiry from a man we had. He wanted one and would have been content I believe with something less than a Riesener. He would have paid up to £300. We could not satisfy him. But if he had seen that . . ."

Her eyes glowed at the talk of money.

"My husband brought this furniture from France years ago."

"Yes, it's mostly French." I went on rapidly, because the thought of inspecting this furniture delighted me, and I would enjoy telling Madame that she was not so poor in worldly goods as she believed herself to be. "I could make an inventory of what is in the house. This could be sent to dealers in England. I am sure with . . . results."

"But I did not know. I did not realize." She was sober suddenly. "To make an inventory," she said, "that is a professional thing. You would need to be paid."

How the thought of having to pay for something worried her!

I said quickly, "I will do it for pleasure. It shall be my hobby while I am in this house. Madame, I should not ask payment. I will teach Edward something about antiques at the same time so I shall not be neglecting his studies. These pieces of furniture are allied to history."

"Miss Brett, you are a most unusual governess."

"By which you mean I am not a real one."

"I am sure you are more useful to Edward than what you call a real one would be."

I was excited. I talked about various pieces in the house. I thought: Those two months will pass quickly because I shall have so much to do.

"Have some more coffee, Miss Brett." A concession. Usually one had only one cup; and the rest was taken away and reheated for the next occasion.

I accepted. It was excellent coffee and I believe grown on the Island, not in large enough quantities to be exported, but very pleasant for the people of the Island.

She became confidential, telling me how the furniture had been brought over.

"My husband was of a good family, the younger son of a noble house. He came to the Island after he had fought a duel in which he killed a minor member of the French royal family. It was necessary for him to get out of the country quickly. His family sent out the furniture for him at a later date. He arrived here with some money and little else. I met him and we married, and then he started the sugar plantation which prospered. He had wines sent out from France and this house was very different then. I had lived on the Island all my life. I had never lived anywhere else. My mother was a native girl; my father a remittance man who was sent out from England because his family wished to be rid of him. He was charming and I think would have been clever, but he was lazy. He liked nothing better than to sit in the sun. I was his only daughter. We were poor. He wanted to spend everything, on the drink that is brewed locally. It is very potent. Gali. You will hear of it, I am sure. And when Armand came, we were married, and we lived here and we entertained and there were few richer than we were on the Island."

"There is a social life on the Island?"

"There was . . . and still is to some extent, but I cannot afford to entertain now and I would not accept invitations which I could not return. There is quite a colony of French, English, and some Dutch. Mostly they look after the industries and the shipping branches here. They go back after a while. Not many stay long."

She had given me a clearer picture of the Island than I had before. It was in fact a strange picture of the commercial and the uncultivated. Down by the waterfront there was activity in the mornings and late afternoons, and in parts of the Island among the thatched huts many lived in a primitive state.

"My husband was a good businessman," she said, "but fiery tempered. Monique takes after him in many ways, but not in her appearance. She looks like my mother. Sometimes she looks as though she is of pure Island blood. But she has inherited her father's impulsiveness and alas his physical state. He had consumption and nothing the doctor could do could help it. He grew more and more ill until he died. He was young. Only thirty-one. And then I had to sell the plantation, and very soon after we started to be poor. I do not know how I manage. It is only with the utmost care . . ."

An insect with glorious blue wings had come in and began to flutter about the lamp. She stared at it as it flew faster and faster in a mad frenzy.

"He will drop in time. He cannot resist the light. How did he get in? The shutters should keep him out."

He was like a glorious dragonfly, too beautiful to smash himself senselessly to death.

"Could I put it outside?" I asked.

"How will you catch him? You should be careful. Some of these fly-by-nights are dangerous. Their sting can make you very ill. Some are fatal."

I stared in fascination at the insect, which with a final gesture of abandon had flung itself against the shade of the lamp and fallen onto the table.

"Foolish creature," said Madame. "He mistook the lamp for the sun and killed himself in trying to reach it."

"There's a moral in it," I said lightly, and I was sorry because it had interrupted our interesting conversation, and we did not continue with it. Instead she asked me to tell her more about the pieces of furniture I had noticed

in the house, and we talked of that until I left her and
went to my room.

Monique was better the next day. Chantel told me that
the belladonna treatment seemed to suit her, but she
herself preferred the nitrite of amyl which she had in
England and which it had not been possible to get on
board.

"We have to remember that she's consumptive too.
She's a very sick woman, Anna. I always wonder whether
she might . . . do something to herself."

"What on earth do you mean?"

"Take an overdose."

"How could she?"

"Well, the drugs are here. There's opium, laudanum . . .
and belladonna."

"How . . . alarming."

"Don't worry. I keep my eyes on her."

"But she is not of suicidal tendency, is she?"

"She's mentioned it, but that's nothing. People who talk
of it rarely do. They like to frighten us, blackmail us into
giving them their own way. She's not the type. But she
talks about the Captain not wanting her and Edward too,
and that Suka woman encourages her. She's been worse
since she's been here."

"Chantel," I said, "if she did, it would be said . . ."

Chantel gripped me by the shoulders and shook me.
"Don't worry. I won't let it happen."

She could not comfort me. I said: "It's so odd. Sometimes I think of it at night. Aunt Charlotte's dying . . . I
can't believe that she took her own life."

"That bears out my theory. The people who do are
those you'd least expect. They don't talk of it. Our Monique likes to dramatize herself. She would never take her
own life."

"Suppose she did. There has been gossip . . ."

"About you and the Captain?" Chantel nodded agreement.

"It would be said that it was because of that. It might
even be said . . . Oh Chantel, it's terrifying. It would be
remembered that Aunt Charlotte died and that I was
suspected."

"You're working yourself up about something which is not going to happen. You're as bad as Monique."

"It *could* happen."

"It *won't* happen. I promise you. I'll watch her. I'll see that she never gets a chance."

"Oh Chantel, I never cease to be thankful that you're here."

She comforted me. I started to make my inventory which I found absorbing. I was certainly justified in my theory. There was a small fortune in furniture in this house, though I was appalled by the condition of some of it.

I called Pero and told her what she must do. Dust was dangerous, I insisted. Insects bred in it. There were termites. I had seen them in the garden—they marched in little armies, but they could be big armies. I imagined them marching over some of this valuable furniture. I knew that they would eat their way through it and leave nothing but a shell.

Pero said: "Polish is so expensive. Madame will never allow me to use it."

"Shortsighted folly," I said.

Poor Pero. She was nervous. I discovered that she wanted to go on working in Carrément House where she received a very small salary, but it was more than she could have got working on the sugar plantation or gutting the fish. She was not quick enough with her fingers to make the shell necklaces and earrings. She wanted to be kept on in the house, so she saved the candles and followed Madame's orders and scraped the plates clean after meals. No food was wasted; it could always be used up. She was a good servant, her one idea being to please.

Since my outburst Suka had seemed less truculent, but often I was aware of her watching me as I examined the furniture and added to my list. Once I looked up and saw her face at the window looking in at me; often I heard her raffia sandals padding away when I went quickly to the door. She seemed to have a new respect for me; perhaps she believed I was going to bring a fortune into the house. I could imagine the garbled stories which Pero and she and perhaps Jacques might contrive between them. The furniture was more grand than they had believed. I was going to sell it for them and the house would be rich again as it had been in the lifetime of Monsieur de Laudé. And the fact that I was to do this gave me new standing in their eyes.

I had seen them looking with awe at the most crude wooden candlestick and old basket chairs.

Pero polished a little now, using the polish very sparingly.

But it was more pleasant in the house and I began to feel more at ease. The days were passing and Monique became more subdued. I had asked Edward to spend a little time with her now and then and to remember that she was ill and that was why she wanted to be assured of his love some days and at others was too tired to see him. He accepted this as he calmly ticked off the days in his calendar and watched with satisfaction the gradual approach of that Red Letter Day.

He was with his mother one day when I slipped out on my own to walk along by the sea. I found pleasure in these solitary walks. The scenery was breathtakingly lovely and I was constantly discovering some new beauty. Making the inventory had had a soothing effect. I could lose myself in the task and forget the unpredictable future and the gloomy present by involving myself in the consideration of a settee or a cabinet which I was sure was the work of a certain artist but which lacked the sign of identification.

It was afternoon; the heat of the day was past, but it was too hot to walk under the sun. I wore a big hat which I had bought at one of the thatch-covered stalls near the waterfront; it was plaited and made of native straw and being wide-brimmed and light it was excellent for the climate.

I had walked a little inland seeking the shade of trees and had rounded the bay and come to a spot which I had not visited before. It was very lovely here. I could hear the pounding of the surf against the shore, and now and then the sudden buzz of a winged insect cruising past.

My attention was caught by a rock in the water, not very far from the sandy shore. It stood erect almost like a human form with blue clear water all about it. I was high on the cliff and I could see for a long way out to the curve of a new bay; there were evidently many bays on the Island. I had heard that it was thirty miles by six which meant that it was one of the larger islands of the group—one of the reasons, I suppose, why it had become inhabited and to some extent cultivated. Far out to sea I could make out in the distance what looked like other islands but which were probably pieces of volcanic rock which had been thrown up centuries before.

The cliff sloped down to a valley which was thickly wooded. The flowering trees were so colorful that I wanted to take a closer look at them; moreover the climb had made me very hot and I longed for the shade they would give me. I would rest a while there and perhaps gather some of those exotic blooms which never failed to enchant me. I kept them in my room in pots which Pero found for me.

I was soon under the shelter of the trees and took off my straw hat and fanned myself with it. Both Chantel and I had acquired cotton dresses of the same color pattern as those worn on the Island, but we had altered them a little to make them more suitable.

Among the trees a mud wall had been built. Strangely it wound its way in and out of the forest in a manner which struck me as being significant. But then I was always finding something unusual on the Island. There was a gap in the wall and I went through this. The trees grew thicker. I came to another wall, high this time. There was some enclosure in there and my curiosity was aroused. I walked round the wall until I came to a gate. I unlatched it and stepped into the enclosure. Inside the trees had been cleared and the grass carefully cut so that it looked like a newly mown lawn. In the center of this lawn was a stone figure. I went closer and saw that all round it were stones in various colors—mauve that looked like amethysts and a dark blue which could have been lapis and pale green agate; there were also big shells. These made a circle round the figure.

And suddenly I was conscious that there was some tribal significance to this and that I had strayed into a secret place.

I was overcome with dismay and I turned and ran from the place. I then began to wonder whether the copse itself was some private place and I had the horrible fear that I was trespassing. I tried to find my way out but I seemed to be farther and farther in the forest. I knew it was not large because I had seen it from the clifftop; but it seemed like a kind of maze from which I could not find my way. There were several paths which were considerably worn by use. I decided to keep to one of these and as I went on turning a bend I saw a house. It was a typical native house of mud and wood built on props with the roof of straw and branches. There was only one story of course but this was a long house and large by native standards.

I was becoming very hot, largely because I was so uneasy. I had the distinct feeling that I was trespassing in no ordinary way and that my presence here would be most unwelcome. The forbidding figure in the ring of stones and shells had made me feel that.

I turned and hurried back in the direction I had come. Every crackle in the undergrowth alarmed me. I had been warned of snakes and deadly insects but it was not them I feared. I was beginning to feel a mild panic.

I found my way back to the walled enclosure and tried to work out what path I had taken to reach it, but there were so many paths and they all seemed to lead in different directions. I tried several. I visualized myself trapped in this maze of trees; then suddenly I saw a glimpse of the sea and I made for it. The trees were thinning. I was free. My relief was intense—far more, I told myself, than the occasion warranted. I was ashamed of my near-panic which had been inspired by that stone encircled figure and the certainty that I was prying into something which was not meant for me to see.

I fanned myself vigorously. I was very hot—far more so than if I had stayed in the open.

It was getting late. I glanced at the watch pinned to my cotton dress. It always looked incongruous there, I thought, but it was certainly useful. Five o'clock. I had been in the enclosure over twenty-five minutes. It had seemed much longer.

I climbed the slope and as I reached the top I saw a familiar figure seated there looking out to sea.

It was Suka. I was certain in that moment that she had followed me.

"Suka," I said, I hoped sternly.

She turned her gaze on me.

"I see you, Miss Brett," she said.

"How long have you been here?"

She lifted her shoulders. "I have not this . . ." She touched her dress to indicate the spot where I wore my watch.

"I thought I was lost," I said.

"You have been where you should not."

"I'm afraid I was guilty of trespassing, but unwittingly."

She looked at me as though she did not understand, which she probably didn't. Chantel and I often had to simplify our language.

"You went into Ta'lui's land."

"Is that what it's called?"

"The land of the Flame Men."

"Oh, I've heard of them."

"They are very wise men."

I sat down beside her. I was exhausted with my panic, the heat and the climb.

"They dance through flame. Fire does not hurt them. They can do what none others can."

"I saw a figure . . . perhaps some sort of idol . . . surrounded by stones."

Her face was blank as though she had not heard me.

"They dance. You will see them dance. Fire does not harm them. They came from the Fire Country . . . years and years ago when there were no white people on Coralle."

"Where is the Fire Country?" I asked.

Again she ignored my remark. "Fire does not harm them as it does other men."

I could see that this was some native superstition.

"I shall look forward to seeing this flame dance."

"They are clever. They are wise." I had the impression that she was placating them in some way. "I will tell you something. When there was a fire . . . a big terrible fire . . . twenty houses were burning and the earth was blazing and no one could stop it, but the Flame Men did."

"That's interesting."

"They fight fire with more fire. They turn people out of their houses and they blow them up. They understand fire and flame. Up went the houses and then there was nothing for the fire to burn. It could not reach the gap between the houses when the fire had taken those in between away."

"I see," I said.

"So Ta'lui made a big explosion and the fire stopped. Fire will do as the Flame Men wish. They are very wise."

I sat beside her, thinking how close she was to the primitive and how so often there was a logical explanation to the miracles of wise men.

I gazed at the rock in the sea and Suka smiled and said: "You like it."

"I can't help looking at it. I haven't seen it before."

"Ka'kalota has been here since the world began."

"I daresay," I said. "Ka'kalota. That's a strange name."

That was a fatuous remark because all the Island names seemed strange to me.

"It means Woman of Secrets."

"Oh," I said sharply.

"There was a ship once," she said. "It was *The Secret Woman*. It disappeared one night. It blew up . . ."

"As the Flame Men blew up the houses?" I said.

"*Two* secret women in the bay might have been unlucky."

I was excited. Was this the answer? Had these strange Flame Men who evidently knew how to handle gunpowder gone out and blown up *The Secret Woman*? I wanted to know more.

I said: "Tell me about that night . . ."

"What night?"

"When the ship . . . disappeared."

"I do not know of it. It was there, and it was gone."

"But you said that she . . ." I nodded toward the figure, "would not have another secret woman in the bay. How could she have made the ship disappear?"

"I do not know. I am not wise."

"Perhaps the Flame Men have the answer," I said.

She was silent. Then she said: "She sees all . . ."

"What?"

She nodded her head toward the figure. "She watches us now."

"Really," I said comfortably.

"She watches me . . . you. She knows we sit here and talk of her."

"But that is a piece of rock."

Suka put her hand to her lips and shook her head vigorously.

"The spirit entered her fifteen years ago."

"Only fifteen. I thought she had been there for centuries."

"That spirit for fifteen years only. There were others before. She is impatient. She wants to depart. It is the spirit of Caro'ka."

"Oh?"

"She coveted another woman's husband and she went out gathering the herb that grows in the woods. She knew how to make it into the brew she wanted and she put it into the cup of her mistress. She murdered and then she was murdered too. We hanged her high on that tree down there facing Ka'kalota. And there we left her and in the morning when we cut her down her spirit was trapped in the rock and there it will stay until another takes its place."

"That's a strange legend!"

"It is the secret woman ... the woman who loves and covets in secret and plans in secret and goes and gathers the deadly herb and makes a brew in secret. There have always been such women ... they live all over the world. They covet another's husband and they kill, and when they kill they are discovered and hanged on the tree there ... near the statue and their souls are entrapped in stone until another takes their place."

I felt as though a cold wind had swept over me, but the sun was as hot as ever.

Had she followed me here to tell me this?

I stared ahead at the stone figure and as I looked it seemed to take on the distinct shape of a woman. It was always as though it stretched out arms to me ... to *me!* I coveted another woman's husband. It was foolish. I had panicked in the copse and it was so hot and the air so still and this woman beside me was an evil creature who hated me.

Was she trying to hypnotize me?

I should certainly not allow that.

I yawned. "How tired the heat makes me. I am not used to it. I think I will make my way back leisurely."

She nodded.

I rose and walked off. I felt an impulse to look round and see if she were following me, to take another look at that stone rock jutting out of the sea.

But the farther the distance I put between Suka and her woman of secrets the more I seemed in possession of my common sense.

Island legends! Was I going to be influenced by them?

21

I couldn't resist telling Chantel.

"The old ghoul was trying to frighten you."

"But I must say I felt very uneasy. It was straying into that place and then coming upon her sitting on the cliff like that. She looked like an avenging stone figure herself."

"That's what she intended. Would you like a nice little pill to calm you?"

"No thank you. I'm perfectly calm."

"As ever!" She smiled. "Or . . . almost ever. Anna, you're not yourself since we came here. You're allowing yourself to be bothered."

"It's this place. It's so strange."

"You were born in India. You ought to be able to adjust yourself. You can't expect the place to be run like an English town, can you?"

"Everything seems so strange here. There's a hidden barbarity."

"Without the conventions imposed by our dear Queen." She spoke ironically. "Don't fret, we shan't be here much longer."

"What of Monique when you are gone?"

She shrugged. "I was engaged to bring her out here. I gave no guarantee that I would stay. She could die tomorrow but on the other hand she may live for years. I do not want to waste my golden youth in this place I do assure you. So don't fret. You and I will be leaving here on the good ship *Serene Lady*, depend upon it."

"I believe you have some secret plan."

She hesitated. Then she said, "I feel it in my bones. Did

I ever tell you, Anna, that I have a very reliable set of bones?"

Talking with Chantel after Suka was like coming back to civilization and sanity.

She went on: "You do want to leave here, Anna?"

"I should feel quite desperate if I were left here. It would be like being shut away, imprisoned. Chantel, what will your patient be like when her husband goes away for a long time?"

"Murderous," said Chantel lightly.

"I might try to find a job in Sydney."

"Why? But I don't need to ask. You *are* deeply involved with your Captain, aren't you? And being you, Anna, you have come to the conclusion that the only decent thing to do is to get out of his life ... quickly."

I did not answer and she murmured: "Poor Anna! But you'll get over it. I promise you you will."

"I could put an advertisement in the papers."

"You're panicking, Anna."

"I think I am. It's that woman Suka and what she said about the stone figure. Suppose something happened. Suppose Monique died and ..."

I could not go on and Chantel said: "I wouldn't let it happen. Not the way you think it might. I wouldn't let it."

"You talk as though you are all powerful. That woman is threatening me in some way. And Monique hates me. What if she killed herself and made it appear that I ..."

"Anna! What a notion."

"It seems to me the sort of sick revenge she might take."

"I repeat I wouldn't let her."

"Don't forget I was suspected of committing murder once."

"And I got you out of that, didn't I?"

"Your evidence saved me. Chantel, sometimes I wondered."

"What?" she asked softly.

"Whether it was true."

"I told you it could have been true."

"But you said you had seen her on one occasion get out and look at the cabinet."

"It was the only way, Anna."

"So you didn't see her."

"I said so. It was possible that she might. I believe she did."

"But you said you were sure."

"I had to do it, Anna ... for you. We're friends, aren't we?"

"But ... you said what wasn't true."

"I'm sure it *was* true."

"I don't believe she killed herself."

"If she didn't, who did? Ellen perhaps. She desperately wanted her legacy and Mr. Orfey was wavering."

"I can't believe Ellen would ever kill anybody."

"There was Mrs. Morton. She was a mystery woman. What was that about having a daughter?"

"Do you think ... ?"

"It's no use worrying about something you'll never know, Anna. That's over. Don't let it worry you now."

"It's something one never forgets. I almost felt guilty. And it comes back to me now. I thought I'd forgotten it. I should have known I never should. But I thought I had. And now this place and Suka and her hints ..."

"You were an heiress then, little knowing that it was debts you were inheriting. And now you are in love with another woman's husband. Anna, what dramatic situations you get yourself into."

I was silent. Then I burst out: "I shouldn't have come. I'll have to get away. It's the only thing to do. I'm afraid of what will happen if I stay. I sometimes feel that there is a great threat growing bigger and bigger every day. It's getting nearer and nearer. And when you talk of her threatening to take her life ..."

She took me by the shoulders and shook me.

"Anna. Stop it, or I shall have to slap your face. The treatment for hysteria. I never thought I should have to give it to you. That foolish old Suka has got on your nerves. She's a silly old woman. Take no notice of her. Listen to me. When *Serene Lady* comes in we are leaving on her, you and I. You've nothing to fear. I'll see that Monique behaves well till then. It's less than five more weeks. Half our stay has gone. We are going to Sydney, the pair of us. You will be with me. I will take care of you. I

will make you my companion and I'll find a rich husband
for you and you'll forget all about your Captain."

"You . . . Chantel. And how?"

"Fairy Godmother. I shall turn the pumpkin into a
coach and hey presto Prince Charming will appear."

"It's nonsense!" I said.

"Listen Anna, get the Captain out of your mind. But
for him you'd be enjoying this adventure now. You'd have
nothing to worry about. It's only because of this absurd
passion. What is it? He came to the Queen's House. You
were lonely. Aunt Charlotte was maddening and he
seemed romantic. You endowed him with qualities he
doesn't possess. You're living in a dream. He's not the
Captain of Romance you imagine him to be."

"What do you know of him?"

"I know that he came to you in the beginning and he
did not tell you that he had a wife. He led you to expect . . ."

"He led me to expect nothing."

"You defend him. He's weak and selfish and wants a
good time. He is tired of his wife and fancies a romance
with you. Don't you see that even if he were free and you
married him he would soon be tired of you?"

I was shattered. I had never heard her talk like that
before.

She said: "He's not good enough for you, Anna. I
know. Listen, in time you'll forget. It's because you have
seen little of the world. I know it is true. In time I'm
going to make you see this."

"I don't know what you're talking about. It's the most
utter nonsense in any case. How are you going to defend
me? By chance we are together now, but we both have to
earn our livings, don't we? If we left here it's hardly likely
that we would find positions together again."

She laughed.

I cried angrily because I almost hated her for the
manner in which she had spoken of Redvers. "You talk as
though you're some Oracle . . . some all powerful goddess."

Again she laughed and she turned on me, her eyes
blazing. "I'll tell you something, Anna, something that will
startle you. I am not the poor little nurse you think me. I

am rich because I have a rich husband. I didn't mean to tell you yet but you've goaded me into it. I married Rex before we left England."

"You ... married ... Rex."

"I married him."

"Secretly!"

"Certainly secretly. We have to placate my obstinate old mother-in-law. We have to make her see what an excellent match her son has made."

"But you never said so."

"It had to be a secret, for obvious reasons. We married on the spur of the moment when we knew Rex was going to Australia. That was why I came out, and I couldn't leave you behind, could I? Everything worked out to suit us, and that's the way it is going to be in future. Oh Anna, my *dearest* Anna, you are to me as a sister. I always wanted a sister."

"You had sisters."

She grimaced. "We weren't in tune. You are the sister I want. You have nothing to be afraid of. When *Serene Lady* comes here I shall go to Sydney and you with me. Rex is there. From Sydney we shall write to tell Lady Crediton that we are married and in time she'll see reason."

"And Helena Derringham?"

"She hadn't a chance once he'd seen me."

She began to laugh. "There, you're a witch, Anna. You've got the secret out of me. I didn't intend to tell you yet. You're so confoundedly analytical. You'll want to know details of this and that. But I had to comfort you, didn't I? It seems to be my mission in life. Comforting you!"

I was completely and utterly bewildered.

I imagined that no sooner had Chantel told me her secret than she regretted it. I must not whisper a word to anyone, she told me. It was our secret and she knew she could trust me.

Of course she could trust me, I retorted.

"We trust each other, Anna," she said.

"Do we?" I asked.

"You're thinking that I kept this from you. Only because I had to."

"In your journal you gave no indication."

"How could I, when it had to be an absolute secret."

"But I thought we were to be absolutely truthful to each other."

"So we were, but this was something I dared not tell. I had sworn to Rex. You understand, Anna?"

I said I did but I was disturbed. There was something else. It was the first time she had admitted that she had fabricated the story of Aunt Charlotte's being able to walk when impelled by some great desire. It was the very pivot on which the evidence against me had been quashed.

It seemed that I owed her even more than I had believed. And although I knew that she had done it for my sake I was uneasy because she had done it.

I tried to comfort myself. I was getting on with my inventory, and I was watching the calendar as closely as Edward was. I was wondering what was really going to happen when *Serene Lady* arrived. Chantel was going to join Rex in Sydney; they were going to openly announce their marriage; they were going to write to Lady Crediton. And Chantel would be the future mistress of Castle Crediton.

I thought of her and Rex and why I had not seen his complete absorption in her. They were married; it was for this reason that he could leave her knowing that he would not lose her by doing so. I wondered what Helena Derringham was thinking and if he had confessed to her as Chantel had to me.

I tried to be with her as much as possible. I never went near Monique's rooms if I could help it. I was always afraid that she would be reminded of her grievance against me and start a scene.

So I asked Chantel to come to my room, which she did often. She would lie on my bed while I sat in the armchair and she would laugh at me and what she called my simplicity which, she hastened to explain, was what she liked.

"How could you bear to be parted all this time from your husband?" I asked.

"Only because there is a fortune at stake. My stern old

mother-in-law needs to be wooed. Don't forget she had chosen Helena Derringham as her daughter-in-law and she hates to be thwarted."

"And how are you going to pacify her?"

"Rex will do well in Sydney. He will show her that we don't need the Derringhams. We can do very well without them."

"He must hate being separated from you. I wonder he agreed to it."

"He didn't. He wanted to tell her right away and take the consequences. But I said no. We must not be foolish."

"And he . . . obeyed you?"

"Of course."

"Isn't that rather . . . weak?"

"Of course," she repeated.

"I should have thought you would have loved a strong man."

"That is where you think along conventional lines, my dear Anna. I could only love a weak man, because I am strong enough for one family."

I laughed at her. "You always amuse me," I said. "But I can't help thinking of your journal. You didn't tell the truth."

She lifted a hand. "I swear I told the truth and nothing but the truth. You note the omission. The whole truth. Truth is not a straight line. It's an enormous globe with hundreds of facets. One of these contained my marriage to Rex. You didn't see it because it was turned the other way."

"I can't believe it, Chantel."

"My marriage? Why not?"

"You'll be the mistress of Castle Crediton."

"I always wanted to be."

"Was that why . . . ?"

"Now you are becoming too inquisitive. I'm very satisfied with my husband. When I return to Sydney I shall go to him and we shall write to his Mamma and tell her what has happened. She will be shocked, horrified, and then she will realize that she must be resigned and in a very short time she will be admitting to herself if to no one else that Rex has made the perfect match after all. Imagine me, Anna, seated at the head of the table in black velvet—or perhaps green velvet would be more becoming—sparkling with diamonds. Lady Crediton, for of course he will have his title in due course."

"So you have decided on that too?"

"I have. And he'll be a baron. None of your knights. I want my son to be the second baron. I shall learn about the business too, just as my dear Mamma-in-law did. And Anna, my dear Anna, there will always be a home for you at the Castle if you need it."

"Thank you."

"And my first duty will be to get you married. I shall give balls for you. You shall be known as my sister. Don't be afraid that I shall make a poor relation of you. I shall want to make up to you for everything ..."

She stopped and smiled at me.

I said: "You are an adventuress, Chantel."

"What's wrong with adventure? Sir Francis Drake, Christopher Columbus, they were adventurers and the world applauded them. Why shouldn't I set out on my own voyage of discovery?"

"You never think that you could possibly fail?"

"Never," she cried vehemently.

I was glad for her, and I laughed at myself for worrying about her loss of Rex. She was right. I was a simpleton. And she was right when she said that she achieved what she set out to do.

There was one thing I noticed in her conversation though; she always talked as though Redvers did not exist. She was determined to take me out of his reach. Dear Chantel! Her concern for me—while she planned such glorious adventures for herself—was touching.

It was late afternoon. I had been out for a short walk and had come back to my room to wash before dinner. As soon as I entered the room I had the odd feeling that everything was not as I had left it. Someone had been here. I dusted it myself so there was no need for Pero to come in. What was it? The cushion which had been on the Louis XV chair was now on one of the crude wooden chairs. I had not left it there. I was certain of that because

I was always conscious of that chair. So someone had moved it.

It was not important. Pero could have come in, disturbed the cushion and put it back in the wrong place. All these thoughts were passing through my mind as I went to the drawer and, in accordance with my usual custom, felt for Redvers' letter.

It was not there.

So someone had been in my room! They had disturbed my things. I could tell that because the drawer in which the letter had been was not quite as I had left it. Someone had been in here spying and had found Redvers' letter.

There could never have been such a revealing letter. I knew it word for word. It was engraved on my memory and would stay so forever.

I went cold at the thought of anyone's reading that letter.

I went through everything, frantically searching. But I knew it was gone.

I thought of Monique's reading it. I imagined Suka creeping into my room, searching through my things, taking the letter to her mistress.

What damning evidence! I should have destroyed it.

There was a knock at my door and Chantel came in.

"I thought I heard you come back. Why ... what's wrong?"

"I've ... I've lost something."

"What?"

I was silent.

"For goodness sake, Anna," she said sharply, "pull yourself together. What have you lost?"

"A letter," I told her. "Redvers wrote a letter before he left. It was in this drawer."

"A *love* letter?" she asked.

I nodded.

"Good God, Anna," she said. "What a fool you are. You should have destroyed it."

"I know, but one doesn't destroy such things."

"He had no right to send it."

"Please, Chantel, let me manage my own affairs."

"You don't seem to be able to," she said angrily. Even she was shaken. "If *she* has it ... then there'll be trouble."

"I believe Suka has stolen it. She'll give it to Monique. And she will think . . ."

"She may not give it to her."

"For what other purpose would she take it?"

"How can we know what goes on in that mind of hers? She's an old witch. Oh Anna, I *wish* this hadn't happened." She bit her lip. "I'll find out if she has it. And if I find it, Anna, I'm going to tear it up. I'm going to burn it and see the end of it with my own eyes."

"What shall I do, Chantel?"

"Nothing. We'll just have to wait. Are you sure you've searched everywhere?"

"Everywhere."

"I wish," she said, "that we were out of this place. I wish I had you safe in Sydney. For Heaven's sake don't give any sign that you're uneasy. It may be that Suka couldn't read it. I'm sure she can't read. If she hasn't yet given it to Monique, we must get it and destroy it before she does."

I felt limp with apprehension; but the fact that Chantel knew was of some small comfort.

That night Monique had a very bad attack and I was certain that she had seen the letter.

I felt sick with anxiety, wondering what would happen next.

I lay in my bed sleepless and it was midnight when the door softly opened and Chantel came in; she was wearing a long white nightdress, her hair loose about her shoulders, a lighted candle in her hand.

"Not asleep?" she said. "Monique's quiet now."

"How is she?"

"She'll recover."

"Did she . . . ?"

"See the letter. No. It was nothing to do with that. She worked herself up to a fury because she said Edward never wanted to be with her. She shouted that nobody wanted her and that the sooner she was out of the way the better pleased some people would be."

"It's terrifying, Chantel."

"It's typical. She talked about you, too. She said you usurped her place and when the Captain returned she would not be here because she planned to kill herself."

"She said that again?"

"She'll say it again and again and again, you'll see. It's becoming a parrot cry. Don't take it to heart."

"And when she sees that letter . . ."

"Clearly Suka has it."

"Why should she keep it?"

"Perhaps she thinks it some sort of spell. We have to stop her showing it to Monique. If she did show it all hell would be let loose. I suppose it's no use my telling you to sleep."

"I'm afraid it's not."

"Well, remember this. In a few weeks we shall be in Sydney. It's not long now, Anna."

And that was my comfort.

22

All through the day I could hear the sound of distant drums. They unnerved me. They seemed to me as though they heralded some fearful climax. It was a week since I had lost the letter and Monique had given no sign that she had seen it. Chantel said that she had searched her room and it was not there. Suka must have it—that was unless I had put it somewhere else.

I was indignant. As if I would.

"Of course not," said Chantel, faintly mocking. "You'd think it too precious."

But she was worried as always by my relationship with Redvers.

And now the great feast day was with us. There was an air of tension throughout the house—indeed throughout the Island. People were already converging from all sides and as soon as it was sunset the great celebration would begin. In each native house great vats of Gali had been stored and these would be brought out when the feasting started.

Carts, the sides of which were decorated with branches of leaves, had been trundling up to that cliff where I had come upon Suka sitting staring at the rock in the water. This was where the feast would take place and the dances performed.

Madame had explained it all to me. We should not join in until after the feast which was for islanders only. We would go later and we would drink Gali from coconut shells and she advised us to drink sparingly as it was very potent. We should find the dances interesting she was sure, and in particular the flame dance which was the great event of the evening.

"It is really well worth seeing," she said. "It's a tradition. The secret is passed down from generation to generation."

"I have heard of these Flame Men," I said.

"It's one of the sights of the Island. They will perform it only once a year. I suppose they think it would lose its importance if it were done too frequently."

"Do the drums go on all day?" I asked.

"All day and all night."

I shivered involuntarily.

"You do not like them?"

"I don't know what it is. There's something ominous about them."

"Don't let them hear you say that. They say it is only the guilty who fear the beat of the drums."

"They say that."

"My dear Miss Brett, they say many strange things."

Guilty, I thought. Guilty of loving another woman's husband. Every morning when I awoke I wondered what the day would hold for me. By night I dreamed often of Aunt Charlotte. I could not have been more haunted by Aunt Charlotte's death if I had been guilty of killing her.

And I asked myself, if I stayed with Chantel, how could I avoid meeting Redvers? It was strange how Chantel refused to consider this and always seemed to behave as though he did not exist.

Lucky Chantel, who had married the man of her choice!

The drums had started again. I pictured it ... the scene on the cliff, the sound of the surf on the golden sand, the dark figure of the Woman of Secrets waiting for a spirit which she could capture that she might escape.

I wished that *Serene Lady* was already in the bay.

That night we rode to the spot in the carriage. Monique was with us. Chantel had not wished her to come but she had grown hysterically imperious and Chantel gave way. She wore a long white flowing dress and red hibiscus in her hair which was loose all about her shoulders. Her eyes were alight with excitement. She looked completely Polynesian, like the spirit of the Island. Her eyes mocked me. It amused her, I knew, to witness my discomfiture; I think she thought it a joke that one so prim as I should be the "other woman" in her drama.

Chantel wore green—long and flowing. She had bought the dress on the Island and although the material was not rich it was soft and clinging and became her. She had plaited her hair and the thick braid was over one shoulder. I had not bought anything for the occasion. I wore my blue silk dress and my hair piled on top of my head in the normal way.

We rattled along the road and left the carriage with the others. We then walked up the slope to that plateau on which the dancing was already taking place. I had seen some of the native dances before. They were often performed near the waterfront on those "houses without walls" which were really platforms covered with a roof of leaves and branches to keep off the sun.

The music was played on the guitarlike instruments with which I had become familiar. We sat down on the rug which we had brought for the purpose and coconut shells of Gali were handed to us. One sip—which I took warily—was enough to make one's veins feel as though fire was running through them. I knew it was highly intoxicating.

I glanced at Chantel beside me, her lovely eyes dilated. She was interested and amused, but I believed she was elated because she was thinking that she would soon be in Sydney with Rex.

Oh, lucky Chantel!

We applauded the dances, clapping our hands in the slow rhythmic way they did on the Island. They seemed interminable, those dances, and it was not very comfortable sitting on the rug.

But when the time came for the flame dance the excitement was so fierce that I caught it. I knelt as so many did and was unaware of my aching knees. Two young men were stripped to the waist and wore loincloths only trimmed with flame-colored beads that flickered in the torchlight. Round their necks were rows of beads—red beads; on their arms more red beaded bangles; on their heads were beaded bandeaux of the same glittering red.

The dark sky was dotted with thousands of brilliant stars; the moon threw its pale yellow light on the great circle—dark faces, pale faces, all intent. I was aware of the scent of flowers, the pungent smell of the torches, the flaring light from them, the faint buzz of insects fatally attracted to the flame.

And the flame dancers were waiting. Their torches were brought ceremoniously to them by their old father—two for each man; the music started and the dance began. At first they twirled the flaming torches lightly; they threw them up into the air and caught them effortlessly. They stamped as they danced and threw the flaming sticks through the air, high up to fall and be caught as they fell. This could be done by any man who was ready to train for it. The real flame dance had not begun.

I do not know how they did it. They were so quick, so skillful. I only knew that at times we saw what appeared to be whirling balls of fire and inside them were the all but naked bodies of the dancers. They danced wildly, madly, and again and again the watchers caught their breath; they did not believe any man could be in the midst of such flame and be unhurt.

As the music slackened the balls of flame moved more slowly and it was seen that there were four flaming torches and two dancing men. We were spellbound.

This was the miracle the Flame Men had learned in the Fire Country and brought with them to Earth to be danced by none but men of their blood.

It was over. For one second there was a hushed and impressive silence, and then the wild applause broke out, the slow rhythmic clapping and the sudden shout "Kella Kella Ta'lui."

It went on and on. There was an excited buzz of conversation. It was not natural. They had witnessed a miracle; the flame had grown cool for the sake of the Flame Men.

Chantel looked at me and grinned. I was afraid she was going to say something flippant and although her words might not have been understood, her mood might.

But there was a rustle of excitement. The two Flame Men were leading out a boy.

He was the son of one of them and he was going to dance the flame dance for the first time. As the son of his father the flame would grow cold for him too.

I felt my heart start to beat wildly. He looked so small and pathetic standing there in his little red-beaded ornaments, and with dawning horror I was certain that he was afraid.

I felt an impulse to stand up and shout: "This must not be." But I did not. I knew I could not. The boy was going to perform as his elders had, and I knew that I was going to sit there in an agony of apprehension because I could sense his fear.

He stepped forward. Two torches were handed to him. He took them. He twirled them; he threw them into the air and caught them. I felt better. He was as agile as his elders.

The music had started—slowly at first but building up to a crescendo. The torches started to whirl, they were turning themselves into a ball of flame.

He can do it, I thought. They have taught him well.

Again that spellbound silence—the brilliant night sky, the impressive silence, and all eyes on that whirling ball of fire.

And then it happened, the most fearful scream I had ever heard. One of the torches shot into the air and the other followed and we saw the writhing figure, the flames enveloping his body, his hair on fire. He looked like a flaming torch himself.

Chantel was up. She was dragging the rug on which she had been sitting; she had reached the boy, wrapped him in the rug and was beating out the flames with her hands.

I was moved. It was a wonderful sight, but most of all because it was Chantel, Chantel the angel of mercy.

People were rushing forward. The two men in their glittering red ornaments were screaming.

I heard Chantel say in that authoritative tone of hers: "I'm a nurse. Stand aside."

The boy who had been shrieking in pain stopped suddenly. I thought he was dead.

Chantel commanded one of the men to carry him into the nearest house, which was their own. She turned to me. "Go back and bring my bag, quick as you can."

I didn't wait for any more. Jacques went with me to the carriage. He drove the horses back to the house with a speed that must have been very unfamiliar to them. I ran to her room, picked up the bag in which she kept her remedies and came out to the carriage.

All the way back memories of the boy's screams kept ringing in my ears.

We came to the house by a different route from that which I had taken on the day I had trespassed. The doctor was there, but considerably fuddled by too much Gali and it was Chantel who was in command.

She took the bag from me. "Don't leave, Anna," she commanded. "Wait for me."

I sat down on a stool. I kept thinking of the boy. I had known he was afraid. He was only a child really, and it was cruel to have submitted him to such an ordeal. And how magnificent Chantel had been in her flowing green and the plait over her shoulder.

It was hot in the room and I stepped out into the open. The trees looked eerie in the moonlight. The scent of their blossoms filled the air.

I thought, if he lives Chantel will have saved his life and we shall not have come to the Island in vain.

I walked round the house thinking of these things. I had no desire to go in again; it was much more pleasant outside. But after a while it occurred to me that Chantel might be waiting for me, so I went in. It was some moments before I realized that I had not returned through the door by which I had left. I groped my way across a floor on which I could faintly see rush mats. I was in a dark passage. This was not the way. I went through a room telling myself that I would get out of the house and walk round until I found the door by which I had left. The last thing I wanted to do was walk into the room where Chantel and the boy were. I must find my way back as carefully and silently as possible.

I groped my way along the passage and I saw in the dimness a door. I listened for the sound of voices. There was no sound. I tapped gently. There was no answer, so cautiously I opened the door hoping to find the room in which I had first waited.

But I was wrong. Two small rush lights were burning in this room. I caught my breath because it was arranged like that walled space I had seen out of doors. In the center of the room was a figure and round it a ring of glittering stones. One stone, larger than the rest, twinkled in the rush light; it seemed alive with red fire. But perhaps I was still seeing that nightmare outside. I felt as though I were impelled forward. The figure in the center was different from the one which I had seen outside; there was a look of familiarity about it.

I went close to it, stepping over the ring of stones. I knew it well. I had seen it many times. I had first discovered it in the escritoire which had come from Castle Crediton; I had kept it in my room; I still had it. It was the figurehead of *The Secret Woman;* only this was no replica. This was the real thing.

Her face was bland and smiling; her hair long as though flowing in a breeze and on her robes were the words *"The Secret Woman."*

I could not believe that this was really so. A crude wooden stand had been made to support the figurehead and the surrounding stones sparkled with red and blue fire.

Then a blinding understanding came to me.

These were the Fillimore diamonds.

In the early morning we came back to Carrément. I was longing to tell Chantel about my find but I must wait until we were alone. She was in an exalted mood because she believed she had saved that boy's life, and undoubtedly it was her prompt action which had enabled her to beat out the flames. She talked of him. Everything had happened so quickly; he was not really so badly burned; his legs and arms would carry the scars through his life and he was very shocked, but she was certain that he would recover.

"Chantel," I said, "you were magnificent."

"I was ready," she said. "I knew it was going to happen. No one could perform such a dance without the certainty that he was going to succeed; and that boy was afraid."

"I sensed that too, but I was not prepared."

"In fact," said Chantel, "I was ready with the rug. That was why I reached him so soon, but I think when anything like that happens one acts without thought. What a sight ... that poor child a mass of flame!"

"I shall never sleep tonight," I said, "or what is left of it."

"Nor I," she replied.

When we reached the house Madame was waiting for us.

"What of the boy?" she asked.

"We think he'll recover," said Chantel.

"He will owe his life to you," she said. "It is something he will never forget."

Chantel smiled. "He's shocked," she said. "I've got him sleeping now. I shall go over and see him in the morning. The doctor will be there then."

"But it was you ..."

"I had drunk no Gali."

"You must be very tired," said Madame.

Chantel did not deny it. We said goodnight to her.

"I must speak to you, Chantel," I said. "Something fantastic has happened."

I lighted the candles and turned to look at her. I thought she had never looked so beautiful and in spite of my excitement I could not help pausing for a few seconds just to gaze at her.

"What's wrong?" she asked.

I shook my head. "You look . . . elated."

"It's having succeeded against death. I feel I've snatched that boy from death tonight."

"What a night. But something happened to me too, and I must talk of it."

I told her of my discovery.

She gasped. "Those diamonds? Are you sure?"

"I feel certain. It was the figurehead. I had seen a replica of it. In fact I have one. And the name was on it ... And those stones were all round it."

"They may not have been diamonds."

"I feel certain they were. You see, Chantel, if they

really are the diamonds it means that Redvers will be cleared of this suspicion. So many people thought he had stolen them."

Her face had hardened a little. I could not imagine why she disliked him so much. Did she know something which she had kept from me? It seemed strange.

"You can't be sure," she said. "There are a lot of weird figures around and stones, well ... They sound too big to be diamonds. They'd be worth a fortune."

"The Fillimore diamonds *were* worth a fortune. Chantel, what can we do?"

"It looks to me as if they treat it as though it were some sort of goddess. That could well be. They have this story about coming from the Fire Country. It may be it has something to do with that. Diamonds flash fire."

"I am sure they attach some significance to this but the point is what shall I do? Shall I go and tell them? Shall I ask them how the figurehead came into their possession with the stones?"

"They'd probably be furious because you'd seen it. You were after all wandering about their house unknown to them."

"Yes, and I'd trespassed before." I told her about the day when I wandered into the grounds. "Perhaps *you* could do something. They'll be grateful to you."

She was silent.

Then I cried suddenly: "We will do nothing until the ship comes. I will tell the Captain then. I will leave it to him."

She did not speak for a while; her mood of elation seemed to have passed.

I felt it had something to do with her dislike of Redvers.

The next weeks were the hardest to live through. I was in a fever of impatience, terrified that something would happen to the diamonds—for I was sure they were the diamonds—before the ship came home. I studied the calendar with greater eagerness than Edward did. Even the thought of Redvers' letter in the hands of Suka or Monique was pushed to the back of my mind.

The whole household knew that we would be returning

to Sydney. There was an unpleasant scene with Monique when she demanded to know what I was going to do. Chantel managed to quieten her; since the flame dance incident Chantel had acquired a new authority. I had seen both Suka and Pero look at her with special respect; when we went out I was aware that people watched her in a different way. Some of the European residents congratulated her and wondered why they had not met her before. But the fact was that we were at Carrément where Madame de Laudé lived like a recluse. Chantel was delighted with this attention, I could see. I thought: What a wonderful Chatelaine of the Castle she will make. I told her that when she was as old as Lady Crediton she would be every bit as formidable. This amused her.

I said to her once: "Chantel, it's a mystery about that letter. Nothing has happened."

"It's a good sign. Perhaps it wasn't stolen after all. What if it fell into your wastepaper basket and was lost that way. It's probably been destroyed by now."

"But I was sure that someone had been in my room."

"Guilty conscience, Anna," she said.

I protested. "But there is nothing . . ."

She gave me a quick peck on the nose. "I like to think that you are just a little guilty, Anna. It makes you more human. But stop worrying about the letter. It's lost."

I had finished the inventory and had calculated that there were several thousand pounds worth of treasures in the house. I told Madame that I would see that the account of them was sent to dealers, and I was certain that some business would result.

She was delighted; she became quite animated contemplating what a difference it would make.

There was a big scene with Monique one evening and I wondered then whether she had the letter and was holding it for some purpose.

She was going back on *Serene Lady*, she said. She was not going to stay when we left. And Edward was coming too.

It was necessary to call in the doctor and he and Chantel between them managed to calm her.

Edward believed that he was going with us. I said to Chantel: "But what of Madame Laudé. She will not want Monique to go surely?"

"Madame is thinking chiefly of the fortune you promised her. Edward is delighted at the prospect of going back. He would have been heartbroken to stay on here. What is there for him but his hysterical Mamma, his parsimonious Grandmamma and mad old Suka."

"Can these matters be so quickly decided? I thought that Monique had come out here to be with her family and because the climate was more suited to her than ours is."

"No climate would suit her. She would never be happy. That's part of her trouble. There are too many tensions in her life. Now she is buoyed up by the Captain's return. She wouldn't let him calmly sail away with you, Anna, she's working up for something. I haven't told you before because I didn't want to upset you. She talked of little but you and the Captain."

"Then she has the letter."

"I'm sure she would have said. And I've looked everywhere. She's even a little quieter than usual, as though she is planning, plotting."

"Oh Chantel ... it's rather terrifying."

"She is sure you and the Captain are lovers. She said that you were planning to murder her to get her out of the way."

"I don't know what to do, Chantel. There's Suka watching me as though she suspects I'm going to do Monique an injury. Pero too. Something is building up against me. I believe that is what Monique intends should happen."

"She loves drama and of course wants to be in the center of it, but there's a lot of play-acting in it."

"What if she were to carry this play-acting too far?"

"How?"

"Suppose she killed herself and made it seem that I ... or the Captain ..."

"No! How could she enjoy the drama if she were dead?"

"If there were a ship that called here before *Serene Lady*, Chantel, I think we should be wise to get on it. To go to Sydney, to try to find some post there ..."

"But you can't just take a berth on a ship like that. And no ship will be calling in any case. You're here, Anna."

"Yes and I feel ... trapped."

"I thought you wanted to stay to tell your Captain you think you have cleared his name?"

"I do but I'm afraid, Chantel. There is something menacing hanging over us."

"A wild hysterical and passionate woman, a straying husband, and the woman he loves. What a situation and who would have believed it of you, my dear calm practical Anna!"

"Please don't joke about this, Chantel. It's a very serious matter."

"A very serious matter," agreed Chantel. "But don't worry. I'm here, Anna, now as I was before. Is that a comfort?"

"It's a great comfort," I assured her fervently.

As the days passed Monique's condition worsened. The attacks were more frequent and one followed another. They were not severe attacks, Chantel told me; but she was alarmed for her patient's health. She never left her and when she was bad I know she often sat up during the night. She was a wonderful nurse.

She told me that Suka sat in the room watching her with great mournful eyes. "I'd like to get rid of her but it upsets Monique when I suggest she go and I mustn't upset her when she's in that state. The old lady's furious at the prospect of losing her Missy. I believe she blames you. I heard her mutter something. She thinks that if you didn't exist Monique wouldn't be jealous and would be content to let her husband go without her. Be careful she doesn't slip something into your mint tea. I'm sure the old witch has a store of poisons, tasteless in Gali, coffee and the aforementioned mint tea. Tasteless and deadly. The two necessary attributes."

I shivered and she said: "It was a joke, Anna. What's come over you? You take life too seriously."

"It seems to have become serious," I said.

"Life is real, life is earnest," quoted Chantel.

" 'And the grave is not its goal'," I finished, and wished I hadn't spoken. I hated even to mention death.

"Don't worry," said Chantel, "we'll soon be in Sydney."

Edward was frankly excited. When *Serene Lady* came we were going to sail away on her.

How many more days to the red letter day? We counted them, Fourteen, thirteen . . . and then ten.

Each morning I awoke wondering what the day would bring. I used to open my door and look out into the corridor. Sometimes I heard her shouting and my name would be mentioned. At others there was silence.

And in my thoughts too was the precious letter I had lost and the memory of that room in which was the figurehead of *The Secret Woman* and what I believed to be the Fillimore diamonds.

Why were the days so long? I was living for the time when I should see *Serene Lady* in the bay. I would not think beyond that. I just wanted to sail away from the Island and when I reached Sydney I would find some post and reshape my life.

Tension was mounting. I longed to tell the Captain of my discovery. I should be so proud and overjoyed if I had been the one to find the diamonds. I longed for his return and yet at the same time I feared it.

Monique grew quieter. A sly calculation had taken the place of unreasoning wildness which was even more alarming and I could not get out of my mind that we were moving toward some tremendous climax. This Island had been but lightly touched by our Western ways. Beneath the veneer there was something deeply savage. These people believed in strange gods; a stone rock to them was a living thing. Curses and spells were commonplace. And I believed that Suka had marked me down as her enemy because she believed that I had come between Monique and the man she loved.

There was no one to whom I could speak of my deep disquiet, Chantel treated the matter too lightly. She refused to accept it as serious. I believed that her thoughts were far away in Sydney when she would be reunited with Rex. Even the discovery of the diamonds meant little for the clearing of Redvers' name was a matter of indifference to her. When she talked of the future she never mentioned him. She didn't trust him. She had plans for me. Dear Chantel! She was concerned for me. I knew she was planning to launch me in society, to make a grand marriage for me. She did not want me to be involved with Redvers. This slipped out in her conversation and although it hurt me in a way I knew it was a measure of her affection for me. She really believed she had to look after me and in her usual determined manner had decided to do it.

I could not look into the future. I could only wait for the return of *Serene Lady*. So the uneasy days passed and one afternoon when we had all been resting behind shutters because the heat was intense, I rose, opened my shutters and saw it in the bay—the white gleaming ship.

I ran to Edward's room and cried, "Edward. She's come. *Serene Lady* is in the bay."

23

The events of the days which followed were so dramatic that it is difficult now to remember the exact order in which they occurred. I could scarcely restrain my impatience. I wanted to go out to the ship. I wanted to tell him of my fears, of the lost letter and most of all my discovery of the figurehead and the diamonds.

But I had to curb myself.

Chantel came into my room, her eyes gleaming.

"There'll be a scene tonight," she said. "Missy's working up for it."

"She must be delighted that he's here."

"She's madly excited. But she's got a devilish look in her eyes. She's planning something. I wish I knew what was in her mind."

I waited in my room. He would come soon. I put on my blue silk dress and piled my hair high on my head. I had worn that dress many times; my hair was dressed in the usual way. Yet I had changed. My eyes shone; there was a faint color in my cheeks. Would others notice the change in me?

I heard his voice below and my emotions were almost unbearable. What a fool I was! Was Chantel right? Could I trust him? The understanding came to me that it would make no difference whatever she could tell me of him. I loved him and I would go on loving him forever.

I opened my door. I wanted to stand there listening to
the sound of his voice.

Then among the shadows I saw the crouching figure.
Suka! She was listening too. She had seen me. I could feel
rather than see her baleful eyes fixed on me.

I went back to my room. When I get to Sydney, I said,
I must find a post. Perhaps I'll stay there. Perhaps I'll find
some people who are returning to England. But I must get
away.

Pero was beating the gong in the hall. It was time to go
down to dinner.

We dined as we had on that first night—Madame,
Monique, myself, Chantel, Redvers, the doctor, and Dick
Callum.

Dick had changed. He was subdued and had lost that
air of truculence which I had so often noticed. I was
aware of Redvers—in fact I was aware of little else. Now
and then I would find his eyes on me, but I dared not
return his gaze. Monique was watching us, I was sure. I
wondered whether she would suddenly talk of the letter. It
would be like her to produce it at such a time.

Conversation was conventional. It centered round the
voyage and of course an account of the flame dance.

As we went through to the *salon* I was able to whisper
to Redvers: "I must see you. It is very important."

Dick talked to me while we drank our coffee but I
scarcely listened to him. Madame de Laudé was talking
about my discovery of the antiques in her house. Dick was
very interested and she asked if he would like to see a
French console table which I had declared to be particularly valuable. He rose and I slipped out with him and
Madame but instead of following them I went out into the
garden and waited in the shadow of the trees. It was not
long before Redvers came out.

He took my hands in his and looked at me but before
he could say anything I began to pour out the story of my
discovery. I said: "You must go to that house. You must
make some excuse to see the figure. I am sure it is the
figurehead of *The Secret Woman* and that the stones are
the diamonds."

He was as excited as I knew he would be.

He said: "There's something I must tell you. Dick

Callum confessed to me. He couldn't get over the fact that I had saved him from the sharks. He's told me everything—who he is and his jealousy of me. I had no idea. He wanted some sort of revenge on me. I was under suspicion but what greater disgrace for a captain than to lose his ship! He suggested to those people that the ship should be blown up. It was something to do with the name. He arranged that no one should be on board, which was not impossible in his position, so at least he made sure that no lives were lost. But Anna, if you're right about this ..."

"I'm sure I am. And if *I* have made this right for you, I shall be so proud and so glad that I was that one."

"Anna," he said, "you know nothing can be right for me without you."

"I must go in now. They will notice that we are missing. They mustn't. I'm afraid of what could happen. But I had to tell you this. I must go now."

He was holding my hands tightly but I pulled them away.

"Please," I said. "Go as soon as you can. At least make sure of this."

I turned and ran into the house.

I had told him nothing of the letter. Later I must do so; but let him first go to the house and discover the diamonds before I told him that I had been so careless as to lose that letter which could be so incriminating.

Madame de Laudé was still showing Dick pieces of furniture and I joined them; so that when we returned to the *salon* I hoped the impression was given that I had been with them all the time.

Redvers was not in the *salon*. Monique said that he had business to attend to on the ship and would be away for a while.

Dick talked to me of the voyage and how dull it had been.

"I missed you," he said. "I thought of you often. It's hot in here. Let us walk in the garden."

I asked if he would excuse me as I was very tired; he seemed disappointed.

I sat by my window. There would be some sign from

Redvers, I knew. Sure enough it came. I heard the light rattle of pebbles against my shutters.

I went down to him to that spot among the bushes which we had made our meeting place.

Redvers was there. He was elated. It was wonderful, he said. I was right. I had made this great discovery. I, Anna, whom he had loved from the moment he had seen her!

I was caught up in his excitement, and once again I experienced the ability to shut out everything past and future and live entirely in the moment. For years he had been under suspicion and I had dispersed that cloud almost effortlessly and by chance. What did it matter now? I had done it!

It was a wonderful moment. "It's significant," he said. "It proves that your affairs are mine and mine yours."

"I must know what happened," I said. "How did you persuade them to show you the figure and give you the diamonds?"

"It was not difficult," he explained. "There was great shame in the house of the Flame Men. One of them had failed. They waved aside the fact that he was only a boy not so skilled in his art as they, and looked on it as the sign of some divine wrath. This gave me my opportunity and I took it. I had to. I suggested that there was an evil influence on the house and I talked of the ship that had been blown up in the bay. I took a pencil from my pocket and drew the figurehead. 'You took this goddess from the sea,' I said, 'and she is an alien goddess.' They told me that they had been promised good fortune if they destroyed the ship. I knew this already because Dick had told me. And when the ship blew up, the figurehead, as they said, leaped from the ship and floated on the water and came to rest near the rock of the Woman of Secrets. They took that as a sign. So they brought in the figurehead and set her up as they set up their own gods. They told me that in the figurehead was a concealed cavity and in this had been the bag of stones. This convinced them, because their custom is to surround their statues with stones and shells. And these were such bright and beautiful stones. They set her up and waited for the good fortune. But it did not come. Instead there was great misfortune for nothing could be worse than for the fire to cease to be a friend of the Flame Men.

"I have the diamonds," he went on. "I told them that there would be no luck until they were taken to those to whom they belonged. Ta'lui will destroy the figurehead and I told him that there will be a reward for finding the diamonds which will enable him to set up a new statue. He is completely satisfied. I will take the diamonds to England and the matter which began when Fillimore died of a heart attack will be settled. If only he had told someone that he had hidden the diamonds in the figurehead a good deal of trouble would have been saved."

"But at last it is over."

"No one can talk of the fortune I have salted away in some foreign port now. And Anna . . ."

But I could hear voices and I believed that we were closely watched and it might even be that now it was known that I was in the garden alone with him. I could hear Monique's voice. She was on the porch and Chantel was with her.

Chantel was saying: "You should come in. Come in and wait."

"No," cried Monique. "He is here. I know it. I will wait here for him."

"Go quickly," I whispered to Redvers.

He went toward the house while I cowered among the bushes, my heart beating wildly.

"What did I say? Here he is. So you are back."

"It appears so." His voice was cold when he spoke to her. How different when he addressed me!

"You look as though you have been having an exciting adventure," said Monique, her voice shrill.

"I should go in," said Chantel firmly. "I am sure the Captain would like that coffee you said you would make for him. No one makes it quite as well as you do."

"Yes, I will," she said. "Come on, *mon capitaine*."

The silence was broken only by the hum of insects in the garden. I waited for some minutes then went swiftly into the house.

There was a tap at my door and Chantel came in. She looked excited. Her eyes were enormous.

"I had to tell you, Anna," she said. "She has the letter."

I put my hand over my heart, and half-closed my eyes; I felt as though I was going to faint.

"Sit down," said Chantel.

"When did you see it?"

"Not till tonight. She was reading it and when I came in she put it on the table and pretended it was nothing. I had a quick glance and saw your name on it. Then she picked it up and put it inside the neck of her dress."

"Chantel, what do you think she intends to do?"

"We can only wait and see. I was surprised how calm she was. And she has said nothing."

"She will."

"I think she will say something to him tonight."

"But she calmly went up to make coffee for him."

"I don't understand this calmness; but I thought you should be prepared."

"Oh Chantel, I feel terrified of what may happen."

She stood up. "I must go back. I may be called in. But don't worry. I promise you, Anna, that it's going to be all right. We have nearly finished with this place, with all of it. You've always been able to trust me, haven't you?"

She came up to me and kissed me coolly on the forehead.

"Goodnight, Anna. Only a little while now."

She went out and left me.

I knew that sleep was impossible. I could only think of Monique reading that letter which had been intended for me alone.

A night of strange emotions. This tremendous tension had to break sooner or later. It could not last. That was my only consolation. I must get away, get away from them all. Perhaps even Chantel for she was bound irrevocably to the Creditons. A few weeks now and I should be in Sydney, and there I must find the courage to break away, to start a new life of my own.

I heard Monique's voice raised in anger and tried to shut my ears to it. A little later I heard footsteps in the garden and looking through my shutters I saw Redvers striding across the garden. I gathered he must have been called back to the ship and that Monique was protesting. Had she shown him the letter? What was she planning to do with it?

I undressed and got into bed but sleep was naturally impossible; I lay as I had often lain in the Queen's House listening to the sounds of the house.

As I lay there my door was opened silently and a figure

stood in the doorway. I leaped up. I cried out in relief when I saw that it was Chantel.

She looked strange; her hair was loose and she wore a soft silk dressing gown of her favorite shade of green; her eyes were dilated.

"Chantel," I cried, "what's wrong?"

Her voice sounded high pitched and unlike itself.

"Read this," she said. "And when you have read it come to me at once."

"What is it?"

"Read it and see."

She threw some papers onto the bed and before I could pick them up had glided out.

I jumped out of bed and lit my candles; then I picked up the papers and read.

Dearest Anna,

There is so much you don't know, so much I have to tell you. I don't think there is much time so I must be brief. You remember I told you that there were so many facets of truth and that I had told the truth but not the whole truth. You don't know me, Anna; not all of me. You know only one little bit of me; and you are very fond of what you know, which pleases me. You read my journal. As I said it was the truth but not the whole truth. I would like to have read it through so that I could have rewritten pieces for you, but that would take too long. You see, I didn't tell you that Rex fell deeply in love with me. You knew that he was attracted by me but you thought it was mild flirtation on his part. You were sorry for me, anxious for me. I loved you for that, Anna. You see as soon as I entered the Castle I wanted to be mistress of it. I saw myself as the future Lady Crediton and nothing else would satisfy me. I am insatiably ambitious, Anna. In almost all of us there is the secret woman who does not appear for her friends and acquaintances, perhaps not even for the man she marries. But Rex must know me fairly well now. It has not changed his devotion to me. You will remember that I was interested in Valerie Stretton; there was the occasion when she came in with her muddy boots. There was the letter in her bureau. I wrote that Miss Beddoes came in and found me with it in my hands. That was not all the truth. I had read the letter; I had read other letters; I had discovered that Valerie Stretton was being blackmailed. I married Rex and when he was to go to Australia I was determined to go with him. He wanted me to go openly as his wife. I was not going to alienate Lady Crediton at that stage. She could have diverted a large part of her fortune from Rex and I wanted him to have complete control. I knew it was better to keep our marriage secret for a while so I put the idea into Dr. Elgin's head that our climate was killing Monique. Then I made Monique decide that she wanted to go to see her mother. As this meant sailing on the Captain's ship she didn't need a lot of persuading. But I had to have you with us, Anna, and poor old Beddoes was very incompetent. I helped to get her moved on. She sensed it. Who would have believed that? But adventuresses learn to watch for opposition in the most unexpected quarters.

So I rid us of Beddoes and got you into the Castle. Anna, I *am* fond of you. I intended no harm to come to you. I saved you before, didn't I? And I was determined to save you whatever happened. But I needed you, Anna. Your friendship, I wanted that, yes ... but you were part of my plan.

Now this is where I have to tell you something which will hurt you. It hurts me too. I thought I was hard and strong. And you are what shall I say ... conventional. Right is right and wrong is wrong, black is black and white white. That is your creed. You won't understand this and like a fool I'm putting off telling you till the last minute, although I know there is not much time.

I have to tell you why Valerie Stretton was being blackmailed. She was not the only one. Rex was being blackmailed too. Rex is not exactly an honest man, but he hasn't got the criminal instincts. He's too frightened. So far and no farther for Rex. I always knew he was weak. Gareth Glenning was blackmailing Rex. That was why the Glennings were taking the trip. They wanted to keep Rex under supervision. They weren't going to lose sight of him. He was their chief source of income.

And Valerie Stretton's secret? It is this: Her son was a few days old when Lady Crediton's was born. Lady Crediton was very ill, so that she knew there was a very good chance of her plan working. Valerie wanted *her* son to inherit the Crediton empire. Why not? Sir Edward was his father. It was merely a matter of marriage lines. Lady C. had them, Valerie hadn't. It was not so difficult. She was in the house. She knew when the nurse was resting, when the baby was asleep in his cot. You can guess what happened. She changed the babies and Rex is her son and Redvers Lady Crediton's. That's how it all started. But she did not get away with it. There was someone in the house who knew the difference between the babies, young as they were. It was the nurse. She knew what Valerie had done.

She hated Lady Crediton; she was fond of Valerie. In fact she may have helped her in the exchange, very probably did. The boys grew up. Valerie couldn't hide her preference for Rex, which was stupid of her because it could have given the game away. It was three weeks or so after the birth before Lady Crediton was able to take much notice and by that time the boys had decided personalities of their own and everyone—except Valerie and the nurse—believed Rex to be the heir.

It's always unwise to share secrets. The only safe secret is the one that is never told. That is why I did not tell you all the truth.

The nurse fell on hard times and asked Valerie to help her; Valerie did and as the years passed the friendship between them was forgotten and every now and then Valerie was asked for money in exchange for keeping the secret. The nurse had married rather late in life a widower with a son. She could not resist telling her husband what she knew; and the husband told his son. That son was Gareth Glenning. He was smart. He saw that there was a better source of income than Valerie—Rex.

When Rex was approached he tackled Valerie who confessed; he was horrified. He cares passionately for the business, Anna. He has worked all his life with one aim in view: to take it over. Redvers was just one of the captains. He would not know how to manage such a business. His job was sailing the seas. Rex could not endure to lose what he had always thought would be his. So he allowed himself to be blackmailed.

Now I come to the hardest part of all. I have put off telling you this because I fear you will change toward me. Why should I care? But I do, Anna. It's strange, but I care very much. You see I'm truly fond of you. I meant what I said when I told you that you were to me as a sister.

It was in a way this secret which brought Rex and me so close together. If I married him it would be my concern as well as his and it was as important to me as to him that this secret should never be known. That was the point, Anna, it must never be known. And how could we make sure that it never would be? It was already in the possession of three people—the nurse, Claire and Gareth Glenning. You see even if they died how could we be sure that they had not passed it on to someone else?

We should never be safe; we should live our lives in a state of uncertainty. Imagine it. At any time someone could appear to tell us that they knew our secret. I have often pointed this out to Rex. He saw my point. You can see that there was only one way by which we could be completely safe. The terms of the will—I had looked them up in Somerset House—were that in the event of the death of the heir and his heirs the estate would pass to that other son of Sir Edward's—believed to be Redvers but in fact Rex. Therefore in actual fact Rex was not the heir but he would be if Redvers and his heirs were dead.

You see, Anna, everything we do has its effect on us. We take some action after a great deal of consideration and when it is done successfully we repeat it without the same qualms; and in time it becomes a commonplace. When Lady Henrock died she left me two hundred pounds; she was in pain; she could not recover; it seemed a kindness to help her to oblivion. That's what I told myself. Your Aunt Charlotte would never have recovered. She would have grown more and more impossible; your life would have been a misery, and I knew that she had left me a little money. She told me so. I have a way of worming these secrets out of people. I didn't realize there would be all the fuss. But I did save you, didn't I? Believe me I should never have allowed you to have been found guilty of murder.

And then of course, the voyage. I had talked of our affairs with Rex. We had discussed them from every angle. I made him see that there was only one way in which we could be safe to enjoy our inheritance, safe

forever. And that was if Redvers were removed. But of
course there was Edward. Rex is weak, and I am glad
he was. I was fond of Edward. Rex bungled that business on the boat. I always said that a ship should be the
easiest place in which to get rid of an unwanted child. I
drugged his milk. Rex carried him out of the cabin. He
was in his burnoose so wouldn't have been recognized.
Johnny spoiled that. But I don't believe Rex would ever
have done it even if Johnny hadn't appeared. He seized
the opportunity of Johnny's appearance and I know
that he was pleased that Edward was safe. It's harder to
kill a child than disgruntled old women. So Edward
lived; but I knew we could not ignore him forever. He
was not so important yet though, because even if the
secret were discovered he would be unable to take his
place as heir for years and Rex would be in charge.
There would be time then to arrange something. But
Redvers was our immediate concern.

Redvers had to die. How? How could a strong man
suddenly be seized with illness? That was impossible. He
couldn't suddenly die of disease. But I always adjusted
my plans to the circumstances: A man with a hysterical
jealous wife; another woman with whom he was in love
and who loved him; and the wife was insanely jealous.
I'm sorry Anna, but he was no good to you. I intended
to look after you. You would have forgotten him quickly. I was going to have you at the Castle, my sister, my
cherished sister. I would have found a husband for you;
you would have had a happy life. That was what I
intended. But Redvers had to die. And I had made up
my mind that there would have to be a murderess.

She will not live long. She could die next week . . . in
two years' time perhaps. I don't think from the state of
her lungs alone she can live another five years. Her
asthmatical attacks are as frequent as ever; they are
aggravating the lung condition. I knew that this voyage
could not do her any lasting good. So, why should she
not take this rôle? There would be compassion for her,
particularly in Coralle . . . the sick and jealous wife.
They wouldn't have been hard on her. And you, Anna,
you would be involved in scandal again, but I would be
there to protect you. I would have power and position,
which I longed for, and I would care for you. And
although you would be pointed to as the Other Woman,

just as you were as the Niece with a Motive—you see that passes. It is a necessary inconvenience in which I had to involve you then, as now.

But I am fond of you, Anna. It is something I never thought possible, so perhaps there are yet more secret recesses of my mind which I don't understand myself.

So I decided that when Redvers came home he was going to die.

And that is what I intended tonight. I had worked on Monique. I had deliberately roused her jealousy, oh very subtly. I had seen how useful Suka could be. It was going to be easy. His jealous wife was going to murder the erring husband and that murder was going to take place either tonight or tomorrow night, when the Captain was in this house. I was waiting my opportunity. I knew it would come because she loved to make coffee. She was proud of it because it was her only domestic virtue. I had told her that she made it better than anyone else in the house. I only had to wait for the moment. Tonight he had been talking to you in the garden. Suka knew it and she had told Monique, who made coffee for him in her own room where she had a spirit lamp. She made it and I put something in his coffee, Anna. I shall not tell you what. It was something that would act quickly. Something which was comparatively—but not quite—tasteless. He was excited. He was thinking of you. I didn't think he would notice that slight acrid taste. When she had made the coffee I said that I thought her blue negligee was more becoming than her red, and she acted as I knew she would and went into the adjoining room to change it. I then did what was necessary. I put the deadly drug into the coffee, stirred it well and when she came back in the blue negligee everything was set.

I went away to wait. I was so excited, so tense. I paced up and down my room waiting.

I have never done anything as big as this. It was very different helping sick old women out of the world. I was not entirely sure what effect a large quantity of the drug would have. I must be ready, prepared to say the right thing, to do the right thing when the time came. I was trembling and apprehensive.

I thought some coffee would steady my nerves. I was

going to make some, but as I came out into the corridor I saw Pero; I did not want to risk talking to anyone in my state. I did not want to go to the kitchen. I most dreaded seeing Suka. She has an uncanny way of guessing. No, I could not face that old woman—which I might well do if I went to the kitchen—not when I had just made a murderess of her darling Missy.

So I said to Pero: "Would you make me some coffee and send it up to my room. I am very tired. It has been a busy day."

She is always eager to please; she said she would; and ten minutes later she came back.

I poured out the coffee; it was very hot but I never cared for hot coffee. I gulped down a cup and poured out another ... and then ... I began to taste that unusual taste.

I looked at the fresh cup I had poured out. I sniffed it. There would be no odor, but a horrible suspicion had come to me. I told myself I was imagining it. It couldn't be.

But I had to satisfy myself. I found Pero in the kitchen.

I said to her: "You made me some coffee, Pero."

"Yes, Nurse." She looked frightened; but then she always looks frightened, always fearful of complaint.

"You made it yourself ... ?"

"Why, yes, Nurse."

I felt better. I realized that my skin was cold although I felt as though my body was on fire. I reminded myself that I must be careful. People were going to be talking about coffee a great deal in this house.

"It was not good, Nurse?"

I did not answer.

"Missy Monique made it," she said.

"What?"

"For the Captain, but he did not drink it. He was called to the ship. So, I heat it up for you."

I heard myself say: "I see."

So now you understand. You can see how one must take every possibility into consideration if one is to be certain of success. This house of economy! It was something I had forgotten. You have to think of everything, and the most irrelevant details can prove your downfall.

And here is your letter, Anna. I took it. I was going

to use it. I had not yet put it where she could find it. She will never see it now. It would have been useful, you see. It would have been found in her room and would naturally have been part of the motive.

But everything is changed now. The truth will come out. It is better for Rex this way. He could never have gone through with this without me, and now he will stand alone.

"A long farewell to all my greatness." You see, I quote to the end. Goodbye to you, Anna. Goodbye to Rex.

I dropped the sheets of paper and Redvers' letter to me; I ran to Chantel's room.

She was lying on her bed.

"Chantel," I cried. "Chantel."

But she lay still unheeding. I knew that I was too late, but I knelt by her bed, taking her cold hand and crying:

"Chantel, Chantel: come back to me."

That happened more than two years ago, but the memory of that terrible night will never leave me. I could not believe what she had written. It was only the sight of her lying there dead that brought home the reality to me. Redvers took charge of everything. I think I lived in a bemused state for weeks afterward. I kept going over parts of my life with Chantel. I dreamed of her gay mocking beauty. To me she had been the sister I had always wanted; I suppose I had been that to her. She had had an affection for me; there was softness in her; there was kindness; and yet how could she have planned such diabolical actions? The murderess was the secret woman in her, the woman I should never have believed existed if she herself had not shown her to me.

Events happened fast. A week or so before Chantel's death that old nurse—Gareth Glenning's stepmother—had died and when she knew her end was near she confessed to Lady Crediton what she knew. Chantel had been right when she had said that it would have been impossible to ward off the inevitable discovery by the blackmailers.

Lady Crediton wanted Edward brought back to England without delay and later I took him back to England but not on *Serene Lady*.

Lady Crediton received me with some respect. She said that in view of what had happened and the shock it may well have been to Edward—he had become very important to her now—she hoped that I would stay with him for a while in my old capacity for it would be somewhat *inconvenient* if I did not. So I stayed on at the Castle.

Monique had remained on the Island. Madame de Laudé, with whom I was in communication about her furniture, wrote to me often; she said that the new doctor —a young man with modern ideas—had charge of Monique and was very hopeful of her case.

I had not seen Redvers; he had reached England before Edward and I arrived and was gone again on another voyage by the time we came. He was the heir to the vast Crediton empire but he extended to Rex the same generous treatment he had accorded Dick Callum. Rex remained in the same capacity to the firm that he had before it was known that he was not the true heir, and stayed in Australia for the rest of the year and I heard that he had married Helena Derringham.

Madame de Laudé, who was delighted because I had been able to arrange for the sale of some of her furniture, kept me informed. The Flame Men had received their reward for recovering the diamonds and what was more important they had convinced themselves that it was an alien goddess who had caused the accident so that when the injured boy reached manhood he would lose nothing by bearing the scars of going into battle against an enemy and surviving. They believed that the Fire Goddess had sent their servant in the form of a nurse who now lay buried in the Christian cemetery. The Flame Men laid red flowers on Chantel's grave at the time of Grand Celebration and had vowed to do this forever.

I often thought of Chantel. My life seemed empty without her. Once I went up North and found the vicarage where she used to live. I went into the graveyard and there I found the grave she had told me about. The stone had slumped to one side and it was scarcely possible to read the inscription on it. *"Chantel Spring 6 6."* I thought of Chantel's mother coming here and reading the name on that stone and deciding that if the child she carried should be a girl that would be her name. I made inquiries in the neighborhood and called on Chantel's sister Selina. We talked for a while. She did not know all

the truth. There had been no need to tell her. Chantel had
accidentally taken an overdose of some sleeping tablet, she
thought. She spoke of her with pride. The truth but not
the whole truth, as Chantel would have said.

"She was beautiful, even as a baby. And she was different from the rest of us. She knew what she wanted and
she wanted it passionately. We always said she would get
what she wanted. Of course she was so much younger
than the rest of us. Our mother died when she was born
and I think we were inclined to spoil her, but she was
always gay and affectionate. We were so surprised when
she took up nursing. She told us she looked on it as a sort
of gateway. And as she married that millionaire I suppose
that was what she meant. But it didn't last, did it. Poor
Chantel—to have so much and to lose it."

And I came away sadly and I continued to mourn for
her . . . and Redvers.

I should not stay at the Castle. I had made up my mind
that I should be gone by the time Redvers returned. I had
to plan a new life for myself.

In making arrangements for Madame de Laudé I had
come into contact with several antique dealers whom I
had known in the past. One of these told me I was wasting
my time at the Castle. I had an expert knowledge. If I
cared to join his company they would have a place for
me. I said I would think this over.

I went and sat on the cliff and looked over the river to
the docks where the ships lay at anchor; the barques, the
barquentines, and the fast moving clippers now being
ousted by the modern steamers and I thought of the days
when I used to come here as a child with Ellen and listen
to stories of the grandeur of the Lady Line.

I had come full circle. And now there was a decision to
make. Edward would soon be going away to school; there
would be nothing for me at the Castle—besides to remain
was to cling to the old life, the life that was over.

How strange is life. Suddenly when one has almost
made up one's mind to a certain action it casually throws
an opportunity into one's path. One morning I received a
letter from my tenants at the Queen's House, asking me to
go and see them.

It was almost summer and when I stepped through the

iron gate into the garden and saw the waxy beauty of the magnolia tree I felt that I had come home and that if I could not hold that ecstatic happiness for which I had longed at least I could find a certain peace in this house. I knocked; a neat maid took me into the hall. It was furnished as I would have furnished it with the Tudor refectory table and the pewter ornaments. On the turn of the stairs where I had once stood with Redvers to face an infuriated Aunt Charlotte stood a tall Newport grandfather clock. "Tick tock. Come home!" it seemed to say.

My tenants were apologetic. They had a daughter in America who had just had twins and who had wanted them to go out for a long time; they had now decided. They wished therefore to give up the tenancy. They had done the repairs and they would sell the furniture at a very reasonable price; but they wished to leave.

I knew at once what I was going to do. I was coming back here. I was going to buy and sell antiques. I had had the usual commission on the sale of Madame de Laudé's goods; I had saved from my salary. Was it enough? There was no need for immediate payment, I was told, and I realized that my tenants' one desire was to get away as quickly as possible.

Could I do it? It was a challenge. I walked through the Queen's House—up the staircase straight into the room. How beautiful it looked now! It should never be cluttered again. I would begin in a small way. I should put pieces where they belonged. I could do it. I knew I could.

I went to the Queen's room. There was the precious bed. I turned and looked in the mirror. I remembered how I used to look in that mirror and see myself years hence. "Old Miss Brett. She's a bit odd. There was some story about her. Didn't she murder somebody?"

But I could not see that old Miss Brett now. Everything had changed. There was no mystery. I knew how Aunt Charlotte had died.

I knew too that I had accepted this challenge.

Ellen came back to me. Mr. Orfey was not doing so well that she could afford to live a life of idleness. She brought news from the Castle.

"My word, Edith said you could have knocked her down with a feather. So it's Captain Stretton who's the big man now ... Captain Crediton I should say. Mr. Rex has come home and Mrs. Rex ... she's a bit of a madam. She'll keep him in order, but Edith says she's all right at heart."

I tried to concern myself completely with my business affairs so that I had no time for brooding. It wasn't possible of course. I had found a new way of life, but I should never forget.

One day Ellen came in with the news. "Mrs. Stretton, I mean Mrs. Crediton, is dead. Out on that island place. They've been expecting it for months. It's what you might call a happy release."

Autumn had come. There were big ships in the docks. I never tired of climbing the cliff and looking down on them—the ships of the Lady Line into which one woman had crept—*The Secret Woman*.

I still treasured the figurehead. I looked at it every day and asked myself: Does he still think of me?

Then one evening when the mist was on the river and the dew drops were clinging like tiny diamonds to the spiders' webs draping the bushes in the garden, I heard the gate open and footsteps on the flagged path.

I went to the door and waited there. He was coming towards me.

I thought: He has changed; he has grown older; we have both grown older.

But when he reached me and took my hands in his I saw that he had not changed. There was the same lilt in his voice, the same eager smile in those slightly uptilted eyes. But after all, there was a change. He was free.

And there, in the garden of the Queen's House on that autumn evening I knew—and he knew—that the future was for us to make.